CANDLEPOWER

Janet Doolaege

New Generation Publishing

This is a work of fiction. Names, characters, businesses, places, events and incidents are either the products of the author's imagination or used in a fictitious manner. Any resemblance to actual persons, living or dead, or to actual events, is purely coincidental.

None of Olivier's statistics should be considered accurate.

– ONE –

Hospital corridors have always frightened me. I came to a stop, undecided, wanting to turn round and hurry back, out of the building and into the sunlight, past the flowerbeds of massed petunias and through the gates to the roaring boulevard. I knew I didn't want to talk about the events of that dreadful night. But perhaps talking would make everything seem true and final.

A trolley of bottles and enamel dishes rattled up behind me, and I stood aside to let it pass. A door opened, and before it closed I caught a glimpse of a high bed festooned with tubes and apparatus. Devices for doing things to people's helpless bodies. The smell of disinfectant made me want to turn and run blindly, as I had done once before. They had run after me and brought me back. "Oh, Stella," my mother said wearily, her face unnaturally sallow against the white pillow, "you are a silly girl. Look at Pascal. He's not frightened, is he?" Pascal looked smug and went on experimenting with the remote control of the TV. He had marched along the corridor, left, right, left, right, unperturbed. But I knew that my mother was going to die. Terrifying men in white masks would do things to her, as they had done to me when I had had my tonsils out, and I had screamed and fought but nobody had come to rescue me.

That smell of chemicals. Barely two years ago I had smelt it again as I lay in the hard hospital bed, not wanting to be there but knowing that there was no alternative, once more under the all-powerful control of the men in white coats and masks. Helplessly, the tears had run out of my eyes and into my ears, on to my neck, soaking the pillow.

What was I doing here now?

At the door of room 214, I paused.

– TWO –

I'm not likely to forget the first time I saw Rose Martin. It was the day that my canary flew out of the window.

The golden October afternoon was so warm that people were still wearing T-shirts and sitting at café terraces, and I had the window wide open as I was cleaning out the cage. Foolish of me, but I'd never owned a bird before. Topaz had been an unexpected present from my office mates when I had invited them all round for a drink to celebrate moving into my new Paris flat, and bubbly Catherine had come straight from the bird market on the Ile de la Cité with canary and cage all complete, announcing that he would be company for me in my new life.

"Birds," she said, "They're decorative. They're discreet. They're not moody, and they don't order you around or make your life a misery." Unlike men, was the implication. True enough, sharing my life with him was nothing like sharing it with Adrien. Topaz never criticized me or made fun of me. He didn't sing, either, which canaries were supposed to do, but he seemed healthy and content, and I enjoyed his cheerful presence, chatting to him when I came home from work. He hopped sedately about, scattering birdseed and saying nothing except for the occasional questioning "Peep?".

Now I was panic-stricken. In a flash of yellow wings he was suddenly gone, past my hand, out of the cage and out of the window. I stared stupidly, then ran to the window calling "Topaz!" No speck of yellow was to be seen in the street or among the leaves of the plane trees. The grey rooftops of Paris stretched to the horizon.

I grabbed my keys and ran out on to the landing, fuming with impatience as the lift made its sluggish way up to the eighth floor. I willed it to take me down fast, but on the second floor it stopped and an elderly lady prevented the doors from closing as she completed her effusive goodbyes to one of my neighbours. I was wasting precious moments.

In the narrow strip of garden between the block of flats and the street I called "Topaz!" again, but could see nothing except the old grey buildings opposite, the leaves of the plane trees lifting in the slight breeze, a blackbird running and pausing, running and pausing on the lawn, and a child whizzing past the gate on a skateboard. I remembered being told that cage birds never survive if they escape. They're too dependent on human beings and can't fend for themselves. Not only that: the other birds attack them and kill them because they're different. They stand out. No city sparrow or starling could compete with that beautiful lemon yellow colour.

He's not used to flying, I thought. Surely he can't have gone far? But the hazy afternoon had swallowed him up. Lost. I was close to tears.

At that moment I noticed a tall figure standing on the pavement opposite, between the Arab greengrocer's and the dry cleaner's. With one arm stretched above her head, she was gazing intently into a tree, not moving – tall, thin, dark and absolutely still. Then I saw him. Topaz! He flew out of the tree, made an arc with outstretched wings and alighted on a twig lower down, swaying. Then he flew directly down and perched on the finger of the woman standing below. I was so relieved that I scarcely had time to be surprised, running across the street and narrowly avoiding a motorcycle.

"That's my canary!" I called.

She turned to look at me, and I saw her eyes for the first time. Blue, that rare true blue, crystalline, rimmed with a darker colour, violet or indigo. Her face was pale, with high cheek-bones, and her hair, drawn back from it, very dark, apart from one pure white streak running back from her right temple.

"Thank you so much for catching him!"

"I didn't catch him." Her voice was soft and musical, with just a trace of an accent that I couldn't place. What did she mean?

I made a grab for Topaz, but he flitted away and landed on her shoulder, saying "Peep?" She placed a hand gently over his wings.

"Does he live with you?"

"Yes," I said eagerly, "He's mine. I live in that block of flats. Oh, please – would you bring him indoors for me? He seems to like you, doesn't he? God, I thought I'd lost him."

Just a second's hesitation, and then she decided. "Why not?" We walked up the path to the door. "We're neighbours, then," she said lightly. "I live right opposite you, in that building," and she pointed to the doorway between the two shops, beyond which a staircase led to the upper floors. It was one of those old, grey Paris apartment buildings with shops at street level, tall windows flanked by shutters and fronted by wrought-iron balustrades or balconies, and dormer windows peeping out of the pitched zinc roof. My own block, by contrast, was modern concrete, featureless and functional.

As we travelled up in the lift, I wondered why I hadn't seen her before; her appearance was so striking. But it was true that I had moved into my tiny flat scarcely more than a month ago, and when not at the office had been busy positioning furniture, hanging pictures, buying a new fridge and getting the shower repaired. I hadn't had time to explore the neighbourhood or to pay much attention to my neighbours, although those who lived directly above me had forced themselves on my attention by the noise they made.

She was standing very stiffly in the lift, her eyes half closed. I wondered if she suffered from claustrophobia. The lift was jerking slightly. Enclosed in her hand, Topaz looked out at me with a round black eye.

"Stella Hayward." On the landing, she read out my name on the label under the doorbell. "You're American? English?"

I explained that my father was English and my mother French, that I had gone to school in England but had moved to France when I started work. We were entering the flat as I spoke, my own private territory, and I chattered rather nervously. I had a brother in England, I told her, "and my grandmother used to live in Aix-en-Provence." But I broke off at that point. I couldn't start to tell a perfect stranger all about Mamie: Mamie who, before she died, had made sure that I had a place of my own – this place.

The sun streamed in across the plain modern furniture that I had chosen. There was still a smell of fresh paint. I had wanted to create a soothing, neutral oasis in tones of white, beige and oatmeal, the only splashes of colour being my Cézanne reproductions and the green of the house-plants. Here, with some electronic gadgets, my guitar and Topaz, I felt calm and safe. I hadn't invited anybody in since the drink with my office workmates, which had been almost an obligation.

Now she was entering the room cautiously, looking to left and right, like a deer stepping into some unknown forest glade. What did she think of my bolt-hole? People, I thought, are always so quick to judge. Ought I really to have invited her in? People judge you by your surroundings and by the clothes you wear. I glanced at her clothes. Jeans (I was wearing jeans myself) and a kind of dark blue smock, with pockets here and there and wide sleeves rolled back. It wasn't the height of fashion, but nor did it look out of date.

I went at once to close the window, berating myself for having left it open, but she said, "He'll be all right now," and sure enough, Topaz hopped meekly from her finger into the cage. I remembered how close I had come to losing him, and was suddenly filled with gratitude. Of course I was glad to have invited her in.

She was holding out her hand to me. "Rose Martin."

Her hand was warm, thin but strong. As I shook it I thought for a fraction of a second that I could hear a singing sound, like high voices in close harmony, very faint and far away; but it faded immediately. I blinked.

"Would you like a cup of tea?" I asked prosaically.

"English tea?"

"Why not?" Tea was tea. What did she mean?

"How lovely. Yes, I would."

As I went into the kitchen to fill the kettle, I heard her add, "I was thinking of escaping to England. For a while."

Escaping? For some reason, I didn't ask any questions. Looking back, I don't know whether I was shy, or gauche, or merely incurious. But I didn't question her.

We sipped our tea and talked about Topaz and how I had acquired him, and how long I had been living in the flat. I began to relax. Maybe it was time I stopped being such a recluse and began to talk to a few more people. And Rose was not gazing around the room, making a mental inventory and noting details that she thought could be improved. Her full attention was on me.

Then the rumbling began above our heads, and I raised my eyes to the ceiling in annoyance. "There they go again."

My upstairs neighbours seemed to spend a great deal of time shifting their furniture around, sometimes very late at night, and dropping hard objects on the floor. They also had a small child which trotted to and fro, and sometimes had tantrums. When it did, they yelled at it. Quite often they used an electric drill on their walls. Rumble. Thump. Crash.

"What on earth can they be doing up there?" I said.

"They go in for weightlifting, that's what it is," said Rose.

"What, even the toddler?"

"Yes. They have a special set of miniature weights for him," Rose said, dead pan. For a moment I had thought she really knew these people. She elaborated on her theory. They were the Dumbbells family, and to keep in training they had contests to see who could move the most furniture across the room in the shortest time. They went in for voice development, and registered how many decibels they could produce. As she talked, I could see them quite clearly, muscular cartoon characters in fluorescent leotards, frowning with concentration. Appropriate sound effects came from above our heads as if on cue.

I joined in. They had special shoes made with weights in the soles so that their child would develop his leg muscles.

The child also had a baby elephant as a pet, and when it was feeling particularly happy, it would gambol around the room. The scenario got crazier and crazier. When they were at a loose end, they would hammer nails into all the walls, because walls looked so much more interesting that way. It was a very silly conversation, but we were helpless with giggles by this time. Rose's eyes were dancing and we were calling each other "tu" like old friends. I had been feeling increasingly irritated with these neighbours in recent weeks, but now the zany picture of life upstairs was making me feel almost kindly disposed towards them.

It was good to laugh. It had been a long time since I had laughed like this.

"I see that you play the guitar," said Rose suddenly, after a pause.

I became serious. "Not really. Not very well, at least."

"Would you play something for me?"

"Oh, no." I shrank into myself. "No, I don't think so." I wished that I had not left the guitar standing so conspicuously in the corner.

"Would you show me how to play it, then? I play the piano myself, you see, but I'm interested in other instruments."

Reluctantly I fetched it, tuned it, and showed her how to place her fingers on the strings. She was wearing a ring with a dark blue stone. Under my guidance she plucked the strings experimentally, then more firmly, and four deep notes broke into the air, sweet and rounded.

From behind me, a most joyful piping started up, and turning round I found that Topaz was singing, trill after trill with his throat puffed out, throwing back his head and singing high staccato notes, then trilling again.

"That's amazing," I said. "He's never sung before. I was beginning to think he couldn't."

"Topaz?" said Rose to him gently.

He gave another ecstatic trill, then stopped and sidled along his perch towards her. "Peep?" he said. He began to preen his wing feathers.

I don't quite know how, but by asking questions and getting me to demonstrate, she eventually coaxed me into playing the guitar for her. When she asked me what the tune was, I had to admit that it was one of my own songs, and then, of course, I had to clear my throat and sing it for her. It was a piece called "Carnival Night", after Douanier Rousseau's painting. All my songs are in my head, and I have a folder full of lyrics.

She sat very still, not looking at me. There was a pause after I had finished.

"So when are you going to share this gift with other people?" she asked.

"Gift – what gift?" I scoffed, embarrassed. "My songs aren't much good. I don't have any illusions."

"Don't be so sure. You have to let others be the judge of that."

"Oh, no…" Nobody would want to listen to my strumming, and my voice wasn't good enough. My mother and brother had made enough disparaging remarks for me to know that.

"Listen," said Rose. "I'm a pianist. In fact, I give piano lessons. I can tell when someone is talented. When you were playing and singing just now, I could feel how much it meant to you."

"Well," I mumbled, "It's what I most enjoy doing, I suppose."

"So you have to develop it. It's not right to keep it to yourself. And music's a wonderful thing to give to the world. It hangs in the air, it takes up no space – it disappears when it's not wanted. Nobody can own it. And you can create it."

"At least the neighbours haven't complained about the dreadful noise!" I tried to turn it into a joke.

It was as if a cloud had passed over the sun. "Not like my own neighbour," she said wryly.

"You have a neighbour who complains about the noise you make? Don't say you go in for weightlifting and hammering, too!" I was still inclined to giggle at the Dumbbells, shying away from the idea that my songs might have any value.

"It's the piano he can't stand. He lives directly below me, and he can be quite … unpleasant." She was silent for a few moments, gazing into the middle distance, her eyes very dark blue. Then she gave a small shake of her head. "I have to take him seriously."

"Why?"

"Because I know him." She shook her head again. "We all live so close together in these Paris flats. We all live on top of one another, so we're bound to be a nuisance to one another. We interfere in one another's lives without meaning to." There was no trace of gaiety left in her voice.

"It would be nice to have a proper house, somewhere, wouldn't it? A house out in the country, on a hill or on the edge of a forest."

"But you wouldn't be able to enjoy it," she said. "Especially not at this time of year."

"Why's that?"

"The countryside's full of men with guns. They shoot birds. You can't even go for a walk without hearing gunfire all around you."

Of course: the hunters. The tradition is still strong in France. In the hunting season, men roam the fields and woods with their dogs, shooting anything, large and small – including one another, by mistake, or people who happen to be out walking. Every year there are reports of accidents. They can hunt birds and animals on anybody's land, even right there in your garden, in front of your eyes. It's a right that was claimed for the common people after the Revolution.

"Some parts of France are almost birdless," said Rose. "They've all been shot." She pushed her hands into her wide sleeves and slowly rubbed her elbows. "But there are men everywhere. You can't get away from men."

By now the sun was sinking, and the outlines of the furniture were blurred as dusk gathered in the room.

I told her that in England and Scotland only the very rich went out shooting birds, but that these were birds specially bred, almost reared by hand, and tame, not expecting the human beings who had fed them to turn on them and kill them. Sometimes they were only wounded, and then they had their necks wrung.

"That's betrayal," she said. Her voice shook. "A betrayal of trust. So it's just as bad in Britain, is it?" She was sitting very stiffly. I could no longer see her face clearly.

I told her about the gamekeepers who shot or poisoned and strung up on gibbet lines any other creatures that might prey on the young pheasants and grouse – magpies, for instance, or crows.

"Crows?"

"They call them vermin."

Rose was sitting like a statue. She seemed not even to be breathing. I noticed that Topaz had stopped hopping about and had put his head under his wing.

"Tell me," I said, reaching to switch on the lamp. I had been about to ask her how she had managed to catch Topaz for me, but just as I pressed the switch the light-bulb flashed and went out again with a loud pop. "Damn. I think I have some spare bulbs in the cupboard." I turned on the overhead light in the entrance, and phut! that bulb also went.

Rose was suddenly on her feet. "I must go," she said abruptly.

"Oh, please don't rush away. I just have to find where I put – "

"No, I really must be going. Thank you for the tea." She was already at the door. "But come over and visit me, won't you?" She put out her hand, almost pleading, but didn't touch me. "The top floor. Whenever you like."

And before I could say anything, she had gone. She didn't even wait for the lift, and I could hear her feet echoing down the concrete stairwell. Topaz and I were left together with the empty tea-cups, in the autumn twilight.

***

When I had changed the bulbs, finished cleaning the cage and eaten some quiche and salad for supper, I stood leaning on the window-sill, looking out into the darkness. There was a nip in the air now, and that autumn smell that still reminds me of returning to school after the holidays: the lingering end of summer, and the start of a new chapter in my life.

Why had Rose left so abruptly? I hoped I hadn't upset her. I could scarcely believe that I had just spent a couple of hours chatting freely, in my own refuge, to a complete stranger. I had even played and sung for her. The people I saw every day in the office didn't know that I played the guitar: I had hidden it when I invited them round. My so-called friends had all been Adrien's friends, and now, after what had happened, I didn't want to see any of them. Friendship didn't mean much, I thought cynically. In fact, I had kept people at a distance for quite a time. But somehow, with Rose, I felt at ease. What crazy things we had said. Why had they seemed so funny?

How had she made Topaz fly down to her outstretched hand? She hadn't called or whistled – not that I had heard, anyway. He had just gone directly to her. And he had sung for her, too. I turned to look at him. "You're a fraud," I told him, "pretending you couldn't sing." He looked at me with a bright, jet black eye. What do birds think about?

Heavy footsteps thudded across the ceiling, followed by the lighter running steps of a child, and a shriek. The television news began to blare. In retaliation I put on a CD of flamenco music and turned up the volume. It was a way of defending my territory.

My home: thanks to my grandmother's legacy. There had been no money left over after the purchase, and I had had to take out a loan to buy furniture, but I had no regrets. Adrien could keep his flowery balcony and his leather furniture and his computer games and his whisky. I would take independence. Mamie had told me that freedom and independence were all-important for a woman, and I had listened to her, but I suppose I hadn't really heard her. I had fallen into that old, old trap: romantic love. "Lerv". Huh.

On one occasion I had taken Adrien down to Aix to meet her, but the visit had not been a success. Her green eyes had seemed to look straight through him, undeceived, and he had become nervous and embarrassingly hearty. "I didn't like the signals I was getting," she told me afterwards. I had resented her disapproval at the time, but on the long drive back to Paris I had worked myself into a furious rage with him over some traffic incident, and had flung myself weeping on to the bed as soon as we arrived home, wishing that I could climb into her lap and let her comfort me as she had done when I was a child and had hurt myself. Well, he always told me that I was immature, and perhaps he was right. But shy, awkward child that I was, I had been Mamie's first grandchild, someone special to her, and I had loved going down to Aix to stay with her.

She had never been quite as fond of Pascal, I knew. She was the exception in that respect. Nobody else was proof against his white-blond angelic looks and mischievous grin. He was so charming that somehow I felt compelled to be more withdrawn and unresponsive than I might otherwise have been. People said I was sullen. But Mamie always seemed to understand how I felt. Admittedly, Pascal tried her patience. She had never forgotten the time in Aix when she had paused to speak to a friend, and while her attention was distracted Pascal had contrived to fall into the fountain in front of the Town Hall. But she could rely on me not to be naughty. I didn't dare.

The Spanish guitar music floated out into the night, and I looked down at the streetlamp shining through the plane trees' dusty, end-of-summer leaves that were just beginning to turn brown. I could see into the lighted windows of the building across the street, where families were having their evening meal and television screens jumped and flickered. Some people had already closed the shutters. Which was Rose's flat? There were three dormer windows opposite my own but at a slightly lower level. I could see a dim glow inside, not like the light from the other windows, and a shadow passed from left to right, then back again. I wondered what she was doing. For the first time in months, I felt a gleam of curiosity about another person.

***

I didn't take up her invitation, of course. You can't just appear unannounced at somebody's door – particularly not in Paris. It isn't a village. I thought that I might try to phone her, but I couldn't find any Rose Martin at that address, either in the directory or online. Naturally, there were hundreds of Martins: it's like being called Smith in England. Several weeks went by, and I had plenty of other things to think about, as we were changing our entire computer system in the office and a great backlog of work built up. This meant that I often had to work overtime, and of course there were teething problems with the new system and tempers became frayed. In the evenings I didn't feel like doing anything except watch television and sleep. The sun was setting earlier and the mornings were darker. Sensible creatures were starting to hibernate.

My mother rang from England and wanted to know what my plans were for Christmas. We always speak French to each other, although she has lived on the other side of the Channel for more than thirty years. "Pascal and Lisa will be coming," she said, as if announcing a special treat. My brother's wife, Lisa, had just learned that she was pregnant with her first child, and I knew she would be the centre of attention. Of course, she would do her best to try and draw me into the circle; she had always been so friendly and sweet – you couldn't fault her. I could just imagine conversations between her and Pascal: she would be so very understanding, making allowances for his sister's glum and unforthcoming attitude. But I found her both dull and silly.

I hesitated and went off at tangents, not keen to commit myself. My mother began to get annoyed. It was only when my father, to my surprise, came to the telephone and said, "Stella – hrrrmm – you must come for Christmas – it's been so long since we saw you," that I finally made up my mind and agreed. My father occasionally writes a very interesting letter, but he never phones, and is not a demonstrative person. He's always wrapped up in his teaching and his poetry, and when you see him he always seems to be either cautiously emerging from his study or swiftly retreating to it – tall, heavy-shouldered and angular, with a quiet voice and a preoccupied expression, quite unlike my plump and vivacious mother, casually elegant with her knotted silk scarves. It was my father who named me Stella, and then my mother chose a French name for Pascal. Odd, really, that with my English name I have chosen to live in France, while Pascal – the brilliant young assistant editor with the BBC – is living in England, indeed in stockbroker-belt Surrey, with a wife who could not be more English if she tried.

I thought irritably, as I put the phone down: there are people all around me still. I can renounce lovers and friends, but I still have a family. It's not possible to cut yourself off and become a total recluse; they won't let you. I would have relished spending Christmas alone in my flat, curled up with a movie and some music and maybe a good thriller. People in books and films don't hurt you. I thought that I could quite easily exist alone, indifferent to other people, keeping them out of my circle, untouched by them.

I was wrong, of course.

***

When I next saw Rose, the weather had turned very cold, and coming home from work I had bought some hot roast chestnuts from the man on the corner by the metro station. With his old supermarket trolley and converted oil drum, he was doing a brisk trade, as the aroma of blackening chestnuts wafted down the steps and along the white-tiled metro corridor to the hungry commuters. The smell reminded me of autumn evenings when my school friend Emma and I used to roast chestnuts over the fire, and sometimes they would explode, frightening our dog. I had no idea what had become of Emma and hadn't given her a thought for years.

Rose was just coming out of the dry cleaner's with a bulky parcel. Her face lit up. "Why haven't you come over to see me yet?" she wanted to know. "Come in and have something to drink, right now. If you can face seven flights of stairs, that is."

The stone lintel of the door into her building was elaborately carved in a design of intertwining leaves and flowers, now worn and blurred. At the centre of the design, half hidden among the stone foliage, was what appeared to be a horned head. I have always intended to photograph some of the richly ornamented lintels that you can see in old parts of Paris. Instead of pressing the buzzer with her finger to open the street door, she used a wooden pencil. I barely noticed it at the time, and held the door for her as we entered her building.

The floor of the entrance hall was of grey and white mosaic tiles, and on the wall on our right were rows of mailboxes. We passed through another door with small glass panels and began to climb the wooden stairs, up past the closed doors that led into people's hidden lives. As I pressed the time-switches on the landings to light our way a dog barked, a couple could be heard having an argument, a child sang loudly and tunelessly, and there was a smell of onions frying. When we reached the sixth floor, a door opened and a stocky man with a bald head and a grey moustache started to come out, zipping up his parka. When he saw us, he stepped abruptly back inside and half closed the door.

"Bonsoir, monsieur," said Rose. A slight grunt, which might have been a cough, was the only reply.

I raised my eyebrows at her.

"My difficult neighbour," she whispered, "the one I was telling you about. He won't even speak to me now."

I was panting by the time we had climbed the last, curving flight of stairs to the very top floor, dark and shadowy, and wondered whether Rose often carried heavy parcels up here. Then she unlocked the door, and for the first time I found myself standing inside her home.

I think I can remember my first impressions. It was dim and warm, and a faint, sweet scent of spices – nutmeg? cinnamon? – hung in the air. There was a glow from the centre of a big wooden table, and moving ahead of me she turned up the oil lamp. Cut-out patterns in the shape of stars shone through its glass shade. She went around the room, lighting several candles, and all the rich, deep colours of the room sprang to life. The long, undrawn curtains were crimson velvet, and on the polished floorboards were white rugs embroidered with bright wools. A manual sewing-machine, black and gold, stood on the table, and everywhere, flowing over the sofa and heaped on chairs, were lengths and scraps of fabric, of many colours and assorted designs. Against one wall stood an upright piano, the old-fashioned sort with candle-holders. It was the first time I had seen one with lighted candles actually in the holders.

She swept aside a heap of materials from the sofa so that I could sit down.

"I didn't have any piano pupils today, so I've spent most of the day sewing. I'm afraid it's a bit untidy." She took off her coat, and I saw she was wearing a dark skirt and a pale golden-yellow blouse that caught the lamplight and seemed to hold it in its folds.

"What are you making?"

"Patchwork. I'll show you." She opened the doors of a heavy piece of furniture – the word "press" occurred to me, for some reason – and took out several folded items. I whistled quietly as she shook them out: two exquisite patchwork quilts, and a skirt and jacket. The combinations of colours and textures made them seem like paintings; you wanted to hang them on the wall. Purple and pink. Leaf green and black. Turquoise and deep blue. One of them was called a crazy quilt, she told me, and the other was made in a log cabin design. The skirt and jacket were a new departure, the colours arranged so that they grew stronger and deeper from top to hem.

"What patience! Do you sell them?"

"Yes, there's a shop in the Latin Quarter which buys them from me. People seem to like them." She tore open the parcel that she had been carrying. "Look at this. Aren't they beautiful?" Her hands caressed velvets and brocades, peacock blue, emerald, gold, scarlet. They spilled out of the brown paper like jewels from a casket. "I know just what I'm going to do with these," she murmured, half to herself.

When I asked her where she found the fabrics, she told me that she knew somebody who worked for one of the fashion houses, somebody else who worked for an interior decorator, and a private dressmaker, all of whom saved scraps and remnants for her. "And sometimes I find really fine things at the flea market. Clothes that aren't wearable – maybe they're torn or stained. Nobody wants them. I buy them for a song and cut up the good parts," she said. "But let me get you some tea. It's my turn today."

She disappeared through a bead curtain into her tiny kitchen, leaving me in the quiet room with the candlelight and all the harmonies of colours. I looked around. It was an unusually large room for an old building, and I thought that at some stage two rooms had been knocked into one. On either side of the piano, bookshelves rose from floor to ceiling, and the gilt spines of the books gleamed dimly. The walls were white, bare of pictures, and the floorboards dark. I could see no sign of any electric lamps or light fittings, but there were various candlesticks, some silver and others china. I glanced out through one of the tall dormer windows at the plane trees' bare branches with their round, dangling fruit, and across the street to my own block of flats and large window, a little higher than Rose's. It was strange to see it from the outside, dark and rather bleak in the featureless façade.

Rose returned with steaming cups, very thin bone china, and we shared the chestnuts as Emma and I had shared them long ago over our homework.

"Hmm! What kind of tea is this?"

"Green tea, with saffron and cardamom. They make it like this in Kashmir."

I wondered whether she had ever been in Kashmir, but before I could ask her, she wanted news of Topaz.

"He's still singing. I think he's happy. At least, I hope so." This thought had been lingering uncomfortably in the back of my mind. "I wonder, sometimes, whether it's right to keep a bird in a cage. Maybe it's wrong?"

"It's not as simple as that. Canaries have been bred as cage birds for generations. They need to be taken care of. They wouldn't survive otherwise."

"Tough to be a cage bird." I hunched my shoulders.

"You mean you want to be free? You don't want anyone to take care of you?" Her direct blue gaze met mine over the rim of the tea-cup.

"I've had enough of all that. Taking care, being taken care of – told what to do. I just want to take care of myself now."

"Good," she said. "That's good. But are you happy?"

Again it crossed my mind that Rose might not be French. For the French, the height of correct behaviour and politeness is to be discreet. You tread carefully around sensitive issues. You don't ask people direct personal questions unless they are close relatives or friends of many years' standing. You certainly don't ask somebody that you scarcely know whether they are happy.

"Why do you ask?" I hedged.

"You're right," she said. "I shouldn't ask. I know you're not happy. You've been hurt."

I nearly stood up and walked out. You just don't tell people truths about themselves so abruptly! But I remembered Topaz singing, and stayed where I was. My throat felt constricted.

"I've been trying to find that kind of balance, too," she said. "Take care of myself. Be independent. Not harm anyone. It's not easy." She put down her cup slowly and precisely in the middle of the saucer.

"It shouldn't be so hard to be independent. The worst thing is to get dependent on that sort of man. On the sort of man I was living with. What a fool." I gulped my tea. "What a mess. God."

"It didn't work out?" she prompted.

I found myself telling her about Adrien, and suddenly it was a relief to talk about it all. After a number of very short-lived affairs, it had been my first attempt at living with a man. I could see him sprawling in his leather armchair, sipping whisky, stockily built and fairish, with fluffy hair, a snub nose, and those eyes that crinkled up when he smiled his boyish smile. It was the smile that had hooked me at first. He had smiled a lot at the beginning, and he seemed to give off a kind of warmth, a warmth that enveloped me when he caught me in one of his bear-hugs that meant, not that he loved me, but that he wanted to have sex. Sometimes it felt as if he was crushing my rib-cage, but I didn't mind because it meant that he wanted me. I wanted to be wanted. And sex was very good at first.

That smile. He still smiled later, even when he said the most hurtful things, so that I was never quite sure whether he was joking. He joked a lot. At first he had made me laugh: he had such a keen eye for people's weaknesses, and he was a good mimic. Later, the jokes didn't seem so funny, particularly when I was on the receiving end. Jokes can be a way of policing people's behaviour, keeping them in line. He started to say that I was over-sensitive, that I had no sense of humour. All right, maybe I haven't. I no longer know.

I do know that he wasn't satisfied with me the way I was. As time went by, he seemed to become more and more irritated with me. I couldn't do anything right, and I didn't look right. Yet I tried so hard to please him. I cooked the food he liked, and I watched the TV programmes that he wanted to watch, rather than the ones I would have preferred myself. I tried not to leave newspapers and magazines strewn around the flat. I didn't play my guitar when he was there, because he said it was an instrument for teenagers, and I didn't complain when he played Berg and Schoenberg full blast on his hi-fi, although they set my teeth on edge. I just wanted him to hold me and love me. I even picked up the dirty clothes that he dropped on the floor. I took care of him. Why? Because I wanted him to take care of me.

But I wasn't good enough. I didn't deserve his love. I couldn't make sparkling conversation at dinner parties with his smart friends, and I'm no good at remembering jokes, or at any rate not the sort that are done up in a package labelled "joke", with a punchline at the end. Nor do I have the gift of repartee. If a barbed remark came across the dinner table, I couldn't send it flying straight back again and make everybody laugh. Although I would smile and pretend not to mind, I would be on the edge of tears. His friends found me pathetic, I know they did, and he used to gang up with them against me, although it was all supposed to be harmless fun.

He started to criticize my clothes and my appearance. Why didn't I grow my nails and manicure them properly? But my nails tend to split, and anyway I have to keep them short for playing the guitar. Why did I never wear elegant shoes? I even bought a pair of high-heeled court shoes to please him, although I hate teetering along and feeling unbalanced and vulnerable. Then one day when we were out together one of the heels got caught in a grating, my shoe came off and I fell over. I felt a fool, the heel was ruined, and he gave one of his heavy sighs as if I had done it on purpose.

"Didn't you defend yourself?" asked Rose

"No. I just kept trying harder. After all, I was living in his flat. I had no particular right to be there. He was putting up with me. I just wished he would be different towards me. I kept hoping things would improve."

"And you weren't angry with him?"

"No. Not at first. Later, I was. Yes, I was angry later."

Even sex was no good after a time. I was so tense that I couldn't let go any more – I couldn't feel anything. That annoyed him, too, because he prided himself on his technique. But it felt as if he was handling me the way he drove his car: push that pedal, pull this lever, and the engine obediently accelerates or changes gear. My body rebelled. I wanted him to hold me, tell me he loved me, take care of me, keep me safe – but at the same time I would get goose-pimples when his hands touched my naked flesh. Even so, I often used to put my arms round him, rub my face against him, try to get close to him. If he wasn't in the mood for sex, he would shrug me off. "Oh, stop pawing me," he said once.

"What happened in the end? What made you get angry?" She was looking at me intently.

If I had been a smoker, I would certainly have lit a cigarette. Instead, I picked up some pieces of fabric and began to place them in overlapping patterns, dark brown corduroy, smooth cream, rust, moss green with a tiny pattern.

"Two things happened," I said slowly.

I stared down at the table. All his friends were elegant and amusing, but Nathalie was the sort of person who could make most other women feel large and frumpish. Tiny, doll-like, with confident arched eyebrows and a shining cap of dark hair that swung when she turned her head, she wore the highest of heels, and her nails were long pink ovals. Her clothes fitted with no bulges or wrinkles, and there were never any snags in her tights. She had the kind of ankles that are so slender they look as if they might snap. I knew Adrien found her amusing, but I didn't begin to suspect that anything was going on until a well-wisher took it upon herself to let me know that she had seen them together in a restaurant one evening when he had told me he was working very late, preparing for an important conference.

"But it was the perfume that clinched it," I said.

"The perfume?"

Nathalie used to wear a rather heavy, exotic perfume. On that particular evening I was feeling almost dizzy with excitement. I didn't know what to do. When I came in, I went into the bedroom and sat on the bed. I remember half noticing that the bed looked as if it had been made rather hastily, not as neatly as I usually made it in the morning, but I was thinking about what to say to Adrien. How to put it. And when to tell him: as soon as he came in? after dinner, when we were in bed? I sat staring at the carpet, and after a while I lay down and gazed at the ceiling. That was when I began to realize that I could smell Nathalie's perfume. I pushed back the bedspread and sank my nose into the pillow. I pulled back the duvet and looked at the sheet.

I felt sick.

It was quiet in Rose's room. The dregs of my tea had grown cold.

"And the other thing?"

"The other thing." I smoothed the pieces of stuff under my fingers. Apricot, lime green, navy, pearl grey. "The other thing was – I'd just found out I was pregnant."

Suddenly I burst into tears. That was the news I had been going to break to him. I'd known that he didn't really want

26

children, but I felt sure that this would change everything. When he realized that he was actually going to be a father he would be pleased and proud – proud of me. I felt so proud of myself, as if for the first time in my life I had achieved something: now I was a real person, a real woman.

I struggled with my sobs, desperately embarrassed at the tears that kept welling up. People are usually so horrified if you cry. Even when I was a child, my mother couldn't stand the noise I made, and used to shut me in my room. Only my grandmother didn't mind. She would just hold me, rocking me gently until gradually I stopped. She must have had strong eardrums, I think. My voice has always been powerful.

"Cry if you want to," said Rose comfortably.

That opened the floodgates. For a while I was bent double, racked by sobs, and when my paper tissues proved inadequate, Rose handed me a white damask handkerchief.

"You don't have to tell me about it."

"I want to!" I scrubbed at my eyes. "I had an abortion."

I hadn't told anyone else about it. I hadn't told Adrien. He had gone away for a few days, supposedly on a business trip, but business or otherwise I knew that Nathalie was with him. And so, after two weeks of the worst loneliness and agony of mind I have ever known, I had it done. I told Rose about the impersonal hospital, the cold questioning, the form-filling, the snooty nurses. And the knowledge, weighing like a tombstone on my head, that I had snuffed out a potential human life. I had made that decision, and yet for some time I had been yearning to have a baby, to hold a small warm human being in my arms and to love and be loved unreservedly. A baby wouldn't impose any conditions: it would just love me for myself, and I would have taken such good care of it. I would have been a model mother.

"But you couldn't have had a child with Adrien. He wasn't right for you," said Rose. "He would have been wrong for the child, too."

"He said he didn't want children, anyway."

Silence.

"You know," she said, "There's nothing worse than being an unwanted child. Even if it's only one parent that doesn't want it. The child always realizes. You carry that with you all your life." There was an odd note in her voice, but I was so full of my own troubles that I remembered it only much later.

"I really did want a baby," I said piteously. If only I could have had one without involving Adrien. If only virgin birth were possible. If only I could have had artificial insemination, at least – though that would have been a hassle. If only men could be kept out of it. But then, I thought – would I have wanted to grow up without my own father?

"Time enough!" Rose broke in on my thoughts. "You have plenty of time still. There's a right time for everything."

"That's another thing – timing." I ran my hands through my hair. "We split up soon after that. I asked him whether Nathalie still wore the same perfume. He didn't deny anything. Well – I moved out as soon as I'd found somewhere to live. All I could find was a tiny, pokey room looking on to a dark courtyard, at an astronomical rent. It was awful." Cramped, lonely. Apart from students, people don't go in for flat-sharing in Paris as much as they do in London. In any case I wouldn't have been good company for flat-mates. Who would want to live with someone like me? "But only six months later – " I gazed out of the window and across the street.

"What happened?"

"My grandmother died and left me some money. Quite a lot of money. As if on cue. So I was able to buy a flat. Strange, wasn't it?"

"Strange? Maybe."

"It was almost as if she knew. But I hadn't told her anything. I was too ashamed. Legally she had to leave everything to my mother and aunt, but she put a clause in her will saying that she wanted me to have a certain percentage of her estate because it was important for a woman to be independent and to have a place of her own until she knew what she really wanted to do – even if it meant being lonely. She said that."

"So we're alike, in a way," said Rose. "Each of us is alone and independent. You know what they used to say about a woman without a man?"

"Oh, that feminist slogan? A fish without a bicycle?"

"Or a neck without a pain."

I smiled bleakly. "So you like living alone? You don't feel lonely?"

"Why should I feel lonely?" declaimed Rose. "Is not our planet in the Milky Way?"

"Wow!" I stared.

"I didn't invent that – I was quoting Thoreau. He was somebody who lived alone, too. I have to be alone, you see. I can't live with anyone."

"It's odd, isn't it," I said, "that when you live with somebody – when you're in love and all that – you try to give the best of yourself, and you expect the man to do the same. But instead of that he just dumps the worst of himself on you, and yet is all sweet and charming to friends that he doesn't even see very often."

"So you don't wish you were still together?"

"I wouldn't go back to Adrien. Not for anything," I said. "But I'd give up my flat, my independence, everything, if only Mamie were still alive. I've made such a mess of the last few years. I know she must have been disappointed in me. She never liked him. No wonder! How could I have fallen for a guy like that? The lousy, sodding bastard. I hope he rots in hell!" My knuckles were white.

"Ah, so you're still angry with him?"

"Yes, I am. I'm bloody furious!" I thought of my mother hurling crockery on to the kitchen floor. She never broke the best dinner service, only the cheap plates and mugs, but every crash made me flinch and cower. I hated things to be broken, but I knew she would be in a sunnier temper afterwards. Anger was dangerous, and yet something about it felt good.

Rose said nothing for a few moments. "Let go of it, if you can. Let it pass."

"Why should I? Haven't I a right to be angry? When I think of the way he treated me…"

"It's not a question of rights. It's more a question of consequences."

"How do you mean?" I added a piece of orange velvet to the pattern I was making.

"It's…" She picked up her tea-cup, turned it around in her white fingers and put it down again. "It's hard to explain. Anger is a – a force, if you like. I read a saying somewhere: who angers me, controls me. If you stay angry with Adrien, you're letting him control you. You're putting yourself in his power. And you mustn't ever give a man power over you. Believe me – I've been through it." Our eyes met.

"Anger is a force, you say?" I stared at her.

"Yes. If you open the door to it, you can't be sure what you're letting in. Hey," she said in a lighter tone, looking down at the table, "that's an interesting combination of colours you've made."

"Oh…" I tossed the pieces aside and went to look out of the window. On the tiny balcony were some withered geraniums in pots and a very small stone statue of a lion, tinged faintly green with moss.

"The best cure for anger – or for loneliness, come to that – is to make something," said Rose's soft voice behind me.

"What can I make? You make beautiful patchwork, but I can't do that," I said despondently. "I was never any good at sewing." Peering down through the wrought-iron balustrade to the street, still busy with the last of the rush-hour traffic, I could see big plastic wheelie bins waiting in lines for the refuse collectors' lorry. As I watched, I saw the old homeless man in a woolly hat shuffling from bin to bin, opening the lids and rummaging inside. He was there most evenings. He had two carrier bags full of pickings. Although I couldn't hear him, I knew he was talking to himself. Was he happy? Was anybody happy?

"Music," said Rose promptly. "Your songs. You have to work on them, record them, let people hear them. Do something with your talent."

"Talent!" I turned back to the room. "You must be joking. Anyway, I haven't touched my guitar for weeks. I've been too tired. We've had so much work at the office." The thought of tomorrow's work was like a grey cloud lowering over me. Work took up so much time, and there was so little left for living – for doing things that I really wanted to do.

"I'm lucky to have a job, I suppose," I said. "I shouldn't complain. My office-mates seem quite satisfied with their lives, after all."

"But maybe you're different," said Rose. "Maybe you're not meant to work on a computer screen all day long. You don't have to be like other people. You can change your life."

"Change my life?" For a second I had an odd sensation, as if hundreds of doors were opening all around me. Then: "No," I said, "No. I'm too tired even to think about it."

"You won't feel so tired if you make something. Put things together. Make a pattern, make harmony. It's just like patchwork, really. Patchwork in the air. I put shapes and colours together, you put notes and words together."

"Patchwork in the air!" A bizarre idea.

Rose narrowed her eyes. "I'm sure you have an idea for a song in your head right now. Haven't you?"

"Well – " I hesitated. "The beginnings of one, actually. Only the first few lines."

"How does it go?"

I sat down at the piano and tried to pick out the notes that I could hear in my mind, but gave up after a few attempts. The song was lurking there, somewhere in the shadows, but it wasn't yet ready to emerge. I asked Rose to play me something instead.

I remember the candlelight on her thin white face, heightening the shadows under her cheekbones as she played, and the sparkle of the blue stone on her finger. The music was Bach's "Jesu, joy of man's desiring", and I knew the English words to it because we had sung it in the choir when I was at school. I began to hum an accompaniment, and then to sing. "Yes, yes," muttered Rose. Then she joined in with the French words. Her soprano voice was thin but very pure, whereas my own is full and rather resonant. I'm a mezzo. Classical music isn't my first love, but I can appreciate it. I stood beside the piano and we sang to our hearts' content, enjoying the melody as our voices soared and blended together. "Do you know, your voice reminds me very much of that singer we hear so much about," said Rose. "Zorinda." There were posters of her everywhere, and I had bought the latest CD, but it hadn't occurred to me to draw comparisons.

Before I could answer, there was an almighty din. Somebody on the floor below was banging with a metal object on the central heating pipes. The whole room reverberated with the clanging.

Rose lifted her fingers from the keys and shut her eyes. "Monsieur Bertrand," she said. "He can't stand it if I play in the evenings. Luckily he's usually out during the day, when my pupils come." She gave a long sigh, closed the piano and stood up, smiling. "One of these days he's going to damage those pipes and cause a leak. He'll have grand waterworks in his flat, like at Versailles. But it's not good," she added, half to herself, "not good being angry. As I said."

"What a pain. It's not as if you were playing heavy metal or rap full blast, after all."

"Some people just don't like music, I suppose. Not even Bach. It seems strange to dislike something so perfect and so…" She searched for the word. "…so intangible. Evanescent. It floats in the air, it's sufficient in itself, but you can't see it or hold on to it. It comes and goes."

"Like happiness," I said, suddenly realizing how closely music and happiness were allied for me. "Like the blue bird of happiness." My father had a copy of Maeterlinck's play, The Blue Bird, in his study. I knew exactly where to find it on his bookshelves.

At that moment there was a shuffling noise at the window, and Rose walked over to open it.

What happened next gave me a shock. I saw a pair of glaring black eyes, and with a rush of cold air a huge bird flew silently into the room. It was not a blue bird, or anything like it. I found myself over by the door with my arms raised to shield my face. Another moment and I would have been outside on the landing.

"It's all right," said Rose hastily. "She won't hurt you. Look, she's perfectly quiet."

I raised my eyes cautiously and saw a great brindled owl perching on the back of a chair. Its round black eyes were still staring fiercely at me. As I watched, Rose stretched out her wrist and the bird stepped on to it, gripping her skin with furry talons that could rend and tear, but apparently not hurting her. The flat, disc-like face bobbed. I stayed where I was.

"It's only Luna," she reassured me. "She lives in the park on the other side of the boulevard, don't you, dear? Incidentally," she grinned, "it's lucky she's not carrying a dead mouse. She sometimes brings me one as a present."

I flinched again as the owl spread its wings and flew up to alight on Rose's shoulder, the claws digging into the gold sheen of her blouse. I thought she looked like Pallas Athene (although I now know that Luna was a tawny owl, whereas it was a little owl that the goddess used to stroll around with). Luna nibbled her ear, very gently. Then she glared at me again and suddenly screeched. If you have never heard an owl screech indoors, you can have no idea how loud it is. I put my hands over my ears. "Kee-vick! Kee-vick! Kee-vick!"

I wondered what Monsieur Bertrand made of it.

Then the bird gathered itself for flight and took off, straight and soundlessly, through the open window. Rose stood with one hand on the window-frame, watching the gliding silhouette dwindle against the sky.

***

Windows, windows. When I look back, I realize how significant they were in this part of my life.

It must have been a Saturday morning shortly afterwards that I stood in my night-time T-shirt by the closed window, sipping coffee and looking out at the pale greyness that is the colour of every Paris street in winter. Slate grey, zinc grey, asphalt grey, cobblestone grey. The sky, the bare trees, the roofs and the building opposite, all were shades of grey, and around Rose's centre window was a great fluttering of grey wings. The pigeons were congregating, jostling for space on the ledge and the balustrade, flying out into the air and swooping back again. I saw Rose open the window and shake out one of her bright rugs, and it seemed to me that several pigeons flew into the room behind her.

I waved, but she didn't see me.

On the floor below, Monsieur Bertrand was diligently scraping his windowsill. As I watched, he clapped his hand to the top of his head, shook out his fingers in disgust and retreated indoors. His window shut with a faint thump.

At other windows, people had hung their bedclothes out to air. It always surprises me that Parisians do this, since the air is so full of fumes and pollution, and windowsills become coated with a layer of greasy grime unless you clean them every week. When my upstairs neighbours, the Dumbbells, hung out their duvets, these sometimes dangled down in front of my window and made Topaz flap about with fright. Safe indoors, he was at present making short flights from the top of his cage to the television screen and back again. He had become much tamer lately, and I could let him out to fly and hop around the room, since he now consented to step on to my finger when it was time to go back into his cage. Of course I was careful, now, to keep the window closed. He had landed on yesterday's edition of Le Monde and was trying to pick up the newsprint with his beak.

I looked back to the street and saw the concierge of my block of flats, Madame Pereira, cross over to the building opposite with a bucket and mop. She prefers to be called the gardienne, I know, but I like the good old French word concierge. Rose's building had no concierge, so Madame Pereira was paid to keep the hall and stairs clean and to wheel out the dustbins, in addition to her work on this side of the street.

Before she could go inside, Monsieur Bertrand came hurrying out, and they stood talking on the pavement.

Naturally, I could hear nothing, but he was making vehement gestures, and she seemed to be trying to edge past him.

Then the main door opened again and a much younger man carrying a tool-box came swinging out. They both turned to him and he joined in the conversation for a few moments. Monsieur Bertrand made a final negative gesture as if pushing something downwards and away from him, then turned sharply and stumped off along the street. He spat in the gutter. Madame Pereira turned back to the other man and they continued to talk.

It was when he flung back his head and laughed that I felt a flicker of interest. Madame Pereira disappeared inside, and I leaned forward to watch as he loped away along the street in the other direction, swinging the tool-box lightly, apparently at ease with himself and the world in general.

He was stronger and brighter than the greyness, and it couldn't touch him.

– THREE –

"**H**ello, you've put on weight, haven't you?" was my brother's greeting to me as he strode into my parents' sitting-room on Christmas Eve. The two dogs romped around in uncomplicated delight, and Lisa, having shed her coat in the hall, followed him, sweetly pretty in a dress covered with rosebuds. She had brought my mother a poinsettia. "Don't tell me you're about to produce offspring too, like Lisa here. How's the emperor?" (He meant Adrien. Ha, ha.) "Ah, but that's off, isn't it – I was forgetting," he said breezily.

I think I must have gone white. I know I sat down rather suddenly and couldn't find a single word to say. Lisa sank down beside me and patted my hand in what was doubtless meant to be a consoling, sisterly fashion; I jerked my hand away. Her pregnancy hardly showed at all yet, but already she looked the part of the young mother, soft and blooming. Of course, Pascal had known nothing about my abortion.

Paying no further attention to me, he caught my mother under the mistletoe and gave her a smacking kiss. She laughed and blushed, pretending to be cross, and pushed past him to the sideboard to fetch the apéritif glasses.

My father was hovering near the door, trying to make himself heard above the din that the dogs were making, asking Lisa whether she would like a drink or whether, in her condition, alcohol was not perhaps...?

"I think I'll risk a very small dry sherry, please," she simpered.

"And you, Stella? A furniture breaker?" This was a family joke of many years' standing, and I accepted an old-fashioned vodka and orange.

"Congratulations on the book, Dad," said Pascal. "I've just bought twenty copies."

"Really?" said my father, pleased. A month ago he had published his second slim volume of poetry, which had been favourably reviewed by one of the posh Sunday papers and ignored, so far, by all the other media. I knew that up in the loft were stacks of remaindered copies of his first volume.

"We're giving away copies to our friends. A bit of publicity for the family name, after all."

"Do you suppose," said my father diffidently, "that they're the sort of poems your friends want to read?"

"Haven't a clue," said Pascal. "I haven't had time to read them myself. You know how it is – life's pretty hectic." He flung himself into an armchair and lounged elegantly, in immaculate trousers and a smart jacket, with his cropped ash-blond hair and green eyes: Mamie's eyes, except that their expression was quite different.

My own eyes are neither green nor brown, but a sort of mixture of both, with flecks in them. I suppose you could call them hazel. And my hair is not properly blond but a sort of brownish fair colour. Not mousy, exactly. Once I had asked the hairdresser for highlights, but the effect had been brassy, to Pascal's gleeful derision. Surreptitiously I slid a finger inside my waistband. Had I really put on weight?

In any case, Christmas is no time for slimming. On Christmas Eve we always have a French meal, with oysters and smoked salmon and turkey and a chocolate Yule log, although we eat earlier in the evening than is the custom in France, since these days we don't go to midnight mass. We are lapsed Catholics, but I know my mother has a hankering to attend mass at Christmas and Easter, and would go to church, except that she has had a row with the local priest. Then on Christmas Day, having exchanged presents in the morning, we have an English Christmas lunch with roast goose and Christmas pudding. Respecting the customs of both countries can be a bit overwhelming.

My mother adores all the cooking and preparations, although she still affects to despise "le pouding", my father's favourite.

"What shall we do this afternoon?" asked Pascal over the lunch-table, while the Christmas rain drizzled down the steamy windows and my mother was in the kitchen setting light to the brandy.

The crack in the dining-room ceiling, I noticed, had grown longer and sent out little offshoots over the years. My parents didn't appear to see it.

"I shall start reading Pepys's diary," said my father. He had received a thick new edition from my mother as a present. "It's a scandal to have reached my age and not to have read Pepys, don't you agree?"

"Merde!" came a shriek from the kitchen, followed by several epithets in French, and Jip the spaniel came hurtling into the dining-room, licking his nose guiltily.

"Diaries are interesting documents, aren't they?" said Pascal in an insinuating voice, glancing at Lisa. "Stella's diary was absolutely riveting, I remember. Had maths test. Got six out of ten. If David doesn't speak to me tomorrow I shall die, I shall just die ..."

"You know you'd no bloody right to read my private diary!" I said, transported in an instant back to school days. "Anyway, what about the time you bought that enormous Valentine card with a great bulbous red heart – "

"Hush, don't shout, Stella," reproved my mother, coming in with the flaming pudding.

"But Pascal – "

He was grinning like a schoolboy.

"Hush! It's Christmas!"

I seethed. The trouble with family reunions is that all kinds of childhood memories and powerful feelings come crowding back. You think you have them under control, and when you are at a distance from your family you can ponder them with detachment and mature reasonableness, but the emotions are still there, only just under the surface, waiting to erupt into childish rages. Pascal loved to wind me up.

"The New Man will proceed to do the washing up," Pascal announced as soon as we had finished eating. I had been on the point of offering my own services.

"Don't put the best glasses in the dishwasher. Perhaps I had better do them," said my mother doubtfully.

"No, no, you're to put your feet up," he said, propelling her into the sitting-room. I followed, feeling superfluous. It was still raining. I sat on the pouffe and fondled Milou's ears, while my father opened Pepys with a sigh of satisfaction.

Red and silver balls hung from the plastic Christmas tree. When we were children we used to have a real tree, I remembered. This year, unlike last, various items that had belonged to Mamie were standing about the room, looking – I thought – strange and out of place: coloured glass vases, an African mask, and a Balinese painting which had always hung on her bedroom wall. Apart from my lump sum, a good deal of her estate had been spent by my mother on long-overdue repairs to the roof of this house, and on a set of rare antiquarian books for my father, to his astonished delight. Most of the old Provençal furniture – "too heavy" said my mother – had gone to Aunt Hélène, and much of what she dismissed as "bric-à-brac" had been thrown away. My mother is a great thrower away. She likes to make what she calls "a clean sweep".

As for my grandfather's flute, it was nowhere to be seen. I wondered where they had put it.

My mother and Lisa sat at either end of the threadbare sofa discussing the obvious subject, Lisa's pregnancy, while sounds of chinking plates and Pascal whistling "The Holly and the Ivy" off-key came from the kitchen. He had never been musical.

"Are you having any morning sickness?" my mother wanted to know.

"Not so far. I feel – "

"I was so sick, so sick when I was expecting Stella. Never have I felt so sick," said my mother dramatically.

I had heard this so many times, nearly as many times as the fact that her pregnancy with Pascal had been wonderfully easy. They rambled on about maternity dresses, and my mother boasted that she had made hers all herself; while Lisa said that knitting was more her line, but pregnant women all wore tight-fitting T-shirts nowadays. As for me, I'm no good at either sewing or knitting. My fingers are all thumbs, except when it comes to playing the guitar. When I was about thirteen, my mother tried to teach me to use her electric sewing machine, and I contrived to get the cotton so entangled round the works that it took her more than half an hour to untangle. She was not pleased. That was my last experiment with the sewing machine. Manual dexterity was one field in which Pascal didn't outshine me, however. He was hopeless, too.

"You can get some lovely knitting patterns for baby clothes these days," Lisa was saying. "In my weekly there was this matinée jacket ..."

I rubbed my nose across the top of Milou's head, and he tried to lick my face. If I had had the baby, how old would it have been by now ...? My mother would have been talking about baby-clothes with me. My eyes blurred. Stop that, you fool.

"... like Stella."

"What?"

"I said, the baby's due in July, so he or she will probably be a moon child, like Stella," said Lisa.

"Moon child?"

"Yes – the sign of the zodiac."

"You mean Cancer, don't you?" I said shortly.

"Astrologers say moon children nowadays. It has more positive energy," she told me seriously.

My father glanced up from his book, peering over his glasses – the broken earpiece mended with sellotape – and his eyes met mine. He shrugged imperceptibly.

"Don't you believe in astrology?" Lisa had noticed the shrug. My father said nothing, keeping out of arguments as usual.

"I believe in good luck and bad luck, oh, yes," said my mother emphatically. "But the French and the English don't always agree about what is unlucky. In England, everybody must take down their Christmas decorations on Twelfth Night, mustn't they? In France, we eat a galette des rois on Twelfth

Night, but the decorations can stay up, even until the end of January. So I don't know what to do. Every year I'm absolutely torn between the two!"

Torn! I frowned, wishing she wouldn't exaggerate.

Lisa nodded sagely. She talked for some time about good and evil omens, horoscopes and clairvoyants, and I stopped listening. What was I doing here? Knitting patterns and superstition. My father was deep in his book.

Pascal burst in, having virtuously finished his task in the kitchen, and the draught he made caused several of the Christmas cards lining the sideboard and the mantelpiece to topple over. I went to set them upright again, glancing at them idly. This year the themes seemed to be stagecoaches and snowmen. I liked cards with angels on them, but there weren't any. Something about angels fascinated me: the tall, graceful, austere kind, not the dimpled cherubs. My favourite carols told of that heavenly host – "Angels from the Realms of Glory" and "It Came upon a Midnight Clear". A real Christmas should have a hint of angels in the sky, I thought, just as a real Christmas should be white. But I couldn't remember snow in December. Usually we had this damp, mild, boring weather.

"Who wants to watch The Wizard of Oz again?" Pascal wanted to know, leafing through the TV programmes. Nobody did, so he immediately suggested that we watch a DVD. He always knew what he wanted to do.

"I'm afraid the DVD player broke down two days ago," said my father mildly.

"I'll try and fix it!"

"You will not!" said my mother hastily.

"Don't touch it, for goodness' sake," I chimed in, "or they'll never be able to use it again. Like my musical box that you took apart."

"What musical box?"

"Don't pretend you've forgotten! You deliberately – "

"Stella, that must have been years and years ago. Fancy remembering a little thing like that for such a long time," protested my mother.

"He ruined it. It wouldn't work after that. Don't you remember, Maman, it was the musical box that Mamie gave me – " I could see it so clearly in my mind's eye. They couldn't have forgotten it: the polished, carved, walnut wood box.

"The box that Mamie gave me!" Pascal mimicked. "Don't you think Mamie gave you enough?" he inquired nastily. He had been furious about the legacy, even though he had already bought himself a three-bedroomed house.

Lisa was watching us and shaking her head slightly.

I was ready with a retort, but stopped myself. Suddenly a memory of Rose's voice was in my ears: "Who angers me, controls me ..." If Pascal wanted to pick a quarrel, I wouldn't give him that satisfaction. Not this time. Nobody was going to control me.

"Oh, forget it. Come on, dogs," I said, "let's go for a walk."

The pandemonium of joy that broke out drowned any further remarks from Pascal.

When I'm old and can retire from city life, I shall have dogs, I think. They are so straightforward and honest and cheerful. They're always glad to see you, and it takes so little to make them happy. Of course, I shan't live in Paris, where there are too many dogs already and you have to watch where you are stepping on the pavement.

We set off through the drizzle, across the recreation ground, where any number of people were also out with their dogs, walking off the effects of their turkey or goose. I didn't feel like talking to any of them, but Jip and Milou romped around with the other dogs. Then we went up the new road to the housing estate, where there were vacant lots and half-built houses on land that had been wilderness when I was a child, and beyond again to real, muddy fields. Coloured Christmas tree lights winked in distant windows, and it was already beginning to get dark. A cloud of gulls rose and fell over a ploughed field. Jip turned back to make sure that I was following, then lolloped ahead again, his tail waving in a circle. I breathed in the damp, clean air that smelt of earth and trees.

Paris is a polluted city, yet I was feeling homesick for my flat and for Topaz. I had left him with Rose. "Of course," she had said, "I'd love to look after him." I wanted to be back in Paris, but I didn't want to go back to the office. Nowhere felt right. I had begun to look forward to coming to England for Christmas, but then my mother had told me at length about several former class-mates who were doing very well: they were pursuing brilliant careers or had married wealthy men. I got the message. And Pascal made me feel as taut as a wire; he couldn't touch anything fragile without breaking it. That musical box incident seemed as vivid as yesterday: I had never forgotten the lovely, melancholy vanished music.

I had left my guitar in Paris, too. It would have been awkward to carry on Eurostar, and I didn't want to hear any of Pascal's comments about my "twanging". But I wished I had a small electronic keyboard. The song that had been in the back of my mind was definitely starting to take shape. Words and melody were beginning to come together, but I needed to try them out. "Rain in Another Country", I called it. I played it over in my mind, beginning to feel better. "Make something," echoed Rose's voice in my memory.

I threw sticks for the dogs for about a quarter of an hour, then called them to heel and started for home, humming, singing under my breath, repeating and altering a phrase, humming again.

Yes, I felt better.

***

Later that evening we switched off the television and played Scrabble. My father wanted to go on reading, but was forced to join in. "English *and* French words are allowed," stated Pascal bossily.

"Talking of Twelfth Night," said my father suddenly. We stared at him, because we had been talking of no such thing, but he went on serenely: "It's very interesting. I've been reading in Pepys that in seventeenth-century England people used to bake a special cake for Twelfth Night, just like the galette des rois in France. It had a dried pea and a bean in it, and those who found the pea or the bean in their slice were the king and queen for that night."

"How funny," said my mother. "Just like the fève – what do you call it? – the charm! The charm in the galette. The lucky charm. Or unlucky. Do you know, once, when we were children, your aunt Hélène swallowed the charm. And believe it or not, we had such bad luck for the next twelve months."

Lisa was nodding gravely.

"I wonder why the custom died out in England. I thought it had never existed here," mused my father.

"I knew about that. I knew it existed in the seventeenth century," said Pascal.

"I bet you didn't," said Lisa, rather sharply for her.

"Yes, I did. I learned it in school."

"Pascal has such a good memory," said my mother fondly.

– FOUR –

Back in Paris, the wet Christmas gave way to a white New Year. Snow began to fall in the night, and on the Monday morning, as I hurried carefully along the slippery street towards the metro, late for work, I looked up to see Rose hobbling toward me, leaning on a crutch. Snow powdered her dark hair, matching the white streak in it, and her face looked thin and pinched.

"It's just a sprain," she said dismissively, when we had exchanged New Year greetings, "but it does make it difficult for me to carry things."

"I can do any shopping you need on my way home from work," I offered. "Why don't you go home and rest your ankle? They really ought to clear the snow off these pavements."

So that was how, on my way back from the office, I began to buy the few groceries and oddments that she needed: bread, vegetables, fruit and rice mainly. She never asked for any meat or dairy products – not surprisingly, perhaps, since she actually had no fridge, and I wondered how she managed without one. Then we would chat for half an hour or so before I went back to my own flat. I talked a lot more about Adrien and about the shock of my grandmother's sudden death of a stroke. She listened sympathetically, but she often managed to make me laugh at myself, or at men and life's problems generally, and I would go home feeling cheered.

Sometimes one of her piano pupils would be there, often a solemn, shy girl of about twelve with protruding ears, or a frizzy-haired woman in her fifties who seemed more eager to gossip than to play the easy pieces she was supposed to be learning. I listened to their stumbling efforts and wondered how Rose, who could play so well, had the patience to teach these beginners, none of whom, in my opinion, would ever be a pianist. But she never lost her temper, even when they made the same mistake five times in a row. Monsieur Bertrand might well have objected to the halting noises they made, but he gave no sign of life, and as Rose pointed out, her last pupil had always left by six-thirty or seven. At other times I would find Rose busy at her sewing machine, or stitching away at her patchwork with a pair of fine half-moon gold spectacles on her nose.

After a brief thaw, it had started to snow again. On that particular evening, I panted up the last flight of stairs with the shopping and heard a man's voice talking inside the flat.

I thought Rose looked ill at ease as she let me in. "Ah – uh – Stella, this is Olivier. Olivier, my friend Stella from across the street."

A tall, lean man in jeans and a leather jacket unfolded himself from the armchair. By the light of the oil lamp I thought I recognized his face, and a moment later I realized he was the man I had seen leaving the building with a tool-box, just before Christmas. His unruly hair was like a mane, curling low on the nape of his neck. His whole face was alive and alert. His eyebrows were straight and level, flicked up at the outer corners like wings, and his eyes were dark and bright at the same time, rather like an animal's eyes, but full of gleaming intelligence. I thought that I had never seen a face more alive.

"Enchanté," he said, taking my hand in a warm, dry grip, and in his voice I heard that accent. The south, the Midi. I could hear the mistral blowing around my grandmother's house, I could feel the hot sun blistering the shutters that in summer she kept closed until evening, I could see the wistaria tumbling in amethyst opulence over the wall of her courtyard and smell the wild thyme on the hills above Aix. It was all there in his voice, the happiest days of my childhood, and the hidden promise of some happiness not yet out of reach. Or so it seemed to me. I think I closed my eyes for a second.

"Olivier has brought a galette des rois," said Rose, still sounding slightly put out. "I'll make some more tea and you must share it with us." I wondered whether I was intruding, but I couldn't take my eyes off him, and I started asking polite questions so as to hear his voice again.

While Rose was making Kashmiri tea, he told me that he was an electrician and had a small electrical sales and repair shop in the next street. Since moving in, I somehow hadn't had occasion to walk along that street, so I didn't know the shop.

"I belong to a dying breed," he told me. "You'd be amazed how many people need small electrical repairs done, but they can't find anyone who will do them quickly. Nowadays you have to send your appliances back to the makers, and they keep them for months. Or the things are just not worth the cost of repairs, and people throw them away. Built-in obsolescence."

I told him I could well believe it. I was fascinated by his voice, and by his eyes, which didn't gaze vaguely in my direction or wander around the room, but looked straight at me.

"The average household now owns at least twenty electrical appliances," he said, "but flats in these old buildings often have only half a dozen sockets. People overload their circuits and blow fuses all the time. You'd be surprised how many people don't know about fuses. Of course, some of these buildings should really be completely rewired."

I was not at all interested in electrical wiring, but I listened intently, watching his lips. I expect I had a gormless expression on my face.

Rose hobbled in with the tea. She could manage without her crutch by now, but had to be careful how she put her weight on her foot. She had placed the galette on a gold-rimmed plate and cut it into three. Twelfth Night was long past, but bakers go on selling these cakes throughout January, complete with gold cardboard crowns for the finders of the charms.

"I wonder how this custom began?" I said, to fill a pause, and told them about my father's discovery in Pepys's diary.

"It's for the solstice," said Rose. I waited for her to enlarge on that, but she said nothing more. The solstice. The turning-point, when the days start growing longer and begin to draw out again into the light.

"Who's got the charm?" asked Olivier after a minute.

"I have." Rose held up the small china charm. It represented a babe in swaddling clothes.

"So!" he said, fastening the flat golden crown into a circle, "Allow me to crown you queen." He placed the crown slowly and solemnly on her dark hair. "Now you must choose a king."

"I haven't a lot of choice, have I?" said Rose drily, standing up to join him. I saw that they were exactly the same height. They kissed each other on both cheeks. "Ouch!" said Olivier. "Static." King and queen then looked at each other gravely, and I felt that I should be elsewhere. Who was I: a kneeling courtier, perhaps, outside the charmed circle? The candles guttered, and beyond the tall windows millions of snowflakes softly fell.

"I must be going," I said, gulping the last of my tea.

"No," said Rose quickly. "Don't go yet – there's something I want to talk to you about. Olivier, thank you for the galette, but I have to talk to Stella now."

He took the hint, winding a long scarf around his neck and moving towards the door. "Remember," he said to me, shaking hands again, "Sanchez is the name for electrical repairs," and a moment later we heard him clattering down the stairs.

Rose briskly cleared away the cups and plates, tossing the charm into the dustbin with the crumbs. Her kitchen was large enough for only one person, and she talked to me through the bead curtain in the doorway. A hurricane lantern made her figure seem darker, bending and straightening in the cave-like alcove, and its glow cast huge shadows of the strings of beads on the opposite wall.

"Isn't it unlucky to throw the charm away?" I said, half jokingly, as she emerged.

She looked at me for a moment. "I don't believe in luck," she said shortly. "What's coming to us is coming to us. We cause what happens. We're responsible."

I didn't much want to follow this line of thought, which seemed full of foreboding.

"Olivier seems a nice guy." I changed the subject. "I feel you rather pushed him out. Don't you like him?"

"No. Yes. I just didn't expect to see him again so soon. He was round here yesterday. He keeps finding some pretext to come round. He just..." Her voice trailed away.

Out of the corner of my eye I noticed a movement in a cardboard box by the side of the piano. "What's in there?" I looked more closely.

"This is what he brought me yesterday." She moved a piece of old blanket aside, and I saw, cowering in the bottom of the box, a very ugly bird. It looked like a badly plucked chicken, tailless and almost featherless, with just a little yellowish down here and there. Its feet were huge, and it had a big beak, purplish and bulbous looking.

"What ever is it?"

"A young pigeon, fallen out of the nest."

"What, in the middle of winter?"

"Pigeons nest all the year round. He said he found her on the pavement and was afraid people would tread on her."

"How did he know it was a she?"

"He didn't," said Rose, "but I know. Her name is Blanche." She fetched a bowl of porridgy stuff from the kitchen and held a fistful over the bird's head; At first it didn't react, but then it began stuffing its beak urgently into her curled fingers, making a faint squeaky whistling noise. Rose explained to me that young pigeons feed, not by opening their beaks, but by thrusting their heads into their parents' throats, and I watched, fascinated. The bird withdrew its head, looking much more wide awake now, bits of food clinging to the down on its head.

"She's rather sweet," I said. "Will she survive, do you think?"

"Oh, yes. She wants to survive, you can see. And pigeons can live thirty years or more."

Thirty years in the street, I marvelled. Thirty years, seeing different models of car come and go, watching the same office-workers leave their homes every morning, seeing them get older and greyer until retirement swallowed them up. A pigeon pecking around my feet might be as old as I was. But could they really survive for so long in the city?

"You wanted to talk to me about something," I reminded her after a moment.

"Yes." She rummaged in a drawer and took out a letter. "What do you think of this?"

It was a typed letter from the administrator of the building, quoting a by-law and reminding her rather pompously that pigeons' droppings caused damage to the façade and that, as she was doubtless aware, it was forbidden to feed them on the premises.

"What shall I do?" she asked.

"Well," I said, surprised, "I suppose you'll just have to stop feeding them on your balcony. It does seem a bit hard in this snowy weather, but still – "

"But I don't. Apart from Blanche. I don't feed them."

I told her that I was sure I had seen pigeons flocking around her window.

"I know. They come, but I don't feed them. They just come to me. Pigeons and other birds."

There was a silence. "I see," I said.

"I'm sure it was Monsieur Bertrand who put the authorities up to writing to me." She walked to the window and rested her forehead against the glass. In the yellowish light from the streetlamps, the snow whirled past endlessly, crystals of purity to be trodden into slush and furrowed by the crawling tyres of the traffic. She seemed to have forgotten the gold coronet still on her head. "I don't know what to do," she said. "How can I stop doing something that I'm not doing? They just come to me. I'm not a threat to them."

***

It can't have been more than a week, at most, before I found an excuse to go round to Olivier's shop. After all, why shouldn't I explore the neighbourhood? I didn't know what shops were to be found in that street. Moreover, I needed some new light-bulbs. It made sense to have a stock of bulbs, I told myself, since if a bulb blew, it was sure to be at an inconvenient moment, when the shops were shut. I was also thinking of buying a low-energy reading lamp. It would be just the thing for my flat, and the prices had fallen quite a lot recently.

The shop was an old-fashioned one with a double frontage, glowing with lamps in the late winter afternoon, and a string of fairy-lights still ran around the window display of plugs, switches, hair-driers, kettles and microwaves. The name "Sanchez" was picked out in faded lettering over the door, which opened with a loud ping.

Olivier, carrying a pair of pliers, emerged from the room at the back of the shop.

"Well, hello! It's Stella, isn't it?" he said at once. He remembers my name, I thought, and those dark eyes fastened on mine again with such intensity that I nearly forgot what I had planned to buy. All around us the lamps shone, their shades ranging from imitation art nouveau to classic parchment, golden, white, pink, pearl.

He had a large stock of light-bulbs, the boxes stacked up on shelves behind the counter. I bought two perfectly ordinary bulbs – the sort that you can buy in any supermarket, in fact – and then inquired about reading lamps, which he proceeded to show me. I looked at several, hesitating, and he switched them on and off, making shadows scurry across the floor. I could feel his eyes on me as I hesitated. I compared prices, hesitated again, began to examine a toaster. Nobody else came into the shop.

"I'll tell you what," he said, "it's nearly closing time. Why don't I shut up shop, and we could go for an apéritif or something."

He'd guessed that I had sought him out. Well, why not? I felt reckless.

We walked down the street, cold and dry now that the snow had gone, towards the boulevard. He had turned up his collar and thrust his hands deep in his pockets. I asked him where he came from originally.

"Perpignan," he said, "the Roussillon. Catalan country. And the climate is a lot warmer down there, I can tell you."

"So why did you come up to Paris?"

"Oh, I'll be going back eventually. It's my uncle's shop, and I'm looking after it for him for a year while he travels round the world. When he comes back, maybe I'll go round the world myself."

He told me about his red-bearded, eccentric uncle René, who had set off with a backpack like a student. He related several funny anecdotes about his escapades, and I was laughing as we reached the café on the boulevard. I started to tell him about my connections with Provence, but the waiter came up and Olivier couldn't decide whether to order a hot or a cold drink. I asked for a diabolo-menthe and he finally settled for a beer. Then there was a pause as we sat looking out through the glassed-in terrace at the traffic and the hurrying passers-by.

"How long have you known Rose?" he asked abruptly.

I told me about our first meeting, and he listened intently, nodding as I spoke, as if hanging on to every word.

"Rose makes problems for herself," he said.

"What do you mean – problems?" I felt protective towards her.

"She's an unconventional person." He looked around the café at the boys playing a noisy electronic game in the corner, at the waiter in his black waistcoat and long white apron giving change, at the people queuing at the counter for cigarettes and lottery tickets.

"Paris is full of unusual people," I said. "That's what makes it interesting. Where my parents live, in England, everyone is so bland. It's really boring." I could visualize their puddingy faces. I tried to imagine Rose among them, and failed.

I wasn't sure that he had heard me. "For instance," he said, turning towards me again, "do you know how I first met her? I went to do a job at her flat. I couldn't believe it: she wanted all the electric light fittings taken out. All the switches removed. I had to cover up all the plug sockets with plastic. You can't use a single electrical appliance in her place."

"Well, I've noticed that she always uses an oil lamp and candles, but it's rather attractive isn't it? What if she prefers it like that?"

"For a start, she's ruining her eyesight, trying to sew her patchwork by candlelight. I've tried to persuade her to have a reading lamp, but she won't." He drank some beer and spilled a few drops on the table top.

"I wonder how she irons the patches before she sews them," I said.

"I'll tell you. She has one of those heavy old flat-irons. You have to go to the flea market to find such things. She heats it up on the gas stove. At least she didn't ask me to disconnect the gas! And another thing," he went on, "I had to go round to her building recently to repair the time-switch on the sixth floor landing. So of course I checked the whole system, and I found that the time-switch on her landing, the seventh floor, was out of order, too. So I started to repair it, and guess what? She came out and did her level best to persuade me to leave it alone. Told me she could see perfectly well in the dark. And there she was, hobbling up and down those stairs with a sprained ankle, in the dark! She's unreasonable. I tell you, she makes life complicated for herself."

I thought about this. "Perhaps she has a sort of phobia about electricity," I suggested.

"Some phobia!" He seemed outraged – I suppose because electricity was his trade and his living, and here was Rose perversely showing that she could manage without it. But she was hardly a threat to him. Everybody else depended heavily on their appliances, as I did myself. Nothing in my flat would work if there were a power cut, and I didn't relish the prospect of walking up eight floors if the lift was out of order. Work in the office would come to a halt – no computers, no fax machines, no photocopiers.

"She hasn't even got television, of course," I commented.

"She's out of touch. Only one per cent of the population hasn't got television. The average adult spends twenty-seven hours a week watching television, did you know that?"

"God, I hope I don't!" It was hard to believe that people were so passive. I watched it, naturally, but one good thing about living alone was that I could switch it off as soon as my interest flagged. Adrien had always wanted to watch programmes that I found boring – athletics and game shows and Formula 1 racing.

"She won't discuss it, though," said Olivier. "And yet she's not stupid, not stupid at all. You can talk to her for hours, about all kinds of things. But with Rose, everything has to be on her own terms."

I wondered when he had had opportunities to talk to Rose for hours. How well did they know each other? What exactly was their relationship? She had certainly hustled him out that day, and she had never mentioned him to me before. Why not? We had talked about men. Or at any rate, I had talked about men, and she could easily have said something. Did she not want me to know him?

I wondered if he had met Luna, the owl, and started to tell him about Topaz as a way of leading up to the subject. But after a few moments I realized that he was not listening. He sat turning his glass round and round with a brooding expression. There was something unconsciously fierce about his profile, the way a tiger or a hawk looks ferocious even in repose. His hair made little curls on the nape of his neck and under his ears, and his lean face was beginning to look in need of a shave.

He glanced at his watch. "I'm afraid I have to go – I have a karate class tonight," he said, reaching into his pocket for change. We had a brief argument over who should pay for the drinks, and then we were walking back up my street. I made another attempt to talk about Aix, and this time he was alive and interested, asking me questions and telling me about Perpignan, which I had never visited. He told me about the pink marble pavements, and how the people danced the sardane in the streets on summer evenings, forming circles within circles. I felt a nostalgic longing for the south.

"I don't know the sardane," I said.

"I'll have to teach you, some time."

"Why not?"

It was, he told me, a uniquely Catalan dance, and so old that nobody knew its origins. Some people claimed that the circle of dancers symbolized the sun.

We had come to the entrance to my building, and I hesitated, clutching my light-bulbs, wondering if he would suggest that we meet again. But he merely said "Goodnight," putting one hand on my shoulder and leaning forward to kiss me on both cheeks. I could feel his stubble and smell the leather of his jacket. It seemed a very long time since I had been physically close to a man. There had been no one since the man who had made me pregnant, two years ago now.

Of course, if I'm honest, I have to admit that I was lonely.

As I entered the building, I glanced back, but he was not looking at me. He was standing with his head tilted back, gazing up at the faint glow of candlelight in Rose's windows.

***

When I was a child, our road was very quiet. The neighbourhood children used to ride their bikes freely along it, and we played on the pavement. I was walking sedately along the pavement that day, pushing my doll Angelina in her pram, and telling her in a solicitous voice that I had just given her her dinner and changed her nappy, and that when she was asleep I would leave her in the garden while I went round to the town to do some shopping and change my library books.

I loved Angelina. She had a sweet, pretty face. Her blue eyes, with long, stiff eyelashes, opened and closed. Best of all, she had real golden hair that I could comb and tie up with ribbons, and she never cried – unlike Pascal, who bawled the place down if he hurt himself or was thwarted in anything. Today she was wearing a pastel blue dress that I told her suited her very well. "It's just your colour," I said, as I had heard my mother say to her friends.

Pascal came pedalling up behind me on his tricycle, ringing the bell and shouting "Beep-beep!" Some boys, older than he, were riding their bikes and doing tricks, making the bikes rear up like horses or cycling with no hands, zig-zagging. Far ahead along the pavement, two girls whom I knew were skipping. I would go up to them and have an earnest discussion about Angelina's ailments.

"Come on, get a move on!" shouted Pascal. Then, "Hey, I know. Let's tie the pram to my trike. I can pull it along. It'll be a – like a – a trailer, see?"

"I don't know," I said doubtfully. "It might be dangerous. Angelina might not like it."

"Oh, come on, Stell. I bet she will. I'll let you have a go afterwards, if you want." He had already produced a piece of string from his pocket and was tying the pram to the back of his tricycle. I watched uncertainly. I was sure real mothers didn't let their prams be pulled along like trailers.

"Don't go too fast," I warned.

But Pascal was already pedalling and gathering speed, shouting "Brrrmmm, brrrrmmmm! Beep-beep!" The pram bumped along behind him, rocking from side to side. Angelina was being jolted about.

I started to run after them, calling "Not so fast!" but Pascal didn't slow down. He was heading for the skipping girls, showing off.

Then one of the trick-cycling boys came veering towards Pascal at top speed and mounted the pavement. "Look out!" I heard him yell, and Pascal gave a shriek. The boy swerved violently to the right and Pascal swerved to the left. I saw the pram career behind him, tilt and topple over sideways. Angelina shot out, straight into the stone wall of a neighbour's garden. The pram lay on its side, two wheels spinning.

I was beside it in an instant. Angelina lay still in her blue dress, her back to me. I turned her over. Her plastic face was cracked right down the centre. I could see inside to the pink plastic hollow of her head. I picked her up, and her eyes flew open, looking at me grotesquely from either side of the great crack in her face.

Pascal was standing by his tricycle, scuffing the pavement with his toe.

"It wasn't my fault," he said. The other boy paused to look for a moment, then cycled off, shouting to his friend.

I was frozen. "You've killed her."

"I haven't! It's only a stupid old doll, anyway," said Pascal.

"You have," I said. "You've killed her." My hands felt very cold and my heart was thumping. A great lump formed in my throat and I began to cry.

Later, my father explained to me gently that even if he glued the two halves of her head together the join would show, and there were some little jagged pieces of plastic missing, so it would not be a neat join. She would not look like my perfect Angelina any more.

"Pascal breaks everything," I sobbed bitterly.

"He didn't mean to," said my father.

I told my mother that I didn't want the doll any more. I bundled up her clothes almost without looking at them, and my mother, shrugging, put everything in the dustbin. Later, when I was in school, I thought about her lying in the bin, sad, damaged and rejected, and as soon as I came home I ran to rescue her. But the dustbins had been emptied, and she had gone. There was nothing left inside except a foul smell and a few potato peelings.

Several times after that I awoke in the night screaming, seeing Angelina's reproachful blue eyes staring at me from her cracked and irreparably damaged face, filled with horror as I tried in vain to push the two jagged halves together.

Although my mother came into the bedroom and tried to comfort me, I could never tell her what was wrong.

***

The traffic lights were on the blink again, I noticed as I hurried towards the supermarket. It was a cold, sunny Saturday morning, and both sets of lights at the intersection were flashing amber. It had been happening a lot recently.

Just as I was about to enter the supermarket, Rose came out, carrying a bottle of disinfectant. She had a cloak flung around her shoulders, and her hair was caught back at the nape of her neck with a black ribbon. She looked as if she should be booted and spurred, about to ride away across some wild plain.

"I have to get back," she said almost immediately.

"What's the hurry?"

"I have to – oh, it's so disgusting," she grimaced. "I have to clean out my mailbox. Somebody put dog shit in it."

"Dog shit! Who could have done that? Children, maybe, playing a practical joke? I hope they don't start doing it to everyone."

"I don't think so. It was meant for me."

"Not that anybody could cram anything into *my* mailbox. It's always overflowing with junk mail."

"Mine's usually empty, but this morning…No, I don't believe it was children."

"Who, then?"

People passed us in both directions, pushing their way through the swing doors of the supermarket. A car backed on to the pavement and we moved to avoid it. Rose was looking towards the flashing traffic lights, her eyes distressed.

"Monsieur Bertrand," she said very quietly. "I'm fairly sure of it." She rubbed her forehead with her knuckles.

"Surely he wouldn't do such a crazy thing."

"I don't think you realize how much he hates me," she said.

"But why? Just because you play the piano? It's ridiculous."

"I know. Well, there is the piano, and there are the pigeons. But there's another reason."

The deafening blare of a horn drowned her voice. Almost simultaneously there was a crunch, and we saw that two cars had collided in the middle of the intersection. I winced. The wing and front bumper of one was severely dented, and there was glass all over the road. This happens all the time, of course, because there is an unwritten rule in Paris that when the lights turn red, three or four cars can still go through. Unfortunately there is also a rule that the very second the lights turn green, you must shoot forward, otherwise you get honked at from behind. It makes life hazardous for pedestrians.

Now, one driver clambered out of his car and began shouting at the other, who soon got out too and stood facing him aggressively, but we couldn't hear what he was saying. The first driver yelled louder and slammed his left hand down on his right arm, punching upwards with his right fist – the *bras d'honneur*. People paused on the pavement with their shopping, waiting to see what would happen. A cacophony of hooting began from motorists at a standstill in all directions.

"So much anger," said Rose ruefully. "Such a waste of energy."

"It's a pity they can't harness that energy somehow," I said. "They could probably run their cars off it."

"It would be non-polluting, too," said Rose. "Environmentally friendly." We grinned at each other for a second.

Now the second driver suddenly kicked the first car, whereupon the first driver grabbed him by the lapels and started to shove him backwards. Other people intervened, and three men began to push one of the cars to the side of the road.

"You were saying, about Monsieur Bertrand?" I prompted.

"I was saying that he hates me for another reason. You see, he wasn't always like that. At first he was very friendly – much too friendly. He kept asking me to go out for a drink with him, and I had to make him understand that I wasn't interested."

"But he's so old!" I was appalled.

"Only in his sixties, I should say. That's not so old. I think he's lonely since his wife died. I was sorry for him, in a way, but he misunderstood that. Then one day he – he put his hands on me, and I, well, I sort of pushed him. He was furious. I think he got the message, though."

"How awful. So you mean – since then he's been making life difficult for you?"

"It started then. But it's been worse since Christmas. You remember when I sprained my ankle? You thought I had slipped in the snow, but in fact it wasn't that. What happened was – he tried to grab me on the stairs in my building. I'm not really sure what he was trying to do – whether he meant to hurt me or just grope me. I'm not sure he knew himself. But this happened in the dark, and we had a violent scuffle on the staircase, and I slipped and hurt my ankle. I'd pushed him hard against the wall, and he tried to turn on the light – and when he pressed the time switch, he got an electric shock. He yelled."

Two sparrows flew down out of the nearest tree and fluttered around her head as if about to alight on it. She lifted her hand and one of them perched on it briefly, turning its head to look at her with one eye and then the other, before flying back into the tree.

"My ankle hurt, and I shouted at him, too. I shouldn't have done. I told him to leave me alone, or I wouldn't answer for the consequences."

"And what did he say?"

"Oh, he said 'merde', and a few other things." She smiled rather wearily. "But ever since then he's been determined to get me out of the building. He wants me evicted."

"Can he do that?"

"Not officially. No, I shouldn't think so."

Another sparrow hovered, then swooped away. Rose said that she must hurry back and clean her mailbox, so we parted and I went into the supermarket.

When I re-emerged with my week's groceries, I noticed that the traffic lights had started working normally again.

***

"Eef I go to ze market, I buy som flowairs."

"No, no. If I go to the market, I *will* buy some flowers."

I was helping Madame Pereira's young son with his English homework. She had asked me if I could give him some extra coaching, since his marks were so bad, and he now sat, flushed, bored and resentful, with his books spread over the kitchen table, while his mother peeled vegetables and stirred saucepans. Why had I agreed to do it? I was rubbish at teaching.

"Eef I will go – "

"No. If I go, I will. All right, Francisco, why don't you just learn these constructions by heart? Don't try and figure out why the rules are like that – just learn the pattern, OK? Then I'll test you on pages 92 and 93 next week."

"OK." He jumped up and grabbed a can of soda from the fridge, swept his books together, turned up the volume on his MP3 player to a tinny shrillness and crashed out of the door.

"He has no patience, that's his trouble. Just like his father," said Madame Pereira. Her plump hands sliced and chopped. "Not like me, you see. When I was at school, I was very conscientious. Persevering, I was. I could have gone on to college if I hadn't got married. Oh, yes, I could have had quite a different life."

"So do you regret getting married?" I asked, watching her. I like watching people who can cook, and sometimes think that I ought to be able to do it myself, but in fact I never do. I choose speed and convenience every time, and thank God for the microwave.

"Regret it? Oh, no!" Her black, button-like eyes were emphatic. They were round and bright, and her teeth protruded, giving her the permanent appearance of a grumpy squirrel, although in fact she was perfectly amiable. "Men are difficult creatures, oh là! They're difficult. But it's only natural for a woman to want to settle down, get married and have a family. I may be old fashioned, but it's what suits us best, I say. I don't hold with all these godless young career girls living alone, living like men themselves, not having any children." The black mole on her right cheek moved as she talked.

"Like me," I put in drily.

"Well, I wouldn't wish to criticize, it's not my business, but take yourself now. Isn't it awfully lonely, not having a man around to take care of and depend on?"

Taking care? Depending? I had seen some of that.

"Being single seems to be the new way of life," I said. "More and more people are living alone these days." I was not about to tell her of my failed attempt at living with somebody else.

"Yes, but are you really happy, all you young girls?" she demanded. She waved her knife. "Take that Madame Martin across the street. I don't want to be indiscreet, but I've seen you talking to her. Such a sad, strange lady. So secretive. I sometimes wish she could find a nice husband. Have children." She flung vegetables into a sizzling pan, and the kitchen filled with the smell of hot olive oil. "My husband, now – he may have his faults – what man hasn't? – but I know he would defend me to the death if he had to. He'd risk his life for me. Isn't that worth having?"

"I think Madame Martin prefers – "

"And then poor old Monsieur Bertrand – he's unhappy, too, come to that," she went on. "He's so lonely, he comes out and talks to me while I'm cleaning the stairs. It's not good to be cooped up on your own all day, thinking your own thoughts with nobody to talk to. You start going a bit funny."

"I don't think Madame Martin – " I began.

The door opened and the head of the household came in. He grunted a surprised greeting at me, said nothing to his wife and went through to the bedroom. He has some kind of job in the building trade.

"Of course, he was different when his wife was alive," said Madame Pereira. "She wouldn't stand for any nonsense. A bit of a battleaxe, she was. Very respectable. Teetotal, too. Went to mass regularly, every Saturday night. So did he, in those days, but not any more. She had him under her thumb. If you ask me, he hasn't been quite himself since she died."

"How long ago was that?" I gathered up my pen and notepad.

"Two years – three years? It was cancer. Very slow. Cruel, really. They say she was like a skeleton at the end."

Monsieur Pereira re-entered the kitchen, having changed out of his working clothes. He had lost most of his hair, but sported a comb-over that surely fooled nobody. As if to compensate, he had a bushy moustache. Lowering himself on to a chair, he reached for the remote control and flicked on the television.

"When was it, now, that Madame Bertrand died?" asked his wife.

"Eh? Three years ago." He had a strong Portuguese accent, unlike his wife, who was from the Ardèche.

"I was just saying, he's been a bit odd since he's been by himself. I don't think he should be living all alone."

"Eh? Old Roger? He's all right." He was watching the commercials, not glancing at his wife.

"He talks to me a lot, but he's not what you'd call sociable. He's always complaining. And he doesn't play boules with you any more, does he?"

Monsieur Pereira looked at the ceiling. "You don't play boules in the snow," he said witheringly. "It's a summer game. Anyway, what is all this? What have you got against him? He's all right. He's a good bloke. Always willing to lend a hand. Remember that time when he helped me shift that wardrobe your brother wanted? We wouldn't have been able to move it without him."

"That was a long time ago. And I didn't say, did I, that I had anything against him – "

The bell rang in the lodge, and she hurried out, wiping her hands, to give a parcel to one of the residents. We could hear their muffled voices until they were drowned by a burst of music from the TV and the beginning of the news.

"Always chinwagging," muttered Monsieur Pereira.

"I gather Monsieur Bertrand complains about Madame Martin?" I ventured.

His eyes swivelled round. "He reckons she makes too much noise," he said loudly through the newscaster's voice. "That tinkling piano all day long and half the night. And she doesn't have fitted carpets, like normal people, just floorboards. He can hear her walking about."

"Surely people have the right to walk about!" I tried to keep the indignation out of my voice.

"And all those pigeons making a mess on his window-sill. He's lived there these thirty years. He has a right to complain. That Madame Martin had better mend her ways, I say." His eyes veered back to the screen, and I looked at it for a few moments, not paying much attention. On a shelf above the TV stood a plaster Madonna. Next to it was a framed wedding photograph of the Pereiras in which both were slimmer and he still had dark hair.

"The rubbish chute! It's blocked again!" announced Madame Pereira dramatically, coming in. "It's those people on the fifth floor. They will put newspapers down it. Great fat copies of the Figaro. Last time there was even a broken umbrella. People have no consideration. That chute isn't designed – "

I didn't want to hear about the rubbish chute.

"I really must be going," I said. "But believe me – Madame Martin is fine just the way she is. She's a friend of mine."

"Hmm," said Madame Pereira.

"Nothing wrong with old Roger Bertrand, at any rate," said her husband, standing up and scratching himself. He went to peer into one of the saucepans. "He's a good old boy. He still goes off hunting with his cronies, doesn't he? Not past it yet. I saw them all going off in a van the other day. He's all right."

I left, with Madame Pereira's thanks ringing in my ears for having tried to knock some English into her son's head.

I travelled up in the lift, staring at myself in the mirror. Why were people so quick to draw conclusions about others, and so sure of their own judgement? I felt tired of hearing Rose criticized just because she was alone and had chosen a slightly unorthodox way of life. I felt that I, too, had been attacked for failing to conform.

Opening the door to my flat, I slipped inside like an animal returning to its lair. Everything was just as I had left it that morning: a newspaper lay open on the table, a blouse hung over the arm of a chair waiting for me to sew on a button, and the scent of a single pink hyacinth that I had bought yesterday filled the room. Beyond the uncurtained window the sky glowed dark blue, and the roof opposite was etched sharply against it, with the black silhouettes of five pigeons, all facing the same way, on the television aerial. The evenings were getting lighter, and there were fine days ahead.

Topaz gave a welcoming trill as I switched on the lamp. I wondered if he was lonely and whether I ought to get him a mate, but Rose had warned me that canaries were not very sociable birds and tended to fight intruders. "Let him settle down for about a year," she had told me. "Then you can try him with a female, but you'll probably have to buy a larger cage. They need space around them."

"I don't want anyone sharing my cage, either," I told him, as I wandered around, watering the plants. "I'm not very gregarious. I want my own space." Adrien's flat had been large, and his king-size bed more comfortable than my sofa bed, but I had never felt really relaxed. Now I was enjoying sleeping alone. I could stretch out in all directions, and if I woke in the night I could switch on the light without disturbing anybody. But …

I took an apple from the kitchen and lounged across the table as I ate it, skimming through the remainder of the newspaper that I had been reading with my breakfast coffee. If I were married, I reflected, I would probably be busy preparing the evening meal now, whether I felt hungry or not.

Footsteps thundered across the ceiling, and there was a scream, followed by desperate bawling and Mrs. Dumbbells's voice raised in exasperation. "Put a sock in it," I muttered in English. Not a very maternal sentiment. Could I ever cope with the reality of a yelling, grubby, demanding toddler? I didn't know any more. I would probably knock it about, do it an injury. But if I didn't want children, what would be the point of getting married? Why were people so anxious to marry me off, anyway? I remembered how thrilled my mother had been when Pascal had announced his engagement. I suppose, if you're married yourself, you're glad to see others follow suit. They're validating your own choice, even if it's a bad one.

"But I don't have to do the same as everybody else," I told Topaz.

I reached for my guitar and tuned it. I played a riff through the sobs from upstairs, then sang and played "Rain in Another

Country". It now occupied a page in my notebook, and I was not displeased with it, but there was still something lacking. It needed another verse, I decided. The lyrics were always more difficult than the music, but they came eventually, and they had to be my own words. Once I had tried to set one of my father's poems to music, but it was a failure. A song had to be all my own work. And my songs had to rhyme, unlike his poetry.

***

I sat at the big dining-room table, my ankles wrapped around the chair legs, listening to the rain tapping gently at the window, and trying to write a song. I was eight years old. It was one of the first songs that I had tried to write, and I had the tune fixed firmly in my head, but not the words. Daddy wrote poems, but I knew that songs were different, and that it was songs I wanted to write.

My mother swept into the room, picked up newspapers from the floor and arranged them deftly in a stack on a side table. Whatever she did was brisk, but today she seemed particularly vigorous.

"I hope you can put that together again," she said to Pascal, who was doing something on the hearth rug, out of sight.

"Of course I can," said Pascal's voice loftily.

"What rhymes with love? I've already got above," I said.

"Shove?" offered Pascal.

"Really, Stella, what do you know about love at your age? How ridiculous." My mother walked into the hall with hasty steps that made the floor shake slightly, and I could hear her pick up the telephone and start to dial.

I looked back at the words of my song. I didn't care. I knew a lot about love: I had read stories and seen films on television, and one day I would live a grand, tragic love affair. I might even die for love. That would show her.

The rain whispered at the window.

"It's outrageous," I heard my mother expostulating into the telephone. There was a pause. "I know, I know, but I won't put up with it. There must be a by-law about bonfires. I had to wash it all again, and as for drying things indoors in this weather – What? Of course I spoke to them. I asked them most politely, but I might as well have saved my breath. I tell you, when I saw all my husband's white shirts that I'd hung out to dry – What? No! I want to know my rights. I demand to know my rights!" Her French accent, always became more pronounced when she was angry.

I sighed. All this trouble was about our nextdoor neighbours, the Kershaws, and Emma Kershaw was my friend, although she was still only seven. Before the bonfires it had been their cat, which used to come into our garden and dig up my mother's bulbs. And there had been some disagreement about dustbins, although I was hazy as to the details. The upshot was that my mother and Mrs. Kershaw were not on speaking terms.

Getting up from the table, I wandered across the room, my mind still half on the song which wouldn't come right. Pascal was lying full length on the hearth rug, quietly intent.

Suddenly I saw what he was doing. My musical box, the beautiful polished walnut musical box, that played Aux Marches du Palais, a present from Mamie, was in pieces around him. He had wrenched the works out of the box itself and taken them apart completely: all the fine strips of metal, the spiky metal cylinders and tiny, neatly interlocking parts that together had made the ethereal music, each note round and gleaming, now lay separated and scattered meaninglessly on the floor.

"Oh! You've broken my musical box!"

"I'm just seeing how it works," he said hastily.

"It won't work at all now! You've broken it! Oh! I'll kill you!" In a second we were rolling on the floor, I trying to pull his hair, hold him down and strangle him, he struggling and yelling and kicking me with his hard lace-up shoes. We rolled on pieces of metal, and I heard an ominous cracking of wood under my elbow. A mad rage was in me.

"Stop that! Get up at once, do you hear me?" My mother's furious voice broke through Pascal's yells, and I felt rough hands yanking us to our feet. "What's the meaning of this?"

"Stella hit me." Pascal was crying pathetically now, whereas a moment ago he had been punching me.

"He broke my musical box! He stole it and took it apart! He – "

"Stella, you must not hit your brother. How many times do I have to tell you? He's only little, he doesn't know any better. Pascal, now don't cry. That was a silly thing to do, wasn't it?"

"It's not fair! You always say he's only little. He does know better!"

"Stella!" The full heat of my mother's anger was turned on me, and I wilted. "You will not answer back! And I will not have the two of you fighting and brawling on the floor like animals, do you hear me? Now go to your room, this minute!"

Upstairs in my room, I hid under the bed with my teddy bear Benjamin, sobbing against his comforting furry face. Officially I no longer played with dolls or teddy bears, but he was always there when I needed him. Nothing was fair. Pascal was younger than me, and always would be, which meant that he could get away with anything all his life. When Mamie had given me the musical box, I had said to myself that I would keep it forever, and already, just a few months later, it was broken beyond repair, and I would never, I thought, hear that tune again, those beautiful notes like an angel's harp. Lost. The hot tears fell.

Later, in the early evening, when the rain had stopped, I buried the pieces in the garden. My father had offered to try and mend the box, but I refused. What was the use of a box which wouldn't play? The whole charm of it had been the hidden music. I stamped the damp earth down with my feet.

"What are you doing?" It was Emma, looking over the fence at me.

"Nothing."

"Yes, you are. You've been crying, haven't you?"

I looked away, embarrassed. "My Mum beat me up," I mumbled.

"What?"

"My Mum beat me up. She shook me, and slapped me, and pulled my hair, and – and -" I invented wildly. "And she shut me in a dark cupboard for three hours!"

Emma's eyes widened. "I don't like your Mum. She's scary."

"It didn't hurt," I boasted. "Do you want to come round and play?"

"No!" She shook her head firmly and stepped backwards. "I don't want to see your Mum. She's horrible to children, and she shouted at my Mum. She's a – I think she's a terrorist. So there."

"Oh – no... Not really..." Too late, I saw the trap I had fallen into.

"My Mum says she's got a fiery French *tempiment*," she announced, as if talking about a disease. "That's what my Mum says."

"Come on round, and we could play jumping – "

"No, I'm not playing." She started to run back towards her house. "I'm telling my Mum what your Mum did. She's an old witch!" she shouted, emboldened by distance.

"So's your own Mum," I yelled ineffectually. I turned round and trudged back to my own house in despair. I hadn't meant to besmirch my mother's name. I had just wanted someone to recognize my pain.

Nothing was fair in the whole world.

– FIVE –

Spring was suddenly here. In the park, purple and yellow crocuses opened on the lawns, and the trees were misted with green. In the early mornings, blackbirds sang, their mellow voices carrying from afar and echoing over the sleeping rooftops.

All day Saturday I had been spring-cleaning the flat, and now I decided to iron some lightweight clothes. I plugged in the iron, whistling to myself, and noticed that the flex was very worn in one spot and the wires were exposed. I must have wound it around the iron while it was still too hot, and the outer covering had become scorched and fragile. It still worked, but it was probably not very safe.

I ironed a dress the colour of new beech leaves, then unplugged the iron and allowed it to cool while I went into the bathroom, neatened my make-up and combed my hair. I could do with a stroll. It was such a fine day, after all.

"Stella," said Olivier, smiling as the door pinged shut behind me. "What can I do for you today?" He had remembered my name. He turned down the radio in his workroom.

I showed him the iron, and he said that he would change the flex for me if I cared to wait.

"It's a day to be outdoors," he said, "but duty calls." He was wearing a blue checked shirt, open at the neck, and I could see the dark hairs on his chest.

"How is Rose these days?" he asked, as I followed him into the back room.

The window gave on to a small yard, full of dustbins and broken boxes, and in front of the window was his workbench.

It was littered with wires, screws, plugs, screwdrivers, a soldering iron and various other electrical bits and pieces, some of them in neatly labelled jars, others strewn around untidily. He had apparently been repairing a broken toaster. Despite the clutter, the room was not unpleasant. There was a sagging sofa with a blanket over it, a sink, and a gas-ring on a table in the corner. I could see half a bottle of wine and a chunk of bread on the draining-board.

"Oh… Rose? Haven't you seen her yourself?"

There was a pause as he unscrewed the heel of my iron.

"She and I," he said, not looking at me, "haven't been seeing so much of each other these days. But it's nothing. Only temporary."

I looked past him to the yard. The sun seemed to have gone behind a cloud. Whenever he saw me, he talked about Rose. Of course, it was natural, I told myself. After all, she was our mutual friend, and she had introduced us. But what did he mean: not seeing so much of each other? Compared with what?

"I've a feeling she just wants to be left in peace," I said.

"Yes, that neighbour of hers gives her a hard time. He's a pain in the arse." He scowled at the wires.

"I think he may be slightly off his head," I said.

"It's the piano that's the problem," said Olivier. "Pianos reverberate through walls. She'd have to have her flat completely soundproofed to prevent him from hearing it."

"Wouldn't that be terribly expensive?"

"You bet it would. No, the only rational solution – "

The door pinged in the shop. Olivier went to see who it was, told the customer that he was just coming, and stepped back into the room to put my iron down on the bench. "Talk of the devil," he muttered.

I followed him into the shop. There, holding a large old-fashioned wireless set in his arms and puffing and blowing slightly, stood Monsieur Bertrand. It was the first time that I had seen him properly at close quarters. His bald head was covered with a flat cap, and grey hairs sprouted from his ears.

His watery eyes in his sagging face met mine, glanced away and then back again.

"Bonjour, mademoiselle," he said. I bristled. I hate being called mademoiselle: it sounds so condescending – as if I were ten years old.

He seemed unsure of himself. He dumped the wireless on the counter, and I noticed his beefy forearms. He was a man past his prime, but I could imagine him heaving wardrobes about, not so long ago.

"What an extraordinary radio," said Olivier. It was made of shiny Bakelite, with a woven front panel and large round knobs.

"Ah, they don't make them like that any more," said Monsieur Bertrand. "Thirty years I've had this one, and it was my father's before that, and never any trouble till now. Thirty years I've lived in that flat, and never any trouble. And now there's nothing but trouble."

"I'll have a look at it, but it may take a while if I need to find spare parts on the Internet."

"Worked like a dream, and now nothing but trouble," insisted Monsieur Bertrand. "It's the interference, see, and now it's gone dead. Can't get a peep out of it."

"Interference? Well, of course, you can't expect the reception to be as good as it was, now that you're surrounded by high-rise buildings," said Olivier.

"High-rise be damned!" he glared. "I tell you, it's that woman upstairs that did it. It's the interference. She told me she would, and now she's done it, sure enough. She's got some powerful machine or other up there. I'll give her interference! It's what makes all those black lines on the telly, too."

"I'm sure it's just a simple breakdown", said Olivier soothingly. "Leave it with me, and I'll see what I can do."

"I tell you, my life's not my own since she moved in." He seemed determined to tell us about it. "Not a minute's peace and quiet. It's not like the old days. She'd have been out – they'd have evicted her quicker than that!" He snapped his fingers.

"If you mean Madame Martin – " began Olivier coldly.

"Ah, that's what she calls herself, but if her name's Martin then I'm an Eskimo. She's foreign. The place is full of foreigners these days. We aren't at home in our own country any more, that's what I say. Layabouts, living off social security – "

"This lady," said Olivier, putting one hand on my shoulder, "is English, and my grandfather was Spanish. Have you any objections to us?" His tone was positively frosty now. I was very conscious of his hand through the thin material of my dress.

"No, well – what I mean is," said Monsieur Bertrand, "it's all these blacks and Arabs, see? Two or three wives, some of them, all claiming handouts."

If he had been trying to improve matters, he had failed. Olivier's grip tightened on my shoulder, and I glanced up at him, shaking my head very slightly. His eyes met mine. He breathed out slowly through his nose.

"Just leave the radio, Monsieur Bertrand. Call in next week, why don't you? Thursday, say."

Monsieur Bertrand looked flustered, aware that he might have put his foot in it but not quite sure how. He started to say something, stopped, wished us a formal good afternoon and shuffled towards the door.

"Oh, by the way," said Olivier.

"Eh?" He turned.

"I should give Madame Martin a wide berth if I were you. I happen to know something about her. I'm telling you this in confidence, mind." He lowered his voice and leaned forward. "She has certain powers."

"Oh?"

"She's what they used to call a witch," he said, very quietly. He nodded.

Monsieur Bertrand looked at him fixedly. Then it was as if shutters came down. His eyes went blank and dead, and turning without a word he left the shop.

"Why on earth did you say that?"

"Racist bastard," growled Olivier, carting the wireless set into the back room. "If you hadn't been there, I'd have called him one to his face."

"Would it have done any good?"

"Of course it wouldn't. Might have relieved my feelings, though." He dumped the set on the bench next to the toaster and the iron. "Don't worry," he smiled swiftly at me, "I wouldn't have picked a fight with him. I may have Spanish blood, but karate teaches you self-control."

"No, but why did you say she was a witch, for God's sake?"

"Give him something to think about. Well, she's different, isn't she? Make him think twice before he bothers her again. People are very gullible, you know. There are forty thousand registered clairvoyants in France, and five hundred so-called witches and warlocks in Paris alone. How about that?" He jabbed a finger at the ceiling. "There's one in this very building. He's put his card in my mailbox before now. He offers to remove curses, protect you against demons, guarantee the return of affection – for a price. Oh, there's money in it all right."

Witches and wizards – surely they belonged in children's storybooks. I shook my head. "I'm not sure what I think about clairvoyance," I said slowly, trying to be fair. "Haven't they done scientific studies on it? I believe… well, there's still a lot that's unexplained in the world."

"Believe in Father Christmas, too, do you?" said Olivier.

I felt rebuffed and said nothing. I didn't believe in horoscopes, like my mother and Lisa, but to me it seemed as unreasonable to claim dogmatically that supernatural phenomena were a load of rubbish as to claim dogmatically that they really happened, in the absence of insufficient evidence. I thought of my father calmly remonstrating with me in my argumentative teen-age years. "How can you prove that, Stella? Where's your evidence?" He hadn't studied philosophy for nothing.

"You have to consider the evidence – " I began.

"Are you in a hurry?" interrupted Olivier. "It won't take me a minute to finish your iron, but I'd really like to have a look inside this museum-piece here."

74

No, I was not in a hurry. I was quite content to sit on his broken-springed sofa, chatting to him and idling the afternoon away. Outside, the traffic was reduced to a murmur, as many Parisians had taken their cars and headed for the country on this warm spring Saturday. Tomorrow evening they would all converge on the city again, creating traffic jams that stretched for miles.

"Look at this. What a beauty," said Olivier, who had carefully unscrewed the back of the Bakelite wireless set and was peering inside. "Uncle René would have liked to see this. It's a real collector's item. Art Deco, isn't it?"

I went to stand beside him and looked at the mass of wires and valves. He explained the difference between it and a modern transistor radio, but I couldn't really understand him. In fact, I was looking at his hands. There is an etching by somebody – Dürer, is it? – of two hands clasped in prayer: you see it reproduced on Christmas cards. Olivier's hands were like that – long, strong, sensitive. But not particularly tranquil: active and skilful.

"I don't see why it shouldn't work," he was saying. "These old models are pretty sturdy." He unscrewed something, and stopped, looking puzzled. He whistled. "That's odd."

"What is?"

"That shouldn't have happened. Theoretically, it can't happen." He took a screwdriver and began to point at various components, explaining, but then glanced up at me and realized that I was not following him. I felt ignorant, but I have never been interested in taking things apart to find out how they work. My view is: as long as something works, leave it alone. If it doesn't work, call in an expert.

"Look," said Olivier. "You see this bit here, where it's burnt and black? Well, basically it's as if there had been a big surge of power through this connection here. But how can it have happened? It's impossible, and yet somehow ..." He scratched his head.

"Can you repair it, do you think?"

"Oh, I can probably repair it. It's just..." His voice trailed away in puzzlement.

I went to sit down again, and he looked over his shoulder. "It'll be a tricky job, though. I'll do your iron now."

It fascinated me that he could repair things, that he could figure out what was wrong and put it right. I wished that I had the gift.

As he worked, I asked him how long he had been practising karate, and he told me that he was a brown belt and hoped soon to be a black belt. He belonged to a club out in the suburbs where he lived in a rented room. "Why don't you take it up?" he asked. "You women need to be able to defend yourselves, living alone in a big city."

Why didn't I take it up? I could not quite picture myself hurling anybody to the floor. I suppose I hoped that, in the event of an attack, if I screamed loud enough, some man would come to my rescue. Not a very independent thought. I had a feeling that Mamie would have approved of karate lessons. I thought of Rose, struggling with Monsieur Bertrand on the stairs, and shuddered at the thought of him touching her. I wondered whether Olivier knew what he had tried to do.

"About Rose," he said, as if reading my thoughts. "Her best solution is – "

The telephone warbled in the shop, and he went to answer it with a sigh. I could hear a brief exchange.

"Somebody has a problem with a washing-machine," he said, coming back. "I said I'd go round right away, as the woman's a good customer. I'll just put the answering machine on. Really I could do with an assistant to take over the shop when I'm called out like this." He gathered tools together. "Here's your iron."

"How much do I owe you?"

"What? Nothing at all. You can buy me a drink some time. About Rose," he went on. "What she really needs is one of those Japanese electronic pianos. They're beautiful little jobs, neat and compact, and they sound exactly like a real piano. Or you can make them sound like an organ, or even a choir. And the big advantage is that you can turn the sound right down if you want to. Or use headphones. For old Bertrand, it would be as quiet as the grave – where he might just as well be," he added viciously.

"Are they expensive?"

"I know a dealer. I could get her one cheap. No problem at all."

"But don't you have to plug them in to the mains?" I asked.

"Of course you have to plug them in. Oh, I see what you mean. Hell," he scowled. "She really has to get over this phobia, or whatever it is. She could surely have one electrical socket in that flat. I could fix it for her, easily. Look, Stella," he said, as he turned the sign on the door round to read Closed, "won't you talk to her? I'd be glad if you would. She won't listen to me at the moment, but you're a new friend of hers. She likes you. Try and persuade her that this is the answer, will you? It would be so simple. All she needs is to adjust to the modern world a little bit." His dark eyes held mine.

I said that I would try to talk to her about it and let him know what her reaction was. I have to admit that I was thinking that this would give me an excuse to see him again.

He took his tool-box and I carried my iron as we left the shop. We walked as far as the corner, and then he said goodbye, as he was going the other way. As he kissed me on both cheeks, he gently pinched my left earlobe, and a great wave of warmth went right through me, from my ear down through my body. I had difficulty breathing.

"Happy ironing," he said, and I set off along the boulevard, looking at the bright pavement, not seeing it.

I had extricated myself from one painful relationship, and now here I was rushing blithely over another precipice. He already had me in his power.

***

On the Sunday I went across the street to call on Rose, but she was out. I knocked several times (she had no doorbell) but no sound came from inside, and I turned back down the stairs disconsolate. It would have been easier to phone her, but she had no phone and certainly no Internet connection. I wondered how she managed without. For me, the phone and email are my chief means of keeping in touch with people..

In the evening I looked across from my window, but there was no light in her flat. Quite late, just before going to bed, I looked again, but her windows were still dark. Most of the other windows in the building were lit up, the wrought-iron balustrades etched in filigree against the yellow rectangles of light. People were not closing their shutters so early, now that there was a breath of spring in the air. I could see figures moving about in their little homes, one person stirring a saucepan, another slumped in an armchair watching the bluish glow of a television. In sharp black profile, a woman was standing behind her daughter, brushing out the girl's long hair. From my vantage-point, the building had the charm of a dolls' house. So many different lives, separate and compartmentalized. People went about their business, only a few feet away from one another, but totally unaware of their neighbours, ignorant of their joys and sorrows and even of their names. Or else, on the contrary, their lives impinged on one another, clashing and overlapping and making sparks fly, as in the case of Rose and Monsieur Bertrand. People pounded on walls and wrote furious notes to one another.

Then came Monday (Mondays come around much more often than Saturdays, I could swear) and the whole long, tiring week at the office. Again I had to work late, as a crisis had blown up. I was also working more slowly than usual and made some errors which I subsequently had to correct. Of course, it was because I was thinking about Olivier. His eyes, his hands, the way his hair curled against the smooth brown skin of his neck – all came between me and the screen. His voice with its southern accent masked my boss's voice, and I misheard his instructions, with unfortunate results. I gazed out of the window at the sky, daydreaming. In short, I behaved like a teenager.

Now and again I scolded myself, telling myself that I was crazy to go overboard like this, and that he probably wasn't interested in me anyway. I reminded myself of all the bad times with Adrien, and all the unhappy times before that, with shallow, unreliable men – but somehow those times had become hazy. And anyway, Olivier was so different. What did he think of me? What was he doing at this moment? When would I see him again? Catherine made jokes about my absent-mindedness and asked inquisitive questions, her smiling mouth V-shaped.

The week wore on.

Saturday again dawned fine. I knew that Rose was at home, as her windows were open and I could see the pigeons flying in and out. Suddenly a magpie emerged from among them and flew off down the street at rooftop level with its lazy, undulating flight, its long diamond-shaped tail seeming to float straight out behind it. "One for sorrow," I said, remembering the old rhyme, and then half bowed, saying "Good morning, sir." This, I had read in a book of English country lore, was a means of averting the bad luck brought by seeing a single magpie. I pulled a wry face at myself, thinking how embarrassing it would be if someone saw me. I was not superstitious, was I? But perhaps you can't be too careful.

As soon as I had taken a shower and dressed, I hurried across to talk to Rose. Her smile welcomed me. The sun streamed in through her windows, lighting up the colours of some of her fabrics, fading other to ashen paleness. The plants on her balcony were beginning to sprout, and the stone lion gazed serenely down through the balustrade at the sunny street.

She was feeding Blanche, the young pigeon. In fact, Blanche was perfectly well able to peck at food for herself by this time, but she still liked to be fed. I watched her thrusting herself upwards towards Rose's hand, flapping her wings and making her piercing, squeaky whistle. Her feathers had grown, apart from a few on the back of her neck and wings which were just bristly spikes, and her tail was still quite short. Her breast and tail were slate grey, but her head and wings had grown feathers of the purest white, like a mantle of snow. Nor were her eyes orange like other pigeons' eyes, but dark and shining like black mirrors of vitality.

"She's got unusual colouring, hasn't she?" I said.

"She's an unusual bird," said Rose. "That's enough, now, little one. You mustn't be greedy."

Blanche gradually subsided, still whistling and flapping. She peered at me, then at Rose, then back again at me.

I suggested that we might take advantage of the fine weather and go on a trip out of Paris, to Fontainebleau, perhaps, on the train. She looked regretful. "I've got some urgent sewing to finish," she said. "I can't really spare the time."

"Oh, come on, Rose. It would be so lovely to get out into the countryside."

"There are pylons in the countryside."

I was nonplussed. True, pylons were an eyesore, but they weren't to be found everywhere. And what difference did pylons make?

She made a concession. "We could stroll in the park for an hour or so, if you like, and you can tell me your news. What have you been doing lately?"

I had suggested on previous occasions that we go on an excursion, but she would never leave the city. I didn't know why.

In the park the horse-chestnut leaves were beginning to sprout, velvety pale green, and dewdrops sparkled on the grass like diamonds. Poplar trees were already thickly misted with a more acid green, and a flowering cherry was in full bloom. A gardener was raking the gravel paths. There was a rich smell of earth and growing things. I wished we could have gone for that country walk. I thought of England, of my mother's garden and all the gardens round about, and the countryside beyond where the dogs could race and frisk through the water meadows. I thought of London's parks, the grass dotted with people sunbathing in summer. In France, there's a tendency to treat grass as if it were some rare and fragile carpet. Paris needs more parks, bigger parks, wilder parks. What was I doing in Paris, anyway? There are times when I feel neither English nor French, and neither country is home. Where was Rose from, originally? I had never asked her.

Rose sat on a bench. "Ah, the sun is a blessing," she said, lifting her thin white face to it and closing her eyes. The traffic made a distant hum.

"Fear no more the heat of the sun, Nor the furious winter's rages," I quoted dreamily.

"What?" Her blue eyes flew open.

"I was quoting Shakespeare, my father's first love. It's a dirge for somebody dead."

"You are so lucky to have a poet for a father."

"Is your own father still alive?" I asked.

"I don't honestly know. I expect so. Anyway," she said shortly, "there's nothing to say about him. He's just a man."

Just a man! The faint scorn burned through her words. What did she have against men, I wondered? Why did she not want to see Olivier – not at all, or less than in the past? And how often had that been? I longed to ask, but couldn't bring myself to speak his name. I was afraid of giving myself away. Had they been lovers? Did I really want to know that? Yes, I wanted to know everything, but I didn't want to be jealous of Rose. Nor did I want her to be jealous of me – but there was no reason for that, was there? Nothing had happened – yet.

"Don't you like men?" I asked.

"It's not that I don't like them. It's that… when they come too close, I injure them."

How? I didn't ask. I wish, now, that I had.

"I think I could be a sun-worshipper," I said, holding up my arms to the light and noticing how wintry pale they were.

"Like the Aztecs?" said Rose.

"Yes. Well, no. I remember my grandmother telling me about the Aztecs. They had a very gory religion, didn't they? They used to practise human sacrifice – tear people's hearts out while they were still alive."

"They did it for the sun," said Rose. "They thought it wouldn't rise otherwise. They believed that the sun needed constant sacrifice, a constant supply of fresh blood and hearts. Their chosen victims had to die to keep the sun alive."

"How could they believe that?" I shuddered.

Rose didn't answer.

"I suppose people have to believe in something," I said.

"Do they?"

A robin came flitting out of a bush and perched on her knee, plump and round on spindly legs, its eye like a black dewdrop. Then came a pair of blue-tits, perching on the back of the bench beside her, and half a dozen sparrows with hoarse cries. I watched, fascinated. There was a harsh "kaaa!" and a shadow crossed the sun, causing the other birds to flutter into the bushes, and a glossy black crow landed on the gravel in front of us. He walked forwards, very large, his tail wagging from side to side, and I could have sworn he bowed.

"Hello, Jacques," said Rose.

The crow gave a run and a bouncing series of hops, and, half opening his wings, landed on her wrist. "Bonjour. Kaa!" he said.

I stared in astonishment. "Did you hear that?"

"Didn't you know crows could talk? They're very intelligent birds. Some people say they can live to be a hundred."

They said "bonjour" and "kaa" to each other several times, to my amusement. Further down the path I noticed an old lady sitting on another bench. She was wearing a very long dark skirt and a cloche hat, and was casting glances in our direction. The ground in front of her was scattered with crumbs, and the sparrows squabbled and pounced, some flying up to feed from her hand. But gradually they were all leaving her to congregate around Rose.

"I wonder how long wild birds generally live," I said.

"They have short lives. But it's not length that matters, is it? They live in the present."

"It's funny," I said. "You hardly ever see a dead bird, apart from pigeons that get run over."

"Pigeons that human beings have killed," said Rose.

"So I wonder where birds go to die?"

"Who knows?"

Jacques eyed her, the short feathers on the top of his head standing straight up, so that he looked like an urchin with a crew-cut. "Fear no more the heat of the sun," she mused. "I wonder why he said that? Could we still be aware of the sun after we're dead? The world goes on, and maybe we go on with it, in a different form. The sacrificial victims thought they were sure of eternal life."

I was not certain that I could follow her down that path. For me, despite my Catholic upbringing, death was a sudden cutting off, the awful finality of a slamming door. Like my grandmother's front door with its knocker in the shape of a hand. One day Mamie had been alive, sprightly for her age, warm and interested in everything. The next she had been in a coma, and then gone. The green-shuttered, crinkle-tiled house in Aix had been sold, and I could never go back there. My childhood was gone, sealed in the past, unattainable.

"You're very thoughtful," said Rose. "And I'm getting much too philosophical. How are things with you? Tell me."

"I saw Olivier the other day," I blurted out.

"Oh. Olivier." Her voice was expressionless.

The crow flew up into the branches of a horse-chestnut tree and began to preen his feathers.

"He seems to be keen to help. I mean, he knows you have a problem with the piano and Monsieur Bertrand. He – er – I thought I would ask you – have you ever considered one of those Japanese electronic pianos?" I had not led up to it very tactfully, I cursed myself.

"But I haven't got a problem with the piano! I like my piano, and I want to keep it. I wish Olivier would stop trying to interfere in my life."

"He just seems concerned about you," I protested.

"Oh, I know he means well, but the trouble with men is that they will barge in and try to change things. They always have to impose their own ideas. They want to control everything – but some things can't be controlled." She turned her blue ring round and round on her finger. "I just want to be left alone and live in peace."

"I know how you feel." Hadn't I felt the same, when I left Adrien? However, I was not sorry to hear her talk like this. The electronic piano had seemed a good idea to me, but in a way I was glad to hear her reject Olivier's suggestions – and reject him with them, apparently.

"You don't like electrical gadgets?" I probed.

"He just can't accept that, can he? Oh," she exclaimed, "Look at the poor creature."

A pigeon came hobbling up to us, its legs so entangled in grey thread that it could not walk, but moved forward in a series of clumsy hops. She bent to pick it up, and it didn't resist.

"People don't think twice when they throw things away," she said. "Nylon thread is the worst." I found a pair of nail scissors in my bag, and she carefully cut and removed the thread. Placed on the path, the newly released bird shook itself and ruffled its feathers. Then it began to walk about normally, its head nodding like a mechanical toy. With a rush of wings, seven or eight more pigeons landed and began to walk about too, peering at the ground in search of food. I could no longer tell which had been the first pigeon, and said to Rose that they all looked alike.

"But they're not. Each one is unique," she said. "That's why I give them names."

I could see now that there was a difference between the males and the females, at any rate. The males paraded and pirouetted, bowing, puffing out their green and mauve neck feathers and sweeping the dust with their fanned tails. The females dodged them, hurrying away unimpressed.

"Silly thing," I said to one of the males. "Can't you tell she's not interested?"

Rose laughed rather sourly. "When a female says no, she means yes, doesn't she? That's what males think."

The harassed female took off across the lawn, and the male deflated, looking rather foolish. Then he again started examining the ground for something to eat.

Now the sparrows were arriving, nipping in and out among the larger birds. One landed on Rose's head and chirped loudly until she put up a gentle hand to remove it. The old lady down the path was glaring in our direction.

Some of the sparrows were thinking about nest-building. I watched one of them wrestling with a long piece of dried grass, much too big for it: it carried it a little way, then was forced to land again.

"But don't you find life very difficult without electricity?" I persisted.

"I'm not afraid of it, if that's what you mean. I'm not like the person in the funny story who would go around screwing bulbs into empty light sockets to prevent electricity from leaking into the room. It's not an irrational fear."

I had rather thought that it was indeed irrational, and felt awkward. Well, Rose doubtless had her reasons for her lifestyle, and she had a right not to tell me. I could scarcely cross-examine her.

"So you haven't seen Olivier lately?" I asked casually.

"No, not for a long time."

My heart lifted. Whatever their connection, it now seemed to be over, on Rose's side at least. I would not be coming between them. He would soon realize that I was genuinely interested in him, whereas she was not.

A shadow fell across us. It was the old lady in the cloche hat, trembling with rage. Her jaws worked.

"You're taking my birds away," she accused Rose.

"Your birds? But, madame, they're not yours," said Rose without heat.

"They're my little ones! Every day I come here to feed them. They all know me. And now you're tempting them away with some expensive food, and they won't come to me any more."

"I'm not feeding them," said Rose. "You see, it's better not to feed them now that the nesting season is starting. It's better for the young ones to have natural food."

"Don't you tell me what to do!" shrilled the old lady. "You're feeding them. It's not fair!"

"Kaa!" said Jacques above our heads. I wondered what would happen if Luna the owl suddenly swooped down from a tree. That would cause a sensation, and who could be accused of feeding owls? I almost wished that it would happen.

"All right, I'm sorry, madame. All right," said Rose, suddenly resigned, standing up, "I didn't mean to interfere. I'll leave you to your birds."

The old lady stumped away, muttering, and we set off in the direction of the gates. Coming towards us was a large woman in a drooping cardigan, with a tiny dachshund trotting on a lead behind her. It was wearing a little tartan coat. As we approached, the dog stopped in its tracks, stared at Rose, then began to bark frantically. Its owner pulled on the lead, but it backed away, cringed, then wound the lead around its owner as it skittered to the farther side of her, still barking.

"Let's go," said Rose to me. Her voice sounded tired.

***

I ran up the metro steps and headed for Olivier's street. All day I had been waiting for this moment. The evening was overcast, but I thought how attractive the street looked. A greengrocer's displayed racks of shiny red and yellow fruit. The green cross of a chemist's sign flashed like a beacon. Just opposite his shop was an old-fashioned bakery, its tiled frontage elaborately decorated with pastoral scenes like my grandmother's pâtisserie, and already an array of home-made Easter eggs and chocolate "April fish" tied with pink ribbon filled the window. I remembered my mother hiding chocolate eggs in the garden so that Pascal and I could hunt for them on Easter morning when they had been "brought by the bells from Rome". Our little English friends used to find this an intriguing custom.

Olivier was serving a short man in a navy beret as I walked in, and a middle-aged woman was also waiting to be served. He winked at me, and I felt that joyous fluttering feeling in the pit of my stomach. I pottered about, examining a rack of batteries, glancing at him covertly. The man in the beret left, but the woman took an interminable time, repeating herself constantly, telling him about some plug which would fit certain sockets but not others. I admired his patience.

"So how's the iron?" he asked when at last we were alone.

"Fine," I said, smiling up at him. I felt like a flower opening in the sun. He must realize how I felt.

He turned away and straightened a wrinkle in his wrapping-paper on its dispenser.

"So did you talk to Rose?" he asked.

"Yes, I tried."

"And?"

"I'm afraid she won't hear of having an electronic piano. She wants to keep her old one."

"You didn't say it was my idea, did you?" he demanded.

"Well, I …"

"Oh, Stella, I told you! I said she wouldn't take advice from me. You're her friend, I told you. She'll listen to you, I said." He walked to the end of the shop and came back again, his arms tightly folded.

I stood there abashed. I felt I had let him down.

"What did she say exactly?" he asked.

"She more or less told me she didn't want anyone interfering in her life. You know, I don't think I can influence her any more than you can," I protested.

"Influence! Interference!" he snorted. "She's so – so closed to the world. Cut off. Defensive. I can't get through to her. She just pushes people away, even when they're trying to help her."

There was a pause. I wished that he would try to influence me: I would gladly buy every appliance in his shop if it would make him happy.

"Why does it matter so much to you?" I asked, desperation giving me courage.

"It doesn't matter to me. I don't care what she does. It just bothers me to see someone being so obstinate and irrational, that's all."

"But she must have her own reasons," I began.

"Oh, all right. Take her side, why don't you?" he snapped. "I can't understand, can I? I'm a mere male."

"I wasn't going to say – "

The door pinged open and a harassed, heavily made up woman came in, hauling two squabbling children. She started

87

to ask Olivier for something, but could not make herself heard, and turned to yell at the children, jerking the arm of one of them, who was screaming and trying to sit down on the floor.

"Excuse me. I'll see you around," said Olivier to me with a taut smile.

I was dismissed. I left the shop feeling as if he had slapped my face. I was useful to him only as a go-between.

The street looked very drab.

– SIX –

I learned a lot about birds that spring. As soon as Rose opened the window they would come, and if the window was closed we would see them queuing on the balustrade. With every rush of wings I would look round to see who the newcomer was, but Rose seemed to know without looking. I had always found pigeons rather dull and slightly repulsive, congregating rat-like around dustbins, but now that I came to look at them properly I changed my mind. There is nothing quite as beautiful as a pigeon coming in to land, with its wing and tail feathers fanned out translucent against the light, making the lovely shape that has inspired so many artists to paint the dove of peace or the holy spirit. A wing, with its perfectly overlapping feathers, is a graceful thing, fragile yet so strong. No wonder angels are supposed to have wings. Pigeons are docile birds, harming nobody. They're scavengers, but scavengers are useful. And their wing-tips are the exact shade of grey of the pitched zinc roofs of Paris. Another thing: birds usually drink by taking a sip and tilting their heads back, but pigeons lower their heads and suck up the water as if through a straw. Why hadn't I observed that before? It was Rose who made me notice them.

Blanche, fully fledged now, had learned to fly.

"I taught her," Rose told me.

"How did you do that?"

"Oh, I kept climbing on the table and jumping off it, flapping my arms." Rose looked sideways at my cautious, half-believing face and burst out laughing. "No, she didn't really need teaching. I held her on my wrist, up high like this, and then lowered my wrist quite suddenly, so that she had to flap her wings, and after a while she got the idea and took off spontaneously."

Blanche tended to queen it among the other pigeons, advancing on them aggressively and aiming pecks at them if they came too near Rose, but she would also fly out of the window with them and go wheeling around on short flights. With her snowy white head and wings, she was conspicuous in the grey flock. Then she would reappear on the balustrade, shaking her feathers comfortably, and fly to Rose's shoulder to croon in her ear.

I also learned to distinguish between male and female sparrows at that time. It was strange that I hadn't noticed the smart black bibs of the males, and the funny way they have of showing off, with wings trailing and tails cocked high, chirping raucously. Then there were the chaffinches. I knew vaguely that they had some colours on them, but I hadn't seen, for example, that the feathers on their backs, between their wings, were a soft olive green.

I liked the chaffinches. All these birds came confidently to Rose, but they seemed wary of me at first, darting away if I moved suddenly. The chaffinches soon got used to me, however, and would even perch on my hand. There's something fascinating about the feel of those light dry claws on your skin and that tiny weight, poised for flight – a wild thing trusting you, just for a moment.

"This place is like a bird sanctuary," I said.

"A sanctuary?" Rose looked thoughtful. Then she gave me a radiant smile.

She had a favourite blackbird who sometimes used to sing from the top of her bookcase. Blackbirds, now – have you ever noticed that a blackbird's eye has a gold ring around it? And the females are brown and speckled. I had confused them with thrushes, but Rose told me that there were scarcely any thrushes in Paris – in fact thrushes seem to be dying out, perhaps because the French hunt them and make them into pâté. I began to find the idea of any bird being made into pâté unbearable, particularly when they started to bring their young to visit Rose. They were so sweet. The fledglings would sit on the backs of chairs, looking slightly bemused, soft and round, with their stumpy tails and the little tufts of downy feathers on their heads, every now and then opening big orange-yellow beaks and demanding food. I have to admit I found them more endearing than human babies.

"How do you attract them?" I was intrigued.

Rose shook her head. "They've always come to me. Perhaps because they know I won't harm them. When you think about it, isn't it remarkable anyway that they live so close to us? When you look at the world we've made for ourselves – huge concrete buildings, plate glass, cars everywhere, noise, pollution – yet here are these creatures, still wild and natural, living right here."

"Yes, we make strange neighbours all right."

"That's it. Doesn't the Christian religion say that we should love our neighbours?" she asked uncertainly. Did she really not know?

"Yes. Love thy neighbour," I quoted, and stared at her. She was deftly threading a needle. Surely she knew the gospels? "Love thy neighbour as thyself, love your enemies, do good to them that hurt you, turn the other cheek. It's a hard ideal to live up to. And," I said meaningfully, "it's not so easy to love some neighbours, is it?" The phrases were there, imprinted in my memory as a child; but how many true Christians did I know?

Rose sighed. "I don't hate him."

"Has he been bothering you lately?"

"Well, a little while ago he started leaving his radio on all day, with the volume turned right up. I think he stood it on top of a wardrobe, or something, because it seemed to come straight up through the floor. It made it difficult for my piano pupils – they could hardly hear what they were playing."

"You mean he left it on all day while he went out?" Such petty vengefulness was hard to believe.

"Yes, and so I ... It's stopped now, anyway." I didn't make the connection. She said: "I don't expect he'll do it again. I'm not angry with him."

"Hell, Rose," I said, "I think you've a perfect right to be furious with him."

But she just shook her head.

She had started to copy an Amish quilt design at about that time. It was a big undertaking. The background was black, and the centre would be occupied by a great star, all made from diamond shaped patches. The colours were sky blue, purple, ruby red and a soft green, all glowing together. "Lone Star" was the name of the design. We would sit talking by her open window, and I would sort her patches and take out tacking threads for her. I was incapable of imitating her tiny stitches, or the amazing speed at which she sewed. But I did have a gift for making interesting combinations of colours, patterns and textures. Sometimes she would exclaim with approval when I produced just the right pieces of deep maroon with pale blue, turquoise with royal blue, or plain scarlet cotton that picked up the narrow stripe in another patch – and I felt useful and pleased with myself.

You might think that birds and fine needlework would be incompatible, since birds are not usually noted for being – well – clean and tidy. But they seemed to realize that they were not supposed to make a mess indoors. Only once, when two robins had fought furiously all round the room, did one of them leave a dropping on the table, and she shooed them both out to cool off.

Jacques the crow was a regular visitor. He was so big that the smaller birds would beat a retreat when he arrived. Sometimes he would perch on her shoulder and lay his black beak against her cheek, looking touchingly devoted. At other times he would march up and down, showing off, and pick up her thimble. I was always afraid that he might fly away with it, but he never did. Sometimes, as a treat, she gave him a small pat of butter. He simply adored this, and would dance with impatience when he saw it coming.

Once, Luna appeared, causing general panic. She had brought a mate with her, but he was mobbed by the sparrows. They actually chased him out of the window, and the other birds disappeared, leaving Luna to glare around the room in solitary dignity. I was no longer so nervous of her, but afterwards we found a terrified blue tit cowering under the flap of the sewing machine.

We talked a bit about the Amish one day as Rose worked, and about their quilt-making tradition.

"They live in a time-warp, don't they?" I said. "Did you ever see the film Witness?"

"No," said Rose, "I don't go to the cinema."

"Brilliant film," I said. "I've seen it twice on a satellite channel. It really shows you how they live – as if the industrial revolution had never happened."

"Yes. They don't have cars, or telephones. They lead a quiet country life. And they all help one another."

"They do," I said, and described that wonderful scene in the film when the whole community spends the day building a barn for a neighbour, the great structure rising against the sky and the little figures working on it all together.

"Just because he's a neighbour?" mused Rose. Her sewing rested in her lap and her eyes seemed to be gazing through the wall.

"You sound as if you'd like to join them," I said. "Would that kind of life suit you? Actually, I can imagine you in an Amish village."

She said nothing for a moment.

"There's another side to it." She began to sew again. "They're very strict. You must conform. If a woman steps out of line, for instance, then she will be – shunned, as they call it." Shunned. It was an old word, and not a good one. Total rejection by your own kind. I thought again of the film. Surely she must have seen it.

"You mean you're not allowed to be different?"

"That's right."

"I love their quilts, though," I said.

"The Amish women made the quilts together," said Rose. "They sat in a circle, sewing away through the long winter evenings, and telling stories. A quilt was always a joint creation."

"I wish women still did things together, don't you? It must have been a very companionable way of working. They must have told one another all kinds of things, I should think. I'd love to hear a recording of one of those evenings."

"Women still quilt together in some parts of the States," said Rose. "But nowadays it's dying out."

"And here you are, doing it all on your own."

"Well, not quite alone," said Rose. "You're here, aren't you?"

I felt privileged. What had I done to deserve her friendship? Nothing at all.

Sometimes I would wander over to the piano and pick out a few bars of Rain in Another Country, which was nearly finished. Once she asked me to sing it to her, and as I played she came over to the piano and added some deep base notes. They were a definite improvement, and I jotted them down on a piece of paper. It was strange – I had no objection to her co-operating with me, yet usually I was very jealous of my own work.

Then the inspiration came to me for a new song. It came all in a rush, with the first three lines complete (it's the song I now call Wings), and to that she had no improvements to suggest. I could tell she liked it a lot, right from the start, and I felt elated by her appreciation.

"You know, you must do something with your songs," she told me again. "Why don't you start by recording them?"

"I might," I said. I was doubtful. Inspiration seemed such a fragile thing that I was afraid it might vanish altogether like smoke if I tried to capture it as a definitive sound file, properly arranged. And nobody would want to listen to what I composed. It was faulty. It wasn't good enough.

"Why do none of us ever fly as high as our dreams?" Rose demanded suddenly, passionately, and I looked at her startled. For a second, it was as if I were breathing clearer air, and great vistas were opening up around me, fold after fold of glittering mountain ranges.

Later, as dusk fell, she put away her sewing and sat at the piano. She played the andante from Mozart's piano concerto no. 21 in C major – the theme from the old film Elvira Madigan, which she said she had never seen either – while the blackbird above her on the bookcase fluted in soft counterpoint, and far away, from a rooftop, another blackbird sang. As I listened to her play, it was as if all my muscles and joints were unlocking and relaxing. I breathed more easily, letting the music flow through me like the spring thaw melting a glacier.

Mozart, and pure birdsong, and the luminous sky. I suppose those days with Rose were some of the happiest I have ever known.

***

I hadn't stopped thinking about Olivier all this time, despite the coldness of our last meeting. I blamed myself for not trying more subtly to persuade Rose that she needed an electronic piano. He had been relying on me, and I had let him down. Naturally he was annoyed. But perhaps he still wanted to see me. I wasn't even sure that he knew my surname, in which case he would not be able to find my phone number, and if he and Rose were not seeing each other then he wouldn't be able to ask her about me, would he? I imagined him trying to find me, and my mind would wander off into other scenarios, unlikely conversations, fantasies. But I was too proud to walk down his street and make it obvious that I was seeking him out.

May Day being a holiday, I decided to give the flat a thorough clean. It needed it, as I had skimped the cleaning recently. Housework is a bore; but I put on some rousing rock music and flung myself into scrubbing, scouring and polishing. At least I was cleaning up mess of my own making, not someone else's. When you live with somebody you make discoveries, like whether he cleans the toilet bowl or leaves his underwear on the floor. Adrien's speciality had been leaving hairs in the wash basin (he was losing his hair, to his consternation) and toe-nail clippings in the bath tub. It would have taken him only a second to swish them away with the shower attachment, but he never did.

Outside, the morning was grey and windy, and having gone out for a loaf of bread I was not tempted to stay in the open air. On the corner by the metro was a man selling bunches of lily-of-the-valley, his eyes watering in the wind and his hands blue. I nearly bought a bunch, but decided against it. On the first of May, lily-of-the-valley should be given as a gift, not bought for oneself. If nobody would give me any, then – tough! I would do without.

When I had finished the housework, I felt pleasantly tired and virtuous. The flat was spick and span. It seemed a pity that there was nobody to see it except me and Topaz. "Don't you dare scatter your birdseed!" I told him sternly. He whistled back at me. I wondered if Olivier was watching the May Day parade. I switched on the radio, switched it off again, played a few notes on the guitar and put it down again.

Sometimes, late in the evening when I knew he had shut up shop and gone back to his rented room, I would phone the number of the shop, just to hear his voice on the recording. I would never leave a message, but would listen to him asking me to leave one, with all the warmth of the Midi in his voice. I would close my eyes and imagine us sitting on some dark red rock with a pinewood behind us, the scent of needles in the air and the blue sea not far away, listening to the cicadas, a loud, dry sound, the quintessence of summer heat. I could listen to his voice now, if I liked. It was a public holiday and the shop would be closed. Dreamily I dialled the number.

"Hello?" said Olivier.

I nearly dropped the phone. "Hello -er – um – this is Stella," I faltered.

"Stella! How are you?" He sounded perfectly friendly. "What can I do for you? Trouble with something electrical? I haven't seen you lately."

"No," I said in a small voice.

"You haven't been avoiding me, have you?"

"I..." I hesitated. "I didn't think you would be in the shop today," I said.

"Then why are you phoning, if you didn't think I would be there? You are a funny girl."

"Woman," I retorted crossly. I felt that he had caught me out.

He didn't react to my correction. "I'm here because I'm so behind with the repair work. There's been a flood of it lately. I'm drowning in a sea of broken appliances. But it's quite boring, sitting here with no customers coming in to distract me. Your call makes a welcome interruption."

"Really?"

"Really. Tell me, you haven't been avoiding me, have you?"

"Well, I got the distinct impression you didn't want to see me," I said.

"Come on, you mustn't let my quick temper put you off. I have Spanish ancestry, remember? We're both bloody foreigners." He chuckled. Then he spoke the magic words: "What are you doing tonight?"

I was not doing anything, and if I had been, I would have cancelled it. My time was his, and I would go with him wherever he liked. He arranged to pick me up at eight, and as I put the phone down the whole room seemed alive. With a whoop I flung myself on to the settee, alarming Topaz. I buried my face in the cushions, then leapt up and opened the sliding doors of the wardrobe, wondering what on earth I could wear. He had said something about going dancing. I held up one dress against myself, then another, looking in the mirror. They all needed ironing, and I must wash my hair. But I had plenty of time. The day stretched ahead full of promise, and I was Queen of the May.

I had been ready for some time, but still I jumped when he rang the door bell. He thrust a bunch of lily-of-the-valley at me as he came in, and I smelt their strong scent as I looked at him standing there in my flat, just as I had often imagined him, but even taller and broader, this time wearing a white shirt and dark tie with his usual leather jacket.

"Nice place you have," he said, looking appraisingly around my cream and beige room with its shiny-leaved pot plants and reproductions of Cézanne on the walls. Cézanne's washes of luminous, translucent colour remind me of the south. "You have good taste." It was a banal thing to say, but I basked in his approval.

"Aha!" I heard him say, as I was in the kitchen putting the flowers in water, "I see you don't live alone." He was bending over Topaz's cage. "Does he sing?"

"Yes, he does, ever since – Yes, he does," I said.

"You know that bit of Mozart's Magic Flute – the Queen of the Night's aria? It was inspired by a canary's song," he informed me. He whistled some of the staccato notes. Topaz retreated to the far end of his perch and eyed him beadily, but made no remark.

So he liked opera, did he? I would not have guessed it. There was so much about him that I didn't know, that I wanted to learn: his likes and dislikes, his hopes and dreams. Another person is like an unexplored country. O my America, my new found land, I quoted to myself as we left the flat and waited for the lift.

The metro was quite full, but we sat on the folding seats. Opposite us sat a middle-aged man who kept twiddling his fingers in his hair, jerking about and talking to himself vehemently. "Either Paris attracts crazy people, or else it drives them crazy," said Olivier in my ear as we roared through the tunnels. "What do you think?"

"A bit of both, I expect." From time to time our thighs brushed against each other, and each time that old, powerful thrill went through me.

On the platform a vagrant shuffled up to us, one grimy hand outstretched, the other holding half a bottle of red wine. To my surprise, Olivier gave him a whole handful of change and wished him luck. He noticed my glance. "Well, he looked pretty miserable," he said, "and here am I, young and fit and going dancing with an attractive girl. Why should I have all the luck?"

"Woman," I corrected again, but quietly, loving him for his generosity. He didn't hear, anyway, as he was striding towards the exit.

It was a long time since I had been in a club. As we went down the winding stairs, the powerful beat of the music engulfed us like a flood, and I nearly lost him in the semi-darkness as we pushed our way to a table. Coloured lights jumped and flashed and the air was thick with perfume and the hot scent of humanity. Adrien had not liked dancing, and it was the atmosphere of my intense teen-age years that it brought back to me, the wild gyrations in the dark, the special boy, the soaring hope and searing pain – all that emotion wasted and vanished now like yesterday's weather.

I was older and wiser now. Or was I?

Olivier turned out to be a good dancer. I was a bit stiff at first, as it was so long since I had danced, but they were playing that wonderful rock and roll from the Fifties and Sixties, and soon we were really moving. Realizing that I could follow him, he started doing more and more elaborate steps, spinning me round until I lost all sense of direction, and we were caught and powered by the compulsive beat, his body and mine, and nothing around us but a blur of other dancers and lights.

Breathless and sweating, we sat down and sipped ice-cold vodka and tonic, talking as best we could through the noise, our heads almost touching. His lips brushed my ear when he spoke to me, and when I turned to him I could see the moving coloured lights reflected in his dark eyes. Resting on the table top, our arms touched. The black light came on and we laughed as his white shirt and the stripes on my dress suddenly glowed an unearthly blue. Then we danced again.

Later the music changed, engulfing us in a sound that was rich and slow, and we danced close together, gently moving in a sea of entwined couples. At first he held my hand in his, but then he guided it to his shoulder and put both arms around me. Slowly, slowly we swayed to the music, and above us the multi-faceted mirror ball revolved, sending flakes of light spinning round the walls like a slow-motion snowstorm. For the next dance he held me closer still. My face was against his shoulder and I could smell the warm cotton of his shirt. My arms were around his neck in the warmth and darkness. I could feel him trembling very slightly, and with one finger he caressed the nape of my neck. Like that song by Fred

Astaire, I was in heaven, though we were not dancing cheek to cheek, as Olivier was too tall for that. Something inside me was unfolding, saying yes. It was so long since I had been in a man's arms like this. To feel that a man wants you, and to want him too, with that sweet ache – those moments of realization and blissful anticipation can be almost better than making love.

We took a taxi back to my place, and in the car he sat with his arm around me, pulling me against him so that my head rested against his shoulder. I blinked at the soaring columns of the Madeleine moving past, the pearly lights of the Place de la Concorde, the rows and tiers of dark shops and empty offices behind the plane trees with their new spring leaves.

As soon as I had closed the door of the flat behind us, he took me in his arms again, not saying anything, and kissed me. His unfamiliar mouth explored mine, gently at first, then more urgently. He began to unbutton my dress.

"Bonjour!" said a loud, hoarse voice.

I broke away from him with a gasp. There was somebody in the flat. "Bonjour!" The voice seemed to be coming from the window. Some madman must have climbed up the outside of the building. I thought in panic of the man in the metro twiddling his hair.

Olivier strode to the window and yanked the curtain aside. I had left the window slightly ajar. There was a black shape on the window sill. "Kaa!" it said.

"My god, it's Jacques." Olivier opened the window.

"Jacques!" I joined him, weak with relief. "What are you doing here?"

"Kaa! Kaa!" said the crow loudly. He walked up and down the window sill, looking agitated, then took off, wheeled above the street and came back to us, still cawing. He rapped on the sill with his beak, then stood on tiptoe, as it were, flapping his wings and rasping "Bonjour". Now that I knew he was not a dangerous intruder, I was inclined to find him funny. But Olivier suddenly leaned out of the window and jerked back into the room, looking at me grim-faced.

"It's Rose!" he said. "Something must be wrong with Rose!"

"Do you think – ?" I began, but he was already out on the landing. He cursed the slowness of the lift, then gave up and ran two at a time down the stairwell.

I followed him as fast as I could, rebuttoning my dress, fumbling for my keys and locking the door behind me.

Parked cars lined the street, but no traffic was passing at this hour. Olivier had already vanished into the building opposite. It's odd, the things you notice in moments of stress. Nearly everybody was asleep, but further down the street, on an upper floor, a man stood silhouetted in a yellow window, wearing a felt hat and playing a saxophone. The smooth notes of Petite Fleur poured softly out into the night.

I entered Rose's building hesitantly. I could hear no sound from above, and on tiptoe I started to climb the stairs, feeling my way, not daring to press the time-switches for the light. Where had Olivier got to?

I had reached the third landing when a commotion broke out above me. There was a muffled shout, the sound of a struggle and somebody falling – one person or two, I couldn't tell. A thud, a grunt, another strangled yell, and then someone was running down the stairs towards me. Petrified, I pressed myself against the wall. The man passed me so fast in the darkness that I scarcely saw him, but I did glimpse his face, and that was what frightened me.

It was dead white, absolutely dead white, with slanting eyes and a slit for a mouth.

I heard Olivier running down after him, then stopping and going back upstairs as Rose's door opened. I climbed the remaining flights on shaking legs.

"Are you all right?" he was saying, his hands gripping her shoulders.

Rose was wearing a long white nightdress, with her hair in two black Victorian-looking plaits. In one hand she held her heavy flat-iron.

"Of course I'm all right." She shrugged his hands off her shoulders. "You really didn't need... Stella! You too!" she exclaimed as I came panting up the stairs and stood there speechless. "Well, you'd better come in."

We stood inside her flat, looking at one another in the dim light from the street.

"I was perfectly all right," she said to Olivier. "You needn't have done anything." She sounded so annoyed.

"It was Jacques," I explained. "He came to warn us. It's true."

"Jacques is a busybody," said Rose, for all the world as if she were talking about a person. She went to the window and immediately the crow flew in. She scolded him.

"But the guy was trying to break in. What would you have done?" demanded Olivier.

"Hit him with the flat-iron. He didn't know I was waiting behind the door."

"But Rose!" I protested.

"I'm sorry," said Rose, her voice suddenly warm again, "I'm being ungracious. I know I'm lucky to have such good friends who come running to help me. I'm just used to taking care of myself, that's all."

"He's damaged the lock, at any rate," said Olivier, bending over it. "It's completely jammed. I can change it for you later, if you like."

Rose was lighting the oil lamp, and the little stars around the shade shone out, sending a pattern of larger, golden stars swimming around the white walls as she moved the lamp.

"But who was it?" I said. "Did you see his face? It was – "

"Of course I didn't see his face," said Olivier. "He was wearing a mask."

"A mask!" Of course. I sat down suddenly.

"Don't you remember that bank robbery the other week? Three men wearing Mickey Mouse masks," said Olivier. "People didn't realize it was a hold-up at first. They didn't know how to react. It seemed like a carnival stunt."

"I suppose you didn't try to tear off his mask," said Rose.

"What, and take his name and address while I was about it?" Olivier sounded injured. "It was as much as I could do to get him away from your door and down the stairs. Well, I'd been waiting for a chance to try out some of those karate techniques. Now I know they work."

"It was somebody trying to get at me," said Rose.

"Could it have had something to do with Bertrand?" I said. "A friend of his, trying to intimidate you?"

"Oh, come on," said Olivier. "It was just a burglar. You can't blame Bertrand for everything. There's a burglary every five minutes in Paris. You can't prove anything."

Rose's face was blank. "Well, now he's gone. And I had my iron as a weapon."

"He might have turned it against you," I said. Or raped you, or killed you, I thought. "Suppose he comes back?"

"Then we'll be waiting for him," said Olivier. "We'll stay right here until it gets light."

Rose hesitated a moment, then laughed rather wearily and said "Why not?" With Jacques on her shoulder she went through the bead curtain to make us some coffee.

Blanche, who still slept here at night, had woken up and was perching on the back of a chair, bobbing her head at us and giving a bubbling coo from time to time.

Now that the danger was over we felt relieved and talkative, describing to one another again and again what had happened: how Rose had heard a stealthy noise on the landing, how Olivier had crept up the stairs and seen a figure bending over the lock, the sudden struggle, how I had seen the white-masked man hurtling down the stairs. Soon we were joking about the whole thing, and talking about burglaries in general, ingenious crimes, remarkable escapes from prison, blunders by the police. We discussed whether criminals were born or bred, and whether one chose the life one led or had it thrust upon one.

Then Olivier started to talk about Rose's way of life, and I could see her beginning to look evasive.

"I think that ... that you're given certain clues as to which way your life should go," she said. "Hints about talents that you can choose to develop or ignore. Stella here – she's a singer." Was she trying to distract attention from herself?

103

"A singer? I thought you were a secretary," said Olivier.

I didn't know what to say. Why could I not be both? Was it only one's job that counted? Was I indelibly branded "secretary"? But how far was I really entitled to call myself a singer? I wasn't good enough for that.

"Sing something for us, Stella," coaxed Rose.

After some hesitation, I nipped downstairs and across the street to fetch my guitar. Traffic sighed past on the boulevard, and the man playing the saxophone had gone. The air smelt fresh, and the sky was beginning to lighten. It never gets really dark in the city.

When I returned, the atmosphere was charged, as if the two of them had been having an argument. However, they both turned to me as I came in.

I tuned the guitar for a few moments, shy of singing one of my own songs in front of Olivier. I wouldn't sing one of the more recent ones, anyway. In the end I sang Carnival Night, thinking of the picture of the pierrot couple walking quietly home after a night of revelry. Then I broke into the sweet, sad strains of Danny Boy. I sang it in English, and glanced at Olivier as I sang "O Danny boy, I love you so."

He was looking the other way.

Boom! boom! boom! Monsieur Bertrand was apparently banging on his ceiling with a broom handle. I suppose we were making quite a lot of noise.

"He shouldn't do that," said Olivier. "I once made the mistake of thumping on the ceiling with a broom when my upstairs neighbours were having a shouting match. All that happened was that I made dents in my ceiling and got a shower of plaster."

We talked for a while about ceilings, old buildings and modern buildings, and then Olivier sang a Catalan lullaby. After a couple of verses I was able to pick out a rudimentary accompaniment on the guitar. He had a good voice, a light baritone. Then Rose went to the piano and sang a haunting little song in her high, thin voice. It had strange, sliding notes in it and unusual intervals, nothing like the Bach or Mozart that she usually played. Neither of us could understand the words.

"Oh, it's a dialect," she said, and wouldn't tell us any more.

By now the street was full of grey light, and Olivier announced that he was hungry. He offered to go out and buy croissants, and Rose started to make some fresh coffee as he clattered off down the stairs.

"Kaa!" remarked Jacques from the bookcase. He didn't seem inclined to leave.

"Isn't it amazing that Jacques came to fetch us?" I said.

"It was you he went to," said Rose. "To Jacques, you're the one who's my friend."

"Oh, but it was Olivier who did everything. He realized at once that there was something wrong. I didn't make the connection."

"Hmm." Rose's eyes narrowed. "Olivier likes to think of himself as some kind of knight in shining armour, coming to rescue me. I know I could have managed on my own." Then she shrugged and removed the coffee pot from the flame. "Do you think I'm too independent?" she asked abruptly.

"Well, don't we all depend on one another, in a way?" I said. "All species? Isn't that what the ecologists say?"

"It's true." She cupped her hands together. "Just think of all the millions of beings in a mere handful of air. Millions of invisible micro-organisms, and without them we wouldn't even be able to breathe the air. We depend on them."

I looked at her white hands, teeming with invisible, essential, mysterious life: angels dancing on the head of a pin.

"I'm beginning to think that being dependent may not be altogether bad," she said slowly. "Everyone needs a lifeline sometimes. But the most important thing is to be dependable. Like you. You're reliable."

No, I wanted to say, no, I am not worthy of that honour. Her blue eyes met mine for a thoughtful moment, and then we heard raised voices on the landing below. They got louder and louder, a door slammed and we heard Olivier's feet thumping up the stairs.

"I've just lost a customer," he announced dumping a bag of croissants on the table.

"Monsieur Bertrand?" I asked.

"Who d'you think?" His eyes glittered dangerously. "Noise or no noise, nobody talks to me like that."

"What did you say to him?" asked Rose anxiously.

"I offered to shove his teeth down his throat."

"Oh. Maybe you shouldn't have said that."

"No, maybe I should just have done it, without saying anything," said Olivier, making a fist and punching his palm experimentally. He whistled tunelessly. Then he went over to the piano and gave a spirited rendition of Chopsticks.

By now it was really morning and we could hear the rumble of traffic in the street and on the distant boulevards, and the hiss of a high-pressure jet of water as men in overalls cleaned the pavements. We drank our coffee and ate the almond croissants that Olivier had bought. They tasted all the better for our having been up all night. Jacques and Blanche shared part of mine. Then it was time to think about going to work. I didn't feel at all tired after the night's excitement, but my eyes were scratchy from lack of sleep. I would just have time to get ready for the office.

Olivier accepted my offer of a shower at my place before he went to open the shop, and Rose let us out, thanking us again for intervening. I half expected Monsieur Bertrand to come storming out as we went down the stairs, but his door stayed shut.

"So what did he say to you?" I asked as we crossed the street.

"The man's a fool. Says she's put the evil eye on him. The evil eye, I ask you! In this day and age."

Three pigeons were bathing in the water that streams through the gutters every morning in Paris. With ruffled feathers that stuck out in scallop shapes, they shook themselves vigorously, drops of water flying like diamonds. Three-toed footprints patterned the kerb.

"And what did you say?"

"Me? I asked him whether he'd seen her flying out of the window on a broomstick." Olivier flung back his head and laughed. "He didn't like that."

Madame Pereira was distributing the morning's post in the mail boxes as we entered my building. As usual, mine was all junk mail. She gave me an old-fashioned look: I was still dressed in last evening's finery, my make-up smudged, carrying a guitar and with a man in tow. I don't suppose it did wonders for my image. But hadn't she hoped that I would team up with a nice man?

In my flat, Olivier emerged from the bathroom with the ends of his hair wet, smelling sweetly of my soap. He kissed me goodbye hastily, his face unshaven, as it was getting late. It was almost a domestic scene. It had been quite a night – but not exactly the night I had had in mind.

When I went into the bathroom, I found a fair amount of steam, but no toe-nail clippings in the bath. On the other hand, he had not asked to borrow any nail scissors, had he?

***

I witnessed the next episode from my window. It was a turning-point, although I didn't know it then.

It must have been about ten days later, a Saturday, I remember, and I was cleaning the windows. Now that the weather was sunny, all the dirty marks left on the glass by the Paris rain showed up white and smeary, and it was hard to see out. I haven't a very wonderful view from my window: mainly rooftops and television aerials and chimney pots, and a changing backdrop of yellow cranes on the skyline as new blocks are being built. If I lean out and look sideways, I can just about see the Eiffel Tower. But I like to enjoy the view, such as it is, through windows that are not too grimy.

I had finished the outside and was rubbing vigorously at the inside when I saw Rose at her open window. I waved to her, but she didn't see me. Blanche was perching on her wrist, and the two of them seemed to be having a conversation. Sometimes I could have sworn that Rose actually spoke birds' language.

Blanche spread her white wings and closed them again. A flight of ordinary grey pigeons came swooping down to the balustrade. I saw Rose lift her arm and launch Blanche into the air, like Noah sending out the dove over the floodwaters.

The other pigeons jostled on the balustrade, a wing opening and folding here and there. Then they all took off after Blanche, describing a great curve against the sky, with Blanche leading them, white and shining, way out in front, and in perfect unison they turned and glided down towards the street.

What happened next was very quick. Monsieur Bertrand's window opened and he appeared with a shotgun at his shoulder, aiming downwards. I heard a shot – you might have thought it was a car backfiring – and then another, a pause, and another. A flock of pigeons rushed past my window, flying extremely fast, up and away over the roofs. But I looked down, and lying in the roadway were some bundles of grey feathers. And white ones. Monsieur Bertrand shut his window, and I saw that Rose had vanished from hers.

By the time I reached the street, she was there, kneeling. She was holding one of the limp bodies, and there was blood on her hands.

"Oh, no. No," I said, as I came up to her. The snow-white head was stained with red. The eyes were still open, but sightless, and the beak that had taken food from Rose's hand and mine was half open now, and oozing blood. On the ground lay two more dead pigeons, plump and in their prime, the sun shining on the iridescent feathers of their necks.

Rose lifted her face to me, her eyes blurred, her thin cheeks wet with tears. It was the only time I ever saw her cry.

A car braked noisily behind us and hooted. Beyond it, another car also hooted. Passers-by were pausing to look at us crouching in the road. Still holding the dead Blanche, Rose moved on to the pavement, and I steeled myself to pick up the other two, rather than let the cars run over them. The bodies were still warm, and very soft: it's surprising how soft feathers can be.

"How could he do it?" I raged, looking up at the closed windows above us.

"Men are killers," said Rose, still weeping. "They're killers. And it's my fault. She trusted me. She depended on me, and I betrayed her." Her tears fell on the slate-coloured feathers, the white wings.

"Oh, Rose, don't cry." I was close to tears myself. "She would have died before now if you hadn't saved her life."

"And these others. They probably have young chicks. They'll die, too, of starvation. Oh, what's the good?" she said bitterly. "It all ends in death. Men have to kill and torture – dominate – destroy. Everywhere. They kill and kill and kill. They're murderers."

I put my arm round her shoulders, and for a moment my head swam with the pity of it all. "Don't," I pleaded. I wanted to tell her that not all men were like that, that there were good men who were working to preserve life and save living creatures from suffering; but at that moment I couldn't think of any convincing examples. In my mind's eye I could see only Monsieur Bertrand's bald head, yellowish-grey moustache and strong forearms as he took aim.

When a wild creature dies in Paris, there is nowhere to bury it. Everywhere you look, you see asphalt and paving stones, and even the trees grow up through a circle of immovable iron spokes. The parks are supervised and regimented, and nobody could dig a hole in a lawn or a flowerbed without a keeper blowing a whistle. And at night the parks are locked.

In the end we went through to the yard at the back of Rose's building and laid the dead birds in a dustbin.

If we had been in England, we could have buried them in the garden, even put flowers on their graves and held a kind of funeral service, as we had done for dead pets when we were children. I still know where a flat stone marks the grave of the white mouse that I had when I was nine. But we were not in England. Forlornly we closed the dustbin lids.

"Things will get worse now," said Rose. She had stopped crying, but her eyelids were swollen and there was a smear of blood on her cheek.

With part of my mind I was trying to convince myself that her grief was out of proportion, that Blanche was only a bird.

But what did I mean by "only"? A person was "only" a person. Life was "only" life.

"Things are going to get much worse," she said. "Nothing can stop it now. I can't fight it any more."

I didn't understand what she meant at the time, but later I remembered what she had said.

– SEVEN –

Olivier was sitting on the counter, reading the sports pages and listening to the radio at the same time. I had heard nothing from him since May Day, but had concluded that he must be very busy. Business seemed slack today, however. The newscaster was talking about an erupting volcano in the Far East: in a small village threatened by the lava, a woman had beheaded her two children in order to placate the spirit of the volcano.

I thought he ought to know what had happened that morning. For a moment he looked startled when I described the shooting, but then he shrugged, switching off the radio.

"He's just trying to scare her," he said. "Too bad about the pigeons. Still, they're not an endangered species, are they?"

"Rose was terribly upset."

He folded his paper noisily. "Frankly, she's obsessed with those birds. God, you can't get near her for birds. Birds, birds! She cares more about birds than about people."

I studied his face. Time was, I thought, not so long ago, when someone might have said, in just such an outraged tone of voice: she cares more about 'wogs' than about white people.

"Why shouldn't she, in the circumstances? They – "

"I'll tell you," he interrupted. "In my opinion, they're just a substitute for children. She needs to lead a more normal life."

I didn't care for this pop psychology pronouncement. "You could turn that on its head and say that some people have children as substitutes for birds, or dogs, or cats," I said.

He laughed. I couldn't understand why he was so unsympathetic all of a sudden. He must know how Rose felt. Hadn't he given her Blanche in the first place?

"Hell!" He jumped off the counter. "I promised to have that kettle ready for old Madame What's-her-face. The firm was late sending the element. She'll be in here, complaining, any minute now."

I followed him slowly into the back room.

"Anyway," he added, "pigeons carry disease."

"I thought you cared what happened to her," I said.

"A lot of thanks I get for caring." He was scowling at the kettle. "You saw how she reacted the other night. I went round there, later in the day, to change the lock for her – and what do you think? She'd already got a locksmith to do it. She'd rather pay a total stranger than depend on somebody who's supposed to be her friend."

"She is very independent," I admitted, "but wouldn't you approve of that? You were telling me that women ought to be able to look after themselves."

"But she's never learned a martial art! She's so vulnerable."

"Well, I agree – I think she is vulnerable," I said, trying to placate him, "And I'm worried about her. What about that burglar? And I think this Monsieur Bertrand could be dangerous, too."

"What, just because he shot some pigeons? Plenty of Frenchmen shoot pigeons. No he's just trying to give her a warning. He wants her out, that's all."

"But bloody hell, Olivier – this man has a gun. Supposing he shoots somebody? He was firing a gun in the street, for God's sake."

"Listen," said Olivier. "Do you know how many people have guns? There are one million eight hundred thousand hunters in this country, not to mention all the people who have firearms left over from some war. My own father has a revolver. That doesn't make him a menace to life and limb. Old Bertrand's a hunter, so you can be pretty sure he's a good shot. He knows what he's doing."

"But hunters are always having accidents with their guns," I protested. "I hear about it on the news. They shoot one another, and their dogs and even their children."

"Merde!" Olivier dropped a screw on the floor and scrabbled for it under the bench. He emerged red-faced.

"All right then, so he isn't a good shot, so he missed the fucking pigeons, so what are we talking about? Why are you so argumentative today, Stella?"

I said nothing for a while, and the radio crackled on, pouring out endless information that I didn't want to know. I looked at his hands, remembering them touching me. The memory was like a dream.

"Anyhow," said Olivier, more quietly, "Women can never understand about hunting. It's a male tradition. It dates way back to the days when it was a matter of survival, when men went hunting for food. It's in our nature."

I couldn't let that pass; I remembered Mamie lecturing Pascal about this very question, her eyes like green sparks. "But if you study hunting and gathering communities, you find that most of their food is gathered. And it's the women who do the gathering. It's women who supply most of the food, while the men just sit around," I told him crossly.

His eyes glinted. "Believe that if you like. But hunting isn't only about food. It's something else. How can you understand, though? You shoot, you bring down your prey – it's an end in itself. But women just don't feel it."

"Olivier, you don't go out shooting, do you?" I was appalled at the thought.

"No, not for years. I did when I was a boy." His face was still fierce. "I wouldn't mind taking a pot shot at old Bertrand, though. Stupid bugger. Why can't he leave Rose in peace?"

Why can't anybody leave anybody in peace? Why can't human beings let the birds and animals live? Why can't Olivier let Rose lead the kind of life she has chosen, whatever her reasons may be? And why, I thought, why won't he look at me, smile at me, take me in his arms? If only we could get back to where we were the other night.

I walked over to the work bench and leaned against it. If he just reached out a hand, he could touch me.

"Are you busy tonight?" I asked him.

"Oh, tonight," he said offhandedly, "the guys from the karate club are all going out for a pizza. It's Alain's birthday, and I said I'd be there."

"Or tomorrow?" I suggested in a small voice.

He stared at me in surprise. "Tomorrow? But tomorrow's the Cup Final. I can't miss that."

The shop door pinged and we both came out of the back room. He had finished repairing the kettle just in time, as the woman in the purple jacket, now chattering non-stop, was apparently Madame What's-her-face. She had finely pencilled eyebrows about half an inch above the place where her real eyebrows should have been.

There was no point in waiting around. He waved at me vaguely, and I left without saying goodbye.

It was an afternoon of hazy sunshine, but rain would have been better suited to my mood. The rest of the week-end stretched emptily ahead; I didn't want to go home. I didn't know where I wanted to go. I told myself I had chores to do at home – washing, ironing, paying bills – but instead I walked slowly down the street and across the boulevard to the park. It was full of young couples in T-shirts and jeans, with children in pushchairs or chasing balls or riding tricycles, and I walked faster, trying to find a quieter path.

I was not observing very much, but after a while I became aware that a familiar thin figure was walking ahead of me. The branches of the shrubs on either side bounced and swayed as a retinue of sparrows and starlings accompanied her, and suddenly I noticed that there were swallows in the sky, swooping low over her head. So summer must really be here. It seemed as if forest glades and rides might be opening on either side of her, and trees stretching away into the distance, although in fact the park was bounded by railings.

As if she had sensed that I was following her, she paused and looked back. Behind her rose the horse chestnut trees, now rich green domes of leaves decked with the white candles of their flowers. She was wearing a dark blue dress with ruched lace at her throat and wrists, as if she had stepped out of an old stone castle with turrets and long galleries. She did not belong with the sportily clad couples at all.

"Are you all right?" she asked, looking at me intently as I came up to her.

"Oh, Rose." I didn't know whether to laugh or cry. "I should be asking you that."

"Why?" Her voice was oddly flat. "What's done is done."

"I feel so upset about Blanche." I was growing more and more depressed as I remembered all that had gone wrong today.

"The innocent die," she said. "The guilty go on living."

We moved towards a bench and sat down, not talking for a few minutes as we watched a sprinkler on the lawn a few yards away. It made a ticking sound as it sprayed, and half a dozen pigeons were taking a shower, ruffling their feathers and spreading their wings under the myriad drops that arched outwards, misty with rainbows. But none of them had Blanche's unusual colouring.

"At least all of these are still alive," I said awkwardly, trying to find some kind of consolation. "They should be safe here. And there must be an awful lot of pigeons in Paris."

"True. But if you lose somebody you care about, does it help to remember that there are billions of other people still alive in the world?"

Her white hands were folded in her lap, and the sun winked on her blue ring. A shiny starling landed briefly on her shoulder and peered into her face.

"No," I said, "I guess it doesn't." Why did our wants have to be so specific? Only one bird, only one particular man, and none of the other teeming millions in existence would do. "Even so, birds must be fairly safe in Paris. People don't normally shoot at them. But I hate to think what happens in the countryside. Did you know that there are one million eight hundred thousand hunters in France?"

"That's a very precise figure." She looked at me with sharp suspicion. "Stella, are you getting involved with Olivier?"

There was a pause.

"I don't know whether I am or not," I said, scuffing the gravel with my shoe. "I did go out with him once, that's all – the night you had the burglar, in fact."

"Ah."

I wondered whether to say any more. I wanted to talk about him, to try and make sense of his changing moods, but I was still not sure what Rose felt about him herself. She had said that she didn't want to see him, but had they had a lovers' quarrel? Deep down, did she ache to have him, as I did?

"Were you – " I hesitated. "Were you so upset about Blanche because it was Olivier who gave her to you?"

"What? No!" Her eyes were wide with surprise and pain. "Not at all. I thought you understood that. It's because her death was my fault."

"Why do you say it was your fault?"

"I should have known. I made her too dependent on me, and then I – I let her down. She thought my place was home. She thought she was safe. It's got nothing to do with Olivier. It's because she was – she was an individual. A soul."

I wished she wouldn't blame herself. Only Bertrand was to blame – horrible old man. But at least she wasn't grieving because the bird had been Olivier's gift.

"I see the swallows are back," I said, after a while. "Do they always scream like that? I hadn't noticed."

"Those are swifts. The ones shaped like half-moons."

I watched the incredible speed of their flight, their screams drawn out like thin wires across the blue sky. They traced invisible, intersecting arcs, and the first few lines of my song Wings went through my head.

"I don't want you to get hurt," said Rose abruptly.

"How do you mean?"

"It's none of my business."

"Come on, what were you going to say? You can tell me."

"I just have a feeling," she said slowly. "I feel it's dangerous for you to see too much of Olivier. I see pain and trouble ahead. I know what he's like."

116

I said nothing for a while. Was she warning me off because she wanted him for herself?

"How well do you know him?" I asked.

She gave a brief laugh. "Well enough. But he's not very self-aware. He doesn't realize what effect he has on people."

What effect had he had on her? Had he hurt her? I wanted to know, but couldn't bring myself to ask direct questions. I watched a blackbird hopping on the lawn, closely followed by two brown fledglings who shivered their wings and loudly demanded food. Father bird hopped ahead, expertly rooting out small grubs and turning back to thrust them into one or the other gaping beak.

"Olivier certainly knows how to be charming – sometimes," I said.

"He has very great charm," agreed Rose. "Too great. Too strong. He has too much power, and he doesn't control it because he won't admit he has it. He won't see what he is doing to people."

"I suppose I should be on my guard. But I guess I'm old enough to look after myself."

"It's nothing to do with age," said Rose. "I just feel you're taking a risk. And so soon after your last relationship. On the rebound."

I knew it. But it was too late. I was already too much under his spell. I wanted him to look at me and smile, I wanted his hands on my body, his lips opening against mine.

"I know he has bad moods, but I can probably get used to that. He's not a bit like Adrien," I said.

"Stella," said Rose urgently. "I'm serious. Don't put yourself in his power. Don't let anyone have power and influence over you like that. I can't stand idly by and watch you walk into the fire."

I remember I thought that she was exaggerating. Fire? Surely not. And again I felt that she might be trying to put me off because she wanted him back, even if there had been a coldness between them. I longed to pour out my heart to her, but I knew that she wouldn't give me any encouragement. She

117

would tell me to keep away from Olivier, whereas I wanted to hear that there was still hope. Even if he had hurt her, that didn't necessarily mean that he would hurt me, I told myself stubbornly.

I gave her some light answer, trying to turn the whole thing into a joke about men, and she dropped the subject.

The sun was lower in the sky now, and the lengthening shadows spread across us as we sat on the bench. Rose shivered, saying, to my surprise, that she had been in the park since late morning.

"What time is it?" she asked. She never wore a watch. When I told her, she stood up. "I must go. I have a pupil coming at six."

Together we walked back across the park, out of the gates, across the boulevard and up our street. As we stood between our respective buildings, she said: "I really don't want to go home."

I thought of asking her in. "But you have a pupil, haven't you?"

"Yes," she said, looking up at her own shining windows as they sent back fiery reflections from the sinking sun. "Yes. Well – goodnight."

I looked after her, wondering if she was really all right.

There was nobody about in the entrance to my building, and I removed yet another handful of junk mail from the letter box. I sniffed. The Pereiras would be having fish for supper tonight. I imagined them in their warm kitchen, with the television blaring. Francisco was making very little progress with his English and seemed to find it a huge bore, although I had heard him singing a pop song with a passable imitation of an American accent.

There was nobody in the lift, nobody on the landing. My neighbours' doors remained resolutely closed. And in my flat there was nobody except me and a canary. Topaz, who had been having a nap, woke up and stretched elegantly, separating all the feathers of one extended wing and fanning out his tail. I talked to him as I pottered around the flat.

"Damn Olivier," I said to him. "Why do I bother with men? Eh, Topaz? What's the point of it all? Why do I want to see him? He doesn't want to see me, does he?"

"Peep?" said Topaz.

"The next time I see him, I shall be cold and distant," I promised him. I picked up my guitar and began to tune it. "It would probably have been better if I'd never met him. I tell you, little bird, I don't want men barging into my life and disrupting things. I'm better on my own."

"Peep?" said Topaz. It sounded like an ironic comment.

For the next hour I worked hard on Wings, and began to feel that I was getting somewhere. I now had another verse in a minor key. That was good: there was a change of mood, like a change of season. And then the whole thing swung back into the major key, wings beating and glittering in the light. It was going to be all right. What had Rose said? I ought to make a recording of my songs. She was right – I might forget some of the details I had added today if I didn't make sound files.

I spent some time rummaging in drawers and cupboards for the microphone which I knew I had stored away somewhere; I couldn't remember when it had last been used. When I found it, I connected it to the computer, played a few chords, sang a few lines tentatively and adjusted the volume controls, feeling rather self-conscious. Then I sang Wings all the way through, followed by Carnival Night, followed by three other songs of mine, written some time ago, and finally, very slowly and sadly, Danny Boy, remembering how I had sung it to Olivier that night.

I clicked on the sound file and listened to it critically. Not so bad, not bad at all, although my guitar playing could do with some improvement. Those low notes that Rose had suggested were difficult to get right. I ought to take some lessons, I thought. It would give me something to think about, and take my mind off unsuitable and unreliable men. If only I could find as good a music teacher as old Mr. Evans at my school.

The light was fading, and before the file had finished playing a noise like thunder broke out over my head. The Dumbbells upstairs were shifting their furniture about again. Thuds, grindings and rumblings edged across the ceiling, drowning the music. I lay back on the carpet, looking up at the blank white ceiling, wondering what ever they could be doing. What hopes and longings did they have? Did they feel they could make changes and improvements in their lives by changing the position of the furniture? Were they Feng-Shui enthusiasts, perhaps? Whatever they were doing, they seemed to be having an argument about it. I could hear vehement voices. A door slammed.

"I'm better off alone," I told Topaz again, as I logged off.

It was at least partly true.

***

"I'm leaving school," I told my mother.

"What?" Her eyebrows shot up in incredulity. She had just picked a bunch of sweet peas from the garden and was about to put the vase on the sideboard. "What are you telling me?"

"I'm leaving school in the summer."

"What, without taking your exams? Ma fille, you're mad."

"Oh, I'll take my exams. But that's it. I don't want to go to college."

"Yes, you do. Don't be such an idiot! Of course you do. What kind of a career do you think you'll have? I never heard such nonsense."

"I don't care," I said obstinately. "I'm leaving."

"No, you're not. And why are you talking like this all of a sudden? What's got into you?"

"I'm sick of doing homework, swotting for exams, stewing in school learning stuff I don't want to know. What's the point? It's so artificial. I feel as if my head will burst."

"Don't say such – "

"I want to have my own life. I'm wasting my time. I want to live, can't you understand that?"

"Live! And what kind of life do you think you'll have, without any qualifications, may I ask? What will you do?"

"I want to spend more time learning the guitar," I said. "That's what I really want to do. And then – "

"The guitar! I knew that was a mistake. I told your father from the start. I told him that if he paid for guitar lessons, it would distract you from your schoolwork, and this just goes to show I was right. All you do is sit in your bedroom tinkering with it, when you should be working."

"I work as well! Anyway, what about the choir? You don't mind me singing in that when I could be working."

"That's different, of course it is. That's part of school. Now, listen to me – "

"I won't listen," I said loudly. "It makes no difference. I've made up my mind."

"You have not! Will you listen!" My mother banged down the vase of flowers on the sideboard so hard that it broke. Water and broken china were everywhere. Silently I went into the kitchen for a cloth. When I came back, my mother had swept the whole mess off the sideboard and on to the floor, and was pacing up and down. As I entered the room she started in with a torrent of words, walking around me and making vehement gestures. I hunched my shoulders and squatted on the floor, mopping at the water. Suddenly she was crouching beside me. She wrenched the cloth out of my hand, her eyes blazing into mine, shouting at me that I was an impossible child, that she would not put up with this, that I was throwing my life away.

I ducked my head down. "I'm still leaving school," I mumbled.

There were two milestones ahead of me: the concert and the exams. After that, school life would be behind me and I would say goodbye to that whole tedious, anxious, frustrating period of my existence. Only the choir was a good enough reason for staying on at school until the end of the year. We were rehearsing for a concert of sacred music, and David was also a choir member.

We used to practise in the school hall after hours, with Mr. Evans, the indefatigable music master, alternately playing the piano and conducting. As the evening light mellowed and darkened, our voices swelled to fill the hall, surging past the honours boards and the old cricket and football photographs, up, up to the high latticed windows, and beyond to the sky. Mr. Evans would often make each section practise its part separately: the sopranos, the altos, the tenors and the basses. David was a bass. Whenever they sang, with their men's voices like rich mahogany, a deep thrill went through me. And when we all sang together in harmony, I imagined our voices like threads weaving a rich tapestry, my voice intertwining with David's, light and darkness, silver and black velvet.

One of the songs we sang was by Hilaire Belloc, set to music by Benjamin Britten. It was about Jesus Christ as a child, to whom the angels brought toys of gold. But he refused to play with them, and, instead, made small birds out of clay, and blessed them till they flew away. Alone in my room, I picked out the notes on my guitar, singing the soprano part and imagining David's deep voice joining me in a duet.

But he never talked to me, never joked with me, barely acknowledged my presence. And in the autumn he would be going up to Cambridge to read maths and physics: solid science subjects, not like my own lightweight French and English. My English and French teachers were dismayed when I told them of my decision. But I was adamant. After the summer, there would be no more choir practice, no more David, and no more school. Everything was coming to an end. I felt I was moving towards a blank wall.

Only my guitar was there, real and familiar, something to hang on to and express my feelings through. In my room, I bent my head over it, my hair hanging down, and crooned over it like a mother to a child.

"Can't you play that thing more quietly?" asked Pascal irritably, poking his head round my bedroom door. "Or play it somewhere else. I'm trying to do my homework."

I stopped playing. Nobody in the family appreciated the music I made. True, my father had agreed to pay for guitar lessons, but he never listened to me practising. Only Mr. Evans seemed to think that I had a good singing voice. In fact, he had wanted me to sing a solo at the concert.

"I know you can do it," he had said, in front of the whole choir. "It needs a high, pure voice, but it must be a strong voice. It should by rights be sung by a boy soprano, but none of the trebles here is good enough. A hopeless lot, you are," he said, looking severely under his bushy eyebrows at the first-year boys in the front row, who grinned and punched one another. "Now, I'm going to play a recording of the piece. Pie Jesu, from Fauré's Requiem. And you can see how you feel about it."

The old, rather scratchy recording began. Mr. Evans turned up the volume. The unfaltering voice rose, hitting each note with perfect precision, with the muted organ accompaniment, like birdsong against dark woodland. It was the kind of still, small, perfect piece that made an audience hold its breath. It wasn't difficult. I could do it, I knew I could. I could feel people looking at me. I knew that David's eyes were turned towards me, curiously. Now was my chance to show him what I could do. I could show him that I was not just a nonentity; I could sing. I had been singled out. I was worth paying attention to. He would be surprised, interested. He might even come over and congratulate me.

"Now, then," said Mr. Evans as the music ended. "Here's the score. Come out to the front and give it a try now. It doesn't matter if it's not very polished. We'll work on it."

I didn't move.

"Come on, girl! Now's your chance to shine. I'll tell you something. I'd been thinking of having a word with your parents after the concert, telling them that it would be a good idea for you to have your voice trained. Wouldn't that be a grand idea? And if they hear you sing this, it's my belief they won't take much persuading."

I could feel David looking at me. I was paralysed. I knew that if I tried to sing in front of him my voice would tremble and squawk. I would ruin the music. I would be humiliated forever.

"Come on, then, Stella. Give it a try. Be bold, now." Still I did not move. My neighbour nudged me. I jabbed her savagely with my elbow.

"Stella?"

"No," I said. My face was burning.

"Ah, child, haven't you the courage? I'm disappointed in you." Mr. Evans's fierce eyebrows lowered. "Will you not think it over?"

"No," I said. "No."

***

Every Wednesday I go to the local newsagent's to buy the Officiel des Spectacles, which lists all the new films, plays, concerts and exhibitions. This grey, overcast Wednesday morning was no exception, and as I hurried into the shop I was telling myself severely that I must get out more, keep in touch with what was happening on the arts scene, find some entertainment and stop moping around the flat.

I had just stepped inside when I collided violently with somebody on his way out. He was not looking where he was going, but retorting something over his shoulder at the newsagent. I caught a glimpse of Monsieur Bertrand's grim face as I lost my balance, grabbed at a revolving stand of postcards and crashed to the floor with it. Cards scattered everywhere, and my bag flew open, spilling half its contents. Monsieur Bertrand was already gone, without uttering a word of apology.

"Ah, là-là, mon dieu!" exclaimed the little newsagent, hurrying to help me up. "Are you all right? Are you hurt? Oh là! What a thing to happen. No bones broken I hope?"

"I'm sorry, I'm so sorry, I'm quite all right," I said, gathering up odds and ends and feeling distinctly shaken. I had wrenched my wrist and banged my elbow by putting out one hand to save myself.

"Sit down here for a minute," he urged, producing a stool from behind the counter. "Have a little rest, get your breath back." His round eyes stared anxiously at me through his rimless glasses. He was a tubby, jovial man, with no neck to speak of, and his pink face always looked freshly scrubbed. When I came in, we usually exchanged pleasantries, remarks about the weather, transport strikes and so on.

"Monsieur Bertrand was certainly in a hurry," I said ruefully.

"Ah! In a hurry and in a bad temper. He might at least have stopped and apologised. I'm quite shocked at him." His cherubic mouth was curved downwards.

"I don't think he even noticed me," I said, rubbing my elbow.

"He seems to be in a world of his own these days." He started setting his postcard rack to rights. Cute kittens and puppies, smiling babies, black and white views of old Paris were retrieved from the floor.

"Hasn't he always been like that?" I was content to sit there for a little while.

"Not at all! You mustn't think so badly of him. He isn't quite himself these days, but you couldn't hope to meet a nicer man. Always a cheerful word, always ready to help out."

"Really?" I said. "I've heard he's always complaining."

"Complaining – well, you might say that. He was complaining this morning sure enough, because I hadn't got his magazine for him. Hidden World, it's called. Ever heard of it? No, I don't suppose you have. It's a bit specialized, you see. I told him, if it hasn't come this morning I won't get it till tomorrow, now, and maybe not even then. Sometimes they forget to send it. There's no demand for it, I told him. But he wasn't having it. Spoke to me quite sharply."

Two small boys in anoraks came in, bought chewing gum and went out again, pushing each other sideways and making yelping noises like dogs.

"To tell you the truth, I don't know what's got into him," said the newsagent, looking at me and wrinkling his forehead. "He was a different man while his wife was alive. Now he comes in here knocking down my customers."

"What was his wife like?" I asked.

"Bit of an old sourpuss. Stiff, she was, but very polite, very correct – you couldn't fault her. Always neat, never a hair out of place. You used to see them both on a Saturday night, going down the street to Mass, all dressed up. Mind you," he chuckled, "I don't expect she knew he used to come in here and buy the odd girlie magazine. He had an eye for a nice – " he broke off. I remained stony faced. "But don't get the wrong idea," he added hurriedly. "Always ready to do a good turn, is old Bertrand. I'll never forget the time those young hoodies came bursting in here and tried to rob the till and smash the place up. On drugs, I think they were. He laid into them, he did. Strong, you see! I couldn't have managed on my own. There was one young fellow, he practically picked him up by the scruff of the neck and threw him into the street! I can see him now."

He thrust his hands in his pockets and rocked on his toes, eyes gleaming reflectively.

"I can vouch for his strength," I said. "It was a bit like being charged by a bull."

"He just doesn't seem to have any patience these days, that's the trouble," said the newsagent. "I saw him out there playing boules the other day. Your concierge's husband was there, too – Monsieur Pereira, isn't it? Well, old Bertrand has been playing boules for years, but he lost his rag over something that day. I thought he was going to punch Pereira in the face. Instead of that he just turned round and marched off. Ah, he's changed all right."

A man with a briefcase came in, flung down some coins, grabbed a newspaper and rushed out again.

I glanced at my watch. "I must go, or I'll be late for work."

"Now are you sure you're all right?" He fussed around me, told me I could pay for my Officiel next time, chatted and beamed and held the door open for me.

I walked along the grey streets, thoughtfully flexing my sore wrist. So it was not only with Rose that Bertrand was disagreeable. And yet he had a reputation for being helpful. What had happened to him? A few drops of rain fell and dust whirled in the corners of the steps as I descended into the metro.

I was on the platform and about to step into the train when somebody grabbed my shoulder from behind.

It was lucky that I hadn't studied a martial art, or in response to what seemed to be the second assault in half an hour, I would probably have whipped round and socked whoever it was. In fact, my hand went instinctively to my bag, and I half turned, glaring.

I was looking up into Olivier's lean, smiling face, his eyebrows like level wings, his hand still on my shoulder.

"Oh, it's you," I said, remembering my decision to be cold and distant.

"Don't look so fierce." His eyes locked with mine as if he could read my thoughts.

With a hoot, the train doors closed, leaving me standing there, and I frowned. "I'm late."

"Stella, look – I'm sorry if I was abrupt the other day. I was abrupt, wasn't I?"

"A bit," I mumbled.

"I didn't mean it. Actually, I haven't been sleeping well lately, if that's any excuse."

I looked up into his smoky eyes. I wasn't going to say anything.

"I was going to phone you, anyway," he said. "Are you free tonight? Our last date didn't really go according to plan. Would you like to see a film, or something?"

I agreed, of course. Oh, I pretended to hesitate, but there was never really any doubt that I was going to accept, and we arranged to meet in the evening.

I was late for work that day, but the day was suddenly fine, not very grey at all, and I hummed songs over my keyboard.

"She must be in love," said Catherine in a stage whisper to one of the other secretaries, but I pretended not to hear.

***

That evening I had just finished getting ready and was looking in the mirror, practising an attractive smile and wondering whether a blonde rinse would improve my hair, when the telephone rang. I jumped, praying fervently that it was not Olivier ringing to cancel our appointment.

"Hello?" My fingers were crossed.

"Stella?" It was my mother. "Stella, I thought you'd like to know we've just heard that Lisa's baby is going to be a little girl. Isn't it lovely? Everything's going splendidly. I must say she's having a very easy pregnancy. And so it's to be a girl – a little niece for you."

"Ah bon," I said. My mother's enthusiasm seemed to warrant some further response. "How nice," I added.

"Can you imagine Pascal with a daughter? My naughty little boy! Of course, he would have preferred to have a boy first, then a girl, so that he could look after his sister. I would have preferred to have a boy first myself."

"Oh," I said. "I'm sorry to have disappointed you."

"Oh, Stella, don't be so touchy. With babies, you take what comes ... But I must say, you have disappointed me in some ways. When I look at Pascal, going to Oxford, making a success of his career, and then I think to myself that you never even went to university – just threw away your chances – and yet you could have done so well, you know you could – you could have been a college lecturer like your father – "

I sighed. I had heard this many times before.

"Maman, I've told you, it was my own choice. I just wanted to lead my own life. People have to make their own independent decisions, even if their mother doesn't approve."

"You sound exactly like your grandmother," she accused.

"So what? I hope I am like Mamie. I'd be proud to be like her."

"With all her talk of independence, she still got married and had children, didn't she? She was dependent enough on her husband when your aunt Hélène and I were small. It's fine to talk about being independent when you're a widow and over sixty. But she lived a normal woman's life first. You're too young to be talking like that, Stella. You should be thinking about getting married and settling down. Time is passing, you know. I really thought you and that nice boy, Adrien – "

"I've told you, it's finished between Adrien and me," I said, gripping the phone so hard that my hand began to sweat. "He wasn't right for me. I don't want him. I haven't met the right man. I don't even know if I want any children." Of course, I had told her nothing about my terminated pregnancy. I couldn't bear her to know.

There was a ringing tone on the line, and then a voice said "Hello?"

"Don't be silly, of course you want children," said my mother firmly. "Babies are so sweet, you know they are. Oh! They have such tiny little fingers, and their little ears – mmm! Wait till you see Lisa's baby. And they smell so nice when they've just had their bath. I'm really looking forward to helping Lisa – "

"Hello? Hello?" said the voice.

"Get off the line. We're talking!" shouted my mother.

"How is Dad?" I asked faintly.

"Get off the line yourself!" The voice was indignant.

"What? Dad? Busy, of course, in his study. He's always so busy, dear man. Of course, he's in the thick of exams right now."

"If he weren't so busy, perhaps he'd have time to phone me now and again. He never does," I said.

"Hello? Who is this?" demanded the voice.

"Well, he's letting you lead your own life, isn't he? He's not giving you any unwelcome advice, is he? You can't have it both ways. I thought you might be pleased to have a phone call from me, but no. You always were a sulky, undemonstrative child, Stella. I don't know what to make of you. Now you're not even interested in Pascal's baby."

Outside the window the sky was a darkening blue. Swifts wheeled against it, flinging their high-pitched skeins of sound. If I had gone ahead with the pregnancy, the child would now be – how old? I must not make that calculation.

"I must say, I always thought you would be the one to give me my first grandchild. You're the elder, after all, and boys aren't usually in such a hurry to get married. You ought not to leave it too late, you know."

I ought; I ought not. The other person on the line seemed to have hung up, and the engaged signal bleeped distantly.

"Maman, listen to me." My voice was harsh. "If I ever have a child, it will be because I've decided that I want one. Not because somebody else thinks I ought to have one. My child will be a wanted child, do you hear?"

"Don't shout," ordered my mother.

"Just stop telling me what to do. I'm not going to have a child that I'm not ready for. You made that mistake, didn't you? You had me. You didn't want me, did you?"

"Stella, don't be so silly. I never said that – "

"Yes, you did. You said you wanted a boy. Well, after me you had a boy, and he's now fulfilling all your expectations, isn't he? So I hope you're very happy. I'm just a disappointment."

"Stella – "

The door bell rang.

"I'm sorry, there's somebody at the door. I must go. I'll talk to you again soon, Maman. Give my love to Dad."

I rang off, and went to open the door to Olivier. He stood there, so tall, so reassuringly large, his expression now changing to one of lively concern.

"What's this?" he asked, wiping a tear from my cheek with his thumb.

I rested my forehead against his lapel for a moment.

"Oh, nothing," I said, and smiled up at him shakily. "I just had a bit of an argument with my mother on the phone."

"I argue with my father all the time," he said, and squeezed my shoulder. "We really make each other angry. But we're still very close. It's probably because we're so close that we get so angry."

He could understand me, I thought.

The old film that we saw was Carmen. One advantage of living in Paris is its plentiful cinemas. There is always a wide choice, from old black and white classics in the cramped art houses to the latest blockbusters on the wide screens of the Champs Elysées. It was a good film, and I like Bizet's music, but I watched the second half through an erotic haze, as Olivier had his arm round me and was gently caressing my right breast. He did not kiss me, just slowly teased my nipple until I nearly groaned aloud.

When we emerged from the cinema into the streets of the Latin Quarter, a chilly wind had got up and it was beginning to spit with rain. We went to a café for a drink and a snack, and sat by the window watching people scurry past, the traffic stopping and starting and the dusty horse-chestnut petals blowing in fan-shaped gusts across the pavement, brightly lit by the streetlamps and the shop windows crammed with summer clothes. We talked about the film, and whether opera could be successfully transferred to the screen. It had worked, we agreed, for The Magic Flute and La Traviata. I had reservations about La Bohème, but he had found it quite convincing. He talked animatedly, listened attentively to what I had to say, looked at me frequently. No one could have called him abrupt or offhand today.

In the metro we stood in the crowded carriage, holding on to the central pole and shouting above the noise of the train and the conversation of a group of happy Italian tourists.

"I think Carmen is meant to be a warning to women," I said.

"What?"

I shook my head. There was too much competition, and I didn't want to strain my voice. He looked down at me and smiled, and his hand slid down the pole to cover mine. We stopped trying to talk as the train rattled on through the tunnels.

Down my street, the wind blew cold, and we hurried against it, hand in hand. The leaves of the plane trees danced and trembled in the light of the streetlamps, and the sound of a saxophone came faintly on the wind, then louder, playing "Summertime, and the living is easy ..." In the lighted window, where I had seen him before, stood the man with the saxophone, the felt hat perched at an angle on his head, swaying forwards and leaning back as the rich, lazy notes floated down to us. It was impossible to see his face, as he was silhouetted against the light. He stood there, swaying with his instrument, pouring his whole being into the jazz.

It was draughty in the flat, and I went to shut the window. This time, please God, there would be no interruptions from Jacques.

Olivier was behind me, his arms around me, his voice in my ear.

"Are you cold?"

"No."

"Are my hands cold?"

"No. Oh, no."

Some time later we unfolded the sofa-bed and I switched on the bedside lamp.

"Did you know that only 17 per cent of women prefer to make love with the light on?" murmured Olivier, helping me to step out of my skirt.

"I didn't know," I said, unbuckling his belt. I must be one of them I thought: I wanted to look at him. And that was the first time I saw his naked body, long, smooth, the black hairs on his chest tapering downwards to his flat stomach. A man's body can be so beautiful. I had almost forgotten.

And then everything went away, as it does, and there was nothing but the warmth of him, his hands and his mouth, the sound of our rapid breathing, and I was clutching at him, fusing with him.

"Just a second," he said, reaching out of bed for his jacket, and I realized that he was going to take precautions. He's being careful of me. He's kind and wise, I thought, with part of my mind. It didn't occur to me that he was also protecting himself.

Then he was back with me again, holding me close, on top of me, inside me – and we began that journey upwards, upwards, through the darkness and the storm, to that point where the stars explode and time falls away. He held me until my shuddering ceased, and I could have wept at the pleasure and the comfort of his hands. It had been so long, a whole year of loneliness, and now here he was – Olivier. We were together. There were, it seemed, no more barriers between us.

Later things became more prosaic again, as they do. I found that I had a hair in my mouth, and he had to shift his arm from under me, as he was getting pins and needles. But those are good times too, lying companionably together, limbs intertwined, talking quietly. I nestled my head against his shoulder and stroked his chest, warm and contented at the nearness of him.

First we talked some more about the film. Then I talked a little about my family. I told him about Pascal: the way he always taunted and ridiculed me, and took my most prized possessions apart. I told him about Pascal's successful career, and the fact that he was soon to be a father, and how fond my mother was of him. I told him about my mother's quick temper. "She flares up so suddenly." Her rages never lasted long, but her outbursts shook me so much that I remembered them long after she had forgotten them. She expected me to forget them equally quickly, and couldn't understand it if I did not. I told him how fiercely protective she was of my father, who always withdrew from conflicts and valued peace and quiet.

He told me a little about his own parents and his childhood in Perpignan. "My father gets angry with me. He thinks I ought to settle down and find a proper job." He made an impatient movement. He was more eager to talk about his uncle René – the one who was now travelling around the world. At one time, his uncle had been outraged when a local winegrower planted vines across a public footpath where he had been accustomed to walk. He had applied to all the appropriate authorities, writing letters of protest and thumping official desks, but had obtained no satisfaction. So somehow he had managed to get hold of an earth mover, and early one morning he flattened the offending vines himself – and then gave the local schoolchildren a lift along the main road, loudly singing the Internationale.

"You should have seen the face of the chief of police," said Olivier, as we laughed together.

"Wasn't there terrible trouble?" I asked.

"There was trouble. But sometimes you have to take the law into your own hands."

I was not so sure about this, but I didn't want to disagree with him.

Afterwards he got on to the subject of cars, and the type of car he hoped some day to own – and here he lost me, as I know nothing about cars and find them very boring. You don't need a car in Paris. It's almost impossible to park and anyway the metro goes everywhere. I tried to say this at one point, but he just told me that in France there were 386 cars to every thousand people. I was content, though, to listen to his voice, to say "Mmm" and "yes" occasionally, and just to be there with him. After a while I let my hand wander further downwards, and he gradually stopped talking.

This time it was slower and more luxurious, not like great flashes of light, but a steady glow, gradually growing brighter and brighter, until it engulfed us both in excruciating pleasure. How had I lived for so many months without this?

At last we agreed that it was very late, and that we had better sleep, since we had to go to work in the morning. So I brought him a glass of water and watched as he drank it, in a cavern of lamplight, the pale colours of the room in shades of muted gold curving around the darkness of his naked body and his darker, wild hair, here in the bed where I had slept alone for so long. He smiled, and kissed me, and held me again. Then I turned out the light.

That's the thing about happiness. It comes out of nowhere, like a comet, blazing and wonderful, but it speeds past you, unstoppably, vanishing into nothingness, trailing glory. You can't hold on to it. However real it is, the present moment becomes the past, and soon everything is different.

I don't know what time it was when I woke up. I was suddenly totally awake, as if I had fallen from a height. Everything came back to me immediately, and I reached out for Olivier, but he was not there. I opened my eyes and sat up. The bed was empty.

Then I saw him.

He was standing, naked to the waist, looking out of the window. He was quite still, but there was an intensity, a clenched, taut look about him, outlined there against the dull night radiance given off by the city, where it never grows completely dark. I was about to speak, but said nothing, watching as he stood there gazing outwards and downwards. What was he looking at? The lower half of the window was slightly misted, and as I watched, his right hand moved slowly, the rest of his body still intent and motionless, as he traced a letter with a long curling tail on the misted glass. I saw it before he wiped it away. It was a letter R.

Very quietly I turned and lay down again, pretending to be asleep. He had noticed nothing. For what seemed a long time, he did not move. Then I heard him turn away from the window, and I felt his weight as he sat on the bed. I could have reached out and touched his naked back, but I didn't. I could hear rustling sounds, and realized that he was putting on his socks and shirt, and I heard the clink of his belt buckle. Then there was a silence, and I felt that he was bending over me. I lay quite still, my eyes closed. Very gently he pulled up the sheet over my bare shoulder. A few moments later I heard the door of the flat shut quietly behind him.

I turned over and buried my face in the pillow.

I don't know how long I lay there, willing myself to go back to sleep, sometimes drifting into an uneasy doze with snatches of meaningless dreams. I heard the hum of traffic and the hiss of tyres, people moving about in the flat above, a radio; and it became obvious that sleep was impossible. I must have slept for about two hours that night, not more. I got up and took a shower, looked at my haggard face in the glass, looked away. There were a few black hairs on the sheet when I made the bed.

I drank strong coffee, tried to eat some buttered biscottes, couldn't eat, threw them in the bin. I sat with my palms pressed hard against my eyes for a while, then phoned the office and told them that I was ill and would not be coming in to work. From above my head a stentorian newsreader made the ceiling tremble, and a high-pitched drone came from outside my door as Madame Pereira vacuum-cleaned the landing. Topaz found this stimulating, and began to sing enthusiastically.

It was raining and blowing. I stood looking out, at the sky and the buildings opposite, dull and flat in dismal shades of grey, and the raindrops trickling down the pane. I clenched my fist. I felt like punching it through the glass, but didn't, of course. A blue plastic bag whirled past on the wind, and Topaz fell off his perch in fright.

Neither of my two umbrellas was anywhere to be found, but I couldn't stay in the flat any longer. Large raindrops from the trees fell on me coldly as I walked to the metro. The train was packed, people smelling of garlic, sweaty bodies and unwashed clothes, even alcohol at that early hour. Jammed against them, I had a close-up view of boils on necks, hairs sprouting from nostrils and ears. Only inches away from my own ear, somebody was chewing gum. When I was finally able to sit on a folding seat, I found myself next to the tinny percussion of a leaking mp3 player. After a while its owner began to drone a tuneless accompaniment. I got out at the next stop.

The oversized hoardings all along the platform shouted with garish colours, except one, advertising a chain of opticians in black and white. It showed a couple, kissing passionately. I looked away. People were streaming through the white-tiled corridors and up the steps to the street, grimly determined not to be late for work, leaning forward aggressively. I pulled open the heavy door at the exit and immediately several people barged through, almost treading on one another's heels as I held the door.

"You're welcome! Don't mention it!" I said at the top of my voice; the last person through cast me a vaguely startled glance.

Still it rained. I found myself at the Arc de Triomphe, which loomed into the rainy sky with the little black heads of tourists bristling along the top of it like extra statuary, even in this weather. I walked down the Champs Elysées, fighting the wind and the oncoming tide of people who used their umbrellas like lethal weapons, trying to poke out one's eyes. Litter lay sodden underfoot and swirled in the gutters. Across the Place de la Concorde and into the Tuileries gardens, where the leaves of the horse chestnuts were vivid green against their black trunks, and the round pond was dimpled with raindrops, but no children were sailing their boats today. Through the Tuileries, crunching across the wet gravel. Out into the rue de Rivoli, on to Châtelet with its fountains, and the Seine. The murky water flowed fast under the bridges, totally opaque with the filth of human civilization.

Still it rained, with stronger gusts of wind now, and chilled to the bone I went into a steamy café for warmth, but couldn't stand the noise of electronic games, the hissing of the espresso machine, the shouted inanities and guffaws of the men at the counter, and went out again. I bought a crêpe from a pinched and tired-looking stall vendor, and walked on.

I don't know how many miles I walked that day, and the rain didn't let up once. As I waited at traffic lights, great shiny buses passed within inches of me, my wavering reflection looking back at me from the glass doors. The buses' bow-wave from the gutter soaked my legs and skirt. Above the street the plane trees' branches clashed and tossed. I walked and walked, drenched, turning down side streets, retracing my steps, staring unseeingly into shop windows, and in the end I travelled home in the rush hour as if I had gone to work, smelling the damp stale smells on the metro, crushed against repellent bodies in raincoats, hearing time after time the dreary hoot that signalled the closing of the doors.

At one stop a man with a guitar pushed his way on board, and the carriage was subjected to a deafening session of bellowing and strumming. It was a song of Zorinda's that I recognized, but he was ruining it. I couldn't imagine how he dared sing and play so badly in public. He even had the nerve to shake a tin under people's noses, but they pretended not to see him, just as they had pretended not to hear him, staring woodenly ahead.

Back in the flat at last I fed Topaz, stripped off my wet clothes and heated myself some milk with honey and cinnamon. It had been Mamie's comforting remedy for sleeplessness and nightmares, but Mamie was no longer here to talk to me soothingly as I sipped it, and I drank it too fast, scalding my throat. It was only early evening, but dark and stormy. I went to bed.

I lay there, shivering, listening to the wind, with the same thought hammering in my brain that had hammered there all day.

Olivier was in love with Rose.

***

137

My grandmother's real name was Thérèse, but to me she was always Mamie, the name that French children give to their maternal grandmothers. I have very faint memories of her wearing her hair in a bun, but later, in the days when Pascal and I used to go to stay with her, she wore it cut very short. It was not grey but pure white, crisply framing her broad, brown face with the deep crow's feet around the eyes – those green eyes that were her most striking feature. I have old photographs of her, but they don't do justice to her eyes. A light seemed to burn behind them, especially when she was excited about something.

She often was excited about something. She was passionately interested in all kinds of subjects, devouring books and magazines, but her special enthusiasm was social anthropology. She went to extramural classes at the University of Aix, joined an anthropological circle which organized talks and film-shows by visiting lecturers, and borrowed books from the library about obscure and threatened tribal peoples whose way of life fascinated her. She read Lévi-Strauss and disagreed with him sharply on many points. She read philosophy, too: heavy books in tiny print. She should really have been an academic or an explorer, I thought.

"No," she said. "I don't regret anything in my life. I did what I wanted to do. That's the most important thing, Stella, my love. To find out what you really want to do, and do it."

One thing that she had really wanted to do was to marry my grandfather, Raoul. He died when I was only two, and I don't remember him, but he looks out unsmiling from faded photographs, a small, slight man with a neat moustache. In my grandmother's house hung a map of the stars that had been his, and his flute lay enshrined in a glass case. "He was unique," Mamie used to say sometimes, her eyes gazing softly into the past. I wondered about him and wished I had known him.

Together they ran a little pâtisserie-confiserie, a cake and sweet shop, in one of Aix's narrow streets, and Mamie kept on the business after his death. How can I forget that shop? I loved its beautiful old tiles showing rural scenes, all looped about with garlands of flowers. Even the ceiling had a central oval panel of rustic harvesting, against a sky of ethereal blue. When the shop was closed for lunch, with the blinds pulled down to protect the window display, I used to gaze up at that scene, imagining the little figures moving, thinking myself into that golden landscape, which was how I imagined heaven to be.

Mamie trusted me not to touch the cakes, but she had to warn Pascal repeatedly and keep a stern eye on him. On Sundays, after mass (Mamie looked upon mass as a harmless social ritual), we were allowed to choose a cake for tea that afternoon. Ah, the chocolate éclairs, the meringues, the millefeuilles, the strawberry mousses, the macaroons, the fruit tarts glistening with glazed fruits like red, purple and green jewels! I was always in an agony of indecision. French cakes are so much better than English ones, and there are some very good pâtisseries in Paris; but I watch my weight now. And they can never be as delectable as those Sunday afternoon treats.

Then there were the calissons d'Aix, the speciality of the town, little elongated cushions of iced marzipan, in a variety of flavours (in Paris I have only ever found the plain sort), to be handled with tongs, packed carefully into boxes and tied with ribbon. Mamie always gave us a box of them for birthdays and Christmas, in addition to our other presents.

But later she sold the shop. It was taking up too much of her time, she said, and she didn't know how much time was left to her. She wanted to spend it doing things that really interested her, not serving customers all day. "But Mamie, you're not old. You have lots of time," I told her. I just couldn't imagine her dying.

She didn't move away from Aix. She kept the tall stone house where she had lived with her husband, and where my mother and her sister Hélène had grown up. "Such a gloomy old place," said my mother, but I didn't think so. True, it could look forbidding. A tall iron gate admitted you to the little gravelled courtyard, and steep steps led up to the front door, surrounded and overhung by wistaria with its dangling mauve droplets of flowers in the spring. On the door was a knocker shaped like a hand grasping a ball, which echoed in the hall. The door and shutters were painted dark green, and the shutters were often closed against the fierce sun of the Midi, so that the tall rooms inside were bathed in twilight – but I liked it. There was a quiet, serene atmosphere, lavender-scented, as if the old house were dreaming of the past. Almost as if it might be haunted, but not in any frightening way, as it was so full of the generous personality of Mamie. When all was quiet, I could imagine the sound of my grandfather's flute twining through the high-ceilinged rooms. It had been my mother's house, too, the home where she had grown up, but somehow she had left no trace. In the bedroom that she had shared with Aunt Hélène there was nothing that she had once owned except some old, fragile books by the Comtesse de Ségur, which I had tried to read and found boring.

At the back of the house was the long walled garden, with the fig tree and the mulberry tree that we used to climb, and the three cypresses casting shade by the honey-coloured wall where I liked to play and read and dream, or where Pascal and I would chase each other round and round in the dust. Somehow, we quarrelled less when we went to stay with her.

One day, however, I remember, we were in the kitchen, with its tall grey cupboards, blue tiles and copper saucepans. It must have been the spring half-term holiday, because I remember the grey, racing clouds and the mistral keening endlessly around the house, sharp as a knife-blade if you ventured outside. In Provence they say that the mistral drives you mad. I must have been about fourteen, that uncomfortable age, full of restlessness and frustration, hot desires and quaking fears, when you oscillate between bold forays into adulthood – boyfriends, make-up – and sudden retreats into the familiar world of childhood – tree-climbing, and books about children having adventures that all ended happily.

In a way I wanted to be here in Aix, where I had spent so many childhood holidays, but in another way I wanted to be back at school, where I could see David every day. Even if he didn't speak to me or even notice me, I wanted to have the blissful torment of seeing him wheeling his bike through the school gates, crossing the playground with a pile of books, or running down the stairs just as I was walking up, so close that I could have reached out and touched him. The wind howled on, mockingly, and I couldn't settle to anything.

Pascal was sitting at the scrubbed table making a model plane. The glue gave off a stench.

"You've stuck that wing on crooked," I said, wanting to find fault, wanting to point an accusing finger at everything that was askew and out of joint in the world.

Pascal didn't answer. He blew out a sigh, making his blond fringe flutter.

"And that bit's all wrong," I went on. "Look!"

He was trying to glue on the nose cone, but under my critical stare his hand shook and he stuck it slightly to one side. He tried to wrench it off again, but the glue was strong. The plastic cracked under his fingers.

"Now look what you've done!" he accused.

"Me? I haven't done anything. You're just clumsy. I don't know why you keep trying to make those models. You're not good at it. You know they never work out right." He exasperated me, sitting there making a botched job.

"I'm learning. I'm preparing for my future career with Air France," said Pascal grandly. "Anyway, what are you good at, I'd like to know? Nothing. You won't have a career at all. You'll just get married and have babies, like all girls do."

"No, I won't," I retorted, stung, because with part of my mind that was exactly what I wanted to do: to be David's wife. "I'm going to be an international singing star."

Pascal gave a prolonged hoot of laughter. "Pull the other one! And I'm going to be President of the Republic."

"You can't. You have to be French for that. You're English." I knew this was a sore point. Pascal had, in fact, been born in England, but he liked to boast to his friends that he was French and show off by speaking the language so fast that his class-mates couldn't understand him – not difficult since, like me, he had been bilingual from birth. I myself had been born in France, because, despite the personality clash between them, my mother had wanted to be near Mamie when she gave birth to her first child. "I'm French," I insisted.

"Yeah, you're a frog. You croak like one, too," said Pascal, suddenly switching tactics. I knew that I was annoying him, but something in me took a sneaking delight in it. If I wasn't happy, why should he be so smug and contented?

"You're just a wimpish English boy," I said. "The English are traitors and murderers, anyhow. Who burned Joan of Arc?"

"The French handed her over. They betrayed her!" said Pascal fiercely.

"No, they didn't. And it was the English who burned her. Burned her as a witch and a heretic! What does that say for the English? They're no better than one of Mamie's primitive tribes."

"She deserved to die. There was a war, and she was raving mad."

"She was not mad! She heard angels' voices. How dare you insult our national heroine!"

We were both furious, and the insufferable wind droned and wailed, with no let-up.

"Alors, alors! What are you two shouting about?" asked Mamie, coming into the kitchen and putting down the National Geographic and the English-French Larousse on the trolley in the corner. Her glasses hung round her neck on a cord. She had never learned English in school, but, nothing daunted, had taken it up in her late fifties, although languages were not her forte. My mother was the linguist of the family.

"Pascal says the French handed over Joan of Arc to the English," I said.

"Stella doesn't know any history," said Pascal scathingly. "You tell her, Mamie."

Mamie began to wash vegetables in preparation for one of her soups.

"As far as we know," she said slowly, "the French did in fact betray her to the English. The Duke of Burgundy and his men surrendered her."

142

"Told you!" Pascal was triumphant.

"But it's not as simple as that. If she had been fighting on the English side, they would probably have betrayed her to the French. She was that sort of person. She was different and awkward. She stood out from the mass. She was bound to be a scapegoat."

"Why a scapegoat?" Pascal was not convinced.

"Because when things go wrong, people get angry, and they always look around for someone to blame. Someone different from themselves. And the Maid was different – very different. She was the obvious choice."

"This is beyond me," said Pascal. "I'm just interested in what really did happen, that's all. Facts."

"Yes, but," I said in a lecturing voice, "you have to think about the sorts of things that happen. Tendencies. Things that might happen again. Isn't that right, Mamie?" I sounded like my English teacher when she tried to make the class feel stupid.

"I'm going out," said Pascal, losing patience with the whole argument. "I'm going round to call for Pierre." And, scraping back his chair with a horrible grating noise, he left the kitchen and slammed the door.

I went on staring through the kitchen window at the grey garden, lashed by the wind. Mamie shot me a glance.

"Come and help me chop these vegetables," she suggested, making space for me by the sink. "And tell me what's bothering you."

Haltingly, chopping onions, I told her about school and about David, my obsession and his indifference. As I spoke, I wondered why I had been so critical of the English when I was half English myself and my beloved David was wholly English. I hadn't meant what I had said, but when things were going badly I felt the need to hit out, regardless of truth or justice. I sniffed and winked hard – partly because of the onions.

Mamie told me that I was just starting my life, and that my life would be what I made of it. Did I want to narrow it down to this one boy, and perhaps some day marry him? Or did I want

143

to learn, study, travel, gain experience, create, taste life to the full? "The world is such a big place," she said. "This boy, now. Is he what you really want? Look into your heart and find out what you really, truly want. You have to do something with your life, something that nobody else can do in quite the same way. Now, what is it?"

I didn't know. I didn't know anything any more, except that I would surely love David until I died. But something in Mamie's words had sown a seed of doubt. The future opened ahead of me like a great plain, shifting, grey, formless as mist. What was my life's work? Who would be part of my life? I felt very lonely.

"Work!" I said. "I don't see the point of working to earn money – just so that you can eat, and stay alive, and go out to work and earn more money. What's the point?" I scraped onion skin off my fingers morosely.

"You don't work just to earn money, you work so as to be free and independent," said Mamie. "When I was young, it was much harder for a girl to have a career, or even a proper job. Now you can have independence and self-respect. You can take care of your own needs. You don't have to ask a man for anything."

"Mmm." I thought about this. "But you chose a man, didn't you, Mamie? You chose to marry Grandfather. Is that what you really wanted to do with your life?"

Mamie stopped peeling a potato and rested her hands on the sink. "It was my own choice. It was what I wanted to do. But I never depended on him, and since he died I've lived my own life. It was as if ... when I decided to make my marriage the centre of my life, everything else fell into place around it. And I'll tell you something." She turned to look directly at me. "I loved your grandfather dearly, but I never needed him. He needed me. I knew I was the only woman – the only one – who could make him happy. Or unhappy. I had that power."

That was one of the things I liked about Mamie. She talked about big things, life and love and death, as if I were another adult, not someone too young to understand.

I tried to imagine them as a young couple. I saw my grandfather in the old-fashioned clothes of the photographs, going down on one knee and giving her a rose, saying that she was the only woman in the world for him. It all seemed romantic, and quite irrelevant to my own situation.

"Did he say that? That you were the only one who could make him happy?" I asked.

Mamie snorted. "Of course he didn't say it! Men never admit such things." My romantic picture evaporated. "But this boy, David. Do you feel – Do you know, deep down inside – that you are the only person in the world who can satisfy him?"

I sliced through another onion. Of course I didn't know that. His whole behaviour seemed to indicate that he would be perfectly happy if I didn't even exist. I didn't count for anything.

Mamie put her arm around me and hugged me. "Promise me you won't give up your independence and get married just because you're lonely, ma puce," she said. "If you can learn to be alone, you can do anything. You'll be in charge of your life. But to be lonely in a couple, always wanting something he can't give you – that's the worst thing." She gave me a little shake. "I know he's part of your life. But only a part. You'll see later how he fits into the whole pattern."

What did I want? I felt as if there was a great hole of nameless wanting at the centre of me, like a crying, hungry mouth that could never be filled, wailing like the mistral. Mamie's arm was warm and comforting, and I leaned against her sturdy body as I had done as a child, when I had bumped my head or grazed my knee; but she couldn't shield me from the world.

I wished that the wind would drop. It blew on, endlessly, wordlessly.

– EIGHT –

pparently I had made a self-fulfilling prophecy. When I phoned the office the following morning, I really was ill, with a soaring temperature and an aching throat. I burned and shook, my nose began to stream as the day wore on, and my head felt as if it were filled with cotton wool, but I almost welcomed these symptoms. They forced themselves on my attention, and I could concentrate on them, pushing thoughts of Olivier to the periphery of my mind – where they stayed, like a persistent tooth-ache.

Eventually I phoned down to Madame Pereira and asked her if she would mind going to the chemist's for me when she went out to do her shopping. I was dozing when she rang the doorbell, and must have looked a sight when I opened the door, with puffy eyes and nose, my hair uncombed and an old black sweater on top of my T-shirt.

"You ought to call the doctor!" she exclaimed, handing me the box of tissues and the vitamin C that I had asked her to buy. The black mole on her cheek had fine down growing on it, I noticed with vague distaste.

"It's not serious," I croaked. She insisted volubly, and to get rid of her I promised that I would call a doctor if I felt any worse, and would phone her again if necessary.

I took the vitamin C and two aspirins, and tried to eat something, but it was like eating cardboard. I crawled back into bed, but the sheets were full of lumps and creases, and I was too hot and then too cold. Every time I began to drift into sleep I had to sit up and blow my nose. The walls seemed to be sloping inwards, and at last I dreamt that I was at the bottom of a well, floundering around in the darkness with some huge and shapeless creature like a whale.

I struggled out of sleep to find that it was late afternoon, a watery sunlight was filling the room, and someone was knocking at the door. I had a feeling that they had been knocking for some time.

"Oh, Rose. Come in." I nearly fell into her arms.

There she stood, tall and straight, holding some kind of bundle, her clear eyes looking at me with concern.

"I met Madame Pereira in the street, and she told me you were ill," she said. "Get back into bed. No, wait." She started to remake the bed with deft movements, straightening out wrinkles and plumping the pillows. Topaz was singing piercingly.

"What happened to you?" she asked, sitting on the bed as I slid gratefully back between the sheets.

"I got chilled in the rain without an umbrella." I didn't tell her how long I had walked in the rain. "The silly thing is that I have two umbrellas, but I think I must have left them both at the office."

"Ah! That's the trouble with umbrellas," said Rose, shaking her head. "They don't like getting wet. If it rains in the morning, you find your umbrella has already gone to the office. But if it rains in the evening, you look for your umbrella in the office and you find it's gone home. They're very good at forecasting the weather."

I laughed and coughed. "They're gregarious, too," I said hoarsely. "The two of them always end up in the same place."

We grinned at each other. Dear Rose. Was it any wonder that Olivier was in love with her? I didn't blame him – at least, not for loving her. I blamed him for pretending to love me. But then, had he done any such thing? He hadn't ever said that he loved me. Surely I ought to know by now that a man can hold and kiss and caress a woman and make love to her passionately, and it doesn't mean anything at all.

That was it. He had just wanted me to go to bed with him, the bastard. And in doing that, perhaps I had wronged my friend. Perhaps he was her true love. Did she care about him? I still couldn't bring myself to ask her – especially not now. How could I confess that I had made love with her man? Yet he had wanted me. He had found me exciting. I didn't know what I felt: guilt, elation, anger, confusion.

"Now," said Rose, "what can I get you? Have you eaten today?"

I was about to ask for a cup of tea, but then it occurred to me that she would have to use the electric kettle, so I asked for a glass of water instead. She extracted something from her bundle and disappeared into the kitchen. I could hear her moving about, and lay back against the pillows. Topaz hopped from perch to perch, singing all the time.

"Drink this." Rose handed me a glass of water that was faintly tinged with green. "It's a herbal remedy. It works."

Obediently, I drank it. It had a lemony flavour. On a plate she had brought me some little cakes, spread with butter and honey, and at first I refused them, but after a few minutes I began to feel slightly hungry and was able to swallow them. She sat there chatting to me as I ate, telling me about her pupils and their oddities, telling me how her Amish quilt was progressing.

"And I've brought you this," she said, removing the paper from her bundle.

I couldn't speak. She was holding up the most beautiful patchwork jacket, the patches all fine triangles in shades of peach, moss green, dark green, rich brown, cream, and here and there a gleam of orange. Everything was beautifully finished – collar, cuffs – and the design was elegantly fashionable.

"Your colours."

"Rose," I croaked. "Why?" I reached out a hand to touch it.

"Let's say it's an advance birthday present."

"But my birthday's not until June."

"Who knows where we shall all be by June." She sounded unaccountably wistful.

"Oh, Rose – thank you," I said inadequately. "Can I try it on?"

148

"Not now. Tomorrow," she said firmly.

"It's so beautiful." The colours ran and blurred as my eyes filled with tears. "It must have taken you hours and hours to make it." I reached for a tissue and blew my nose. I imagined her sewing away, straining her eyes during the long hours while I dreamed about Olivier and yearned for him. Perhaps she had been putting the finishing touches to it while we were actually making love, oblivious of everything except our own fierce pleasure. I wanted desperately to know whether she loved him. I also wanted desperately to believe that she did not. It was bad enough that Olivier was in love with her. I couldn't ask her. Olivier, Olivier. The tears spilled over.

"Come on, now," said Rose. "You must get rid of this fever, and then everything will seem better. Lie down now."

I closed my eyes and could feel her moving round the bed, tucking in the bedclothes just as Mamie used to do, with small, comforting jolts.

"Don't go yet, Rose," I said faintly.

"I'm right here."

She began to talk, quietly, about patchwork, about mosaic quilts and all the different colours that she pieced together. I could see the colours flowing past me like a river, gleaming and melting into one another as they poured into the darkness. Then she was talking, still in the same low voice, about the snow-capped Himalayas, and the blue lakes and the kingfishers. Her cool hand rested on my forehead as she talked, and I could breathe the pure air. I was floating, high above the range of peaks all glistening with snow, and Rose was with me in the air, still talking. Not floating, but flying. How had I failed to notice that we had wings? We flew effortlessly, above the untouched drifts and deep folds of snow shadowed with blue, and far ahead of us, ringed with wisps of cloud, rose the peak towards which we flew, the highest peak, the pinnacle of the world.

When I opened my eyes, it was morning. I was alone in the flat, my head was clear and my temperature was down to normal.

***

I suppose about a week must have passed after that. I know I went back to work, still slightly hoarse and needing to blow my nose frequently, but feeling perfectly well – physically, that is. The pain in my heart was still there, but I tried not to let it affect me. Life was like that, wasn't it? X loved Y, and Y loved Z. People's feelings didn't match, people passed each other in the dark and failed to meet. I had been through this before. The acts of love were so powerful – they were like weapons that could destroy someone's world. But the person performing those acts often had the best of intentions, and didn't realize what destruction he was causing, even as he gave such intense pleasure and joy. It was not his fault. Olivier had received the message that I wanted him, and he had responded like a man. I had hoped for that, hadn't I? What right had I to expect any kind of exclusiveness or commitment?

I wasn't even sure that I wanted to be committed to anybody. It was good to be free and single again, I told myself. I didn't want possessiveness and jealousy coming into my life. And I had other things to think about.

I worked hard on the guitar accompaniment to several songs, although my throat was sore and I couldn't yet sing. I watched a long-running talent show on TV, and was struck by how painfully untalented the competitors were, though bursting with self-confidence. I would never have dared to take part in such a show, but – if I was totally honest – I did believe that my own songs were better.

I also went with Catherine after work to see a new film, and she invited me back to her flat for a drink afterwards. "Your jacket is fantastic!" she said several times, and I let her try it on, although it was too large for her. She wanted to know whether Rose took commissions, and I said vaguely that I would introduce her, at some stage. But I couldn't imagine them together. Catherine was always so exuberant, brimming with enthusiasm, a bit noisy – a different person from Rose altogether.

The night I arrived home late after the cinema, there was a message from Olivier on the answering machine. "I just wondered how you were. Why don't you give me a ring?" said his voice, that voice from the Midi.

"And why don't you go to hell?" I retorted, wiping off the recording. There was more to life than Olivier, and I didn't want to see him. Not yet, anyway.

Topaz watched me, and scratched his head vigorously.

It was June now, and warm, and the evenings were long and light. The sky was full of swifts and swallows. Long grasses tried to grow where they could, pushing up between the iron spokes around the trees and transforming into meadowland corners of the park that the mower had missed. The smell of freshly mown grass held memories of summers stretching back into the past, and wasps began to come indoors, where they hung like small torpedoes, trying to escape again through the glass. I began to think of holidays, but had no precise plans. I wondered whether Rose would join the general exodus of Parisians in summer, leaving the place to a minority of office workers and teeming crowds of tourists.

She took some time to answer the door when I knocked. When she opened it, I knew at once that all was not well. As usual, the last time I had seen her I had been engrossed in my own problems – my bad cold, my heart-ache – and I hadn't really looked at her. She had given nothing away, and had been brisk and reassuring, as she knew so well how to be. But today there was definitely something wrong. Her eyes were very blue and sharp. I could see the crystalline formations in the irises, the deep indigo of the pupils.

"Come in," she said. "Sit down. Uh ... I won't be long, if you don't mind waiting." She withdrew into her bedroom.

It was stuffy in her living room: only one window was open a crack. The Lone Star quilt was about two-thirds finished, but other materials lay jumbled about in disorderly heaps, orange clashing with pink, yellow looking sickly against sludge brown. No other work seemed to be in progress. The piano stood open, and piles of sheet music lay on top of it and on the floor. Rose was not usually so untidy. I went to the window. On the ledge, geraniums thrust up their vigorous bunched flowers; half hiding the stone lion, who sat as ever gazing down through the wrought iron balustrade into the street. I wanted to open the window, but didn't like to do so without asking Rose. Silence. What was she doing? Was she all right?

At last I tiptoed to her bedroom door and knocked softly, then peeped in. Her small bedroom was bare, almost monastic, with white walls, the only splash of colour the quilt on the brass bedstead. High up on a shelf stood a small black statuette of what seemed to be an Egyptian goddess. Like an Egyptian statue herself, Rose was sitting motionless on the bed, her hands on her knees, eyes closed. As I looked in, her eyes opened, and she gave a small strained smile.

"Are you OK?"

"I hope so. I'm just trying to redirect it."

"Oh." Redirect what?

Her eyes followed my gaze to the statuette.

"That is Hathor," she said, standing up, her hand resting a moment on the shelf. "Goddess of music and love and dancing. And journeys." She sighed. She seemed tired.

We went back into the living room, and immediately the window was alive with wings, as several pigeons, a flock of starlings and two crows tried to get in. Rose shooed them away, knocking on the glass and flapping a length of material at them until they flew off. She did not open the window.

"You don't let them in any more?"

"I can't." Her voice was tense. "They have to keep away from here. I think they're beginning to understand. I don't want any more killing."

"Have you seen Bertrand again?"

"No, but I've heard him. He still bangs on the ceiling. And two days ago he fired his gun in the air. He didn't hit anything. But Jacques had been around all the morning, trying to get in. I'm sure Jacques knows I don't want him here, but he won't take no for an answer."

"He mustn't shoot Jacques! God, Rose, what can we do about this man?"

152

"Nothing," she said. "He's my neighbour. He has a perfect right to live where he does. All I can do is – try not to be angry with him." She closed her eyes and massaged her forehead with her fingers. "And try not to provoke him."

I was tired of hearing this.

"I think you ought to be angry. You can't put up with this."

"No. We should love our neighbours, isn't that right? Anger is not the answer, I tell you. I know anger is not the answer!" She sounded angry even as she spoke, I thought.

"You can't help being angry sometimes," I objected. I knew I was still angry with Olivier. Being angry with him made it easier to think about him. It made me feel stronger.

Rose paced to and fro in front of the windows. "I can't help it," she said at last. "But I ought to help it. I've let it get out of control. Everything's slipping."

She sat down at the piano and started to turn the pages of a book of sonatas. I was beginning to feel oppressed. I understood now why she wanted the windows closed, but there seemed to be not enough air in the room, and the atmosphere was oddly charged. My thoughts returned in their accustomed groove to Olivier, and I wondered if they had seen each other. I could ask her that, couldn't I? I could ask her casually whether she had seen him.

Rose launched into a piece of music that I had not heard before. It was certainly not Mozart or Bach, but slightly discordant, with surprising jumps and pauses.

"That's not your usual style," I said when she had finished.

"Bartók," she said briefly, and stood up to flap at the window again as a little flock of sparrows hovered. "I can change my style, can't I? I have to make some changes."

I said nothing, but watched her as she sat down at the table and began to sew furiously. "I have to change!" she burst out. "I thought things had changed. I thought they were getting better. I'd even made friends with a normal person – with you, Stella. And then it just takes one old man – "

"One stupid old man," I said.

"Maybe. But I can't forgive him. I can't. I can't cope with him being so near. And now I can't let the birds come to me. I admit, Stella, I wouldn't have cared so much if he'd shot a policeman instead of Blanche. Don't look so shocked! How many people do the police themselves shoot every year? I expect Olivier knows the figure. They're trigger-happy men. We're all guilty, we all deserve what we get, especially men. They're the destroyers in this world. But Blanche was totally innocent, she was a different species, and I should never have let her get so tame. She trusted me too much, and – " She choked. Her hands were lifted and dropped in a listless gesture.

I didn't know what to say. I thought about Olivier saying that Rose cared more about birds than about people. Then I remembered Blanche on Rose's shoulder, her feathers fluffed out comfortably, giving little affectionate nibbles to the side of her neck. She had seemed so contented with life.

"All right," I said after a while. "Bertrand is making things impossible for you at the moment. But it surely won't go on like this. Perhaps you should just let some time pass. From what I hear, he seemed to be going off his head – having some kind of a breakdown. Maybe if you can just hold on, he'll go into hospital and you'll be left in peace. Try not to be too upset."

I was finding it hard to breathe, and was panting after this speech, which seemed to become more hollow and meaningless as I went on. Perhaps my cold was turning into bronchitis. But why was it difficult to sit still, and why did I have this prickling sensation moving up the back of my head?

Rose was looking directly into my eyes. That blue gaze. "It's not just the fact that I feel upset," she said. "It's the consequences."

"What consequences?"

"That... intruder. The man in the mask," she said slowly.

"Oh, but surely you aren't afraid that he'll come back? Not after the reception he got."

She was still gazing at me. "You see, I haven't told you everything. I know who he is. And I know why he wears a mask."

I was sitting with my back to the piano, so I saw nothing. But just as she finished speaking, a note played. I turned round. I recognized it: middle C. But there was nobody and nothing there. It was as if an invisible finger had depressed the white key. The note hung in the air, dying away. I turned back to look at Rose.

She bent over her quilt and went on sewing as if her life depended on it.

***

Who knows what my motives were? I truly wanted to help Rose, but I was at a loss as to what to do, and I genuinely wanted to talk about it with someone else who knew her. Who knew her better than Olivier? I wasn't angry with him any longer – just disappointed and wary. It seemed he didn't really know what he wanted – but such uncertainty was only human. If I had been a man in his position, perhaps I would have acted in the same way. Men were strange creatures, who could keep their emotions and their bodies in two entirely separate compartments. But I was strong enough to cope with that, wasn't I? I wasn't born yesterday. I could accept the fact that he didn't love me, just so long as he still wanted me physically – as I wanted him. There was no doubt about the intense physical longing that I still felt. That at least was real. As for love: it was a source of complications, I told myself. Love could wait. Olivier would make up his mind one way or the other eventually.

Even so, I didn't go straight to the shop when I emerged from the metro after work, but walked slowly around the block, thinking about what I was going to say.

In the gravelled space between the boulevard and the park, the usual bunch of middle-aged and elderly men were playing boules. They were heavy and solemn. I saw Monsieur Pereira in his shirt-sleeves swing his arm back, carefully taking aim. Other men were sitting at the café terrace enjoying the evening sunshine. Monsieur Bertrand, however, was nowhere to be seen.

I walked on, round the corner and up Olivier's street. I was walking more and more slowly, and my heart started to thump.

Ping! went the door as I entered. There were no customers in the shop.

"Well, hello, stranger!" Olivier came towards me with a dazzling smile. "I was just about to close."

He must have felt me draw back slightly, since he didn't take me in his arms but just kissed me on both cheeks as friends do. He looked down at me quizzically. What had I been up to? Why had I not returned his call? I told him, bleakly, that I had had a bad cold and had not been feeling very sociable – which was true.

"But you're here now." There was no answer to that. He flipped the sign on the shop door to read Closed. "Come through to the back and have a glass of wine. I was just about to have one. I need a break."

The work bench in the back room was still piled high with appliances: electric mixers, hair driers and other gadgets. The stream of small repair work never seemed to slacken, luckily for him. I watched him, tall and lean in jeans and a green sweat shirt, as he poured me a tumbler of red wine. Our fingers touched as he handed it to me, making me catch my breath. I wondered if he had noticed.

"I had a card from my uncle René today. He's in India now." I looked at the photograph of domes and graceful pavilions outlined against a crimson sunset. Another world.

Olivier swallowed some wine and gave a small sigh. We were sitting together on the sofa, not touching.

"Next year," he said, "I think I'll take off. A backpack and a couple of guidebooks, and I'll be off on my travels. It's nice to have a regular income, but these regular opening hours get me down – not to mention some of the customers. I'm sick of the metro in the rush hour, too. I hate being in Paris in the summer. Don't you?"

"I have to earn a living," I said. "Won't you be taking a holiday later in the summer?"

"Oh, yes, I'll be taking the regulation holiday," he said.

We were talking as politely as two strangers at a cocktail party.

"Where will you go?"

"I don't know yet."

Possibilities hung in the air between us like smoke. I imagined myself travelling with him, with a backpack and my guitar. Spending whole days and nights with him.

Why was I dreaming?

"I wanted to talk to you about Rose," I said.

"Again?" He frowned. "I can't stay too long. I have a karate class tonight." He looked at his watch.

This was not a promising start. I hardly knew how to address the topic of Rose, aware as I now was of his feelings towards her. I tried to tell him how tense and distraught she seemed, and how she was even forced to drive her beloved birds away because of Bertrand. I didn't tell him what she had confided to me, and I didn't mention the piano incident. I was not even quite sure, now, that it had really happened. But I was sure that Rose was under a lot of strain. I told him about Bertrand firing his gun in the air.

"Can't we go to the police?" I demanded.

"Police!" His voice brimmed with contempt. "The police won't do anything. Somebody has to be murdered before they'll step in."

"But isn't there some way we can stop him intimidating her?"

"I could lie in wait for him in a dark alley." He put his hand on my arm, laughing. "I'm only joking." My arm burned where his hand had touched it. He was looking at my hands cupped around the tumbler of wine. I willed myself not to tremble. There was a pause.

"No," he said, "Rose may be overwrought, but I think it's just a matter of time. I think she's strong enough to cope. But I've a feeling you're right about old Bertrand. He's losing his marbles."

"Other people say he's been acting strangely."

"Mmm. He has a funny look in his eye. I bumped into him coming out of this building the other day. Don't know what he was doing here. He looked decidedly furtive. Of course, he won't speak to me since that – conversation we had. He cut me dead."

"I wonder," I said suddenly.

"What?"

"Didn't you say that a clairvoyant lived in this building?"

"Aha! That could be it. Ha! Paris is full of loony people visiting fortune-tellers, reading tea-leaves, spending all their savings to have their horoscopes drawn up. We're living in an irrational age." He gulped the rest of his wine and glanced at his watch again.

I looked down at the floor, wishing that I could take an equally robust attitude. I was not sure of anything any more. Mentally I could hear middle C floating on the air. Had it happened or hadn't it? And what was Rose really afraid of?

"What are you thinking about?" Gently he removed my empty glass and took my hand. His fingers stroked mine. I began to shake. "What is it, Stella? Have you been avoiding me again? I was hoping to see you."

I didn't believe him, but I couldn't speak. His arm was around me now, and his other hand moved down onto my breast. It was no use, I was lost. My head sank on to his shoulder: you win, Olivier. He raised my chin and our lips met, gently at first, our tongues exploring each other, then more and more fiercely, and I felt myself going, yielding, falling again into that dark and fiery vortex that seems to have no end.

Some time later we were lying on the sofa, our clothes tossed anywhere on the floor. I could feel the hammering of his heart as I struggled to catch my own breath, my eyes closed. He had taken me up so high, and brought me down again, but his hands were still moving over my body, and we were starting all over again. I opened my eyes for a second and the ceiling and walls seemed to be turning in a slow circle. His breath was in my ear: "Like this? Shall I do it like this?"

"Yes – oh yes. Oh, don't stop – "

It did not seem possible to reach a higher pitch of pleasure, but it happened, with everything in the world behind my eyelids straining upwards to that final triumphant explosion, just tantalizingly out of reach – and then it was there, and nothing else mattered but the force of it, and I felt I would be shaken to pieces. And again I began to come down, and to breathe again, but he would give me no rest, and again he forced me on to what my body begged and craved for, yet protested against – no, no, this is too much. Then, later, I was on top of him, caressing him, kissing his eyelids, his neck, his chest and stomach where the hair was wet and matted with sweat. I ran my hand along his hard thighs, my fingers stroking the hardness and hot silkiness of him. In control now, I caressed and devoured him like some fierce Maenad, wild with happiness, and he gave himself up to me, his breathing fast and shallow, until at last I heard that gasp and strangled groan that can be the sweetest sound in the world, and I had given him what, at that moment, he wanted most of all.

Oh, yes. The sex we had was very good. It was like a powerful drug.

We lay for a long time heavy and still in each other's arms. Then I turned my head and found his eyes looking into mine, very close. It was getting dark.

"Ça va?" he whispered.

I hugged him closer. "What about your karate class?"

"I'm not going."

The faint light filtered through the window on to the cluttered work bench. There were broken springs in the sofa, but I was as happy as it was possible to be. We were together now. This was it: the real, the essential bond.

He pulled an old blanket over us and we talked quietly as the light died. He told me about his clashes and reconciliations with his father, and about an unhappy love affair two years ago with a girl called Isabelle, who now lived in Narbonne. He hinted darkly that she had behaved badly, but seemed reluctant to go into details, and I didn't press him. I told him about Mamie, and a little about Adrien, though it wasn't easy to talk about that time.

"What went wrong between you?" he asked.

Then, hesitantly, I told him about the abortion. I held my breath, wondering how he would react. He was very still for a moment.

"But how come this guy got you pregnant? What the hell was he doing?" he demanded.

I explained that the doctor had ordered me off the pill because it was making me gain weight and giving me skin rashes, but that Adrien had always refused to use a contraceptive. He said it spoiled his pleasure. He preferred to withdraw – but of course it only takes a split second's bad timing. I thought about my own stupidity. By that time, I had not even wanted him to touch me. I craved love, not sex. But I had let him do it, all the same.

"Selfish bastard," growled Olivier.

"It was my fault, too."

"Poor Stella." He stroked my hair, again and again, as if he were stroking a cat. It felt very calming.

"But I hope I'll have children one day," I murmured.

"You will. I'm sure you will. Why not?" His words in the darkness were like an unopened flower, a hint of joy to come, a promise hidden in the curved petals.

And we lay there, our bodies pressed together, our arms around each other, breathing together, telling each other small, inconsequential things about our lives. We had become the whole universe, and we didn't talk any more about Rose. I no longer believed he was in love with her. It wasn't possible. He was just fascinated by her, as to some extent, I was myself – and so, perhaps, was Monsieur Bertrand.

Much later, we got up and retrieved our tangled clothes, sorting mine from his and smiling at the haste with which we had strewn them across the floor. He turned on the light so that I could comb my hair in the mirror over the sink. I looked like a scarecrow, but my face was blissful. He stood behind me, folding his arms around me and resting his chin on the top of my head, and we looked at our two faces in the mirror, mine fair, his dark.

"I'm starving – aren't you?" he said.

So we went out to a pizzeria, some distance down the boulevard opposite the park. I can remember it all – the white rough-cast walls, the red checked tablecloth, the artist's impression of Venice on the cover of the menu, the waiter shouting our order in Italian as he returned to the kitchen – and the way Olivier held my hand across the table as we were waiting to be served. Our two hands resting on the table, mine broad with short nails for typing and guitar-playing, his olive-skinned, long and sensuous. All of it, jewel-sharp in my memory.

And I remember, as he walked me home through the warm night, the heavy branches of the trees above us, and between the branches, the pinpoints of the stars. It's not often that the Paris sky is clear enough for stars.

"Rose once told me – " I said, and stopped. But it was all right. I knew it was safe to mention her now. "Rose once told me that we shouldn't be lonely, because our planet is in the Milky Way."

He gave a delighted snort of laughter. "Isn't that just the kind of crazy thing she would say!" Then, tenderly, his arm around me, "Are you lonely?"

"No," I said, turning towards him, "not right now," and we stopped for a few minutes.

"The Milky Way," said Olivier as we walked on, "has a diameter of 109,000 light years and contains 100,000 million stars. We are 32,000 light years from the centre."

What could I say? Figures like that take your breath away. Here we were, spinning in space, insignificant stardust, and yet we were at the very centre of the only universe we knew.

As we turned up my street, we heard the sound of a saxophone, and there was the same man outlined against the yellow light of his window, playing jazz. He wasn't wearing his hat. There was no wind tonight, and the notes fell soft and sweet on the air. A cat's eyes blazed at us for a moment before it vanished between the waiting wheelie bins at the kerb.

"Stella by Starlight," said Olivier.

"What?"

"That tune he's playing. How did he know? And your name means a star."

We kissed for a long time in front of my building, holding on to each other as if we couldn't bear to part. But it was late, and we both needed sleep. He left at last, turning to wave as he walked down the street. He did not so much as glance up at Rose's window.

There were stars all around us that night. And now, looking back, I know that there were stars in my eyes, too. Oh, yes. Starry-eyed, that was me.

***

I was on a continuous high for the next few weeks. I was unbelievably happy, sometimes uncomfortably so, as if I were living on wine and cream. We were wrapped up in each other.

On the evenings when I didn't see him I worked hard on my songs. I didn't sing or play when we were together. Well – he was really only interested in jazz and opera, not in my kind of music (even though I had composed a song for him, called He's the Man Who).

I didn't see Rose at all: I didn't have time. The thought of her did cross my mind now and again, rather guiltily, and I told myself that I really must pop across the street and see how she was getting on. But I didn't go. It would have been so much easier if she had been on the phone.

Like tourists, Olivier and I wandered around Paris together in the evenings and at week-ends. We queued to go to the top of the Eiffel Tower. We leaned on bridges, looking down at the murky flow of the Seine parting against the buttresses as we talked. We sat at café terraces, watching the colourful tide of passers-by. One evening we went to an open-air jazz concert, with moths drifting white in the spotlights and dark leafy branches above our heads. Every day was new and interesting, and every morning I awoke feeling happy because I would see him that day. In the autumn, we told each other, we might get tickets for the opera.

Some time later he was busy for a whole week-end doing an intensive karate course with his friends, and I decided that I would spend Saturday re-recording my songs, and would then take my guitar and go and play them to Rose in the evening, to see whether she thought, as I did, that I had done as much as I could to improve them, and that they were now ready.

But I had reckoned without the pneumatic drills. I had forgotten that it always happens. As soon as the fine weather arrives, out come the drills, like seasonal visitors, and the streets are full of roadworks. My street now had a long trench in it, with workmen on the job from eight o'clock in the morning. Luckily they had packed up for the day by the time I came home from the office, but I hadn't realized that they would be working on Saturdays, too. It was warm, and I wanted the windows open, but the din was unbearable and I had to close them again.

"You might as well take advantage of this, and have a fly around," I said to Topaz, letting him out of his cage. I put a saucer of water on the table and he took a vigorous bath, sprinkling drops everywhere. Then he flew, bedraggled, to the top of the wall unit and preened himself.

It was so hot. It would be wonderful to be on a beach somewhere, and to take a header into the waves. I imagined Olivier walking out of the sea, his bronzed body slick and wet, shaking the water from his curly hair. Perhaps later we could get away somewhere together. I hadn't yet mentioned the idea, but I felt that it was distinctly possible. I sighed and roamed around the flat. A whole week-end without him, and this heat, and the terrible noise from the street. I felt like a coiled spring. It was cooler in the bathroom, but above me I could hear Monsieur Dumbbells, a heavy smoker, coughing and making disgusting hawking noises.

I thought about going for a walk, but the streets baking in a haze of petrol fumes had little appeal. There were cars and traffic lights everywhere; nobody could walk in comfort. The park on a day like this would be heaving with people, and there would be ice-cream vendors and men selling helium balloons.

It would be nice to lie on the grass under a tree, but you aren't allowed to lie on the grass in many Paris parks. The keepers blow whistles and wave their arms at you. Children have to play on the gravel paths, and adults sit upright on benches and little spindly iron chairs. I could have caught a train and travelled right out of Paris, but I wanted to get the recording finished.

Luckily the workmen stopped for lunch, but by then I was thoroughly tense. I made some false starts with the software, and cursed and swore. Then as soon as I started to play, Topaz burst into song, and I had to put him back in his cage and cover it to keep him quiet.

At last I started recording. The first attempt was no good at all, and I did some deep breathing and deliberate relaxation before I started again. But the second time, everything was fine. The new songs were fine. I knew what effect I wanted, and I achieved it – just about. Of course, you're always critical of your own work, and there is always room for improvement. But, all things considered, it was a good recording. I began to feel elated.

I made a cup of tea and stood by the open window to drink it, playing the file through again quite loudly. Yes, those base notes were all right. Luckily my neighbours never complained about my music – or else they were away, which was more likely. Across the street, Rose's windows were still firmly shut, and I could see no sign of movement inside. A crow perched on the television aerial on the roof of her building. Jacques, possibly. As I watched, he began to caw harshly, thrusting his head forward with each "kaa!" I nearly called to him, but then thought that maybe it was not Jacques at all. I still can't tell one crow from another. But Rose would have known.

Rose. It was already early evening, and I would go over and see her. It was unforgivable of me to have neglected her like this. She had always encouraged me with my songs, and I knew she would be interested to hear what I had done to them.

Carrying my guitar, I began to climb the stairs in her building. There was nobody about. In fact, it was remarkably quiet. The closed doors turned impassive wooden faces to the landings, each with a different size and shape of doormat, some with the occupant's name printed by the doorbell, others anonymous. There was a faint smell of the wax floor-polish that Madame Pereira used. I passed nobody and heard no sounds of life. Everybody seemed to be out.

And apparently Rose, too, was out. The time-switch on her landing was again not working, and I stood there in the dark, knocking on her door. Nobody came. I knocked a second time. Well, like everybody else, she was taking advantage of this fine weather, I told myself. Unless, of course, she was ill. With another twinge of guilt, I remembered how she had come to look after me when I had caught that chill. I rested my guitar against the wall and called "Rose!" through the key-hole. My voice sounded unnaturally loud. I put my ear to the door, but could hear no sound of movement inside.

Then I thought I heard something. It was very faint, but it sounded like the piano. Yes, surely it was the piano. There was a strange rippling music, as if somebody were playing notes almost at random. Rose must be in there. I banged on the door, calling her name. Nothing. The door remained resolutely shut, and the music had stopped. Silence.

It was very dark on the landing. I felt an odd, prickling sensation moving slowly up the nape of my neck. Don't be stupid, I told myself, rubbing my neck hard. She's out, that's all. I wished I had brought a piece of paper to scribble her a message. Picking up my guitar, I clattered down the stairs, making a fair amount of noise and humming defiantly.

Apart from the gaping trench, marked out with red and white tape, the street was just as usual, with cars parked all along it and the big wheelie bins waiting at the kerb for the collection. There was even the usual homeless man, hunting for treasure in the three bins that belonged to Rose's building. Wait a minute, though – it wasn't the homeless man. It was Bertrand. As I watched, he delved inside and rooted around. There was a small pile of rubbish at his feet, but nothing that looked salvageable. What could he be looking for? Something that he had thrown away by mistake? As I walked past him he shot me a baleful glance, then continued to rummage, and I didn't like to stop and watch.

I should have said something to him, I thought. I should have told him that the neighbours wouldn't tolerate his shooting birds in the street. I could have threatened to report him. Or maybe I should have been conciliatory, trying to point out that Rose was not deliberately bothering him, and suggesting that people who had to live so close together must surely be prepared to put up with a certain amount of noise. But the moment had passed.

Did he ever regret having shot Blanche, I wondered? But then, for him she hadn't been Blanche; she had not been an individual at all, but just any pigeon. A pest. Vermin.

I crossed the street and passed through the gate into the narrow strip of garden in front of my building. Suddenly, ahead of me I saw something grey and shapeless moving across the path. The blood drummed in my ears and my heart thumped. Then I realized that it was merely a ragged piece of grey plastic, drifting on the evening breeze.

What was the matter with me?

***

On my birthday, to celebrate, I finally decided to do something reckless. I posted a bunch of songs on the social network. Come on, I told myself. Enough dithering. If you're satisfied with them, put them out there.

That morning I had received cards from my parents, from Pascal and Lisa, and from a handful of friends in England, plus some e-cards. There were no presents, and in Paris nobody knew that it was my birthday. In my family, birthdays have never been important occasions. Mamie was the only one who used to send presents and make much of us on those days. If we happened to be staying with her, she would always plan a special treat, and my one and only birthday party had been held at her house, with an iced cake aflame with seven candles. If only I could phone Mamie. One more year gone, and what was I doing with my life?

I had at least recorded my songs and posted them on the Web. What the hell, I thought to myself. I've got nothing to lose. Probably nobody will listen to them, and in any case it's nearly the summer holidays. Nothing happens in Paris in the summer: shops close, businesses barely tick over, the streets are wonderfully empty of traffic, half the population migrates to the coast and the metro is full of foreign tourists. Paris is dead in the summer.

I was on my way home after work when I met Madame Pereira in the garden in front of the flats. She was picking up beer cans and ice cream wrappings that had been tossed over the low wall on to the patch of lawn.

"Have you seen all this mess?" she demanded. "People aren't civilized. They have no respect at all. It's not right."

I murmured something in agreement.

"And the dogs! How many times have I seen people last thing at night, letting their dogs into the garden to do their business on the flower-beds? It's disgusting. People have no consideration for their neighbours."

Picking up a soda can, I put it in her plastic bin-liner.

"In the village where I grew up, people would never have dreamed of throwing their rubbish about like this. Country people have more pride. It's Paris that does it. People start to act like savages when they live here. I've seen too much of it."

"London's just as bad," I told her. "I think it's a problem with all big cities. They're too anonymous. If people don't know their neighbours, they don't care."

"I don't know about London, but I always thought the English were tidy people. Oh, that reminds me." She straightened up – "I meant to tell you about Francisco."

"What about him?"

"He's failed his English exam."

"Oh, no!" I felt disappointed and guilty at the same time. Silly boy – he had made no effort, hadn't taken any interest – but I should have pushed him harder. Some really good coaching would surely have got him through.

"I'm so sorry," I said.

She shrugged. "Oh, not to worry. You did your best. He's lazy, that's his trouble. Takes after his father."

I certainly didn't take after my own father, I thought despondently. He was a born teacher, and I knew how much his students respected him. Clearly, I was not good at teaching. I had never wanted to teach. Was I really good at anything? One more failure on my record.

Just then I saw Rose coming out of her building, and at the same time three magpies appeared from nowhere and started to swoop around her, weaving patterns and making a loud rattling noise. I walked across the street to greet her.

"Three for a letter," I said, half joking, pointing to the magpies.

"What do you mean?" She stared at me with those blue eyes. She was wearing a black and white dress which seemed to be echoed by the bluish-black and white of the birds' plumage, and in the inky dark hair the white streak gleamed like snow. I would have liked to take a black and white photograph of her at that moment.

"It's an English saying. You count magpies and say: one for sorrow, two for joy, three for a letter, four something better – " I babbled.

"Superstitious nonsense," said Rose curtly. "As if magpies wanted to play any part in people's lives! Joy and sorrow? We bring them on ourselves. As if poor magpies had anything to do with it!"

One of the birds perched on her head like some outlandish hat, and the other two sat side by side on a branch above us, gazing down and rattling.

I was taken aback at her vehemence.

"I don't really believe it," I assured her. "It's just folklore."

"Folklore! Don't tell me about folklore. Do you know what they do in Greece?"

"No, what?"

"They shoot down pelicans. Shoot them down, clip their wings and keep them cooped up as pets. Because they're supposed to bring good luck. Pelicans, I tell you – great wild birds."

I made a helpless gesture, and the magpie left her head and suddenly flew almost into my face. I had wanted to tell her about my recording, but this didn't seem the right moment.

"You – uh – seem a bit tense. Is anything wrong?" I asked.

She turned away, shrugging. "Wrong, right – I don't know. I'm sorry, Stella. I must go. Let's talk later, shall we?"

She walked away from me, down the street, tall and narrow in her black and white dress, followed by the three magpies and by a gathering throng of other birds, pigeons, sparrows – and swallows, too, speeding like arrows out of the sky. As she walked past the parked cars, a terrible racket began to arise as the car alarms went off one after the other. Nobody pays much attention to these alarms, as they so often go off for no reason, but now there must have been four or five all sounding at once, and the street was full of demented yodelling. Heads were beginning to turn. The skirt of Rose's dress billowed briefly on the breeze as she and the cloud of birds disappeared round the corner.

As I returned to my block of flats, I saw Madame Pereira standing in the entrance, watching. She crossed herself.

"Did you see that?" she asked in a low voice. "Do you know what Monsieur Bertrand says about that Madame Martin?" She nodded meaningfully. "He says she has the evil eye."

"Nonsense! That's just superstition."

"Maybe," she said darkly, "but I don't like it. You don't always know who you're dealing with. People think they know everything these days, but there's a lot we don't know, I say."

Shit, I thought, as I went up in the lift. I hope Madame Pereira doesn't start spreading gossip about Rose. She has enough trouble already. Then I wondered whether I had got the rhyme right. My aunt Margaret in Torquay had always said Three for a letter, Four something better, but somewhere I had heard Three for a girl, Four for a boy. I checked myself in annoyance. Why was my head so cluttered up with foolish beliefs for which there was not a shred of evidence?

I worried about Rose for a while, but then forgot about her as I was expecting Olivier and had to prepare a meal.

"I've recorded all my songs – did I tell you?" I said when he arrived. "I've posted them on the network."

"Oh, yes," he said.

Then he told me animatedly, and at length, how he had got the better of a customer in an argument about a guarantee.

***

Magpies or no magpies, the letter arrived a few days later.

I wasn't seeing Olivier that evening, as he had gone to his last karate lesson of the season, and the whole class was to take the instructor out to a restaurant afterwards. So we wouldn't see each other until the following day, and in a way I was rather glad to have an evening to myself and relax. I felt quite worn out with continuous passion. I planned to potter about, do some mending and perhaps go on reading a novel that I had started several months ago but hadn't had time to finish.

It was high summer now, the sky light until well after ten o'clock. Topaz would hop about dynamically every evening until about nine, but then would usually stand on one leg and fluff out his feathers, looking sleepier and sleepier until finally he put his head under his wing. If Olivier and I kept the light on too late, making love, he would poke his head up again and glare at us, with a cross and ruffled air, so I usually covered his cage at sunset these days.

I hoped he hadn't been scared by the fireworks on 14 July. We had gone to watch them, but I don't really enjoy Bastille Day: the streets are loud with firecrackers thrown by teenage boys. The noise is just like gunfire, and I could understand why Jip and Milou hated Guy Fawkes night. But Olivier didn't mind the bangs at all. When a firecracker went off right at my feet, and I screamed and leapt back, he was quite unperturbed.

Now I was sorting through a heap of junk mail that had been piling up on the table for a couple of weeks. It was amazing how much of it I received. Catalogues of household gadgets, gardening catalogues, special offers and promises of huge cash prizes galore. The reason I received more and more of it was no doubt that I always sent off the lucky numbers and coupons for the prize draws, even though I hardly ever ordered anything. I kept hoping for a lucky win.

It would be so wonderful to win a huge sum of money. It would change my life. I had no savings left at all after furnishing my flat, and exotic holidays were out of the question; I still had no idea where I would go on holiday this summer. Or perhaps I might win a car, which I could sell – or give to Olivier if he wanted it. I longed to give him a lovely surprise. Somebody has to be lucky, I told myself. Somebody has to win. Why not me, for once? Or how about this: lose five kilos in two weeks. Infallible method. Money back if not satisfied. An attractive brunette in a swimsuit beamed glossily. Anxiously, I pinched the flesh at the side of my waist. Was I putting on weight? With Olivier, I had been eating far more than my usual small meals when I was alone. Did he think I was too fat? Did he prefer skinny women? Rose was so thin. Perhaps I should try one of these wonder diets, and magically transform myself into somebody five kilos slimmer, with perfect teeth and shining hair into the bargain. Part of me scoffed at these proposals, but with another part of my mind I wanted to believe that anything was possible: intractable reality could change and blossom into something new and perfect.

Somebody was knocking at the door. Was the bell out of order? Then I realized that it must be Rose, and sure enough, there she stood on the landing, wearing a pale grey cotton dress the colour of mist, her hair scraped back from her white face. She looked like a wraith.

"Come in! It's great to see you."

"Uh... do you mind? I need – I would rather like – to talk. I'm sorry if I was short with you the other day."

"Don't be silly. I've been meaning to come and see you, but – somehow – I haven't had much time lately."

"I've received – " Rose was starting to say, but as she stepped into the room, my attention was distracted by two things. Topaz burst out singing, and simultaneously a loud hissing and crackling noise came from the loudspeakers of my hifi. But I hadn't been listening to music, and it wasn't even switched on. I started across the room to investigate.

"Just unplug it," said Rose in a strained voice.

"What?" The hissing rose to a whine.

"Unplug it – quickly – and it will be all right."

I couldn't think of anything else to do, so I pulled the whole adaptor out of the socket, and the noise stopped. "How strange. I'll have to – " I had been about to say that I would have to ask Olivier to take a look at it, but I stopped myself. I glanced at Rose. She was pinching the bridge of her nose between her thumb and forefinger, her eyes closed. She looked exhausted.

"Well," I said, "Let's sit down."

We sat side by side on the sofa bed, Topaz still trilling, and she showed me what she had come to see me about. It was the second time she had shown me a letter.

The envelope had her name written on it in blue ballpoint – Madame Martin – but no address. Inside was a single sheet of cheap squared paper, and again in blue ballpoint, in irregular, clumsy writing, a single brief message: THOU SHALT NOT SUFFER A WITCH TO LIVE.

For a second I felt scared. I dismissed the feeling.

"What rubbish!" I said, handing it back to her quickly.

"Yes, isn't it?" She laughed rather unsteadily. "Not a very nice thing to find in one's mailbox, though."

"Any idea who put it there?"

We looked at each other. "Bertrand," we both said together.

"But I can't prove it," said Rose. "I don't want to believe it was him. But who else could it be?"

"Have you any idea what his writing is like?"

"No. But people who send anonymous messages disguise their writing, don't they?"

"Let me have another look." The blue writing on the flimsy paper was almost childish.

"Anyway, if it is Bertrand, he's certifiably insane, I should say. Or else he's guilty of threatening behaviour, and you could take him to court."

"I don't want to take anyone to court," said Rose wearily.

"But look, you have to defend yourself. You can't just let him get away with a death threat."

"But how can I prove anything? I haven't any proof that he put it there. I can't prove that he put dog shit in my mailbox, either, although I think he did. I know he hates me, but I can't prove it if he denies it, and I don't want to hate him, I don't want to fight him, I don't want to fight anybody – I just want all this to stop!" Her voice cracked.

Out of the corner of my eye I saw a sharp movement on the shelf near the hifi. The next moment a pile of CDs had crashed to the floor.

Rose made a faint sound like a groan of pain.

The CDs must have been piled up precariously, and a passing lorry must have caused vibrations which made them fall. This reasoning was already going through my head. But the next thing I saw very clearly. Just behind Rose was the bookcase, and as I watched, two paperbacks moved forward in jerks from the middle of a row of books, toppled forwards, seemed to hang in the air for a long moment like a slow-motion film, and fell one after the other on to the arm of the sofa.

This is not happening, I thought. Help, Olivier, where are you? This isn't real. You are real, Olivier. I can't believe this.

I wanted to say something, but no words would come.

"I'm sorry," said Rose. She stood up. "I'd better go before something gets broken."

"No, wait – wait!" I found my voice. Rose was moving towards the door, and I made as if to hold her back.

"Don't touch me!" she said hastily, and my hand dropped to my side. We stood facing each other.

"You mean– what happened just then – you ...?"

"Yes. No, I didn't do it. Oh, Stella. I can't explain. Things happen around me."

"That noise in the loudspeakers – just now ...?"

She sighed. "Especially anything electrical. It's not deliberate. You have to believe me."

"So that's why ...?"

"Yes, that's why. I didn't want to say anything. I felt I couldn't just announce it."

Certain things were beginning to fall into place in my mind. Olivier, I thought again. You wouldn't be scared by all this. You would know what to do. You would be calm and objective and reassuring.

"It seems to be getting worse. I understand if you can't accept it," said Rose. "I understand if you think it's weird and you'd rather keep away from me. You wouldn't be the first." There was such pain in her voice. "I had hoped you wouldn't find out, you see. I had hoped to have a normal friendship."

"It makes no difference," I said, but I could hear the doubt in my own voice. I glanced quickly around the room, wondering if anything else was going to start moving. Suppose something broke with a great crash? Suppose something that I treasured got broken?

Rose forced a smile. "Anyway, I'd better be going. I'd better not come here. But you know you're still welcome to come over and see me, any time at all." Her voice was faint.

"I'll come, I'll come," I assured her. "Don't worry too much about that letter," I added, as she let herself out.

"I'll try not to."

I think we both knew how empty our words were.

She went down the stairs, and I stood on the landing for a moment listening to her descending footsteps. Then I went back into my flat and closed the door. I leaned against it. The room looked just as usual, apart from the CDs on the floor and the books splayed open on the sofa. Topaz, quiet now, was nibbling a lettuce leaf. I breathed out slowly, relaxing my muscles, then knelt to pick up the discs, rather gingerly, and restore them to their plastic jewel cases. It seemed to me that they felt faintly warm. I stacked them well to the back of the shelf, and eyed them warily, but nothing else happened. The books that had fallen were a science fiction novel and an old French-English commercial dictionary that dated from my schooldays. Nothing special about them. I put them back in place.

"What about that, then, Topaz?" I said. My voice sounded odd.

"Peep," said Topaz, and continued pecking at the lettuce leaf with gusto.

I suddenly felt ravenously hungry myself. Before going into the kitchen I plugged in the hifi again and put on a record of harpsichord music by Couperin. The loudspeakers seemed to be functioning just as usual. The orderly music of another age made a soothing background to my thoughts as I boiled rice and fried some frozen fish. It occurred to me that I still hadn't told Rose about finishing my songs and posting them on the Web. She would have been pleased and interested – or would she? Although she had wanted to tell me about the anonymous letter, she had seemed remote and turned in on herself somehow, as if a door had closed. This bothered me. In the past I had felt that I could talk about anything and everything to her.

"Thou shalt not suffer a witch to live." That sounded like a quotation, but I couldn't identify it. I'd have to look it up. Whatever it was, it surely amounted to a threat of murder. I thought again that she ought to go to the police – but both she and Olivier had been so contemptuous of the idea. I would have to discuss this with Olivier – my gorgeous Olivier. I closed my eyes for a moment and hugged myself, thinking of his nakedness.

My eyes flew open. The Couperin record had finished a few moments ago, but now I heard the opening bars coming again from the other room. A mysterious hand had put the disc on again. My heart thudded. After a few seconds I went to investigate.

Nothing in the room was out of place. I peered suspiciously at the hifi as the harpsichord music filled the room. Relief! The repeat button was pushed in. I must have pushed it accidentally when I slid the disc into place. The mechanism was working perfectly normally, after all. There was nothing mysterious about it. Nothing was broken.

Now a smell of burning fish came from the kitchen, and rather shakily I hurried to deal with it.

Some time later, I suddenly realized that my watch had stopped.

***

"Good news!" carolled my mother's voice over the telephone. "You have a little niece. Isn't that lovely? She was born at six twenty-three precisely. We made a careful note of the time, because Lisa wants to have her horoscope cast."

I had been watching the news, and had turned the sound down when the phone rang. Now helmeted figures ran across the screen, gesticulated, wrestled with hoses. There were rolling clouds of smoke, and the camera focused on a Canadair plane spraying water on the fire. Now the head of a woman filled the screen, talking frantically, her face smudged and distraught. Various camp sites had been evacuated. The picture changed to a map of France with little stylized flames showing where, all over the south, forest fires were burning. Forests were alight in the Var, the Vaucluse, Corsica – and in Provence, not so very far from Aix, I noted with alarm. Because of the drought, pinewoods were as dry as tinder. But most of these fires, if not all, had been started deliberately by arsonists. Rags and bottles of methylated spirit had been found, and one youth had been caught in the act – but only one. Two firefighters, badly burned, were seriously ill in hospital. I watched the living trees burning like torches, and thought of the birds who lived in them, caught by the flames themselves and burned to cinders. Did Rose know what was happening?

My mother's voice chattered on.

I said: "There's a big forest fire near Aix. Have they mentioned it on the English news?"

"Have you listened to a word I've been saying?"

I held the receiver away from my ear. "Yes, of course, yes. I'm very pleased. How is Lisa?" Three for a girl, I thought, and a vision of magpies swam into my head.

"I've just been telling you about the episiotomy, haven't I?"

"Ah... What are they going to call the baby?"

"Jacqueline Stella."

I gulped with surprise. "Is that definite?"

"Yes, yes, of course it is. They decided some time ago. Jacqueline after Lisa's sister, and Stella after you."

"Pascal decided that?"

"I've just told you! You sound as if you're asleep, sometimes, Stella. Don't I express myself clearly, or what? Now, tell me, when are you coming over? You must be taking some time off work soon. Come over and see the baby, won't you? They're dying to show her to you."

"Hmm." I stuck one leg out in front of me and examined my toe-nails. "My holiday plans aren't really fixed yet."

"Well, hurry up and fix them, then. Daddy would be pleased to see you, too."

"Did he say that? Is he there?"

"No, he's at an end-of-term staff meeting. This has been a very busy time for him with all the exam papers to mark. He needs a rest, poor man."

"Well," I said, "Give my love and congratulations to Pascal and Lisa, won't you?"

"Shall I tell them we can expect to see you?"

"I can't promise anything right now. I'll be in touch."

I put down the receiver with one hand and picked up the remote control with the other. The newscaster's voice blared into the room: " – thousand hectares of forest destroyed. The Minister has described it as an environmental disaster."

I thought of the countryside around Aix, of the foothills of the Alps, of walks in the spring with Mamie, and of the charred battlefield that would now be left.

I thought of the new life that had just come into the world, bearing my name.

Outside the window, the evening sky hung colourless and heavy with traffic fumes. Occasional lightning flickered on the horizon, but there was no hint of rain.

– NINE –

I woke up incredibly early next morning, something that I never do spontaneously on a week-day. I reached out to touch Olivier, found the bed empty, and remembered that we had agreed he would go back to his rented room last night after the party with the karate instructor, rather than arrive at my flat very late and possibly slightly drunk. The events of last evening came flooding back, and I pulled the sheet momentarily over my face, but the brilliant morning sunlight filtered through. No chance of getting any more sleep. Anyway, I was already rehearsing in my head all the things I had to tell him. I might as well arrive at the office early for once, and make a better impression than I had been making lately by dashing in at the last minute with circles under my eyes, absent-minded, my body still trembling inwardly with the memory of his caresses. Olivier liked to make love first thing in the morning.

Before I had even finished my coffee, the road drills started up outside. Work on the site seemed to start earlier and earlier. I peered out of the window at the trench, which now ran nearly the entire length of the street, a gash of clay, pale and sickly. It was not clear what purpose it served. Were they repairing sewage pipes or laying cables, or what? The noise was infernal.

Across the street, Rose's windows were closed, and there was no sign of movement behind the glass. On the floor below, however, I could see Bertrand standing at his window, stock still – abnormally still, I thought. I sipped my coffee, waiting for him to move, almost willing him to move. But he continued to stand there like a wax dummy. A magpie winged its leisurely way across my field of vision, and swooped upwards to land on Rose's roof, its diamond-shaped tail fanning out.

"Good morning, Sir or Madam," I muttered. "One for sorrow."

I looked around hopefully for a second magpie. Its mate must be somewhere around, surely? But there was just the one black and white bird, cocking its head to left and right on the roof. One for sorrow. "Idiot," I told myself.

The din of the roadworks hit me full blast as I left the building, and I almost ran along the street towards the metro to escape it. Today was Wednesday, I remembered, and swerved into the newsagent's to buy the Officiel des Spectacles. From the racks of newspapers the headlines demanded in thick black letters: "Forest fires – whose fault?"

"You're bright and early today," commented the newsagent, his eyes crinkling behind his glasses. Ever since Bertrand had knocked me down, we had been on the friendliest of terms.

"It makes a change, doesn't it? I'm more of a night-owl, usually."

His face became serious. "If you're walking home late at night, you want to be careful," he said. "This neighbourhood isn't what it was. Did you hear what happened the night before last?"

I shook my head.

"Some poor woman was walking along the street, about half past eleven, and this fellow came up behind her and pushed her into the roadworks trench. She broke her leg. And he didn't even steal her bag, that's the strange thing. Just shoved her in. She's got a nasty fracture, and had to be treated for shock, too, they say." Despite his disapproval, there was a certain relish in the way he described the incident.

"How dreadful. But didn't anybody go to help her?"

"She was screaming, but there wasn't anybody about, was there? And she couldn't even get a look at his face, believe it or not, because he was wearing a white mask. Imagine it! This chap walking along a deserted street at night, wearing a mask. Gives you the creeps, doesn't it?"

It did. It also reminded me forcefully of something. "It must have been the same man. It was a man in a white mask who tried to break into my friend's flat – my friend Madame Martin." I scowled, remembering those unchanging holes of eyes, that rigid slit of a mouth that I had briefly seen. What dreadful features might the mask conceal?

"You don't say." He shot me an odd look. "Is she a friend of yours, then?"

"Yes, she – Yes. Why not?"

"Well, I wouldn't want to bad-mouth anyone."

There was a pause. I was still remembering that dead white face that had passed so close to me on Rose's dark staircase.

"What do you mean?"

"Oh, nothing, just that there are more and more strange people about. Not quite normal. Not like you and me, if you see what I mean. She's the one old Bertrand says is making his life a misery. In fact, he says a whole lot more than that. You'd be amazed at some of the things he says. I don't know what to think, to be honest."

"Bertrand? Well, he's someone who isn't normal, in my opinion," I retorted. "Didn't you say yourself he seemed different these days? And for some reason best known to himself, he has it in for my poor friend Rose. And yet she wouldn't dream of harming anyone."

"I never said Bertrand wasn't strange. He's strange too, nowadays. That's just what I'm saying. Paris is full of weirdos." He looked at me severely, pushing his glasses up his nose. "I shall be glad when I can retire and go and live in my little house in the Dordogne. I shall be really happy to get out. Stay in Paris? No, thank you very much."

"But really, there's nothing wrong with Madame Martin," I persisted, crossing my fingers behind my back. I felt bound to defend her against everyone.

"Ah, you've a right to your opinions. But you might think different if you'd seen what I saw the other day."

"What did you see?" Oh, no, I thought, not some unusual phenomenon, please. Poor Rose – everybody staring at her as if she were a freak.

"I saw your Madame Martin in the street, talking to a tree. She was standing there in front of this tree, talking to it. Now, would you do that? Would I do that? If that isn't strange behaviour, I don't know what is."

I almost laughed aloud. Was that all? She must have been speaking to a bird. "If trees could talk, they might have a lot to tell us," I said. I picked up the Officiel and my eye fell on a magazine called Hidden World. On the cover a white-robed figure was raising some kind of chalice aloft, and printed across the sky were the words: "There is no such thing as death." So that was Bertrand's magazine.

"What about this strange stuff you're selling? There is no such thing as death. Ha! There's a pretty good imitation, though, isn't there?"

The newsagent smiled, but rather sourly, I thought. "Anyway, you want to be careful if you're walking alone at night. There are some funny people about. Don't say I didn't warn you."

I wished him a pleasant day and walked out into the sunny, deafening street.

**

I rang Olivier from the office and we arranged to meet in a café that evening, since he had a repair job to do not far from where I worked. I asked him how the party had gone, and he said OK. I hinted that I had a lot to tell him, and he said "Oh?" His voice sounded remote, and I wondered if he had a hangover. He could have shown a bit more interest, I felt. But I couldn't go into details over the phone, with people milling around me in the office, so I rang off feeling slightly frustrated. I sighed as I looked at my cluttered desk. Everybody was talking about their summer holiday plans, but the pace of work was not slowing down at all. It would be good to get away.

At lunch time I grabbed a sandwich and went to the English bookshop in the rue de Rivoli. The air conditioning made it blissfully cool inside, and normally I would have been tempted to browse among the novels, but today I was looking for something specific. I had found some very scanty information on the Internet, but a couple of books looked as if they might be helpful. Rather sheepishly, I scrutinized the titles of the "occult" section, glad that my father couldn't see me. Several other customers were quite unselfconsciously leafing through books on astrology, ghosts and the like. How, I wondered, could people believe in magic and talismans, in these days of quantum physics and space exploration? How could they talk about karma and reincarnation when the secrets of DNA had been unlocked? It didn't hang together, somehow. But the contradiction didn't seem to bother people. Catherine had once paid quite a lot of money for a computerized horoscope, and had read bits aloud to me, half laughing but half serious. Anyway, what was I doing here myself? I resisted the temptation to look at a book on the signs of the zodiac and check whether Olivier and I were supposed to be compatible.

I paused only to glance at a book on the symbolism of birds. Under the Mithraic cult, I read, the crow was a sacred bird, considered to be the messenger of the sun. Swallows, too had a symbolic significance: in ancient Egyptian tomb paintings, they represented the afterlife. Rose would have been interested. But perhaps she knew that already.

At last, having found what I wanted, I paid for my two books and left. God, but it was hot outside. I almost longed for some good old English drizzle.

***

I saw Olivier sitting at the café terrace before he saw me. He was screwing up his eyes against the evening sunlight, a glass of beer in front of him, and I felt a rush of tenderness as I made my way towards him and saw his expression change to one of recognition. We kissed briefly. A label was sticking up at the back of his polo shirt, and I tucked it back in for him. It was so nice to be able to touch him in that easy, casual way.

"I'm exhausted." It was true, he did look rather haggard.

"Too much to drink last night?"

"No. I just slept badly, that's all. Have you ever seen me drunk?" He sounded aggrieved.

I assured him that I hadn't, and ordered a citron pressé. The pavements were thronged with people in their lightest summer clothes, and in the stale heat of the day's end the traffic revved its engines and ground its gears. The scene was very ordinary, with people hurrying home from work, carrying baguettes and shopping, dodging cars, tossing cigarette-ends into the gutter. I didn't know how to begin describing what had happened last night, and in fact I was beginning to doubt my own memory of it.

Olivier was asking me whether I wanted anything to eat. "They have hot dogs or hamburgers," he said, glancing down the menu.

"In this heat? I hate hamburgers, anyway. They destroy the ozone layer, or something, don't they?" I said vaguely.

"Do you know what happens every single second in the United States?" he demanded.

"No, what?"

"Two hundred Americans eat a hamburger."

This suddenly struck us both as funny, and when we had stopped laughing I felt more at ease and launched at once into a description of Rose's visit, trying to be as matter-of-fact as possible.

But I felt him turning away, withdrawing into himself. I became more insistent, telling him how nobody had been near the CDs when they fell, and how I had seen the books tilt outwards into the room before toppling forward.

He took a long swallow of beer. "You know, those roadworks in your street have been causing a lot of vibrations. It only takes a touch, or a slight draught, to dislodge something. A box of light-fittings suddenly fell down in the shop, only the other day. Gave me quite a fright. But it didn't mean anything."

"Yes, but Rose herself says she causes things to happen."

"Look, I'll tell you something. What Rose says is very often a smokescreen. She's just trying to be mysterious." There was a note of irritation in his voice.

How could I convince him? I had been going to tell him about my watch stopping, but I knew that he would tell me

I merely ought to change the battery. Again I felt a doubt in my own mind. I hadn't expected him to react like this. I had expected him to be reassuring, not disdainful. Bending down, I produced the two new books from my bag under the table. At odd moments during the afternoon I had flicked through them, reading a paragraph here, a section there. Now I put A History of Witchcraft and The Poltergeist Phenomenon in front of him.

"What's this?" he scowled, picking them up, looking at the back cover and putting them down again.

Of course, I had forgotten. He couldn't read English. That's the trouble with coming from a bilingual family: you tend to forget that other people can't slip easily from one language to the other. I felt frustrated, because I had wanted to show him certain interesting passages. Instead I tried to paraphrase in French, describing how the evidence seemed to indicate that some individuals, especially disturbed adolescents, generated a kind of energy that could cause objects to move about and affect appliances. In one case described, the energy had dialled the speaking clock several hundred times a minute. It sounded improbable, and I could see him looking sceptical. Admittedly, there was no scientific theory on the subject.

"Rose isn't exactly a teenager," he pointed out.

"No, but things do happen around her," I argued. "Other people notice it, too. The newsagent down the street thinks she's odd. So does my concierge. And Monsieur Bertrand seems to have got it into his head that she's a witch. Hell! – you said it to him first. You may have put the idea into his head, for all I know."

"That was a joke, for heaven's sake! Do you think I believe in witches and broomsticks? People are so gullible, it's incredible. Here we are, in the twenty-first century, and you get people believing in witchcraft as if we were still in the dark ages."

"Well, I think people are gullible. And so many people are slightly unbalanced and strange. We've talked about this before," I said.

"There may be a lot of weird, unbalanced people about, but Rose isn't one of them," he said flatly.

That was not what I had said. Why was he twisting my words and not answering me properly? We fell silent. I thought about the book on witchcraft, and how innocent women who had been different in some way, who had not quite fitted the established pattern, who had lived alone and practised crafts such as herbal medicine and healing, had become objects of fear and hatred among their neighbours, and had been shunned and persecuted. They had been denounced, and tortured into confessions of consorting with the Devil. They had been drowned on ducking stools. They had been hanged. They had been burned alive at the stake, all across Europe, the black smoke choking them, the flames eating their defenceless flesh. Again I felt a prickling sensation at the nape of my neck, and shook my head to get rid of it.

"I think we have to take this seriously," I said. "Somebody who apparently believes she is a witch has sent her an anonymous letter. It's a death threat. It says: You shall not suffer a witch to live."

"What's that – one of the ten commandments?"

"No. It's a quotation from the Bible. From Exodus. I found it in the book on witchcraft, and checked it on the Internet."

"No kidding? There's a lot of weird stuff in the Bible, they say," said Olivier off-handedly. "I've never read it."

"Surely this is important, though, don't you think? She may be in danger, Olivier. Do you think Bertrand sent it?"

"Bertrand or some other nutcase. As you so rightly point out, Paris is full of them. I'm sick of them all. I want to get away and breathe some clean air. Look, don't blow all this up into a melodrama, right?" He drained the rest of his beer. "So, Rose is being mysterious. So, she's received an anonymous letter. So what? I think you're getting jumpy, Stella. Things aren't really mysterious when you understand how they work, you know. All kinds of things that we take for granted would have seemed like magic to people living a couple of centuries ago. Holograms, WiFi – television, even. There's some

185

perfectly simple explanation for your CDs falling on the floor, believe me. Nothing supernatural about it. And as for poison pen letters, the only thing to do is to burn them and forget them. I hope you told Rose as much. God!" He banged his glass on the table. "I'm fed up with all this nonsense. Can't we change the subject?"

I put the books away, nonplussed and disappointed. It felt lonely not to be believed. I had hoped so much to be able to talk matters over with him. But perhaps he was right, and I was making a mountain of the whole affair.

I wasn't satisfied, however. It was true that you find explanations for things, but you couldn't explain them away. My mind groped after what I meant. Explanations were all very well, but there seemed to be no explanation for the fundamental fact that there was anything at all in the universe rather than nothing. It was the sort of thought I could have voiced to my father, but not to Olivier. On the other hand, if we could understand a strange phenomenon, really understand it, then we ought to be one step closer to controlling it. Hadn't humankind harnessed any number of natural forces? The difference was that we didn't yet understand this force and couldn't control it, whatever it was. This power. "The powers of darkness," said a voice in my mind, dredging up the words from somewhere.

I found I was staring fixedly at a man on the other side of the street, a middle-aged man with round shoulders and hair the colour of cigarette ash, who was walking slowly on the far side of the row of parked cars, stopping occasionally and talking to himself all the while. He definitely wasn't using a mobile phone. No, he was another crazy person, wildly muttering. What was it about city life that drove people out of their minds? As I watched, he emerged from behind the last of the parked cars, and I saw that he had a fat and elderly black labrador on a lead. The dog had been nosing its way along the gutter, out of sight, and he had been talking to it. He was not odd at all, any more that I could be called odd for talking to Topaz. There was a perfectly simple explanation. I felt suddenly foolish.

I glanced across at Olivier, who was running his fingers around the brass rim of the table, his gaze opaque and brooding. I wished that he would smile, touch my hand, lean over and kiss me – move nearer to me in some way. But he didn't move. He looked up and our eyes met.

"Any other news since we last saw each other?" he asked abruptly.

"There is, as a matter of fact." I told him about my mother's phone call and the birth of the baby.

There was a spark of interest in his eyes at once, and he asked a lot of questions. Were Pascal and Lisa pleased to have a girl? What were they going to call her? Did she sleep well at night? Was she born bald or with hair? Did I really not know? Then I would have to go over to England and see her as soon as possible. Babies changed so quickly that I would always regret it if I hadn't seen her when she was tiny.

I was surprised at his interest. I had thought that most men found babies boring.

We talked of babies' reactions to stimuli when they were still in the womb, and about the use of recordings of the mother's heartbeat to lull them to sleep after birth. I began to wonder, happily, whether he would like to go to England with me and see her for himself, but I didn't think it was quite the right moment to ask him. There was still something guarded about him. Nevertheless, I allowed myself to picture him for a moment, sitting beside me on Eurostar as the plains of northern France sped past the carriage window, and then walking through the pale green underground corridors at Saint Pancras.

I said that it must be awful to be a baby, totally powerless and dependent, but he said that it didn't matter as nobody remembered the experience. We both tried to recall our earliest memories.

He could remember being spanked by his father when he was about four, for turning the oven right up and burning the lunch. "I remember the absolute outrage I felt. I'd been conducting a careful experiment, trying to find out how it worked. I was doing what I'd seen my mother do. Why did different rules apply to me? I was so furious!" He grinned faintly.

"My earliest memory," I said, "must date back to when I was a toddler, I suppose, because I can remember that Pascal was a baby. I was in my playpen. I can remember holding on to the bars and crying and screaming."

"Can you remember why?"

"Yes. It was because my mother wouldn't come and help me build a tower with my bricks. She was breast-feeding Pascal. I remember her sitting in an armchair, wearing a blue dress with big buttons, feeding Pascal and taking no notice of me, until she suddenly flew into a rage and shouted at me that I was a naughty child and that I must stop making so much noise." I broke off and swallowed, my shoulders tense. I could feel my heart beating. The memory was surprisingly vivid. I knew I had had a loud voice when I was small – a singer's voice, as Rose had once pointed out when I told her about this.

"Poor Stella," said Olivier. "One thing about you is that you're not mysterious at all. You're so transparent."

I looked at him suspiciously. That didn't sound like a compliment. I wondered whether I had been too open with him, telling him freely about myself, my childhood, my family, my troubles with Adrien – even the abortion. But surely that was part of the charm of being close to another person: that you could tell him everything. On the other hand, perhaps one ought always to hold something back, some secret room marked No Entry, to keep the other's interest alive. And yet he complained that Rose was too mysterious. Perhaps he thought he knew me too well and understood me. After all, I'm not a very complicated person. But I certainly didn't feel that I knew everything about him; that would have been presumptuous.

"And how does Pascal feel about being a father?" he asked.

"Don't know," I said shortly. "I haven't spoken to Pascal." I never did speak to Pascal, except when our paths crossed at family reunions. He would never have dreamt of phoning me, nor I him.

"It must be quite amazing," he said. "Quite fantastic. To hold a baby in your arms and know that you have created it – brought another person into the world. A tiny, perfect human being."

"I didn't know you were so keen on babies." I felt a glow of affection for him as he sat there gazing at the street.

"I'm not, in general. It's just that – " He scratched the back of his head, embarrassed. "I've been thinking more and more about it in the last year or two. About being a father, I mean. I think it's something I really want to do, eventually. I want to father a child."

My eyes were on his face, and the scene of the café terrace and the street beyond melted into a haze of light and movement as I gazed intently at his unruly hair, his fierce eyebrows, the familiar shape of his nose and mouth – the features that he might pass on to a child. "There," he said, glancing sideways, "I've just told you something I've never told anybody else."

"But you're so careful about contraception," I said quietly.

"Of course I'm careful!" He sounded suddenly irritable. "It's not something to be undertaken lightly. A human life, for God's sake. It has to be the right time for me – and the right woman."

I looked at him with love and longing. To think that he, too, wanted a child. Let me be the right woman, I found myself praying. Let me bear his child. I want this man to be the father of my child. Surely he must sense that I'm the right woman, or he wouldn't have told me all this. He hasn't told anyone but me. I'm the only one he confides in.

I leaned across to touch his hand, but he moved at the same time, picking up the bill, feeling for his wallet.

"Shall we go back to the flat?" I asked.

"Well, maybe not tonight." He glanced away. "I'm dog tired, honestly, and I've got a bit of a headache. I wouldn't be good company. If you don't mind, I think I'll just go back to my place and have an early night." He stood up.

"As you like." I hid my disappointment. I wanted so much to hold him in my arms, to feel his naked body fused with mine, as if we were a single person. The spark of a new life would be part of us both, uniting us ... But there was plenty of time.

We parted at the metro station. I hugged him, but he kissed me briefly and disengaged himself. "I'll call you," he said. People pushed past us into the tunnels, smelling of sweat, apéritifs and Gitanes.

I wanted to ask him again if he was quite sure he wouldn't come home with me, but I bit back the words, telling myself that he felt awkward and vulnerable, as men do when they have just revealed some intimate fact about themselves. It was natural that he wanted to be alone for a while. He needed time. I mustn't crowd him.

Tenderly, I told him to have a good rest, and we went our separate ways.

***

The air was a sullen yellow as I crossed the street to Rose's building. There was a storm brewing, and today had been one of the hottest and stickiest I could remember, stifling in the office and almost unbearable in the metro. I had the two books under my arm. All yesterday evening I had been reading them, lying on the floor with the window open to catch the slightest breath of air, marking certain passages, skipping others. All the while, in the back of my mind, I had been waiting for my phone to ring and for Olivier to say that he had changed his mind and was coming round. But it didn't ring. As I entered the building opposite, there was a faint mutter of thunder, and the staircase was dark.

Rose opened the door a crack, then wider to let me in. She had the same pale, hunted look as the other day. Her hair was loose, like a river of black silk flowing on to the shoulders of her dark red dress. It seemed to me that her hair had a bluish sheen, with the white streak still in sharp contrast, but perhaps it was just the storm light from the window. The room looked different. Books had been removed from the shelves and were piled on the floor, and her sheet music had been thrust into a box. Scraps of material had been sorted into heaps. The Lone Star quilt occupied half the table, the other half of which was stacked with reels of cotton, all different colours glowing dully.

"I thought you might be afraid to come here," she said.

"Afraid? Why?" I said robustly. I held out the two books. "Listen, Rose, I've been thinking about what happened the other night. I've been reading up about – about that kind of phenomenon."

She took the books and leafed through one of them, then the other. She read a passage that I had marked, and put them both down on the table.

"Stella – "she began.

"A lot of research has been done, you see. There are scientific theories now, instead of all the superstitious beliefs that people had in the past, about spirits and devils. Understanding a problem is the first step towards overcoming it. It has to be." I sounded like my father. "If we can explain this thing, we're on the way to controlling it."

Rose walked restlessly to the window, then back towards me, pushing her hair away from her face. She looked at me.

"It's no good," she said, after a moment. A glimmer of lightning lit the room, and seconds later came the slow rumble of thunder.

"What do you mean, it's no good? Look I wish you would just read what it says here." I picked up the book on poltergeists and scanned the index for the relevant passage.

"It's useless. It's not so simple. Books are fine, but they can't help. Not in this case." She sat down at the table, then stood up again.

"But why? What makes you think nothing can help? I want to try to help you, Rose. God knows, you've helped me enough."

"I know, I know you do. I don't mean to seem ungrateful. You've been a good friend and a good neighbour. But it's just that – I'm afraid you don't understand. You can't understand this."

"Why not?"

"Because it's too strong, and I don't understand it myself. Do you think I haven't tried to find out what's wrong with me? Do you think I haven't tried to cure it – or at least to control it?" Her voice was growing louder and higher. "It's *too strong*."

"But at least let me – "

"Nobody can ever truly help anyone else, Stella. I mean, you can never solve somebody else's problems. I'm the only one who can find a solution, and I've tried so hard. I've tried, and failed, and moved on, and wherever I try to settle, things are all right for a time ... and then – I have trouble with people. If you move to a different place, you just take your problems with you, like a brand on your own skin. It's no good."

Her voice rose and broke, and at the same time all the pins in her pin-cushion on the table sprang into the air. They began to circle around her head, glinting like a metallic halo. Round and round. She put up one hand as if to ward them off, then sank drooping on to a chair.

I watched, mesmerised, and realized that somebody was knocking insistently at the door. I don't know why I went to open it. Perhaps I just wanted to escape.

"Excuse us for disturbing you," said one of the two young men standing on the landing. He was lanky and bespectacled, while his shorter friend, as I noticed with part of my attention, was wearing a rather nice embroidered waistcoat. "We're art students, and we need to raise funds for our college fees, so we're offering these excellent reproductions of paintings to discerning persons who would like to have a work of art in their home. Of course, you have no obligation to buy, but if you'll just let me show you ..." He started to open the large green art folder that his friend was carrying and shot me a salesman's smile.

Then he seemed to freeze, looking past me into the room. His friend followed his gaze.

"I don't think we want – " I said, turning back and starting to close the door, but at that moment there was a brilliant blue flash of lightning and a clap of thunder, and with a high-pitched whistling noise several cotton reels and a cloud of pins shot out of the door like missiles, one reel hitting the first student square in the chest as the other raised his arm to ward off the pins.

At the same moment, the large wooden press moved about a foot out into the room, rocked slightly, and slid back again against the wall.

I looked towards Rose, but she was silhouetted at the window with her back to the landing, and beyond the window panes were beating two vast wings. A pair of fierce round eyes glared into the darkening room from the stormy sky.

The faces of the two students were expressionless with shock. Then they turned like one man and ran down the stairs, shoving each other in their haste, their feet clattering, followed by a gust of wind as Rose opened the window to let Luna in. I retrieved the reels of cotton from the corner of the landing, quite ordinary plastic reels of green and blue thread, now faintly warm, and put them on the table, advancing rather warily as Luna flapped and settled herself on Rose's shoulder. There were no pins in the air now, but it was too dark to see where they had gone. I glanced uneasily over my shoulder at the press, now motionless.

"I'm sorry, I shouldn't have opened the door," I said. "They were scared, I think. It was a bit unexpected."

"Yes. They were scared." She picked up the cotton reels and put them down side by side, picked them up and put them down again, tense as a wire. "I'm trying to tell you: it isn't a matter of looking at a problem and finding a solution to it. I *am* the problem, don't you see?" She put the reels one on top of the other, and again the air crackled with lightning.

"But, look," I said, "there's a very powerful force here. Just think how it might be harnessed! If you could only control it – "

"It's too big. It's controlling me."

"I still don't believe nothing can be done," I said stubbornly. "That's why I wanted to show you these books. Look, if you'll let me, I'm sure I can – "

"You? What can you do? Oh, Stella, you're not the first. Why don't you solve your own problems? Tell me that. Why don't you go out and show the world what you can do, instead of being so afraid? I can't make you. Only you can do that. And you can't make me do anything. Oh, why doesn't everyone just leave me alone? Why don't you leave me alone?" She stood up abruptly, and Luna flapped her wings and gave a shriek.

Hurt, I said nothing.

"I'm sorry." Her voice softened. "But maybe it would be best if you kept away from me – for a while. It's not just you – I don't mean it personally. But people either want to get rid of me or else they want to control me. I can never have a normal relationship with people." She rubbed her temples. I wondered whether anyone else could convince her that there must be some solution. Had she no parents, no brothers or sisters? No kind and caring grandmother, as I had had?

"Your family – " I began weakly.

"Oh! My family? If only you knew. But listen, if you have a family, a good, loving family, don't ever let misunderstandings come between you. For me, it's too late. But if you have any problems with your family, make your peace with them. Please. Believe me, I know what I'm talking about."

"Why is it too late for you?"

"I can't explain. If I try, people only get hurt." There was a pause. "I have to be alone. I just want to be free and do what I choose to do." Her voice was a groan.

The window banged in the draught. Her words and her red dress reminded me of something, or somebody – that anguished yearning. Only later did I remember that it was Bizet's Carmen, who had just wanted to be free and do as she chose.

Now Rose was rummaging in her box of sheet music, looking for something. She found it and turned, holding out a letter that had been pushed carelessly back into its torn envelope. It was the third letter that she had shown me. First the warning about the pigeons, then the threat, and now this. Who was her enemy? Three for a letter; three letters. Why was

194

three a magic number? From her shoulder, the owl glared at me.

"Read this," she said. "He won't let me alone. He thinks he knows the answers. I warned you about him – he's a controller. Read it!"

As I took the letter, a loud discordant noise came from the piano behind me, as if someone had crashed their two fists down on the keys. But there was nobody near it. I found that my hands were shaking as I unfolded the paper. It was a single sheet, closely written in spiky handwriting which I did not recognize until I looked at the signature on the bottom: Olivier. There was no reason why I should have recognized his writing. He had never written to me: he didn't need to, as I was always available on the phone, wherever I was.

I began to read, and felt as if the floor was dissolving underneath me.

I don't remember his exact words now, although at the time they seemed to be searing themselves into my memory. He said that he had to see her. He said that he couldn't sleep, and thought about her day and night. He said that she must realize now that they needed each other. He said he would protect her. He said – and this I do remember – "I've tried other women, but I can't forget you, Rose. You're the one I want." I read it to the end, and then started again at the beginning, making out the words with difficulty as it was now so dark. I tilted the paper towards the window to catch the light from the streetlamps. I found I had crushed the envelope into a ball.

Rose had stepped out on to the balcony, and I moved towards her. The wind whipped her hair about her face and made it stream outwards around her head like a dark halo. She held it back with one hand, looking up at the sky, and Luna took off on slow wings and flew up, way up above the roof and television and satellite aerials of my block of flats opposite, whose façade was now a pattern of lighted rectangles where people had switched on their lamps. The flying black shape of the owl seemed to open up far perspectives of grey meadows and dark forests and a long chain of mountains on the utmost horizon; yet there were only rooftops in sight.

I tried to speak, but my voice was husky and the wind took my words. Somewhere a shutter banged repeatedly, and far away in a lower storey a door slammed. The lightning glittered across her upturned face, playing over her cheekbones and the dark sockets of her eyes, and again the thunder crashed as if the sky were full of giant furniture. The rain came then, pelting down in huge drops. And suddenly all the lights opposite went out.

"When did you receive – ?"

Again I tried to ask a question, but the lightning lit up the whole sky and almost instantaneously came a terrible roll of thunder, and I seemed to feel the building tremble. Rose's hand was still lifted skyward, in the direction that Luna had flown, and immediately the lightning came again, revealing her thin figure in livid detail, the raindrops running like tears now down her face and making darker patches on her dark dress. It seemed as if the lightning came forking down to her hand. She looked almost exultant, in the second before darkness fell again.

"Why don't you come in? You're getting drenched," I said desperately through the booming.

She heard me then and stepped back into the room, her hair wet, her face expressionless. The scent of wet geraniums floated in with her.

"You've read it? You see, he's just a man, like all the others."

"He never told me – "

"Of course he never told you. He used you. Men use other people as if they were tools or machines. I tried to warn you, but you wouldn't believe me." Then, more gently, "I'm sorry. I should have known."

I couldn't say anything, and the rain pelted in great gusts against the window.

"He charmed you, but it's better that you should know. It's better to be struck by lightning than to be burned alive slowly. But I didn't want any of this to happen. Damn him!" She startled me by hitting the table with her fist. "If he hadn't given me Blanche, none of it might have happened. I shouldn't have fallen into the trap again. He thought he would get me that way. He started the vortex. If he hadn't interfered, it would have been all right this time. I would have managed – this time."

"Did you receive the letter today?" I asked.

"This morning." Still the thunder growled and rumbled over the roofs, and the façade of my building was totally black.

"I think I'll go home."

"Won't you wait a little? There's no light."

It was true, there was no light. No light anywhere, and I was drowning in a sea of darkness, overwhelmed by the storm, dragged down into the bottomless depths of a bitter sea. But I didn't want to stay. I wanted to go back to my own place, shut the door behind me and hide.

"Stay," she said. "Don't go. I've said things I shouldn't have said. Everything's sliding. I can't seem to – "

"No, I just want to go home."

Silence between the thunderclaps. Darkness.

"Let me give you a candle." She pushed a candle into my hand, and a box of matches, although she had still not lit her own candles or lamp, and I blundered out on to the landing. I started to grope my way down the stairs. She put out one thin hand then, and touched my shoulder, feather-light. In my ears was a sound like high-pitched singing in close harmony. I thought I might faint. I don't believe I even said goodbye. And as I reached the landing below, I heard her door softly close.

I was soaked just crossing the street, in a downpour of tropical intensity. Cars' headlights lit the needles of rain. The lifts in my block were not working, and I had to walk up eight flights of the unfamiliar concrete stairs, lit by dim emergency lighting. There was no power in my flat. I thought that Topaz might have been frightened by the storm, but I could just make out his hunched and sleeping shape in his cage, moving very slightly as he breathed.

I walked from the kitchen to the living-room and back into the kitchen, hardly knowing what I was doing, flicking switches and noting dully that nothing happened. After a while I lit Rose's candle, planted it on a saucer and carried it through to the living-room. It was a beeswax candle, and gradually a subtle scent of honey began to permeate the room, reminding me of the scents and herbal aromas of Rose's flat. I wished that I could stop thinking about her – erase her name from my mind. She had such power, such incredible power over Olivier, that he would write: I can't forget you, Rose. You're the one I want.

And I, Stella, who was I? A passing attachment, a convenience, a distraction from Rose, a female body. He had tried, he said, other women. Tried them. I was one of those women – any woman. I put my hands over my eyes and pressed the eyeballs until stars swam. Maybe I was just one of a series, to be used and thrown aside like paper tissues. With a kind of horror I remembered all that I had told him about my life, the confidences, the endearments – above all our nakedness together, the caresses, the closeness and the holding. In that very room and bed we had made love. Love. I had opened my heart to him, and all the time he had been using me to take his mind off Rose.

I perched on a chair by the window, shaking, wrapping my arms around myself, rocking to and fro. I looked out, waiting for something or for nothing – waiting for the lights to come on. Rose's building opposite was still dark, and I could see her window ajar, but no sign of her. Apparently she had still not lighted her lamp.

How had she drawn Olivier to her? I began to feel, like a small flame in my chest, the beginnings of resentment towards her. How had she done it, and why did I count for nothing? If she had not been around, he might have loved me. Everything might have been different. He had wanted me, that was undeniable, and desire would surely have blossomed into love. Or else, if she had been honest about her relationship with him from the start, I would have kept my distance, wouldn't I? I would not have allowed myself to fall in love with him. She should have told me.

My thoughts kept going round and round.

Listening to music was not possible, nor could I even boil the kettle to make tea. I tried the remote control of the television, but of course the screen stayed blank. The radio, when I tried it, blared into the room with loud crackling from interference, and I switched it off again, but not before I had heard that in the south the drought was continuing, the mistral was blowing strongly, and there were more forest fires, creeping steadily closer to Aix, destroying the pine forests and charring the hillsides of my childhood.

No light, still no light. I couldn't see to do anything, not even read. I could go to bed, but I knew that I wouldn't sleep, and that my thoughts would torment me still more if I were lying down. In the end I picked up my guitar and played a series of notes, descending in semitones. The rain seemed to be slackening now, and the thunder was more distant. Strumming quietly, I looked across the street again. Rose had lit a candle. No – that was not candlelight, those flickering blue flashes from somewhere inside her flat, suddenly blazing out brightly and then going dark. The rest of the building was still lightless; but the odd, irregular flickering continued.

Whatever it was, it was no concern of mine. I had tried to help her, and had got nothing but this shock of pain in return. I sat on by the window, playing my guitar in the darkness, playing a tune that I had never played before. There were no words yet, but phrases of music began to take shape, and then whole passages, as if it were welling up from the depths of my misery, all my rage and grief and shattered trust rising like a river and pouring outwards in sound.

The candle burned lower and lower, the melted wax sliding down the side in a winding sheet, one tiny, wavering flame in the growing immensity of darkness.

– TEN –

The summer exodus was beginning, shops were closing for the holidays, and traffic jams clogged the roads out of Paris as people migrated south towards the beaches, open-air nightclubs, suntanned romance and all the dreams of what a summer holiday should be but never is.

There were no customers in the shop when I walked in. My breath was short and my hands were damp, but I had to confront Olivier. From the back of the shop came the animated voice of a television commentator, and hearing the familiar names I realized that they were broadcasting the finish of the Tour de France. I'm not remotely interested in this cycling race, but in July you can't get away from it, the main news item consisting of men with their heads down and their legs pumping. I couldn't imagine why Olivier was so keen on sports news: before this there had been the tennis from Wimbledon and Roland Garros, and now, doubtless, the football season would be starting. But he would not be watching any loud and tedious televised matches in my flat.

"I want to talk to you," I said without preamble, as he emerged in response to the ping of the door.

"What's wrong? Has something happened? Why don't you come and sit down?"

"Oh, shit." I felt my face growing hot. "Don't put on that caring voice. I can talk perfectly well standing up."

He folded his arms. "So what is all this?"

"Can't you guess? Did you think I wouldn't find out, or something? What kind of a fool do you take me for?"

"Find out what? Talk in plain, language, can't you?" There was an edge to his voice now.

"About you and Rose, of course. What else? Everything you've been hiding from me all this time. All this play-acting you've been doing."

His face seemed to close, and he turned and went into the back room. I followed him. The television screen in the corner showed lowered heads over handlebars, and then a sea of faces shouting and delirious with mindless joy.

"You've just been stringing me along, haven't you?" I said. "If there's one thing I hate, it's dishonesty."

"What dishonesty? What right have you got to know everything about me?"

"I've a right to know what concerns me," I said loudly above the TV. "I've a right to know the most important thing. That you're only interested in Rose, and this whole relationship has been a sham."

"What has Rose told you?" – arms folded, very still.

"Nothing. She didn't need to tell me anything. She showed me your letter."

He turned away and looked out of the back window, at the bins and the piles of crates and flourishing weeds, all bathed in the evening sunlight. "So that's it. Now you know. All right. What more do you want?"

He had admitted it. I felt the pit of my stomach drop away.

"You lied to me!" I yelled.

"I did not lie." He whipped round, his face tight. "What did I ever say to you? I never told you I loved you. I never asked you for anything. I never led you to believe that this affair was anything except just that – an affair. If you don't want it on those terms, right – let's end it. That's fine by me."

"But how could you – do all those things? Sleep with me? Make love? When all the time it was Rose that you wanted?"

"Well, as for sleeping – by which you mean fucking – isn't sex what you wanted yourself? You didn't seem to have any objections, I must say. I didn't exactly have to rape you, did I?"

"But it wasn't like that for me. It meant something. I –
" I couldn't tell him that I loved him: not this hard, angry
stranger. With part of my mind I could still visualize the other
Olivier, subtle, passionate, warm, funny. I could remember so
clearly the time we had made love on that same broken-down
sofa.

"If you thought it was something more important, that's
just a fantasy that you cooked up yourself. I'm sorry, but I'm
not responsible." His eyes veered to the television screen.

"How can you say that when we've spent so much time
together?" I said. "We've talked about so many things. Christ,
you make it sound as if it was just a one-night stand. I've told
you secrets about myself. And you told me – " I had difficulty
in controlling my voice. "You told me about wanting a child.
Why did you tell me that? I even thought maybe we might – if
you wanted – together – " My voice broke.

"You!" The word was packed with venom. "You thought
that! You thought I would let you bear a child of mine? When
you've aborted one child already?"

I gasped as if I had been punched with a fist. He took several
steps forward and loomed over me.

"It didn't suit you, did it, to have that baby? So you just got
rid of it, didn't you?" He snapped his fingers. "So easy, with
the modern methods they have. Not convenient? Right! What's
a human life? Down the drain with it."

I had never seen him so angry. He was practically shaking.
Yet he had betrayed my trust, betrayed my confidence, and was
attacking me where he knew I was most vulnerable. Suddenly
my pain flared into anger.

He began again: "Do you know what percentage of
women – "

"No, I don't! And I don't give a shit about your percentages.
Figures, figures – that's all you care about; I'm sick of your
statistics. You're not a human being – you're a machine.
You're a sodding computer!" I yelled. "No wonder Rose wants
nothing to do with you."

"Leave Rose out of this." His face was white.

"No, I will not leave her out of it. She's at the centre of all this, isn't she? But you needn't think she wants you. She doesn't. She doesn't want you interfering and controlling. She wants you out of her life. She told me so, and God, I don't blame her."

"You don't know what you're talking about. You don't know anything about her and me. You don't know anything about Rose, or about love – you're so bloody naive. Rose is a very special person. She needs to spend some time apart from me right now, but she's on her way back to me. I know her better than she knows herself. She's the only woman for me. It's only a matter of time. But I can't expect you to understand a thing like that, can I? You think people should stick together like chewing-gum all the time. Christ, once you appeared on the scene, I couldn't get away from you. Couldn't breathe. You just threw yourself at me."

"I did not!" The injustice went through me like a knife. I could hear him, in my mind, asking me why I had been avoiding him. "And you weren't exactly reluctant to jump into bed!"

"You offered yourself! You were begging for it! Wise up, Stella. You need to learn a thing or two about men."

"I've just learned enough about them to make me want to throw up."

"Good. So go and be a feminist, why don't you?" He looked back at the television screen. The commentator jabbered ecstatically and the winner in the yellow jersey raised his arms aloft.

"I can't believe you're like this. I can't believe you're really saying all this," I said, and to my intense annoyance the tears came.

He made as if to put his hands on my shoulders, then thought better of it.

"Look," he said, more quietly. "Let's get this straight. I didn't want to have a row with you, Stella. You've just come in here spoiling for a fight. We had a good time together, didn't we? Can't we part friends?"

"Friends?" I spat out the word. "What do you know about friendship? Rose is my friend, and you betrayed me with her – and her with me, come to that."

"Betrayed! You do overdramatize. Listen, I'm telling you that there was nothing important between you and me. We had a fling together, OK?" His voice rose. "It was fun while it lasted. But I knew Rose long before I met you, and with Rose it's different. Get this into your head: I love her." His last words were spoken with an intensity that seemed to make his whole body go rigid.

Again I saw the two stern profiles facing each other, ignoring me, Rose with the gold crown on her dark hair, against the backdrop of softly falling snow.

"I never want to see you again," I wept.

"Then get out!" He strode back into the main shop and made exaggerated movements of ushering me through the door. "It's mutual. Shut up and get out. And you won't be seeing me, thank God. I'm going down to Perpignan. I need a break. I can't stand the atmosphere around here. I need space, for Christ's sake."

"You can go to hell, for all I care."

"Right, maybe I will." He smiled thinly. "Really, you're ridiculous, Stella. All this fuss about a little affair. You're hysterical, coming in here shouting at me like this. Whatever fantasies you've been spinning about me, I'm not responsible for them. I don't owe you anything. I've got nothing to answer for. I think you need to see a psychiatrist, quite honestly. Get your head sorted out before you get involved with some other poor guy and start shouting rape or fantasizing about wedding bells. Your mother must have read you too many fairy tales. Grow up, why don't you?"

"You bastard!" I shouted, pushing past him towards the door.

I turned round and grabbed an urn-shaped alabaster lamp from the window display. It was lit, glowing white, and I yanked the plug furiously from its socket. "I'll kill you!"

I hurled the lamp at him with all my strength.

It missed him, of course, but hit the wall behind the counter and shattered violently in a thousand pieces, bringing down stacks of boxes and another light-fitting with a great crash.

I would have slammed the door behind me, but it was on a spring and shut slowly. My legs weak and shaking, I ran stumblingly in the direction of home, the crash still resounding in my ears. I was furious, despairing, devastated – and yet something inside me felt a sense of release, as if a great tiger had escaped from its cage and was free at last. Tigers, however, are dangerous. I knew, with bitterness, that it was not only the lamp that I had destroyed. Something had ended.

***

I went to England.

There seemed to be nothing else to do with the summer. August was here, the holiday season when everything grinds to a halt in Paris. My boss was going away and expected me to be taking my summer holiday now, but I had made no reservations. For as long as possible I had postponed committing myself to dates, hoping and dreaming that I might be travelling south with Olivier to the Midi, or north with him to introduce him to my family.

Eurostar was fully booked, so I took a train to the coast and caught the ferry. Now I stood, alone, leaning over the rail to watch the churning bow wave far below. Crystal-white foam curled and dissolved on the glossy dark surface, again and again, hypnotically. The ferry was crowded with several parties of schoolchildren. People with backpacks barged into me from time to time. I was carrying only a small travelling bag, and had once again left my guitar behind. I didn't need to take a lot of clothes with me, either. Who was going to see me, after all?

I had hesitated over Topaz, whom I had to leave in Paris. The obvious course would have been to ask Rose to take care of him while I was away, but I couldn't. Topaz was always so happy to see her. If I left him with her for a whole fortnight, who could tell whether he would even remember me? He would probably grow so attached to her that he would become, to all intents and purposes, her bird. And that was more than I could take. I couldn't bear to lose anyone else to Rose. In the end, I asked Madame Pereira whether she would look after him, and since she was not going down to the Ardèche until the second half of the month – for some reason which had to do with a niece's wedding – she agreed, clearing the top of her fridge so that I could stand his cage out of harm's way and stowing a couple of packets of birdseed in a cupboard with repeated assurances that she had kept birds as a young girl and knew all about canaries. Francisco, who seemed at a loose end as usual, wandered over and whistled at him through the bars, and Topaz whistled politely back. I thought he would be all right.

Topaz, the Pereiras' cluttered kitchen, my building with half its windows shuttered and its residents away – all were far behind me now. The coast of France was just a dark line on the horizon to the south, and ahead, somewhere beyond the expanse of bluish-grey water, the cliffs of England had not yet come in sight. I gulped in great draughts of sea air. Below decks, the smell of motor oil and chips was overpowering. I'm normally a good sailor, but I had eaten very little in the past few days, and felt faintly queasy. I was longing to arrive. I wanted to get away from these crowds of holidaymakers and find myself in my old bedroom in my parents' house, with my old children's books and the moth-eaten teddy bear that I had never been willing to pass on to Pascal.

I wanted to go home.

"We're getting up a bit of speed, aren't we? How fast do you reckon these old ferries can go?"

A cheerful, chubby face, straight hair falling into his eyes, a red T-shirt and a backpack. The owner of the voice eyed me. Something about his expression reminded me of Adrien.

"I've no idea," I said frostily, and turned away. I moved further along the rail, and he didn't follow me. I wanted nothing to do with any men, particularly not some chance encounter on a boat. Far away on the horizon a grey steamer was moving in the opposite direction, and I focused on it, blinking hard.

The mornings were the worst, at the moment of waking, my thoughts still blurred and hazy with dreams, when it struck me with the force of a blow: it was all over. Again I saw the lamp shattering in smithereens. My anger in the shop had carried me home on a wave of rage, but it hadn't lasted, and was followed by a strange impression of emptiness and deadness. Everything seemed unreal. Nothing made sense any more. I attended to Topaz and did household chores, but everything seemed flat, grey, two-dimensional, as if a light had gone out. Olivier's hard words kept repeating themselves in my mind with a kind of dull echo. I kept having imaginary conversations with him. In my mind, I pleaded with him not to leave me, kneeling at his feet, embracing his knees, until he realized that I was the only woman who truly loved him, the woman he needed in his life. Or else he came to me and entreated me to take him back, having realized his mistake, but I stayed aloof and cold, and slammed the door in his face. Missing him was a physical ache, a shock, like finding that one of my arms was not there. And yet that didn't make sense either. Nothing hung together, everything was in fragments.

People kept jostling past me on the deck, talking loudly. There was almost a carnival atmosphere: crowds, the smell of frying, children shrieking and pounding up and down the deck, pop music and the noise of electronic games in the saloon. Some poet – Lamartine, I think – says that when you are missing one person, the whole world is depopulated. I think he got it wrong. If the one person you want isn't there, the whole world seems overpopulated, teeming with human beings of all shapes and sizes, with their ugly, grinning faces that are not his face and their silly braying voices that are not his voice, swigging soda from cans, joking, pushing and shoving. Too many people.

I wished them all at the bottom of the sea.

The ferry ploughed its way north. Somewhere, on a train, Olivier was speeding south through the parched countryside to Perpignan – without me.

And Rose was in Paris, alone.

***

I had carried out my teenage threat.

The carnival was always held in late September, when we had been back at school for two or three weeks. But this time I hadn't gone back to school: I had left. I lay in bed in the mornings, imagining bells shrilling through corridors, the chatter in the cloakrooms, the banging of desk lids, satchels and briefcases weighed down with dog-eared textbooks. But I was out of all that. There was no point in getting up. My mother looked at me disapprovingly when I drifted down to breakfast at about eleven, dressed in my oldest clothes and trainers. We had had a few rows about the untidiness of my room, the state of my hair, and the fact that I did nothing to help in the house – to which I had replied with outrage that Pascal did nothing, either. Now she was leaving me severely alone. I would wander around the town, which seemed oddly deserted, the inhabitants all shut away in their offices or in school. Or I would take Rex, predecessor to Jip and Milou, for long walks in the countryside, not speaking to a soul, composing songs in my head which I would later pick out on the guitar, alone in my room. The days melted into one another, pointless, formless. My exam results had come through, and I had done well, but I didn't care one way or the other. Nothing mattered any more.

"Me and my mates are going to the carnival," announced Pascal.

"My mates and I," corrected my mother.

"Didn't know you had mates," he said cheekily. "And then we're going on to the fair, and then we're going to watch the fireworks. I'll need my pocket-money in advance."

"Well, no getting involved in any punch-ups. And keep out of the pubs. You're under age, never mind what your mates say." My father put on a severe voice.

"I know that," said Pascal scornfully. "You going, Stell?"

"I shouldn't think so."

"Old misery-guts!" He pulled a hideous face at me, and I ignored him.

The day of the carnival dawned fine. Avoiding the route of the procession through the town, I trudged through the deserted allotments, along the railway embankment and down to the river. Leaning on the bridge, I looked down at the bright green weed, flowing like the hair of Ophelia, who had drowned herself for love. But I could hear the oompah-oompah music in the distance. Everybody was out watching the procession, laughing and cheering and having a good time. Only I was an outcast.

I went home and sat in my mother's deck-chair in the garden. Pascal came rushing home, demanding tea and bread and butter before dashing out again to go to the fair. I had watched the fair arriving in the recreation ground, the caravans and the great lorries and generators, the scaffolding for the rides and the garishly painted booths. This year there was a Ferris wheel, which I had always loved when I was younger. Now I could hear pop music blaring as the setting sun cast long beams through the trees and across the lawn. There was also an insistent voice like a siren, and a man's voice urging people to have a go, have a go, try your luck. I stood up; sat down again; went indoors and up to my room, where I leaned out of the window. I felt I was going to explode. Why did nothing ever happen? How could I bear this long, long tedium, going on forever? I needed to be caught up in life, whirled around, shaken out of myself.

Grabbing a sweater and my purse, I ran downstairs. My father was closeted in his study. My mother, on hands and knees in the sitting-room, was turning out a cupboard and filling bin-bags with things to be thrown away, making another of her "clean sweeps". I would go to the fair. I would go on all the rides, the switchback, the waltzer – the rougher the better.

As I crossed the recreation ground, the blare of music grew louder and louder, sucking me in like a whirlpool. The hot lights blazed in strings and letters, bright bulbs reflected in mirrored booths. People were everywhere, jostling, shouting at one another above the din, and there was a smell of crushed grass, frying onions and toffee apples. In a moving blur, the rides hurtled people through the air in great arcs and circles and waves, and laughter and screams came from the sky. Once

I caught sight of Pascal with his mates; they had their heads together and seemed to be counting their money.

I rode on the switchback several times, my hair streaming out behind me. I circled through the air on the chairoplane. Alone in an old-fashioned swingboat, I pulled myself higher and higher, to and fro, like a solitary adventurer on a stormy sea. Then I bought a toffee apple. We had never been allowed to have these when we were small. "The fairground people use maggoty apples," my mother always used to say, with what justification I don't know. Now I bit through the hard, sweet casing to the sour apple beneath. Who cared if I ate a maggot?

"Want to come on the Ferris wheel, Stella?" said a voice right by my ear, through the noise. I turned, my mouth full of toffee, and nearly choked. It was David. Behind him, I could see a group of sixth-formers huddled around the shooting gallery, urging on a boy called Darren who was taking careful aim.

I swallowed. "All right," I said. I could feel the chunk of apple going down my throat like the point of a knife.

Only a metal bar that closed the swinging car separated us from the sheer drop into the huge revolving spokes of the wheel. Up we went, backwards and up, the racket of the fair fell away, and we could see right out over the dark tree-tops to distant streetlamps and the grey mist lying on the fields. Then over the top with that sinking thrill in the pit of the stomach, and down into the dazzling lights and deafening music, all jumbled and moving, glowing with colour. Up, over and down.

Once we stopped at the very top of the wheel, while other people were clambering on at the bottom. I looked at David, who was gazing out over the countryside, his face chiselled, serious, a snow prince. His arm rested along the back of the seat, almost as if he had meant to put it around me. I wished that we could stay there forever, in a tiny space of our own, suspended in the sky.

He turned to me with a small smile. "I'm having a last fling, he said. "I go up to Cambridge next week."

When we had finished our ride, a loudspeaker was announcing the fireworks. David looked around for his friends, but couldn't see them. "Shall we go and watch?" he said.

We were caught up in a mass of humanity surging to the other side of the recreation ground, and positioned ourselves near the tennis courts. "Stand in front. You'll see better." He pushed me in front of him. He had put his hands on my shoulders for a second. I was trying to store up every precious moment, every look and gesture a treasure to be taken out later and re-lived.

Above us, the sky burst into chrysanthemums of pink and green and gold. Orange trails shot heavenwards, lights as bright as the sun detonated like bombs. I felt as if something in me was soaring into the sky, exploding too, making great flowers and fountains and coloured stars. And behind me stood David, his warm body only inches away.

Afterwards, he walked me home. We walked slowly across the dark recreation ground, other groups of people at some distance from us, all streaming slowly towards the gates. The air smelt of smoke, and also of the first frosts of autumn, only weeks away. I shivered, and he tucked my arm through his. I had no idea why he was being so different. He must have changed his mind about me. He must at last have realized how I felt, and taken pity on me. I felt sure that we would write to each other during the term, and go out together during the Christmas vacation. The lights of the fair were behind us, and our linked shadows were cast ahead of us on the grass. I was floating. It seemed strange to see my feet, walking in time with his, touching the ground.

After chatting about exams and colleges and his intention to take up rowing, he fell silent, and we just walked: across the grass, through the gates, along the quiet streets. We reached the corner of my road, and my arm was trembling in his. I knew that he would kiss me. We stopped in front of my gate. Don't let Rex bark. Don't let my father or mother open the front door. I prayed silently. Don't let Pascal come charging along the pavement with his friends.

We stood facing each other, very close.

"Well, I guess this is goodbye," said David.

I stood, my face turned up to his, my eyes half closed, my lips parted.

He kissed me briskly on the cheek. "What will you do, now that you've left school?" he asked in a matter-of-fact voice.

"I ..." I felt breathless. I felt as if I had just been slapped. I stepped back a pace. "I'm going to do a secretarial course in Paris," I said. I hadn't thought about it before, but suddenly I knew what I was going to do. I couldn't stay here. I must get away from this town, this country, this whole life that was going nowhere. He might not want me, but there would be others – lots of others – who would.

"Paris? Jolly good," he said. "Well – good night, then, and good luck. See you." He nodded, and began to walk back along the road, away from me.

I stood frozen. "It's all because of you," I whispered.

His footsteps rang on the pavement, fading as his figure dwindled towards the corner.

"It's because of you!" I shouted.

"What?" His voice came faintly as he paused and turned.

"Nothing!" I called, and waved.

He waved back, turned the corner and was gone.

※

– ELEVEN –

"Isn't she lovely?" demanded my mother. "Isn't she sweet? Didn't I tell you she was just perfect? Yes, mon chou, here's your Auntie Stella come to see you. Here you are – hold her." She dumped the pink-shawled bundle in my arms, and there she was: Jacqueline Stella. I don't know what I had been expecting. She seemed so small, no bigger than a doll. Her skin was as delicate as the inside of a shell, and her bald head had just a wisp of brown hair. Her dark eyes of indeterminate colour seemed to focus on my face, as I smiled foolishly down at her, and her fists and feet began to work, her face grew red, her eyes closed and her toothless mouth opened in a surprisingly loud yell. I rocked her awkwardly, nervous of dropping her.

"There, there," said my mother, taking her back. "There, there. Come to Granny, then." She held the baby against her shoulder and patted her back, jogging gently up and down, just as I had seen her do with Pascal so many years ago. She looked immaculate, in a cream dress with a pale gold scarf knotted casually around her neck, and I felt crumpled and travel-stained. If I ever knot a scarf casually around my neck, it unknots itself within the hour.

Pascal was eating late strawberries with the relish of a schoolboy, the sun white on his fair hair. We were having tea in the garden, and the table had been carried on to the lawn, where the trees in full summer leaf made dappled patterns on the white tablecloth. Lisa sat next to Pascal, wearing a daisy-patterned dress, rather pink and puffy about the face. My father leaned back in his chair, a piece of sponge cake apparently forgotten on his plate, the sun winking on his glasses, beaming with vague benevolence at us all.

I had barely had time to deposit my luggage in the hall and wash my hands before my mother hurried me into the garden to see the baby. Now nobody could say anything, as both dogs were leaping up at me, barking and whining as they wagged their tails furiously and ran in circles, and little Jacqueline was yelling at the top of her lungs. Pascal waved his spoon at me, wordlessly. Lisa stood up and took the baby from my mother, and as the pandemonium gradually subsided I could hear my father asking me whether I had had a good journey.

The next quarter of an hour was spent in the usual chit-chat, as I ate English bread and butter and home-made jam, strawberries and cake, and drank tea. How was I? Oh, I was fine. How were they? How was work? Wasn't the garden looking nice? But the focus of everybody's attention was Jacqueline.

I had brought her a present, and went into the house to fetch it from my bag. For a long time I had hesitated, forcing myself to walk around mother-and-baby shops and to look at all the cots, cuddly toys, rattles and pastel mobiles, until I had finally chosen this, which had cost much more than I had originally planned to spend. I had used my credit card and recalculated my budget.

"Oh, look, Pascal," said Lisa, holding Jacqueline in the crook of her arm and pushing back the tissue paper with her free hand. "Isn't it pretty?"

"I'll take her, shall I?" said my mother, and gathered her greedily into her arms again, touching her cheek, smoothing the wisp of hair. The baby gripped her scarf with tiny monkey fingers.

"It's lovely, Stella," said Lisa. "It will just do for her christening, don't you think, Pascal?"

The little white dress had puffed sleeves and a scalloped hem, and was embroidered all over with butterflies, delicate wings shimmering in silks.

"It's quite sweet – but not very practical, is it?" said my mother. The recipient said nothing, quiet now, gazing up at my mother with a round-eyed, unfocused stare. "Your Aunt Hélène sent her a Babygro. Now that's a useful thing to have. She'll get a lot of wear out of that."

"I like it," said my father to me. "Hrrrm. It's like a miniature dream."

I gave him a quick nod. A miniature dream! It was the sort of thing he would say.

"Of course, my mother's been knitting for months. You should see the heaps of little jackets and bootees!" said Lisa. I remembered her mother, an apple dumpling of a woman.

"She's got too much gear, I think," said Pascal. "If she has so much now, what kind of a wardrobe will she have when she's a teenager?"

"Nonsense! Babies need lots of clothes," said my mother firmly. "They make them dirty all the time."

Lisa agreed, and they talked animatedly about washing machines, disposable nappies, bottles, birth weights and colic, and I don't know what else. It was very boring, and I fed the dogs bits of cake surreptitiously under the table. This was strictly against house rules, but, after all, I was only an occasional visitor now. I fondled Jip's ears, and Milou rested his chin on my knee. I kept my eyes on Jacqueline, however. Everyone's eyes kept returning to her as they talked.

Lisa was now saying how lucky it was for a person to be born in a caul, and my mother was announcing at the same time that it was important to place the cradle so that the baby slept with its head due north. Lisa said that she was very careful about that, and added that she had hung a turquoise bead on a silver chain around Jacqueline's neck, under her clothes.

"That's right," said my mother approvingly. "To ward off the evil eye."

My father's cup rattled in the saucer, and he coughed. "Surely, darling, you don't seriously believe she's in any danger from the evil eye. Do you?"

"Oh, yes, Monsieur Hayward," said Lisa earnestly. "There are evil spirits all around us, all the time. And then there are the elementals. They may not always be friendly."

My father's eyebrows rose, and I glanced at him sideways.

"Yes, well," put in my mother. "it's just a custom, really, like wearing something blue on your wedding day, or throwing salt over your left shoulder." She sounded a little embarrassed, but defiant.

"I never throw salt over my left shoulder," said my father gravely.

"Anyway, who knows? It does no harm, and you can't be too careful," said my mother. "We've got to look after this little one, haven't we, my precious? Haven't we, ma puce? Yes, we have!" She seized the teapot and tried to pour out more tea, but the pot was empty apart from the dregs. I half noticed the few last drops dripping into the bottom of her cup, but I was still mesmerised by Jacqueline – her smooth skin, so new and unmarked, almost transparent on her fragile skull. My mother saw me watching. "Stella!" she said irritably. "Can't you see the pot needs topping up? I'm holding the baby, here. Go and put the kettle on, won't you?"

"I'll go," said Pascal, jumping to his feet and grabbing the teapot. He turned towards the french windows, but Milou, thinking more food might be on the way, chose that moment to burst out from under the table and tripped him up. Milou yelped, Pascal stumbled and the teapot went flying.

"Pascal, you really are clumsy," said Lisa, pink and cross, swatting at a wasp.

"Did you hurt Milou?" I asked.

"Is it broken?" my mother wanted to know.

"Just the lid." Pascal rescued it and scrambled to his feet. "Bloody dog!" he roared, and Milou crawled on his stomach, grinning apologetically, while Jip slunk away behind us in case he, too, had done something naughty.

"Oh dear – my favourite china teapot." My mother looked reproachfully at me.

My father was examining the broken lid. "It's a clean break," he said. "I think I can glue it so you'll hardly be able to see the join."

"Oh, thank you, chéri. Anyway, never mind," said my mother to Pascal. "Tea-leaves are good for the lawn."

"I know that," said Pascal.

"I thought it was roses they were good for," I said sourly. "I'll make some more tea." And I marched into the house with the lidless teapot.

"Use the other pot!" my mother called after me. "The stainless steel one." I had been going to do so anyway.

When I came out again, my heart gave a lurch. Pascal was holding Jacqueline and strolling around the garden with her, telling her the names of shrubs and flowers in French.

"You're absurd," Lisa told him. "She can't understand anything we say yet."

"Ah, that's what you think", said Pascal. "Babies can understand far more than we give them credit for. Anyhow, my daughter is going to be bilingual. I won't settle for anything less. Isn't that right?" he asked the baby in French.

"I'll have to brush up my schoolgirl French, won't I?" giggled his wife.

I thumped the teapot down on the table so that a few drops shot out of the spout on to the cloth, and my mother clicked her tongue in annoyance. Why did I have this feeling of anxiety, like a cold hand twisting my guts? I wanted to grab Jacqueline from Pascal and shelter her in my arms. If he hurt her I couldn't bear it. He danced a few steps with her, humming, and I caught my breath. But he seemed remarkably at ease with her, holding her comfortably and supporting her head.

"It'll be your turn next," said Lisa conspiratorially.

"What?"

"To have a baby. As soon as you find yourself a nice man."

"Oh, I shouldn't think so." I bent down to stroke Jip, who rolled on his back with his paws in the air. "I think I prefer animals." Upside down and clownish, the dog thumped the lawn with his tail.

Jacqueline gave a piercing wail, and I jerked upright, aghast. But Pascal had not dropped her or done anything terrible. He talked to her encouragingly, but she was working herself up into a steady bawling. Lisa said that she must be getting hungry, and he deposited her in her lap.

"Or else she has a dirty nappy," said Lisa, peering to see, and sure enough an unpleasant smell was wafting from the tiny screaming creature. Her eyes were tight shut and her face was a dull puce colour. And the noise! The smell was quite disgusting, too. I no longer felt any overwhelming urge to touch her. In fact I edged my chair slightly away.

***

Several days later, around seven in the evening, I was lying on my bed with its candlewick bedspread in my old room, watching the evening sun slant across the faded wallpaper on to the door post, where a series of black pencil marks showed my height on successive birthdays. It was hard to imagine being any shorter and closer to the ground than I was at present, but clearly I must have been. My old teddy bear, Benjamin, sat splay-legged and threadbare on the ottoman, and the shelves held illustrated children's books and a number of sentimental little ornaments that I would not want cluttering my flat in Paris, but which reminded me of the past: a windmill that was a souvenir of a school trip to Holland, and a whole collection of china dogs and horses.

Emma Kershaw had had a little white china horse, something like one of mine. She had said that it was her mascot and brought her luck, and she had stood it on her desk at examination time. At the beginning of the second paper, she had knocked it on to the floor. It had smashed, and she had fled from the room, sobbing – and failed her English exam. I had passed my exams without the help of any mascot. But I used to threaten Pascal with terrible consequences if he ever touched my ornaments.

The window stood open on to the garden, and I could hear peaceful English summer sounds: a neighbour using a pair of shears some distance away, the measured cooing of a wood-pigeon – so very different from the constant undertow of traffic noise in Paris, the background to everything I normally do, not to mention the recent drilling.

Floating through the quiet house, my mother's voice could be heard singing Jacqueline to sleep. The song was "Il était un petit navire", which I could remember Mamie singing to me. I couldn't remember my mother ever singing it before. Earlier, Jacqueline had been bawling, but now she seemed to be dozing off, and the castors rumbled on the floor as my mother pushed the old cradle, which had been Pascal's, to and fro.

Pascal and Lisa had gone to the pub. They had asked me if I wanted to go along, but I wasn't feeling gregarious, and anyway I felt that they probably wanted some time alone together and a rest from both the family and their daughter. She certainly had a loud voice. And she preferred to sleep during the day rather than at night. I was not sleeping very well in any case, with strange, restless dreams about objects flying through the air and disintegrating, doors opening and closing, and after two or three disturbed nights I could almost sympathise with Bertrand's intolerance of noise – though it would have done no good to bang on the wall of the spare bedroom.

You could hardly get into that room, so cluttered was it with baby paraphernalia. I hadn't realized just how much equipment babies need. The kitchen was full of bottles and powdered milk and a sterilizing device, the bathroom overflowed with baby talcum powder, baby cleansing lotion, baby shampoo and giant-size packets of disposable nappies, and in the hall we barked our shins on a carry-cot and a sling – not to mention treading on rattles and rescuing cuddly toys from the dogs, who seemed to like them more than Jacqueline did.

Ohé, ohé, matelot,
Matelot navigue sur les flots, sang my mother.

I alternated between wanting to hold my niece, singing nursery rhymes to her and feeling the warm weight of her little body against mine, and wanting to get away from the noise and commotion and fuss that seemed to spring up spontaneously around her. Why do people have to speak to babies in funny high-pitched voices? I spent a lot of time in my room – moping, as my mother would say, and doubtless did say.

Thump! I sat bolt upright on the bed. Benjamin the teddy bear had fallen off the ottoman. My heart was pounding and

I could feel the sweat pricking my forehead. Hell! Why was I still so jumpy? I picked him up and sat him squarely on the ottoman again. His dark glass eyes looked at me with what had always seemed a kindly expression, particularly on days when I had been scolded. I could hear my mother going downstairs. She must have caused a slight vibration as she walked along the landing – or else his stuffing was sagging and had quite naturally tilted him off balance. Luckily he was unbreakable. And nothing else was moving about, was it? Everything in the bedroom was perfectly still, except the curtain shifting slightly in the breeze from the window.

I stepped out on to the landing. Not a sound from the spare room. Opening the door, I crept in.

She was lying rosily asleep in her cradle, her fine hair faintly damp and flattened against her head. One fist was curled in front of her mouth, the nails like pink pearls, and her eyes were closed, the dark lashes resting on the plump curve of her cheek. My niece. She was adorable, and yet – to see her now, nobody would guess how much noise she could make or how much single-minded fury could be generated by that small person. I wasn't sure that I could have coped with it, day after day. Perhaps my mother had had a point about my own loud voice as a baby. Lisa seemed to manage, but she had a placid nature, and Pascal – I had to admit that Pascal now seemed every inch the devoted father. I still felt a stab of anxiety when he picked her up, but he was so careful.

Something glinted. It was the fine silver chain around her neck, with the turquoise bead. Against the evil eye.

Retrieving a pink stuffed rabbit from the floor as I went, I let myself quietly out of the room, hesitated, and then crossed the landing and tapped on the door of my father's study.

"Come in! Hrrmm. Come in!"

"Am I disturbing you, Dad? You're not still doing college work, are you, in the holidays?" I hung on to the door handle.

"No – I'm just glueing this. Sit down, if you can find somewhere to sit." He waved a vague hand. He was seated behind his desk, flanked by piles of books, carefully mixing glue on an old bathroom tile, with the two halves of the teapot lid placed on the blotter in front of him. Books lined the walls, books cluttered the desk and were heaped on chairs, and any space on the walls between the bookcases was filled with geometrical abstracts painted by a friend of his.

I moved some books to the floor and sat down, looking at him affectionately. His once-curly hair was receding now to greying tufts over his ears, and his domed head was slightly freckled. Those same freckles appeared on my own face when I was exposed to the sun of the Midi. He was attending to his glue, mixing it very thoroughly, but I noticed that the ear-piece of his glasses was still mended with sellotape. Of course, the teapot lid was for my mother, not for himself. He glanced at me over the rims and asked me how things were in Paris.

That was when I started to tell him about Rose.

I didn't say anything about Olivier. I can talk to my father far more easily than to my mother, who always jumps in with some vehement opinion before I've finished speaking. But the memory of Olivier was too fresh to discuss with anybody, and moreover I felt that I had been a fool. Rose, however, was another matter, and the words poured out.

" …And these pins were just revolving round her head, in the air… And then they shot out of the door with some cotton reels – wham. And a piece of furniture moved. And she has this strange effect on anything electrical or electronic." I told him about the loud noise that had come from the speakers of my hifi, and about the CDs and the books falling to the floor.

"You witnessed all this, you say? You experienced it directly?"

"As plainly as I can see you now."

"Well, then." With extreme precision he pressed the carefully glued halves of the lid together, and held them in place for a moment. "Well, then, either you were having some kind of hallucination, which I doubt, or else it really happened."

I let my breath out in a long sigh. I had been afraid of what he might say. It was such a relief to be believed. "I know it really happened. But people don't like these strange things.

And then there are the birds." I told him about Luna, and Jacques, and the birds in the park, and the fate of Blanche. "Rose is so different from anyone else. People are attracted to her, but somehow they're scared of her at the same time. My concierge even thinks she has the evil eye."

My father's eyes rolled ceilingwards. "Don't talk to me about the evil eye. Turquoise beads, indeed!" He snorted. "Luckily these rites are fairly harmless. Hrrmm. You know the saying misattributed to Chesterton? That when people cease to believe in God, they don't believe in nothing, but believe in anything? Spirits! Elementals!"

"And this horrible man Bertrand thinks she's a witch," I said, and told him about the anonymous note.

"Hmm, that's unfortunate." He shook his head. "If you'd been living in a small village, now, I wouldn't have been surprised – but in the heart of Paris...! But then, this is an age of irrationalism. People are eager to hold strong beliefs without a scrap of evidence for them."

"What do you believe, Dad?"

He rubbed his chin thoughtfully.

"I believe that there are more things in heaven and earth, Horatio ... To disbelieve in something is as much an act of faith as to believe in it. Who knows whether the world really exists? Whether we are here at all? But on a practical plane, we should guard against being gullible. If you're gullible, you're open to manipulation."

"That's the sort of thing Mamie would have said. Oh, Dad – I do wish I could talk to Mamie about all this."

"Hmm, your grandmother and I always did have similar views. It used to annoy your mother a great deal. Too Cartesian, she used to say. She rebelled against her mother's rationality, and I must say she seems to have gone to the opposite extreme recently. Horoscopes and such." He shrugged, and the dust motes whirled lazily in the evening sunlight. My mother was not allowed to do any dusting in here.

"I don't know what to think," I said. "If I hadn't actually been there, I would probably have said that it was impossible.

222

But I've seen the birds coming to her, even trying to get in through the closed window."

"It must be rather delightful to be able – literally – to charm the birds out of the trees, like Orpheus," mused my father.

"It's fascinating. It doesn't bother me at all. Well, maybe owls are a bit much. But it's the objects moving about, the piano playing all by itself, and – and stuff. That is quite frightening, and she herself doesn't want it to happen, you see. She hates it. That's the point."

"We're always frightened by what we don't understand." he tapped the desk. "But there's always a cause or a reason for everything. If we understood the causes, we would understand the phenomena, and they wouldn't seem so threatening. Your friend has never actually harmed anybody, has she?"

"Rose? She wouldn't willingly hurt a fly. But I think perhaps she does cause things to happen. Bertrand said she was causing interference on his TV, and I thought that was nonsense at the time, but now I'm not so sure."

"Causes are very hard to determine. And cause shouldn't necessarily entail blame. We all cause things to happen. From what you say, it sounds as if this young woman has an interesting problem of spontaneous psychokinesis." He pushed his glasses up his nose. "Interesting from a scientific point of view, of course. Oh, I'm sure she would prefer to be without it. It hasn't yet been satisfactorily explained, although it's well documented. There seems to be some connection with electromagnetic fields. But she is not deliberately setting out to disturb people – and so should not be held accountable. But unfortunately human beings prefer to have someone to blame for what goes wrong. They like to have a scapegoat."

From somewhere in the recesses of my mind came an echo of Mamie's voice.

"That's what happened to women accused of witchcraft in the Middle Ages, isn't it?" I said. "They were made scapegoats. Oh! Haven't we progressed at all?" I stood up. "I just wish I could do something."

"You know, Stella, if I were you I wouldn't interfere." His voice was mild.

"But it's not interfering – "

"I know, you want to help. But you won't be able to change this problem, whatever it is. She has to solve it or come to terms with it herself. If you want my advice, just offer her your friendship and let her be."

I walked over to the window. The trees cast long shadows on the lawn, and at the far end of the garden my mother was struggling with the hosepipe, watched with interest by both dogs. So I should just let Rose be. Well, all right. She had more or less told me to leave her alone. But she had impinged on my life, too. If it hadn't been for her, Olivier – my thoughts shied away. We all affect one another, I thought, even if we don't mean to cause those effects on other people. She hadn't intended Olivier to fall in love with her. It was not her fault. And Olivier, apparently, hadn't intended me to fall in love with him. We're all at the centre of vortices, I thought, blindly causing storms in others' lives. We don't know what we're doing.

Except that I – I had clearly not impinged on Olivier's life. He was quite unaffected. I had no power to touch him at all.

"Look at the light falling on those copper beeches," said my father, joining me at the window. He smelt faintly of the aftershave that my mother bought for him and that he sometimes remembered to use – a familiar, reassuring smell. Down in the garden, my mother seemed to be having more and more trouble with the hosepipe.

"Madeleine's very pleased that you came over," he told me.

"Really? She seems so wrapped up in her granddaughter, I think she's hardly noticed me."

"Ouch! Don't remind me that I'm a grandfather. I feel old enough already," he protested. "No – she's very glad you came. She misses you, you know."

"Oh, rubbish! Well, maybe she misses having me to boss around. But I can never do anything right. And she only wanted me to come to see the baby."

A magpie flew across the garden from right to left and alighted in one of the Kershaws' copper beeches next door. One for sorrow, I thought, and then checked myself guiltily.

"It's not as simple as that, you know." My father's voice rumbled at my left shoulder. "Hrrrm. I think she feels a bit frustrated over you. You see, you never followed the path she mapped out for you. She would have liked you to have an academic career, and then get married and produce the first grandchild."

"But that's not what I wanted! It wasn't possible! I – "

"Hush! I know, I know. I'm not saying that's what you ought to have done. You did what you chose to do, and I deliberately didn't stand in your way. In fact, I could see that the more she pushed you, the more determined you would be to do the opposite." He gave my hair a gentle tug. "You always knew what you didn't want, right from a baby."

"Like Jacqueline?" I grinned. "She lets us all know when she's not pleased with something."

"So she does. Because she's a person, not just a baby. I think part of the difficulty with Madeleine is that she doesn't always see the person – she just adores babies. And she hates not to be in control."

"I remember she used to adore Pascal when he was little. Well, she still adores him." I could hear the edge of jealousy in my voice.

"But when you were born she was just the same. She was besotted with you when you were tiny. I'd never seen her so happy. She positively – hrrrmm – she positively radiated happiness."

What? The idea had never occurred to me. I was stunned.

"It didn't last, did it?" I cleared my throat. In the evening sky, swallows wove their dipping patterns – or were they house-martins? Rose would have known. A metallic noise rang across the garden; my mother was hitting the water tap with a spanner.

"You grew up, you see," said my father. "But Pascal went on being her baby. To tell you the truth, I think she spoiled that boy, although I can't say he's turned out too badly."

I glanced at him and looked away again. He had always been scrupulously fair in the way he treated Pascal and me, although if fights and quarrels broke out his reaction had been to withdraw from the scene and bury himself in his poetry and his college work. He wouldn't arbitrate.

"He went on being her baby because she couldn't have any more babies, that's the trouble, Stella," said my father. "I think that was the greatest disappointment of her life, loving babies as she does. She would have liked half a dozen. Naturally she was anxious to have grandchildren."

"She couldn't have any more children?" I hadn't known that, either.

"After Pascal was born, she had a miscarriage, and then an ectopic pregnancy. She was deeply depressed for a time. You were too young to realize."

I digested this information. I could remember times in my distant childhood when for some reason my mother had not been there, and I had been bundled off to stay with Mamie or with my aunt Margaret in Torquay. I had asked for Maman and called for her, but she had not come. There were other memories, too, of frightening visits to hospitals, with their bare corridors and strange pharmaceutical smells. My mother had been lying in a strange high bed. I could remember the strangeness and the terror.

"I see," I said.

"There's a reason for everything, a cause of everything," said my father, "if only we could understand it. Your mother is a very frustrated woman in many ways. Her life didn't turn out as she planned and willed it, and it's important to her to plan things and control them. I try to make it up to her."

"But she gets so angry," I said, and could hear the wail in my voice, like a child's.

"She can't help it, though. It's her vitality. Now that you're grown up, I'm sure you can see that. She goes off like a firework, but it's a lot of sound and fury, signifying nothing."

I looked along the garden, where clouds of gnats hovered over the lawn.

"There will be fireworks out there in a minute, I think," I said.

"Or waterworks," said my father.

My mother had stopped hitting the tap and was swearing in French as she tried to twist it with her bare hands. I could hear her, right down the garden. Jip pushed himself under her arm and tried to lick her face, and she jerked her head away. Suddenly the water came on with full force, shooting out of the hose and hitting the fir trees at the end of the garden like a squall. My mother trod on Jip, who yelped – She pulled at the hose, which rolled sideways, soaking Milou, who had been quietly investigating a flower bed – She shouted at both dogs, who had started to bark and run madly round in circles – She made another dive at the hose – The dogs thought this was a fine game, and pounced in the same direction – My mother caught her foot in the hosepipe and nearly fell – The jet of water was spraying straight up into the air like a fountain – The hose appeared to have sprung a leak, and another fountain, a miniature one, started up behind her.

"What accompaniment would you say?" asked my father calmly. "Handel's Water Music or Handel's Firework Music?"

I glanced uncertainly at him and back at my mother. I could feel her fury from where I stood, and out of habit I was stiffening defensively. Her anger had always broken over me like thunder, and was so much bigger than me. But down there at the end of the garden she seemed small, somehow – a miniature virago battling with the hose and the dogs, and making matters worse as she lost her temper. She no longer looked elegant. I gulped. Suddenly the scene began to seem funny. Apparently there was air in the hosepipe, which coughed and spluttered and twisted itself out of her hands like a live thing. Both she and the dogs were now drenched.

I looked at my father and saw that he was starting to laugh, too. "Oh, dear," he said, "I must find someone to repair that thing."

"She's getting so wet," I giggled, "and so cross. Oh, look!"

She had now managed to turn off the water, and was standing with her hands on her hips, her wet dress clinging to her, haranguing the two bedraggled dogs, who stood looking up at her with their tongues hanging out, nonchalantly wagging their tails.

"She'll be all right in a minute, you'll see," said my father. "Her rages – you just have to let them go through you. Let her be angry if she wants to be. It will pass."

"You do understand her, don't you?" I said, wiping my eyes.

"Hmm, we've been together a long time. Tout comprendre, c'est tout pardonner."

I left him hunting for the quotation that was not from Chesterton, muttering "People believe, not in nothing, but in anything," running his finger along the dusty shelves. The teapot lid gleamed in the dusk almost as good as new.

Some time later, when I went downstairs, my mother, her hair still in rat's tails, was placing a large bowl of roses on the oak chest in the hall, and their sweet, cool scent wafted up to meet me. I astonished her by coming up behind her and giving her a hug.

***

"No, not the sheet, the pink cot blanket!" shouted Lisa to Pascal, who had his head in the boot of the car.

"It's not here," called Pascal. "I'm sure you put it in the suitcase."

"Which suitcase?"

"Not the brown one, the one with the – that's funny. It was here a minute ago."

Chaos reigned. They had been getting ready to go home since early that morning, but collecting their stuff from every corner of the house and garden was proving a major operation. The dogs were uneasy, and kept jumping into the car for fear of missing an outing. Jacqueline seemed unsettled by the commotion, and cried and grizzled, although I rocked her, talked and sang to her, waved rattles in front of her and offered her cuddly toys.

"Half a pound of tuppeny rice,

Half a pound of treacle,
That's the way the money goes -
Pop goes the weasel,"
I sang, bouncing her as I danced around the lawn. She stopped crying for a moment and gazed at me bemused, eyes wide and mouth open, dribbling. Pascal, over by the french windows, seemed to be watching me attentively. Then Jacqueline remembered that she was cross, screwed up her face and started to yell again.

My mother fussed around loading the car with home-made cakes and blackcurrant jam. In the middle of packing, Pascal and my father got involved in an intense political argument, and had to be prized apart. At the last minute, Lisa put the butterfly dress on Jacqueline to show me what it looked like, and Jacqueline was sick on it. There was much discussion as to the best way to wash it.

By lunch time I had had enough. I retired to my room, nerves frazzled with the constant yelling. I could still hear the voices from up here, but they were muffled, and a furry bumblebee blundering in the clematis sounded louder.

I sat on the ottoman and took Benjamin on my knee. He felt strange after Jacqueline. He didn't squirm or bawl or dribble, and he wasn't wet or smelly. To tell the truth, I thought, I had had quite an unrealistic idea of what babies were like. They invaded your whole life. They took over. Everything had to revolve around them – except when they were asleep, and then you had to tiptoe about and talk in whispers. I tried to imagine a baby and all its equipment in my neat, bare flat in Paris, and myself looking after it and somehow contriving to earn a living at the same time.

Somebody tapped on the door.

"Come in." I hastily put the teddy bear down on the ottoman.

Pascal poked his head round the door and then edged in, one hand behind his back.

"Maman says lunch will be about ten minutes," he said.

"Oh, all right. Does she want some help?"

"No, I think everything's under control. Dad's giving her a hand. Er ... I haven't really had much chance to talk to you, and now we're leaving."

"Well, your daughter's been the star of the show," I said brightly.

"Isn't she wonderful? She really is the most amazing little girl." He grinned and scratched his ear. "You know, I'm glad you like her. I really wanted you to – to take to her."

"Why wouldn't I take to her? She's perfect," I said.

"I still can't quite believe I'm a father." There was a pause. "Wouldn't you – "

"I hope you – "

We both spoke at once, and stopped.

"Wouldn't you have preferred a boy?" I said at last.

"Boy, girl, what does it matter? When it comes to the crunch, you just want a healthy child, safely born. God! Lisa was in labour for such a long time. I was just relieved that she was all right. Anyway, Jacqueline's fine just the way she is. I wouldn't send her back! We might have a boy next time."

Next time. Pascal as the father of a family. It was hard to imagine – but getting easier all the time.

"You seem different, you know," I told him.

"I feel different. I think being a parent changes you." He looked at me. "So, you see, at last I've done something right, haven't I? Created something perfect."

I didn't say that only God could create life. I didn't remind him of Lisa's share in the process. I smiled, and let him have his moment of glory. It occurred to me that I had never praised him for anything that he had done.

We talked about Christmas, and whether I would be coming over, in which case I would be able to see the video of the christening. Pascal seemed to be beating about the bush, slightly embarrassed about something.

"Yes, well," he said, "What I really wanted to say was – happy birthday," and he produced a package from behind his back.

"But my birthday was in June," I said blankly.

"I know that. So what? I know we don't bother much with birthdays in this family. Odd, really. Why don't we? Jacqueline's first birthday will be a grand occasion. But I mean – you brought her that lovely little dress and everything. And I – Oh, well, why don't you open it?" He thrust the package at me and scratched his ear furiously.

Was this a joke? I vividly remembered the time he had left a beribboned shoe-box of earthworms on my pillow. Gingerly I tugged at the wrapping.

"We'll make lots of videos, I think. She changes so quickly, it's incredible. Already she's got a different look about her. You can see she's got Lisa's nose, and Sandra thinks she's going to have my eyes. They were dark blue at first, but their colour keeps changing." Sandra was Lisa's mother.

"Green eyes?" I said. "Mamie's eyes."

"They're my eyes, too," he said.

I looked at him quickly, but there was no defiance in his words: he was just stating a fact. He was Mamie's grandson. And were his eyes so very different from hers?

"I wish Mamie could have lived to see her," said Pascal.

The last of the wrapping paper was ripped off, and I found myself holding a musical box. It was round and wooden, painted bright blue, and it had several cartoon-like bunny rabbits with yellow bows round their necks cavorting on the lid.

"There's a key underneath, look," he said, turning it for me, and the strains of Auprès de ma blonde came tinkling out.

It was one of the ugliest things I had ever seen. I didn't know whether to laugh or cry.

"It's because I once broke that musical box of yours, you see," he said gruffly. "The one you were talking about at Christmas. I never meant to break it – honestly. I just wanted to find out how it worked."

"I shouldn't have made such a fuss about it," I said. "It was ages ago. We were only children."

"But it's tough, being a child," said Pascal. "You feel things so strongly. Little mishaps seem like major disasters. Children are so vulnerable. It's terrible how vulnerable they are. Before Jacqueline was born, I kept coming across articles about still births and cot deaths. Life is so bloody fragile." He gazed out of the window, then looked back at me. "I couldn't bear her to be hurt. And I realize, now, how many times I must have hurt you when you were only a child."

It was my turn to feel embarrassed.

"We were both horrible to each other when we were children. It wasn't just you."

"That musical box," he said. "Mamie was always giving you things. Why not? You were careful with things and I only used to break them. But I guess I was jealous."

"You were jealous! But I was jealous of you."

"Of me? Why on earth?"

"Oh, because Maman... Because you did well..."

He shook his head. "Families are complicated, aren't they?"

We half smiled at each other.

"We're grown up, now," I said. I hoped it was true of myself.

"Anyhow – " he moved towards the door – "Take it as a present from Jacqueline if you like. By the way, I hope she'll turn out to be blonde, like the two of us."

Auprès de ma blonde, qu'il fait bon, fait bon, fait bon...

"The two of you? But Lisa isn't blonde."

"No, I meant you and me. Her father and her aunt."

I just nodded, unable to speak, holding the tinkling box to my chest. My hair isn't blonde, only a fairish brown. But it was such a nice thought.

"Lunch!" sang out my mother's voice from downstairs.

***

Later, through the kitchen window as I dried the saucepans, I saw the three of them on the garden bench. Jacqueline was asleep, a soft bundle in the crook of Lisa's elbow, and Pascal had his arm round his wife. He bent to rub his cheek on the top of her head, and she turned to nuzzle his neck. With his other hand, he tucked some strands of hair behind her ear, then caressed Jacqueline's sleeping head.

I looked away quickly, painfully. It seemed almost indecent to be seeing such happiness, intimate and self-contained. They were all right, the three of them. They had created their own little world, and Jacqueline would be safe in it.

***

Now that they were gone, it was so quiet. At night the house sank into the soft silence of quiet roads and well-kept gardens. In the grey dawn, only birdsong broke in on my sleep. The dogs seemed disconsolate, lying flat with their noses between their paws or panting and whining restlessly. I decided to go for a walk, but I didn't take them with me. I wanted to be alone for a while and to collect my thoughts. Their doleful faces watched me through the bars of the front gate as I walked down the road. It was a warm, overcast day. There had been a shower in the night, and the air was heavy with clouds of gnats and the rich scent of damp earth and leaves.

Tonight my mother was having a bridge party. People whom I thought of as her expensive friends were coming round, and all morning she had been baking little vol-au-vents. I would never have the patience to make puff pastry. At first I had helped her in the kitchen, and we had worked quite companionably, talking about Jacqueline, Pascal and Lisa. She likes us to be there together, mother and daughter in the kitchen. But gradually I could sense her growing edgy as she eyed me doing things differently from the way she would have done them, and eventually I left before she could shoo me out.

That was all right. I knew she loved me as her daughter, but it was better if we didn't spend too much time in close proximity. We didn't have a great deal in common – but then, why should we? We were different people.

To be frank, I was rather tired of talking about babies. I missed Jacqueline, of course, but it was nice to have some peace. I crossed the road and turned right at the pillar box, walking along the side of the recreation ground, over the railway bridge, and heading for the centre of the town.

I hadn't realized before what it meant to have someone so utterly helpless and utterly egocentric, totally dependent on you. It was terrifying, in fact. I missed her little face, and I would be happy to see her again at Christmas. But I didn't wish that she was mine. Wherever would I have kept a pram? Or a pushchair? And how could I afford to buy all those things? And how could I manage to work if I was woken up every night by a baby screaming and bawling? I supposed I wasn't ready for that kind of responsibility – or that kind of sacrifice.

Hell, I hadn't lived yet! There were other things that I wanted to do first. Like what? I asked myself.

In the high street I looked to see how many shops had changed hands since I had last been there. The names and the ground-floor frontages were different, but the upper storeys with their worn brickwork and sash windows had been the same since my childhood and had probably been the same for a century or two. The shops below were becoming more and more quaint and folksy, selling pot-pourri and tea-cosies, home-made fudge and reproduction Victoriana. Mild-looking people were doing their shopping. They looked so neutral, dressed in shades of pastel and beige, their pudgy faces pleasant and dull, without a trace of passion or oddity or flamboyance. They looked so English. And how unattractive the men were, I thought. Spindly and nervous, with thin necks and thick glasses, or loutish and uncouth with greasy hair, their beer bellies spilling over the tops of their jeans. There was no one who looked remotely like Olivier, for instance. I realized that I was comparing him quite objectively with the men in the street, as if holding him at a distance. I could visualize his broad shoulders, his unruly hair and fierce level eyebrows, his long legs and quick movements – and yet I no longer felt a pang when I thought of him. What he had was vitality. Not unlike my mother, in a way.

I remembered him at the café table – his face as he told me that what he really wanted was to have a child. Surprising that he should feel like that. I had thought that men were concerned above all to keep their freedom and independence, not to become fathers, burdened with responsibilities.

Yet Pascal had done it. And now he seemed a different person, no longer such a loud-mouthed show-off. It was quite amazing that he had given me that musical box, horrible though it was. I couldn't get over it. And after all these years he had actually apologized for breaking the old one. I couldn't remember him apologizing for anything, ever. And he had told me that I was blonde! Maybe my little brother was growing up. He was trying to repair the past. But I had grown up, too, surely, and I didn't want a musical box now. How, I thought ironically, would I have felt if he had given me a doll? He had changed, but perhaps I had changed, too, and was seeing him differently.

And how might fatherhood change Olivier, I wondered. I paused, staring unseeingly into the window of a bookshop. I would never know. Even if he and Rose had once been lovers, I was sure that she didn't want to be his wife, or anyone's mother. She had enough to cope with.

The thought gave me no satisfaction.

The books on display were all about gardening and cookery and do-it-yourself, apart from a few romantic novels and biographies of minor royalty. The people in this town read that sort of thing. They ate their breakfast cereal, they mowed the lawns in their gnome-bedecked gardens, they did the crossword in the paper, they thumbed through charity catalogues, they watched television soaps in the evenings, and, retiring early after a hot nightcap, they laid their blameless heads on their floral printed pillows. I had wanted to come back here, to the comfort of home, but if I had to live here forever I would die of boredom.

Walking faster, I moved on in the direction of my old secondary school. All these streets held memories. And this was where it had all begun. There was the sycamore tree into which Brian Roberts had thrown my school bag when I was thirteen, and it had caught on a branch and hung there, to my intense dismay, until David Grey had heroically climbed up and rescued it.

Ahead of me a young couple moved closer together, and in an easy, natural movement he put his arm around her shoulders and her arm went around his waist. My throat felt tight. Olivier and I had walked like that a few times. But was it really Olivier that I wanted, or was it just that physical closeness, that warmth and ease with a man? It was not for me. Whenever I thought I had found it, it was not for me. She lifted her face to him and he bent to kiss her, as they walked through the dappled light and shadow of the lime trees lining the approach to the school.

Through the railings and at the far side of an expanse of grey playground it loomed, Victorian brick, with sightless windows and locked doors, closed for the holidays. I picked at a flake of rust on the railings. Here, for four whole years, I had been desperately in love with him. David ... I could still remember that anguished longing, those sudden upwellings of hope if he spoke to me, those long hours of despair when he ignored me, or was not around or, worse still, that time when he had seemed interested in Sally Barwell. David, quiet and brilliant at maths, with his clean-cut, perfectly regular features. He had won his scholarship to Cambridge, and I – I had merely left school. God, it might have been yesterday.

It had all begun with that school bag incident. I thought he had done it out of gallantry to me, but most probably, now that I looked back, he had climbed that tree to impress Brian Roberts. At any rate, he had shown no particular interest in me after that, while I had eaten my heart out, gazing after him from afar, and even composing one of my first songs for him. The Quiet Boy. How did it go? I hummed under my breath, recalling it in snatches. It wasn't so bad, after all. Maybe I could do something with it. I would have to work out a proper guitar accompaniment and an arrangement.

A few leaves and scraps of paper rose and blew in a circle in the corner of the playground. All the pupils were far away, living out their own private dramas, having holiday romances, perhaps. The sixth-formers felt altogether grown up, but to me they now seemed young. So much intensity, so much agonizing. With a slight shock, I realized that my short-lived affair with Olivier seemed lightweight beside those years of unrequited yearning for David. That had been real pain. I had let it flood me, take me over. It had filled the universe, and yet he had never wanted me – whereas with Olivier, if I thought about it, I had had a brief period of happiness, and a lot of pleasure. OK, so he had dropped me. I had smashed the lamp. But I wasn't destroyed. I was still here.

As I stood there, it was as if the world came into focus around me. I felt myself becoming clearly defined and self-contained. Those oceans of emotion that had swept uncontrollably outwards towards David, towards Olivier, were now gathered back into myself, held in check, my own. I had frontiers and could choose whether or not to cross them.

I wasn't just Olivier's lover: I was a singer. I was also an aunt, wasn't I? To hell with it – I was my own person, and I would be what I chose to be. There was no point in feeling angry and bitter about Olivier. As long as I felt like that, I was letting him control me. "Who angers me, controls me..." I thumped the railings with a dull sound, and a shower of rust fell on to the low brick wall. Those schooldays were long gone, and today's pupils had never heard of David, or me, or any of us. All gone. All in the past.

Beyond the school I wandered on, up the avenue into the posh part of the town, where the roads were wide and quiet and the large old houses were surrounded by spacious lawns and mature trees. I had known one girl, Gillian, who had lived in this area, but I didn't know what had become of her. All my old class mates had dispersed, in fact – and where was David now? I wondered how I would feel if I suddenly came face to face with him, turning a corner between a privet hedge and a lamppost. Perhaps I would feel quite neutral. I had moved on. I didn't belong here any more.

How smooth the lawns were. Ours had daisies and clover and even the odd dandelion growing in it, but these swards were like green velvet. Blackbirds, no respecters of private property, were busy on the grass, running and pausing, running and pausing, suddenly stabbing the ground with their yellow beaks and gobbling some invisible grub attracted to the surface by the recent rain. They looked sleek and fit. Over on the far edge of the lawn was a song thrush, the bird you never see in Paris, hitting a snail against a stone. There were so many birds in all the gardens. They were happy here, I thought. England might have its boring side, but at least it wasn't the custom for ordinary Englishmen to go into the countryside every autumn and shoot anything that moved. Only next month, the hunting season would begin in France, and doubtless old Bertrand and his cronies would be driving off in their van, bent on killing wild creatures. The woods would be loud with gunfire.

From a tree above my head came a series of plaintive whistling cries, and several birds seemed to be moving in the foliage, but I couldn't see them. I craned my neck. Before knowing Rose, I would probably have paid no attention to them. Rose would have recognized their call. If Rose had been here, they might have flown down and fluttered around her head and shoulders in an airy ballet of flitting wings. Might Rose be happy in England? Suddenly I missed her almost painfully. I missed our long talks and our companionable quilting sessions. I missed the spicy smell of her flat and the rich colours of her patchwork. Sometimes we were serious, almost philosophical, and other times we had utterly zany conversations that ended in gusts of laughter. Other times, again, we sat in silence, and neither of us felt obliged to keep the conversation going. Sometimes I would hum, as I worked on my latest song, but she never minded; yet Adrien had found my humming intensely irritating. When I thought of her playing the piano, and how we had sung together, our voices harmonizing…

From the open french windows of the grand house came pouring a sudden huge wave of classical music. I recognized it. It was Jessye Norman singing Purcell. When I am laid in earth, sang the full voice, flooding out through the frothing clematis and across the lawn. May my wrongs create No trouble, no trouble in thy breast. I stood, transfixed, the street and the gardens blurred, everything around me melting into the singing. Remember me, remember me, but ah! Forget my fate. All the strength and passion of the singer were in her tremendous voice. I stood shaken, the waves of it going through me. Remember me, but ah! Forget my fate. I could see Rose's face in my mind's eye, white like a pale flame against the gathering storm and approaching nightfall, a lonely figure. She didn't know where I was. I had left her alone to contend with Bertrand – and with who knew what other hostility? That frightening man in the white mask, trying to get at her. I felt that people were against her, talking about her behind her back like the mutter of distant thunder. I should have told her where I was going and when I was coming back. What kind of a friend was I? Remember me … Voice uplifted against the impending blackness, the singer implored the one who had abandoned not to condemn her to everlasting oblivion.

The music ended as abruptly as it had begun, and again I could hear the plaintive cries of the birds in the tree, and the engine of a single passing car. I saw a flash of olive green overhead. Could they be greenfinches up there? Rose would have known. A blackbird flew with a chattering shriek into the shrubbery.

Still buoyed up by the power of the music, I turned and began walking back in the direction of my parents' house. Once I would have called it home, but now it was my parents' house. Home for me was Paris, my sparsely furnished flat, shuttered and collecting dust, waiting for my return. I wondered if my plants had survived with the self-watering system I had rigged up. In my flat was my guitar, waiting for me to tune it and play it. My voice was nothing like Jessye Norman's, and my style of music was entirely different. But I wanted to sing. I wanted to get back to my songs and change certain passages, and I wanted to work on that strange wordless lament that had come to me the night of the power cut. It was there, raw material, waiting for me to shape it. I had to do something with it. And Topaz was there, with Madame Pereira. Perhaps he was missing me. I would be glad of his little yellow presence again.

Above all, I wanted to see Rose, urgently. There had been tension between us, and misunderstanding. Helping somebody didn't mean blundering in, taking over their problems and changing them. I couldn't do that, anyway. My father was right, I abruptly realized. I should offer her my friendship and let her be. I must not let Olivier come between us. I had done that already, and I had been wrong. When I had been unhappy, I had gone to see her nearly every day, wanting to talk and knowing that she would listen. Then, when I had been so deliriously happy with Olivier, I hadn't bothered to see her at all. And yet Olivier was a man who didn't give a toss about me and had just been having a good time. Why had I let him take up all the space in my life? What about friendship? With remorse, I remembered that I hadn't even said goodbye to Rose.

I knew what I wanted. I wanted to get back to Paris, and sing again, and straighten everything out. Olivier could go and jump in the lake. Go and fly a kite. Aller se faire cuire un oeuf. Aller se faire foutre. I tried out various – increasingly vulgar – expressions in both languages.

I wanted to go home.

♪

240

– TWELVE –

I panted up the steps from the metro, the strap of my luggage cutting into my hand. The leaves of the plane trees hung limp and dusty in the still air, and I was sweating, although it was past ten o'clock at night. The ferry had been delayed, I had missed the first train, and then the metro had stopped for ages in a tunnel. During the unexplained stop, a woman with bare blotched legs and bushy grey hair had delivered a long monologue from the other end of the carriage, vehement and unintelligible apart from the swear-words. People of all physical types, white, black and copper-coloured, in all styles of dress, robes, T-shirts, headscarves, shorts, baseball caps – all stared into space or consulted their mobiles.

Outside the supermarket a bearded homeless clochard had bedded down for the night, with newspapers and a greasy rug and half a bottle of red wine. A group of people, one of them wearing scarlet trousers and a huge black hat, burst out of the café where I had first gone for a drink with Olivier, talking and laughing loudly and lighting up their Gitanes. Since it was August, there was much less traffic, but as I was about to cross the street a car hurtled out of the distance and jumped the lights, its horn blaring, so that I stepped back hastily and trod in some dog shit.

I was well and truly back in Paris, and England seemed remote.

My letter box was jammed full of junk mail. Curse it, I should have asked Madame Pereira to keep all my mail for me, but I had forgotten, so preoccupied had I been with other matters, and so anxious to get away. It was too late to bother her now, but with luck Topaz was all right, and I would collect him in the morning. Now all I wanted was to take off these clothes, have a cold shower and go to bed.

My plants were alive, though drooping and parched, but the flat smelt like a compost heap, and I realized with dismay that I had also forgotten to empty the rubbish bin. Having crammed the full bin-liner down the chute, I flung open all the windows, and stood for a moment looking out. Across the street, most of the windows were shuttered and no lights were on. Either people were asleep, or else they had gone on their annual holidays. Rose's windows were not shuttered – she never closed her shutters – but they were dark. And Bertrand's windows below were unshuttered and dark, too, the glass sending back crooked watery reflections. Nobody seemed to be stirring. On the roof, in hunched profile beside the silhouettes of the television aerial and the chimney, I could see the black shape of a crow against the deep blue sky, with one very bright star hanging high above. Was that the faithful Jacques, I wondered? He did not move.

"Bright star,"– the words, in my father's voice, unfolded in my mind – "Would I were steadfast as thou art."

Rose must have thought me strange and volatile, disappearing like that without a word. It was too late to disturb her tonight, but tomorrow morning I would go over there and we would talk and get back to where we had been before Olivier screwed things up. I was her friend, and I would be steadfast.

I riffled through my mail and found my phone bill, but there was no word from Olivier, nor were there any messages on the answering machine. Why should there have been? I thought again of the way I had hurled the lamp at him. I didn't even know his address in Perpignan, if that's where he still was. I switched on the computer and waited while it booted up.

Throughout my stay in England, I had been offline. My parents' house was a low-tech space, and there had seemed no point in checking my email or going on to the social network. For me, it had been a time out of time, a period becalmed, when nothing was happening. Now, though, I was going to make a fresh start. The computer hummed and beeped. My inbox was sure to be full of spam.

Sure enough, there were more than 300 messages. Viagra, cheapest insurance deals, Do you need cash? Zorinda manager, Customer survey, Reductions on T-shirts, Your new BMW is waiting… Wait a minute: Zorinda the singer? Was she due to give a concert in Paris? I had thought she was in Germany. Anyway, the tickets would be all sold out by now. I clicked on "Select all", and the cursor hovered over the "Delete" button. I was tired, and thought longingly of a shower and bed. Idly, I scrolled down the page again. Had the message really said "manager"? I clicked on it.

For the next few minutes, I sat motionless, reading and re-reading the message. Somebody claiming to be Zorinda's manager was anxious to contact me because she, Zorinda, had heard my song "Wings" online and would like to record it and possibly sing it at her Paris concert scheduled for December. Or so it said. Could it be genuine?

I stood up and went into the kitchen for a glass of water. Across the street, all was still and silent. As I gulped the water, I told myself that this must be a hoax. Returning to the computer, I checked the Hoax website, but there was nothing about Zorinda. Then I went to Zorinda's own website, with its photographs and clips of her singing passionately into a microphone, wearing a range of flamboyant get-ups. I searched for the name of her manager, and there it was, the same name: Adam Leblanc.

It must be true! I wanted to shout and yell. Where was my guitar? I wanted to begin playing "Wings" immediately. Wait a minute, though. It could still be some kind of elaborate joke. I would have to check that it was an authentic message. Anyway, I realized that I couldn't start playing music at that time of night. Everything would have to wait until tomorrow.

Tomorrow I would phone the number that Adam Leblanc – if it were really he – had left, and above all, tomorrow I would go and see Rose. What a piece of news to give her! If it was true, I knew she would be excited for me. Hadn't she always told me that I had talent?

And maybe, I thought, as I soaped myself under the shower, just maybe my life would now start to change and open out.

Dreams were within reach. Anything was possible.

**

I awoke with a jerk from a dreamless sleep. Something strange was happening. Moving lights were reflected on the ceiling, I could hear shouts in the street, and there was an odd smell. The refuse collectors must have changed their schedule. Normally they came through this street in the evening, with the thud of bins and the vibrating lorry digesting the day's rubbish. Not properly awake, I fumbled for my watch. Twenty past two. Then deafeningly, right outside my window it seemed, came the two-tone blare of a siren.

I was out of bed and at the window.

There was a confused mass of vehicles and hurrying figures in the street below, and blue and orange lights flashing monotonously. Had there been an accident? A car's horn hooted from the end of the street, and another siren blared, farther off. Then I realized what the smell was. Smoke was pouring from the windows opposite. Rose's windows.

The building was on fire.

I don't know how I flung myself into my clothes and downstairs, but I found myself racing out of the main door of my building and across the narrow strip of garden to where dark-clad figures, some of them wearing helmets, were moving around the fire engine, shouting orders to one another and very slowly unreeling a hose.

I dashed out of the gate, making for the door of Rose's building, which stood wide open. I could see shadowy figures moving inside the doorway.

A fireman barred my way.

"Where are you going?"

"My friend! My friend lives in that building! It's her flat that's burning!"

I tried to push past him, but he forced me back, saying something that I couldn't hear because another police car came screaming up the street at that moment. I could just see his angry, ill-shaven face mouthing something at me in the alternating blue and orange light. I struggled with him, and he bellowed in my ear: "We're evacuating the residents. Keep out of the way."

"Have you got her out? Madame Martin? Is she out?"

But he was not listening, already turning back to join the firefighters. I made another attempt to dart across the street, but two policemen bore down on me, and at the same time somebody grabbed me from behind.

I turned, furiously, and found myself wrestling with Francisco, who was wearing a tracksuit. He was surprisingly strong for his age.

"Let me go!"

"Meess! Meess! Please stand back." How many times had I told him that it was not correct to address anyone as Miss? "It's dangerous. You'll be in the way."

"Rose – Madame Martin. Have they got her out?" I demanded.

"They're evacuating the people now."

"But have you seen her?" I could have slapped his face.

"No, I haven't seen your Madame Martin, but I expect she's there in that crowd. They've been getting all the people out by the main door."

There was a huddle of people in the street, some fully dressed, others in pyjamas or with a blanket flung over their shoulders, now being herded like refugees away from the building by the police, in straggling groups. I couldn't see Rose's tall figure among them, but the light from the streetlamps was not bright enough. She must be there – she must be.

"One guy panicked and jumped out of the window. I expect he's smashed his legs to bits," said Francisco with relish. "The ambulance just arrived."

There was a white flash over to our right. Somebody seemed to be taking photographs. How long ago had the fire started?

The street was so crowded with vehicles and people that I couldn't tell what was going on. There was an ambulance, a police car, a police van and the fire engine, all with revolving lights, and in the distance came the siren of yet another fire engine, getting louder and louder. Why were they being so slow with the hose? I could see it, dark red and flattened, only partly uncoiled even now. The building would burn to the ground before they were ready. I was reminded for a brief second of my mother's recent struggles in the garden. Sapeurs Pompiers de Paris, I read on the side of the fire engine.

I craned my neck back, trying to see if there was any sign of movement at Rose's windows. The only movement seemed to be the thick black smoke billowing out of them, and at street level it was creating a light fog which was beginning to make my eyes smart. Francisco was still holding on to my wrists. I tugged ineffectually, whimpering with frustration. She might be suffocating in there.

The first group of firefighters had entered the building and were hauling the hose up the stairs. It was disappearing into the dark interior like a snake.

Those from the second engine seemed to have got themselves into position at last, and a powerful white jet of water shot up from their hose, but it was blasting a torrent of water on to the roof, which was not burning, while smoke continued to pour from the top floor windows.

"Lower down!" I yelled, but they couldn't hear me.

Then a movement caught my eye in the sixth floor window. The window opened. Francisco saw it, too.

"There's somebody still in there!" he said. "Eh – it's that old guy Bertrand. Eh! Oh!" he yelled at the firemen, but they couldn't hear him, either.

A sharp crack rang out. Something in the building must have snapped in the heat. Another crack, and one of the flashing blue lights went out. A great shout went up from somewhere: ATTENTION!

"Get down! He's got a gun!" shouted Francisco in my ear, and felled me to the ground behind the garden wall. Small mossy pebbles and blades of grass were within inches of my nose, and Francisco was practically lying on top of me. He smelt sweaty.

"Get off me." I jabbed him with my elbow and wriggled.

"OK, but keep still. Don't move. The guy's armed."

I struggled into a crouching position. This isn't happening, I thought. I'm having a nightmare. In a minute I'll wake up and everything will be normal. I blinked my eyes hard, several times, but I didn't wake up. My thigh muscles were aching.

The deafening hiss of the hose had stopped, though the sirens were still blaring. Crack! Another shot. I couldn't see what he was shooting at. I couldn't see anything, and didn't dare raise my head above the wall. The sky was thick with smoke.

"They've taken cover," muttered Francisco. "They'll just have to let it burn, or he'll shoot them all down, at this rate." Crack! A bullet crashed through the foliage of the plane tree above our heads. "The whole place will go up like a torch."

"Oh, shut up! Shut up, shut up, shut up!" I put my hands over my ears and shook my head violently from side to side, my eyes tight shut.

I felt his hand on my arm. "It'll be OK," he said, abashed. "They'll figure out what to do." We ducked as another shot rang out. There was a sound of breaking glass. Francisco edged his way up until he could just peer over the top of the wall.

"Oh, be careful," I agonized.

"Quick, he's reloading," said Francisco, yanking me to my feet. "Let's get out of here," he added in perfect American.

He dragged me back across the strip of lawn to the shelter of our building, where quite a crowd had gathered in the entrance, talking and exclaiming.

"What were you doing out there?" yelled Monsieur Pereira, grabbing him.

"Oh – don't – Never mind that now," said his wife agitatedly. Francisco's father was wearing his work trousers and a shirt wrongly buttoned, and his mother was clad in a full-length paisley dressing gown. Somewhere a child was crying hysterically.

"Monsieur Bertrand's shooting out of the window," I said, and my voice sounded strangled.

"Poor fellow, he's been pushed too far – he's cracked up," said Monsieur Pereira, his Portuguese accent more marked than usual.

"He's gone raving mad," I said. "They can't put out the fire while he's shooting. The fire! What about the fire?"

Residents of the building jostled around me, trying to see out without exposing themselves to danger, skulking behind the masonry of the entrance. In the street, there were no longer any figures running to and fro. In the porches opposite I could see vague shapes of people huddled, out of Bertrand's line of fire. The acrid smell of smoke was worse, prickling in my throat. But now there was not only smoke. In Rose's central window a yellow spurt of flame leapt up and fell back. Then more flames, crimson dancing forked shapes mixed with black smoke, and a horrible reddish glow brightened in the room behind. My nails were digging into my palms. Do something, do something, oh God, somebody please do something. I had to know if she was still in there. And even if she wasn't, all her belongings would be burning – her precious piano, her beautiful patchwork, finished and unfinished – her treasures and her livelihood. Everything she had.

Framed in his window, the pale figure of Bertrand seemed to be gesticulating. Then I saw him bring his gun to his shoulder and fire again.

"Why don't the police shoot him down?" I said. This violent thought should have shocked me, but it did not.

"I'll go and talk to him," said Monsieur Pereira.

"You can't!" His wife clutched at him. "You'll be killed! You mustn't!"

"Let go of me." He shrugged her off. "He knows me. He'll listen to me. I'll get the old fool to come down, or he'll be fried to a crisp in there."

"Don't go!" Small and plump, she tried to hold him back. On her pale face, the black mole stood out like an insect.

"For Christ's sake! I know what I'm doing."

"I'll come with you," said Francisco eagerly.

"You'll stay with your mother," he snapped, and he was out of the door, moving down the path at a low, crouching run, his bald head gleaming. He took shelter by the wall, then emerged again and scuttled crabwise into the shadow of the fire engine.

Madame Pereira had both hands pressed against her small, squirrel-like mouth.

"Quick," said Francisco. "Into the flat. We can see better from the kitchen." He hustled both of us ahead of him into the concierge's flat. I seemed temporarily to have become his protégée.

In the dark kitchen we peered around the edge of the window, from which we had a clear view of the street and the building opposite. There was now no sign of Francisco's father. His mother seemed to be praying, gabbling inaudibly behind her hands.

"Peep?" said a little voice.

"Oh, Topaz," I sobbed. I could make out the shape of his cage on top of the fridge. I could so easily have left him with Rose, and now he would be dead. Dead, like Rose? Was she dead? I think I was praying, too, although not in any language.

"Look," said Francisco. "Somebody's coming out of the building."

As we watched, a fireman appeared in the doorway, holding two children by the hand. They hesitated, then made a dash for it. Crack! I gasped as I saw the fireman double over, then straighten up holding his arm above the elbow. The two children flitted ahead of him like ghosts into the shadows, and I saw him run, staggering, to the porch of the next building.

"He shot him," said Francisco, awed.

"Oh, look, look." His mother was moaning.

From the entrance to the dry cleaner's, three figures were edging their way towards the burning building, spread-eagled against the wall. They were moving very slowly – Monsieur Pereira and two policemen. They seemed to be out of Bertrand's line of vision. One after the other they disappeared inside the dark doorway.

Above, the flames made a sinister thudding noise, and all three windows now glowed, a lurid red, mocking Rose's usual soft lamplight or candlelight.

"They'll creep up on him," said Francisco. "If he won't talk to Papa, they'll have to break the door down. He'll have barricaded himself in."

There was still an infernal din going on. Farther down the street, several car alarms were yodelling. There was a police cordon at the end of the street, and traffic was hooting on the boulevard. Even at dead of night, even in August, the traffic in Paris never stops. I glanced towards the boulevard, then looked again. A fight was going on. Three – no, two – figures were struggling. Then one of them made a swift and decisive movement which I recognized: it was a karate chop. The figure broke free and began to race up the middle of the street. A police whistle shrilled.

"Who's that crazy nutter? A decoy?" said Francisco.

Oh, no. Please, no. I recognized that running figure black against the reddish fog. Olivier.

The flames were curling out of the windows now, licking up over the guttering to the dull zinc of the pitched roof.

Bertrand seemed to be reloading again. Somebody was talking through a megaphone. The words were blurred. The message was repeated, and this time I heard them asking him to put down his gun.

Nearer and nearer ran Olivier. He seemed to be shouting something. He was making for the door of Rose's building.

I leaned right out of the kitchen window.

"Olivier!" I shrieked.

At that moment, we saw Bertrand take aim. Olivier had almost reached he doorway. He was never afraid of anything. A shot. Just one. And he fell.

He fell.

"... Mary, mother of God .... mmm ... pray for us sinners, now and at the hour of our death ... mmm ... At the hour of our death ..."

I could hardly hear Madame Pereira's voice above the roaring outside, shouts and yells, what sounded like more shots, and the great searing hiss of water again from the hose.

Somebody in the kitchen was screaming. I wished they would stop.

When I found I couldn't breathe any more, I realized that the screams had been my own.

"... now and at the hour of our death ... "

The walls, orange and flickering, swam around me.

*****

So – they say that nothing happens in Paris in August. You have to walk miles for a loaf of bread, because all the bakeries are closed, like most of the smaller shops. At work, the coffee machine had broken down, and some wit had taped a notice on it saying "Closed for the holidays". The metro is full of tourists in shorts and trainers, humping backpacks and unfolding maps and guidebooks. And if you want to buy a newspaper, it's more than likely that your local newsagent's will be closed. Mine was. A steel shutter, already daubed with graffiti, protected the whole of his shop frontage, and he himself was doubtless far away, enjoying the quiet countryside of the Dordogne.

I was walking home after my interview with the police. In a cluttered cubicle with frosted glass partitions which screened us from sight but did not keep out the sound of voices, telephones, drawers opening and closing and echoing footsteps, a plain-clothes officer had taken down my personal particulars in minute detail, typing directly on to an elderly computer. We had, as they say, a dialogue of the deaf. I wanted him to tell me about Rose, and he wanted me to tell him about her. What was her nationality? I had never thought to ask, and didn't consider it of prime importance to know which country a person came from originally. Her marital status? Her age? he wanted to know. Again, I had no idea. I thought she was quite young, but sometimes she seemed much older. Wearily, the policeman typed with two fingers. My questions – where was she? how could I contact her? did she need help? had any of her belongings been saved from the fire? – all met with a stone wall of bland and non-committal reassurances that did nothing to reassure me. I kept asking questions, insisting that the police must know at least something. Suddenly he became impatient and hustled me out.

My street was quiet, with fewer parked cars than usual. I couldn't bear to look at Rose's building. I turned my eyes away from the blackened top two storeys.

In the entrance to my building, a downstairs neighbour – an old lady with stick-thin legs, whose name I couldn't recall – was pulling junk mail and leaflets out of her letter box with little, irritable jerks, and throwing them into the waste-paper bin thoughtfully provided by Madame Pereira. Murmuring a vague bonjour, I glanced from habit into my own mailbox. There was nothing in it except a small card.

"Marabout," I read. "Medium. Divination. Return of affection. Removal of curses a speciality."

I tossed it into the bin.

Oh, no. The lift was out of order. I would have to walk up all those flights of stairs, and in August who could tell how long it might take them to repair it? I had reached the first floor when I heard Madame Pereira's door opening, and hesitated. I knew she was about to go on holiday. Should I go down and ask her if the lift would be repaired while she was away?

"Bonjour, Madame! Alors! Have you recovered from the events of the other night?" said the old lady's voice.

"Ah! Don't talk to me about that! Such a terrible business. I can't tell you how glad I am to be going down to the Ardèche. Tomorrow we're leaving."

"Your husband's quite a hero, I believe," said the voice ingratiatingly.

"He did what he could, poor man. He never was afraid of danger, never. Never! He would die to defend his family, I swear. Me, I was sick with fright."

"I should think so. And tell me, do you know if they ..."

I couldn't quite hear what they were saying, and leaned over the banisters. The women seemed to be muttering. Then Madame Pereira's voice came again, louder:

"No! Not she! Nothing but candles and oil lamps, you see, and all those piles of old rags lying around. A real fire hazard."

"And did the insurance ...?"

Somebody flushed a toilet behind one of the closed doors on the landing. I had hoped that the occupants were away. If anybody came out, I would look odd standing here on the landing. The noise of rushing water drowned out what the women were saying.

"They do say ... found a book all about witchcraft, all in English, lying on the table. Charred, of course ..."

"Mind you, I'm not saying ... pleasant enough, great charm, in fact ... something funny about the way she looked at you. My husband, he blames the whole thing on her. Says she drove poor Monsieur Bertrand out of his mind. Poor old man, he thought she'd put the evil eye on him. Of course, you can't be too careful, I say ..."

Mumble, mumble. The corners of the stairs were dusty. Madame Pereira apparently didn't clean this staircase very often.

"... that great black crow perched on the roof all day. I saw it in the morning, and I saw it again in the evening, from my window. And I said to myself, they do say that's the bird of death."

"Ah – that's not the least of it. I've seen her walking along the street, just outside here, and a great crow come flying down out of the sky and perch right on her shoulder. I've seen it with my own eyes. Put me in mind of that Hitchcock film, you know?"

"Ah. The bird of death, they say."

"Not that I'm superstitious, mind, but they do say ..."

Mumble, mumble. My hands were gripping the banister, the knuckles white and the metal digging into my palms. I forced my fingers to relax, turned, and continued my long climb upwards.

***

" – So in comes the fireman. Just burst in. Out! he said. You're all coming out, and he picked up my old mother as if she weighed no more than a puff of wind – and her with her weak heart – I tell you, I nearly had a heart attack myself. To tell the truth, I think she was rather taken with him. Handsome chap, he was. Oh, the firemen were wonderful, no doubt about that. So out we went and down the stairs – and the smoke! You could hardly see where you were putting your feet, and it caught in your throat and made your eyes water something shocking. I was terrified, I don't mind admitting it." She paused for breath, a plump woman bulging out of her floral dress.

The other customer in the dry cleaner's was a middle-aged man with a red, broken-veined nose and bristly jowls, who had just handed his ticket to the owner of the shop. The woman talking was lingering on her way out, her arms full of clothes wrapped in polythene. Rows of polythene-encased garments hung above our heads, and with the help of a long pole the owner reached down a pair of trousers.

"A bad business," said red nose. "And poor old Roger Bertrand being taken away. It seems he cracked up. Couldn't take any more. Pushed beyond the limit, you might say."

I waited. I wanted to collect my patchwork jacket that I had handed in to be cleaned before I left for England. Throughout the spring and early summer I had worn it nearly every day until it was grubby.

"Cracked is right," said bulging dress. "Shooting out the window like a maniac. But what do you mean, he was pushed? People are saying some very strange things."

"Ah, and I could tell you stranger," said red nose knowingly. "As a matter of fact, I was having a drink with poor old Bertrand only last week. I've known him for years, just to say hello to – play boules, have a beer, that kind of thing. Well he stood me a drink, and he was telling me – though I don't know that I ought to repeat it."

"Was it about his neighbour?" prompted bulging dress eagerly.

"I can tell you've heard something, too. Well, he told me," he said hastily, not to be forestalled, "that his upstairs neighbour was actually trying to drive him out of his mind. Deliberately. Like – by making a noise all the time, see? Tramping up and down on her bare floorboards, singing, playing music, talking out loud even when she was by herself. Never a minute's peace, he said, not since his wife died. And," he leaned forward conspiratorially, "there was the wailing and screeching, too. Sometimes at dead of night. Screeching like a banshee. Inhuman, he said it was." His eyes were round.

Bulging dress shuddered. "Well, I never heard any noises, if it's that Madame Martin you're talking about," she said robustly. "But I live on the third floor. All I know is that she always wished me good morning or good evening very politely if we passed on the stairs. Not like some I could name. She seemed normal enough to me."

"Madame Martin?" put in the owner in her warm contralto. "She was a good customer. She was always bringing in great bundles of quaint old clothes for cleaning, or sometimes just pieces of cloth. A very charming lady, I should say. Quiet, if anything. Very pleasant. A good customer."

"Ah, but quiet is just what she wasn't, or so old Roger told me. And a temper, too. Oh, a temper. One day he just wished her a good morning, or something, and she tried to push him down the stairs. How about that? If he hadn't had the quick reactions of a much younger man, he told me, he might have tumbled from top to bottom and killed himself."

"Oh? Really?" said bulging dress faintly.

"And another thing. Apparently she had some kind of machine up there – a computer, or something – causing all sorts of interference on his radio and his TV. He couldn't even listen to the news or watch the telly in peace any more. He said they made a noise like a pneumatic drill. No wonder he couldn't stand it."

"Do computers cause interference?" asked the owner. "My son – "

"Oh, really," protested bulging dress, "she can't have had a computer. People say she wouldn't even have electricity in her flat, let alone modern gadgets. If you ask me, Monsieur Bertrand was off his head. Drills? We've had road drills in the street for weeks. That's what he could hear. We could all hear them! It was enough to get on anyone's nerves, I grant you. But enough to drive them round the bend? Well, he was definitely round the bend. Oh, yes, he was far gone, he was."

"He seemed perfectly sane when he was talking to me," said red nose peevishly.

"Sane? Oh, no. With respect, you can't have seen him poking around in the dustbins recently. Poking around and muttering to himself. I never heard Madame Martin talking to herself, but he did – out loud, and not very nice things, either, what I heard. And fishing around in the dustbins! If that isn't disgusting – "

"Well, he told me – " said red nose.

"Always very quiet and polite. A sort of old-fashioned courtesy," said the shop owner, folding busily.

"Well, he told me," blared red nose, "And I wouldn't normally say this sort of thing in front of ladies – but it shows you what he was up against. He told me that she had put a curse on him. Unmanned him. Sort of – shrivelled him up, if you get my meaning."

"Oh, là, là," said bulging dress, giggling and starting to blush.

"What's this you're talking about?" asked the owner sharply. "Voodoo?"

"Call it what you like," said red nose darkly. "There have been some funny goings on, if you ask me. What did she get up to in the middle of the night? Why did she have so many candles around the place, I'd like to know? Just one candle is enough to set a building ablaze. No wonder a fire started. What's the world coming to, if we can't even have a bit of peace and safety in our own homes? Invasion, that's what I call it. Too many bloody foreigners coming in with their barbaric customs and rituals and that. She wasn't French, was she? You can't tell me she was French. Touch of the tarbrush there, old Bertrand reckoned."

The tarbrush. I thought of Rose's pale, almost translucent face.

"My mother," said the owner, "came from Haiti. And I don't care who knows it." Her brown eyes flashed. She folded a sheet of paper around the second pair of trousers and stapled it together viciously.

An awkward silence fell. Murmuring something about having shopping to do, bulging dress sidled out of the door.

"You're not closing this month, then? Not going on holiday at all?" asked red nose, trying to repair the damage.

"No," said the owner shortly. "Some of us can't afford holidays. Business is bad."

As I handed over my ticket after red nose's rather subdued departure with his trousers, she added, "That old so-and-so would probably tell me business is bad because all these dirty foreigners don't want to have their clothes cleaned." She was still bristling.

"People always have to find somebody to blame," I said, as she sorted through the rack of clothes behind her. "A scapegoat."

"What? Blame? Well, I blame the government. This recession... But it's just as well we hadn't closed for the holidays. What if we'd come back and found the place burned to the ground?"

"You must have known Madame Martin quite well?"

"Oh, not really. She was a regular customer, that I will say, and very polite, soft-spoken. But she was a bit – I wouldn't say it in front of that old soak, but she was a bit – different. I can't describe it, really, but it was the way she spoke and moved. You know the way some people are? She had presence, that's what I call it. I noticed it in the shop. People's eyes were – sort of – drawn to her."

I nodded. "Drawn, yes. But not in a bad way."

"Maybe not. But say, like, you're in a room and there's just one candle burning in it. People's eyes are drawn to it. To the flame. D'you know what I mean?"

I knew.

She handed me my jacket, and under the harsh strip lighting I glanced down through the polythene at Rose's tiny stitching. The patchwork pieces were like a rich landscape, a bird's-eye view of fields far below, each burgeoning with corn or pasture or fruit or delicate flowers.

"I only hope she wasn't practising voodoo," the dry cleaner went on. "There are powers in this world that you don't want to meddle with. You open a door just a crack, and in comes something much bigger than you expected, and you can't control it."

It was very quiet in the shop.

"You think she – opened a door? Let something in?"

"Ah, there now!" She lifted her hands in an averting gesture. "I'm not saying anything. I wouldn't want to be indiscreet. Everybody has their own problems, don't they?"

She became very busy sorting a basket of laundry, and I knew she would not say any more.

***

It was the end of the lunch hour, and Catherine was sitting at her desk reading one of the more sensationalist papers that I don't normally buy. She had read the horoscopes and the cartoons and was idly leafing through the news. "Man, 82, fathers triplets," she read out, and chortled. "Can you imagine going to bed with a man of 82?" Then, "Say, isn't this your street? There's a piece here about that fire. Look out! Mind my envelopes!" She retrieved the pile from the floor where they had scattered in a fan-shape when I lunged for the paper. I stood in the middle of the office, reading the article in the bottom right-hand corner of the page.

"THE LADY VANISHES. The residents of this modest Paris apartment building will need time to get over the shock. Not only were their lives and homes threatened by an unexplained fire in the middle of the night, but the event escalated into drama and near tragedy when an armed man barricaded himself into his flat on an upper floor and began shooting from his window at firefighters and police. Meanwhile the building blazed. It was some time before the police were able to persuade the man to give himself up, but not before he had shot one fireman in the arm and severely wounded a bystander. One resident panicked and jumped from an upper window, breaking both his legs. Why the shooting and the fire should have occurred simultaneously is a cause for speculation. The occupant of the flat which was totally gutted by fire, a Madame Rose Martin, has not been seen since that night, and her whereabouts are a mystery. It was initially feared that she might have been trapped inside, but the firemen found no trace of her. The gunman, who appears to have been in a mentally disturbed state, was arrested with severe burns to his face and hands. He was unavailable for comment."

The telephone shrilled and Catherine answered it. She put her hand over the receiver. "It's for you. It's Monsieur Chardonnier."

"Tell him I'm not in the office," I said urgently. Next to the article was a smudgy photograph of Bertrand with his gun, framed in the window.

"... some electrical fault in the building. Residents had complained of very poor TV and radio reception for a number of weeks before the fire, and it was thought that this might have been connected with recent roadworks in front of the building, but ErDF denies any possibility of interference. The roadworks themselves, in that very street, were recently the scene of a mysterious night attack on a local nurse by a man in a white mask, who pushed her into the deep trench. Odder still, there have been reports that such a man had been seen crawling out of the same trench, always at dead of night! Could workmen have unwittingly hit an entrance to the catacombs, where secret societies are known to hold illicit meetings? The mystery thickens. A resident had this to say: "I don't know where Madame Martin is, but there has been a strange atmosphere in this building ever since she moved in." Whereupon her five-year-old daughter, bright as a button, who had been carried downstairs in a blanket on the night of the fire, piped up: "I saw her! She was flying through the sky." – and the little girl held out her arms like a bird's wings. Children, as we know, have vivid imaginations. But the fact remains that Madame Martin has vanished as surely as if she had indeed flown off the face of the earth. What caused the blaze? Why did her neighbour lose his mind? Who was the man in the white mask? Alas, these are some of the strange happenings of the month of August that are probably destined to remain forever unexplained."

The article was signed A.K.

I searched through the paper for the phone number of the editorial office. When I rang, it was engaged. I kept trying, and eventually got through to the switchboard. When I asked how I could contact A.K., who had written the article in question, I was put through to another extension, made the same inquiry again, and was transferred to yet another extension which did not answer the phone. I eventually got back to the switchboard, and was advised to try again later.

I tried again later. After three transfers, I was put through to a bored-sounding woman who said, talking against a lot of background noise, that the journalist I wanted was a Monsieur Klein, who was on an assignment. I should try again tomorrow.

I tried again the following day. After several fruitless attempts I finally spoke to Monsieur Klein, who denied all knowledge of the article. When I insisted, he eventually said that the author must have been a certain Monsieur Karsten. When I asked to be put through to a number where I could speak to Monsieur Karsten, I was told that he was a freelance journalist and that it was not the newspaper's policy to give private telephone numbers to members of the public. I asked if he might be reached at the office, and was told to try tomorrow at three.

I tried the next day at three. There was no reply. I tried again at three-thirty. I eventually spoke to a man who brusquely told me that Monsieur Karsten no longer worked for that newspaper, and hung up. I was left staring at the bleeping telephone. Trying the Internet, I found that there was no A. Karsten in the whole of the Paris area, or, if there was, then he must be ex-directory.

I rested my chin on my hands and looked across the office with unfocused eyes.

"I wish you would tell me why all this is so important to you," complained Catherine.

I shut the now crumpled article in a drawer of my desk.

The city was a maze of streets, a labyrinth of criss-crossing telephone wires, radio waves, fibre-optic cables. Nameless masked men slipped round corners, melted into doorways, did evil by stealth for inexplicable reasons, vanished. I couldn't loiter around the building in the hope of cross-examining a five-year-old child with a vivid imagination.

In my mind I could almost hear the doors shutting in my face, one after another.

– THIRTEEN –

The door of room 214 had a little window in it, but I could see nothing through it except the end of a regulation hospital bedstead. Further along the corridor, a man with a child carrying a huge bouquet of flowers disappeared into another room. I looked again at the varnished surface of the door, and knocked.

The room had two beds in it, one of them flat and unoccupied. In the other bed, nearest the window, lay Olivier.

He was lying back against the raised pillows, wearing a blue pyjama jacket that I had never seen before. It looked old-fashioned, and for a fraction of a second I wondered whether it belonged to him or whether the hospital had supplied it. When we were together we had always slept naked. His face was pale, but his eyes locked with mine in the same intense gaze as always. I saw that his wrist was attached to a drip. Worse, a tube was sticking out of his chest, between the buttons of his pyjama jacket; it led down to some kind of container under the bed, which was making a bubbling sound. But he was alive.

"I didn't expect you to come," he said, with an awkward half smile, as I bent to kiss him on both cheeks as if he were family or an old friend. He didn't smell the same. He smelt of hospitals and medication. I stepped back and looked at him, tethered by tubes like a trapped animal.

"How are you feeling?" I asked, taking some sports magazines out of my bag.

"Better. I'll soon be out of here." He saw me eying the tube in his chest. "Another couple of days and they'll take this thing out. It's to prevent the lung from collapsing."

"Did the bullet – ?"

"It grazed my lung. A lucky escape, wasn't it?" Another half smile. "It should have healed a lot faster, but I developed an infection and my temperature shot up, so they put me on antibiotics." He tilted his head towards the drip. "I'll have a scar, of course." I thought I detected a faint note of satisfaction.

"But are you in any pain?"

"Not now. Just uncomfortable. And bored. Bored out of my mind!"

"Any visitors?" I had noticed a box of pâtes de fruits and another sports magazine on his locker.

"Oh, yes. A couple of guys from the karate class." His voice tailed off, and his eyes bored into my face. "Stella," he said. "Tell me. Tell me about Rose."

I stepped over to the tall window and looked out across a corner of sunlit lawn to the dingy brick wall of another wing of the hospital. It had been built in the nineteenth century and resembled a prison.

"I don't know what to tell you," I said.

"Don't fool around," his voice snapped. "Is she – come on – is she alive?"

I turned to face him.

"I don't know," I said.

"What do you mean, you don't know? You must know!"

"I can't be certain," I said. "The police won't tell me anything because I'm not her next of kin. I don't think she's dead. I think ... they just didn't find her. They would have found her – found her body, I mean – in the flat, if she had died in the fire."

"What about her flat, then? No clues there? Nothing?" He glared.

"Everything was destroyed by the fire and the water. It was all black and ruined, and the place stank of burning. They threw everything out and loaded it into great skips in the street. All her furniture, her clothes, bits of patchwork all horribly black and – " I broke off. The window of this room and the windows in the other wing had bars. Almost at the edge of my field of vision, sunlight glowed scarlet on a bed of

263

geraniums. "She's gone," I said. "Vanished. But I can't help feeling she would have got in touch with me if ..."

"If?"

I said nothing.

He let out his breath in a long sigh.

"But why would she have just disappeared?" I asked. "Could she have gone to her family? You've known her a long time. Do you know where her family is?"

"No. I don't even know if she has any relatives."

"I think she mentioned her father, once," I said. "But I don't think they were close."

We looked at each other questioningly.

"What about her piano pupils?" he asked.

"I only saw one or two of them, and I don't know where they live. Or what their names are. Don't you know any of her other friends? What about the people who gave her the scraps for her patchwork?"

"Couldn't tell you who they are. She never mentioned anyone's name, apart from yours. She was always so secretive." He shifted restlessly.

"Was she?" I said. "Why didn't we ask her about herself? About her life? I feel I know almost nothing about Rose."

"Somebody must know. What about the neighbours?" he said.

"Everybody's talking, but I don't think anyone really knows anything. Talk, talk, talk, yap, yap, yap. That's all they do. It's just gossip and speculation. They say she was weird, and stuff like that. They say she used to make a lot of noise in the middle of the night. They say her flat was a fire hazard, and no wonder it caught fire with candles and oil lamps everywhere – "

"Candles, my arse! It was fucking Bertrand who set fire to the place! He was trying to kill her, and he damn near killed me. It's as obvious as – "

"I tried to talk to the police about Bertrand, but they warned me about making defamatory accusations without proof. I told them about the threatening letter, but of course I couldn't produce it. Rose had it."

"The police are as thick as planks. Where the hell is Bertrand, anyway? Is he dead?"

"I think he's in hospital – maybe in a psychiatric ward. But I can't be certain. I can't be certain of anything – that's what's so awful."

A thought struck me with sudden horror. "You don't think he did kill her, do you? Could he have murdered her and hidden her body somewhere before he set the place on fire?"

"No," said Olivier after a long moment. "I don't believe that. He might have killed her, given a chance, but he wouldn't have been able to hide the evidence. How do you get rid of a dead body in the middle of Paris?"

Throw it into the Seine? I thought. No, that would have been too conspicuous, and corpses are fished out of the Seine. I clung to the thought that he couldn't have killed her, although at the back of my mind I knew that he was quite strong enough to carry a dead weight. And the fact that no body had been found proved nothing. Where do birds go to die? What happens to their bodies? They live lightly on the earth, but they are not immortal.

"Ah, I should have known the man was a lunatic," groaned Olivier. "I knew he was a fool, but I should have known he was a dangerous maniac. I should have protected her. We both should have done more to protect her."

"Both! But when I warned you she was in danger, you said it was all nonsense. You just wouldn't – " The blood rushed to my face.

"I know, I know. Shut up! Do you think I don't curse myself?" His face was grim and haggard. There was a silence, and the container on the floor bubbled softly. I thought to myself that he had nearly died for Rose. For Rose – or else to prove something.

"Anyhow," he said, "she must be somewhere. Forty thousand people disappear in France every year. They can't all be dead."

Oh, I thought, so that was all right, then. Rose was reduced to one of Olivier's statistics. I had been on the brink of telling him about the newspaper article, but I knew he would only scoff.

"I should have thought," I said bitterly, " that since the two of you were so very close, you would have some idea of where she might be now."

Olivier closed his eyes as if he were very tired. An expanse of shiny floor, like an ocean, separated his bed from the window where I stood. I looked at his face on the pillow, remembering his sleeping face as I had lain beside him in my bed. This was the man I had held naked in my arms, the man who had made me so furiously angry, the man for whom I had shed tears. We were utterly separate now and couldn't reach out to each other.

"There's something I ought to explain," he said quietly, opening his eyes and looking across at me with a dull gaze. "I told you I loved Rose, and it's true, I love her. I think I'll always love her. I can't help it."

The knife twisting in the wound again. Why did he have to do this? I said nothing.

"But I couldn't reach her."

"What do you mean?"

"I let you think we were lovers. We should have been lovers. But she – wouldn't. She said it was too dangerous. She said she caused harm. I only ever kissed her – once."

"Is that all?" My voice was husky.

"Yes." His fingers clutched the sheet, hard, then went limp. "It was enough."

The indelible memory of that kiss seared itself into the silence that hung between us. Voices passed in the corridor and faded. A car's horn honked distantly in the heat of the afternoon.

I cleared my throat. "Why did she say it was dangerous?"

"Oh, I don't know. I think that was one of Rose's red herrings. She's the most elusive person I've ever known. Then there was that stuff about her cousin."

"Her cousin? What stuff?"

"That guy in the white mask. Didn't she tell you?"

She had told me nothing. What was this?

266

"I finally got it out of her, that he was her cousin, that he had some kind of a grudge against her and he tracked her down. She told me – but it was all fantastical."

"What did she tell you? Olivier?"

"Oh, that he had burned for her, and that he had ... *been* burned, and was disfigured and had to wear a mask ... So she said we would destroy each other, or at any rate she would destroy me. It made no sense."

So much fire, I thought. Burning, burning. The flames leapt in my memory.

"She was totally adamant," said Olivier. "Stubborn. She said we could be friends but that was all. I couldn't sleep any more. I used to walk the streets at night, walk past and look up at her windows, just to be near her. It was – "

"So you turned to me as a substitute, right?" My voice was harsh.

He looked embarrassed. "I wouldn't put it quite like that. You're a very attractive girl, Stella. And you seemed interested in me. Any man would have reacted the way I did." He lifted the hand that was not attached to the drip. "And it wasn't so bad, was it? We had good sex together, didn't we?"

I didn't move. "I trusted you," I said. "I didn't know what was going on. I confided in you. And then you – " I swallowed. "You threw my abortion in my face."

He looked away awkwardly. "I'm sorry," he said. "I guess I ought not to have said what I did. But it touched a raw nerve. When all I wanted was to give Rose the child she needed so much – for her to be the mother of my children – and yet she wouldn't have me. Denying herself and me! And then, after Isabelle – " He broke off.

"Your old girlfriend? What about her?"

"I seem to be telling you the story of my life," he grimaced. "Well, she – to cut a long story short, when I was with Isabelle, she found she was pregnant. And she got rid of it. Without consulting me. Without telling me anything about it until it was all over. And it was my child. She killed my child! I can't forget that. I can't forgive her."

I flinched. "But in my case, it wasn't your child. If you can even call a cluster of cells a child. I didn't even know you at the time. And I wasn't obliged to tell you about it. I bloody well wished I hadn't, afterwards."

"I know," he said. "I overreacted. I ought not to have yelled at you. I'm just trying to explain why, but I'm sorry. There. I'm sorry. What else can I say?"

There was no need to say anything else. It didn't matter now, anyway.

"What makes you think Rose needed a child?"

"Well, it was obvious – the way she mothered those damn birds. And the way she threw herself into all that needlework, slaving at it day and night. She needed something to lavish her attention on. She needed a baby. Oh, she may have said she didn't, but unconsciously she did. She was so creative all the time – and the supreme act of creation is to create another life, you have to admit."

Did I have to admit any such thing? To create another person elbowing their way on to the metro, another polluter, another consumer of the earth's resources, another person unemployed and on the dole? Maybe. Maybe not.

"I think her patchwork was worth creating in its own right," I said. "Her quilts were works of art." In my mind's eye I could see her very clearly, stitching at her table with the little half-moon, gold-rimmed glasses on her nose. "She never finished that beautiful Amish quilt, the Lone Star one. I saw it in the skip, all burned and ruined." It had been half buried under part of her broken piano. She had taken nothing with her, clung to no treasures, relinquished everything. But even if the piano was destroyed, she still had her ability to play, wherever she was. "And her music – what about her piano-playing? Isn't that creative?"

"I know, I know." Olivier had been making little impatient movements. "You don't have to convince me that she's an interesting person. She's the most fascinating person I've ever met. I fell under her spell the first time we ever talked. She's somebody that you can talk to for hours and not even notice the time."

"All right," I said, "but if you talked for hours, she must have told you something about herself. Did she say anything about her past? About where she lived before?"

"Well – no. Not really. I've told you, I think she likes to be mysterious. I guess that's part of her fascination. But she's a good listener. That's a rare quality. Most people just want to talk about themselves. But she really listens to what you tell her."

"That's true," I said heavily. Olivier, then, had talked to Rose for hours about himself, just as I had talked to her about myself. And now neither of us knew anything about her, or had any idea of where she might be. I could so easily have taken an interest in her, could have tried to see the world from her point of view. But I had just taken advantage of her and basked in her presence. I hadn't even looked at the titles of the books in her bookcases. I didn't know what subjects interested her or what languages she spoke. Nothing. And Olivier was just as bad. We couldn't fool ourselves that we had just wanted to be discreet. We were two monsters of egotism, utterly wrapped up in ourselves, when we should have been aware of her needs and her predicament and the dark threat rising about her like a pall of smoke as Bertrand gradually turned into a predator, not to mention the deranged man whose disfigured face was hidden by a mask. She was vulnerable, and we were supposed to be her friends, but we had failed her.

People had been against her. They couldn't accept what she was. They had hunted her down, driven her out.

"She's gone to ground," I said.

"What? Oh, she's hiding somewhere. I'm sure of it. She can't be dead, so she must be hiding. But I'll find her. Once I get out of this place, I'll track her down. I'll put adverts in all the regional newspapers. I'll search the Net. And I know a guy from Interpol – I'll ask his advice."

A pause. There seemed to be nothing much to say.

"When do you think you'll get out of here?"

"Any day now. I can't stand it much longer." He fidgeted. "I'll be going down to Perpignan to convalesce for a while. Look, I'll give you my address and phone number down there. If you hear anything at all from Rose, or anything about her, then let me know, OK? Have you got a pen?"

I rummaged in my bag and found a notebook and a stub of pencil. He grimaced. "There are fourteen billion pencils produced in the world every year. Can't you do better than this?" he grumbled as he wrote down his address in the same spiky handwriting that I had seen on his letter to Rose. "If you discover anything at all, get in touch, all right? It would be nice to hear from you, in any case," he added, after a fractional hesitation. "And try to track her down yourself. Think. Something may suddenly occur to you."

"Mmm," I said. There was no point in his telling me what to do. I knew I would not try to find her. If she had chosen to disappear, then that was her right. If she didn't want to see me, then it was not for me to force myself on her. I hadn't been there for her when she had needed me. I missed her dreadfully, but I would wait.

I would let her be.

Crockery clinked on a trolley coming nearer along the corridor, and a smell of soup reminiscent of school dinners wafted in. It was very early to be eating, but Olivier, a prisoner in his bed, had to keep hospital hours. I looked at him pityingly. He shifted his long legs under the sheet. Taking my hand, he squeezed it.

"We're still friends, aren't we, Stella?" he said. "You know I shan't forget you. I really appreciate you, you know that?"

I withdrew my hand. Friends? Appreciation? It was strange: I felt nothing, not a spark of desire, not a pang. I might have been relieved that he and Rose had not, after all, been lovers. But all I felt was a vague sadness. Where was my ability to suffer unrequited love, hopelessly faithful, year after year, longing for what I couldn't have? Something in me, it seemed, had burned out.

"I must be going," I said.

"And don't forget. If you hear – "

"I'm sorry about the lamp," I said, opening the door to the corridor. "Can I pay you for it?"

He looked at me blankly.

"What lamp?"

– FOURTEEN –

It's October now, and the leaves of the horse chestnuts in the park are a rusty brown. But it's still warm – so warm that the other Sunday afternoon I took my guitar out there and sat on a bench in a quiet corner, playing.

After visiting Olivier in hospital I threw myself into music, to the exclusion of everything else. I had never worked so hard or with such determination. It was as if I had moved on to another plane, and no doubts or distractions could hold me back now. As soon as I awoke in the morning I was aware of my guitar standing there, waiting, shining, calling to me. Since Rose had gone, all my attention was focused on it, drawn to it inexorably as to a source of light, and the songs came of their own accord.

I practised and refined my whole repertoire, and made quite a few changes to the catchy He's the man who, and to The Lights of the City, a very slow piece that I sing almost in a whisper. I kept trying out different kinds of phrasing until it came right. The lament without words, however, I left virtually unchanged, although I practised it. In fact, I went on playing until 2 a.m. on one occasion, and only realized how late it was when my downstairs neighbours rapped on their ceiling. My latest song is called Phoenix, and I think it's the best I've done. It has rising arpeggios that go up and up, with my voice chasing them, and it ends with a great crash of sound, like a sunburst – at least, that's how I think of it. Adam Leblanc hasn't heard it yet.

I phoned Monsieur Leblanc ("call me Adam"), and he really is Zorinda's manager. We met in the bar of one of the posher hotels. Slightly balding, with a bow tie, he was in Paris only briefly, and was flying back to Toulouse that evening to join Zorinda, who was on tour. We discussed a possible contract – but above all, he told me that Zorinda wanted to meet me. "She's very interested in your songs," he said. "She wants to hear you sing live. Then – possibly a duo, possibly a new arrangement, possibly a gig. You must leave it to her. She'll know immediately what she wants. And her new album is coming out next spring, of course."

I've said nothing about any of this in the office. Catherine will scarcely be able to believe it when she finds out.

There were birds in the park that Sunday: blackbirds on the lawns, sparrows pecking on the gravel paths, and pigeons, some of them hobbling on injured feet, lamed by civilization. The thin, sweet song of a hidden robin threaded its way from the shrubbery. But they paid no attention to me. They went about their own business. In the winter, I thought, I would buy some mixed birdseed and come here to feed them. Perhaps they would even grow used to me and feed from my hand again. But I would have to avoid that furious old lady, who seemed to think that they belonged to her. They belonged to nobody. Here they lived, so much smaller than us, so different from us, and yet so close to us. And either they accepted what we gave them, or they ignored us. Mostly they ignored us.

The swifts and swallows were gone, I noticed. Suddenly, with no warning, from one day to the next, they had simply vanished, leaving the sky silent and empty.

The sun was warm, warm and peaceful on my face as I closed my eyes and played the opening chords of Phoenix. Then I began to sing, softly at first and then louder as my voice bodied forth the images of the rare bird, crimson and shining gold, who soared upwards in joy, and burned in suffering, and was consumed and fell, and then – my voice softer again now, the guitar thrumming insistently – then rose again from the ashes, a pure, bright flame, higher and higher, higher and higher, up into the great arc of the sky, immortal.

When I had played the last notes, my face upturned to the sun, there came a burst of ragged applause. Startled, I opened my eyes. About a dozen people and a dog were standing in a semi-circle in front of the bench. How long had they been listening? I heard the chink of a coin. They thought I was a busker! But I wasn't about to pass a hat around. Embarrassed, I stood up and made a half bow, clutching my guitar awkwardly, and strode off.

"Good, isn't she?" I heard someone say behind me, and exulted inwardly. It was a start. Perhaps people would like what I composed. Perhaps, perhaps ...

As I left the park, I heard a crow cawing, with an autumnal sound that reminded me of elm trees and ploughed fields. I turned and squinted upwards against the sinking sun. At least four crows were silhouetted in the upper branches of a plane tree, whose pale green leaves were turning gold. "Kaa! Kaa! Kaa!" One of them nodded its head vigorously as it cawed. Could it possibly be Jacques? It didn't sound like his voice. But I couldn't tell. They still all looked alike to me because I didn't know them, couldn't speak their language, couldn't hope to come close to them as individuals. And yet I was sure they were individuals. No bird was exactly the same as another bird; no person could ever wholly replace another person.

I thought to myself that in the winter I would bring some butter to the park for Jacques. He loved butter so much. But somehow I doubted that he would come to me. The crows took off one after the other and flew over my head, their black pinions spread like fingers against the pale sky.

The man with the tenor saxophone was playing at his open window as I walked back up my street, the melancholy notes of Autumn Leaves floating down like smoke. Under my breath I sang in French the line about the sea washing away the footprints of lovers who have parted – and grinned sourly. This summer I hadn't walked by the sea at all, and certainly not with a lover. Could I, I wondered, work out an arrangement of that song which would make it sound less cheesy? It was too well known. How might a duo of guitar and tenor sax sound? The man at the window had his back to me and I couldn't see him properly. He wasn't wearing his hat today. He and I had lived in the same street for more than a year, but I knew no more about him than if he had lived on the moon.

That's how it is in the city.

The windows of Rose's old flat were boarded up, and so were Bertrand's. I knew that the staircase leading to the top two floors was sealed off. Bertrand's windows reminded me of pathetically blinded eyes. At first I couldn't bear to look at the scorched and smoke-blackened top of the building, and would avert my gaze, but gradually I forced myself to look up, and began to feel less anguish, only sadness, when I remembered how it used to be. For a long time her broken windows had stayed gaping open, dark and empty, and quite often I would see pigeons perching on the balustrade of the little balcony, peering hopefully in. But now that it was all boarded up, the pigeons didn't come any more.

My flat had sunk into quietness. Topaz was no longer singing these days. He had started to moult, and sat hunched on his perch, looking morose and saying nothing, except very occasionally "pee-eep" on a descending, disgruntled note. Next spring I might get a mate for him. It wasn't fair, after all, to deprive him of the company of his own kind.

I was even seeking other people's company myself. Catherine from the office was sunny-tempered, and kept asking me for advice that I couldn't give, about a suave new man whom she had met – a cologne-and-cufflinks type who would probably have hit it off with Adrien. About Olivier I had told her nothing at all, and about the fire very little. Once she asked me whether my friend was still making those nice patchwork jackets, but I told her that she had stopped. I had also written to my aunt Hélène suggesting that I might go down and visit her some time, and I was trying to get back in touch with Emma Kershaw. Old friendships should be cherished, not just allowed to drift. One friend can't replace another.

On the bookshelf stood a snapshot that Pascal had taken of a chubby, beaming Jacqueline. Already she had more hair than when I had seen her in August. Pascal had enclosed a scrawled note, reporting on her progress and saying that they were all looking forward to seeing me at Christmas. Her wide eyes in the photograph shone like glass balls on a Christmas tree. She was growing, finding out about the world. There was nothing wrong with her. When she was older she could come to stay with me, her Auntie Stella, and I would take her out and show her buildings, paintings, trees, birds ... Two weeks ago I had written a song for her.

Fairly regularly, now, I phoned my mother, just to chat – Jacqueline was always a good topic of conversation – instead of waiting for her to get in touch with me because she wanted me to do something.

"I was talking to Mrs. Grey the other day at bridge," my mother had said, as we were coming to the end of an amicable conversation. "She was telling me all about her son's wedding."

"Who?"

"Mrs. Grey. You knew her son David, didn't you? Wasn't he in your year? Anyway, he's just got married, in America. New Jersey, I think she said. Apparently the girl comes from a very wealthy family."

"Oh. I'm glad for him," I said.

So: the remote and perfect David was married and living on another continent. If it hadn't been for him, my life might have been quite different. But he didn't know that. If it hadn't been for David, if it hadn't been for Adrien, if it hadn't been for Olivier ... But when it came down to it, I had chosen to react the way I did to all of them. I had made all those choices that had determined my life, right or wrong. I had chosen to let them control me. I couldn't hold anyone responsible except myself.

I had even received a brief letter from my father, enclosing a press cutting about an association recently set up in England to mediate between neighbours who couldn't stand one another's noise, and who otherwise resorted to feuds and court cases and violence. I hadn't told my father about the fire, either. Perhaps I would write to him, or perhaps I would wait till Christmas.

One day I had walked past Olivier's shop, and had been surprised to see that it was open. I caught a glimpse, behind the counter, of a weather-beaten man with red hair and a red beard, who would have looked more at home on the deck of a boat than in a shop. I supposed that this was Olivier's uncle René, and almost went in, but decided against it and walked on.

Another day, as I was looking idly at my father's first volume of poems, something fell from between the pages. It was a dried sprig of lily-of-the-valley. I tossed it into the bin.

Now, dusk was falling. The days had been growing shorter for some time, and the evenings carried a chill that hinted of the winter to come, thick winter coats, scarves, the smell of roasting chestnuts on street corners. More than a year had gone by since the day I first met Rose.

All over Paris, I watched the lights coming on as the autumn dusk fell and people returned home from work. Windows. Squares and rectangles of light, cold and bare, or tinted different colours by curtains or blinds, or just perceptibly filtering through slatted shutters. Every lighted window was somebody's home; every light meant a person, or a family, each with their own story – and I knew none of them, and would never know them, and they didn't even know that I existed, unless they noticed my own lighted window among so many, like one star among all the billions of stars. How many stars had Olivier said were in the Milky Way? I had forgotten. And if one of those lights out there, in some unknown room, just happened to be shining on Rose, I would never know.

October twilight, the beginning of autumn. Soon it would be Hallowe'en, the time when the gates between the visible and the invisible world are open and spirits roam the earth. I remembered screeching around the back garden with Pascal in the failing light, muttering spells over the remains of my mother's bonfire of dead leaves, pretending to be a witch, and looking behind me fearfully, half afraid of ghosts among the trees. Some attempts have been made to celebrate Hallowe'en in France, but for the most part they have fizzled out. All Saints' Day is quite important, though: the eve of the festival of the dead. Half the population makes a pilgrimage to the cemeteries and puts chrysanthemums on the family tombs. It would be a public holiday, and I could, I supposed, trek down to Aix to put flowers on Mamie's tomb. But I wouldn't go. It made no sense to go to a graveyard and perform rituals over a slab of stone. I knew that Mamie wasn't there. No, there should be no rites for those who had gone. Only remembrance.

And then, in England, it would soon be the fifth of November: gunpowder, treason and plot. Guy Fawkes night. What long memories people had. Fossilized memories. Burning the guy had turned into an entertainment for children, who knew virtually nothing about the plot to blow up the Houses of Parliament and cared even less. But the grudge was still there, the tradition was alive, and on thousands of bonfires the sinister stuffed effigies would sit, gazing out with masked faces, gradually crumpling and collapsing as the flames rose. For his sins, the long-dead Guy Fawkes – the culprit, the ringleader, the scapegoat, the Popish conspirator – must burn.

So much burning.

*****

Now here I am in Zorinda's flat, high above the rooftops of the Latin Quarter, with a view of Notre Dame from the broad terrace, on which I can see stacked carved wooden chairs and a furled blue parasol. I imagine cocktail parties out there, glittering people drinking champagne in the summer dusk among the flowering shrubs in ornate pots. But today it's cool and windy, late morning on a Tuesday, and I've had to take a couple of hours off work to come here. Adam Leblanc met me at the street door and escorted me up in the discreetly sumptuous lift. I had been expecting some kind of bare warehouse with signs that the in-crowd spent time here snorting cocaine. But of course, Zorinda has been successful for years and has probably moved beyond that type of lifestyle.

"Zorinda isn't an early riser," he had told me confidentially, as a Filipino maid let us in and offered us coffee. A maid! How the other half lives ... I feel out of place among the white sofas, the deep pile rugs on the shining parquet floor, the wealth of luxuriant houseplants and the full-size painting of Zorinda that takes up part of one wall. My eyes were drawn to the painting as soon as I entered the room. It shows her dancing wildly with some kind of huge, fiery bird, against a background of dark clouds. Could it be a phoenix? I keep glancing at it and wondering.

But here I am, with my guitar in its rather battered case, and all my demo songs to date on a memory stick in my bag. I'm wearing my patchwork jacket. I am ready.

This will be the turning-point, I think. The palms of my hands are damp, and I wish that I went in for knitting or some such soothing activity. Adam Leblanc chatters away, grumbling about airports and agents and photographers, but I'm not listening to him. I'm afraid I may not be able to remember the words of my songs. I try to go over them in my mind, but different lines from different songs get jumbled together, and desperately I search around for something to distract my attention. Soon that door will open, and Zorinda – *Zorinda* – will come in and speak to me. Will she be polite, off-hand, snooty, relaxed? She wants me to play and sing live for her. If I fail now, it's back to the office-and-metro routine.

Will she look like her photographs? Will she be wearing full makeup and glittery clothes, or an old tracksuit with her hair in a rubber band? How will she behave towards me? Shall we actually sing together?

In a flash of memory, I see other faces, smiling and unsmiling, faces from the past and the present, and see them in my mind's eye, bright and very clear. Friends. Family. Mamie, standing in her high-ceilinged kitchen and telling me that I must do what I really want to do, something that I alone am able to do. Pascal, grinning awkwardly as he hands me the ugly musical box. My quiet father in his study, who always let me make my own decisions and go my own way, and who took time from his beloved books and poetry to try to mend the things that got broken. My mother presiding over the table, clicking her tongue in irritation at my clumsiness, but nevertheless glad that I am there, part of the charmed circle of family and, with all my faults, her own child. And then the men, brief encounters, burning out like meteors. David, turning cold and perfect to look at me against the evening sky at the top of the Ferris wheel. Adrien, joking waspishly over a glass of vodka. And Olivier: Olivier, his face fiercely contorted in orgasm, his long fingers, the smell of his skin and the hardness and gentleness of him – all gone now. I see him as a solitary figure with a backpack, hitching a lift on a distant road, still searching for Rose, believing her to be the mother of his future children. Bon voyage, Olivier. And he never taught me the sardane, after all. Each of those men was himself, unique, even those whose names I have forgotten. But none of them was right for me. Mentally, I kiss my hand to them, without anger, and let them go.

In between the faces and the people, the songs come and go in my mind, each one clear now, separate and intact, contrasting, each belonging to a part of my life. I have created them: they are alive. The people and the songs, sights and sounds, all come together in a pattern in many dimensions, and I am there, my own self, a point at the centre of the pattern.

How long have we been waiting? I breathe deeply. I feel stronger now. Courage flows through me like warmth. I shall be weighed in the balance, but it will be all right. Somewhere ahead of me there is an audience waiting, an audience so powerful that it can either destroy me or, on the contrary, fill me with its power, the sheer size of the audience generating in me the energy to surpass myself and create what only I can create. If the singing voice is Zorinda's and not my own, that doesn't matter. The songs will be out there. Very soon now.

And as the sun rises higher, the wind causing a branch of Virginia creeper to tap on the french windows, I think at last of Rose. Rose at the piano, playing by candlelight, and our voices twining together. I remember her thin smiling face and her eyes as blue as the dome of cloudless sky that stretches high over Paris this morning.

I am sure I shall see her again. Some day there will be a face emerging from the crowd, a light touch on the shoulder, or a knock at the door. In the park or in the street. We shall stand face to face again and greet each other as friends.

And I will do better this time. I may have failed as a student, failed as a career woman, failed as a teacher, failed as a lover, failed as a friend. But I *will* do better.

Why am I sure of seeing her again? Perhaps because something happened the other day – on Hallowe'en, to be precise. I found a message on my answering machine. Well, it was not a message, exactly. There were no words, and at first, listening to the silence, I thought it must be somebody who had dialled a wrong number. I was about to put the phone down. But then I heard it, very faintly: a piano. Playing Bach's Jesu, joy of man's desiring, just as she used to play it. Nothing else, but I feel sure it was a message for me. I can't explain it. I've no evidence. Call it an act of faith, if you like. Anyway, how can we be sure of anything?

Strange things happen in this world.

The sun is dazzling, and Adam Leblanc says "Here she is." I can hear light footsteps outside the door. Picking up my guitar, I rise to my feet.

The door knob turns and the door opens.

THE END

Also by Janet Doolaege:

Fiction:
A Paris Haunting

Children's fiction
The Story of an Ordinary Lion
Flora and the Wolf
Tobias and the Demon

Non-fiction
Ebony and Spica – Two Birds in My Life

Lightning Source UK Ltd.
Milton Keynes UK
UKOW02f0410101215

264435UK00001B/3/P